THE WILD WARFRONT

Vishwas Patil is one of the most acclaimed Marathi writers today. He has written iconic novels like *Mahanayak*, *Chandramukhi*, *Pangira*, *Zhadazdati*, *Panipat*, *Sambhaji*, *Nagkeshar* and *Lust for Lalbagh*. He has also written a literary biography of Anna Bhau Sathe, the founding father of Dalit Literature in Maharashtra, titled *Annabhauchi Dardbhari Dastaan*, which is considered an outstanding work by critics. He has received the Priyadarshini National Award, the Bharatiya Bhasha Parishad Award (Kolkata) and the Sahitya Akademi Award for *Zhadazdati* and the Gadkari Award for *Mahanayak*. *Panipat* has received thirty-eight awards since its publication in 1988. *Panipat*, *Mahanayak* and *Sambhaji* have been published in English by Westland Books. Patil's novel *Nagkeshar* has been adapted into a television serial. In 2020, he was awarded the prestigious Dr Indira Goswami (Mamoni Raisom Goswami) National Literature Award. The *Shivaji Mahasamrat Series*, a quartet of novels on the Maratha Empire, is his most ambitious work thus far.

Nadeem Khan has been a teacher of English since 1973. He retired as Head of the Department of Languages, Shivaji Science College, Amravati in 2010. In 2011, he became the founding director of the Western Regional Centre of the Indian Institute of Mass Communication run by the Ministry of Information and Broadcasting, at which post he remained till 2018.

Other than translating four other novels by Vishwas Patil, he has also brought into English the novels of the young Marathi writer Avadhoot Dongare, as also the works of celebrated writers like Bhau Padhye, Rangnath Pathare and Anant Deshmukh. His translation of the Marathi autobiography of Dr Savita Ambedkar, *Dr Ambedkaraanchyaa Sahavaasast*, has been released by Penguin Random House, India.

Read the first volume of the Shivaji Mahasamrat Quartet

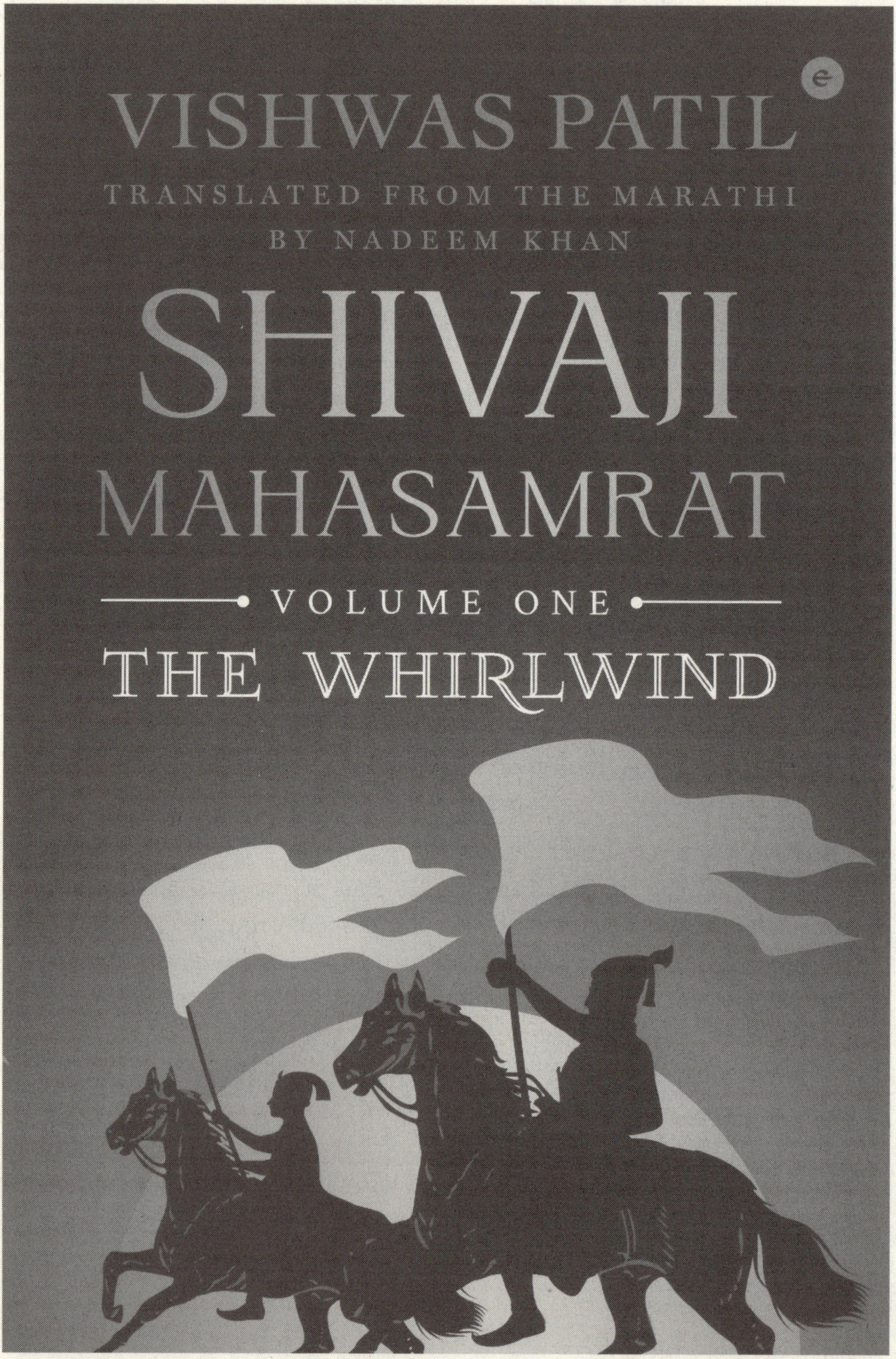

VISHWAS PATIL

SHIVAJI MAHASAMRAT

VOLUME TWO

THE WILD WARFRONT

TRANSLATED FROM
THE MARATHI BY NADEEM KHAN

eka

eka

First published in Marathi as *Rankhaindal* in 2023 by Mehta Publishing House

Published in English as *The Wild Warfront* in 2025 by Eka, an imprint of Westland Books, a division of Nasadiya Technologies Private Limited

No. 269/2B, First Floor, 'Irai Arul', Vimalraj Street, Nethaji Nagar, Alapakkam Main Road, Maduravoyal, Chennai 600095

ISBN: 9789360450854

10 9 8 7 6 5 4 3 2 1

This is a work of fiction. Names, characters, organisations, places, events and incidents are either products of the author's imagination or used fictitiously.

Typeset by Jojy Philip

Printed at Thomson Press (India) Ltd

CONTENTS

DRAMATIS PERSONAE

Afzal Khan	major Sardar of the Adilshahi court, commander-in-chief of the army that attacked Shivaji. Annihilated by Shivaji at Pratapgadh fort
Ali Adilshah	Sultan of Bijapur
Aurangzeb	the last great Mughal Emperor
Badi Begum	Taj-ul-Mulk, alias Ulia Begum, the widow of Mohammad Adilshah and the mentor of Sultan Ali Adilshah
Bahirji Naik	Shivaji's lieutenant and senior official of Shivaji's spy network
Baji Raje Ghorpade	sworn enemy of Shahaji and Shivaji. Sardar in the Bijapur court. Feudal lord of Mudhol. Killed by Shivaji in his manor at Mudhol
Baji Prabhu Deshpande	associate of Shivaji; martyred at Ghodkhind pass
Dara Shikoh	eldest son and the crown-prince of Emperor Shah Jahan and Aurangzeb's eldest brother. He was a learned man who believed in treating the Hindus as equals. He was hounded by Aurangzeb and killed
Vishwasrao Dighe	Shivaji's secret agent and warrior
Doroji Phaakade	a captain of Hindvi swarajya
Dulari Begum	Shaista Khan's wife
Faazal Khan	Afzal Khan's son
George Oxenden	chief of English factory establishment at Surat

Guna maavashi	a milkwoman who helped Shivaji escape from Panhala
Ikhlaas Khan	the wazeer of the Adilshahi Sultanate under Ali Adilshah
Inayat Khan	the Mughal subedar of the port city of Surat
Jaswant Singh	a Rajput king and captain under Shaista Khan
Jijabai Bhosle/Jijau/Jiu	valiant wife of Shahaji. Shivaji's mother and mentor
Kanhoji Jedhe/Kanhoba	a senior associate of Shahaji, who continued to serve under his son Shivaji
Kartalab Khan	a captain of Aurangzeb. Roundly defeated by Shivaji in the battle of Umbarkhind
Khawaas Khan	a senior captain of the Bijapur army
Koyaji	Shahaji's son from a concubine and thus Shivaji's half-brother
Moropant Pingale	One of the trusted sardars of Shivaji
Mumtaz Mahal	Emperor Shah Jahan's wife and Aurangzeb's mother
Phirangoji Narsaala	Shivaji's captain who fought valiantly at the Sangramdurg fort at Chaakan
Netaji Palkar/Netoba/ Netokaka	the most gallant and trusted of Shivaji's captains
Phulaji Prabhu	Baji Prabhu's younger brother: martyred at the Ghodkhind pass
Rai Bagan	a lady captain of Aurangzeb's army
Rayaji Bandal	a hero of the battle at the Ghodkhind pass. He was one of the few who survived
Henry Revington	official in the Rajapur warehouse of the East India Company
Rustam-e-Zamaan	son of Randullah Khan, who was a friend of Shahaji; captain of the Adilshahi Sultanate; a childhood friend of Shivaji and his secret supporter
Sambhaji	Shivaji's valiant eldest son and successor
Santaji Jadhavrao	Jijabai's relative and another martyr of Kanakgiri

Shahajiraje Bhosale	Shivaji's father, who planted the concept of Hindvi swarajya in Shivaji's mind
Shaista Khan	trusted captain of Aurangzeb. Also the brother of Mumtaz Mahal, and thus the emperor's maternal uncle. He was sent to the Deccan at the head of a huge army to subdue Shivaji, but had to finally withdraw in shame
Shambhuji Jadhav	son of Santaji Jadhav, martyred in the battle of Ghodkhind. Shivaji's captain and brother-in-law
Shiva Kashid	a brave soldier belonging to the barber community. A look-alike of Shivaji. A martyr for Swaraj
Shivaji/Shivba/Shivraya (pronounced Sivaji and Siva by his Muslim antagonists)	the founder of the Maratha empire and the Hindvi Swaraj in Deccan
Shivaji's wives	Saibai, Soyrabai, Putlabai, Sakvarabai, Sagunabai, Kashibai, Lakshmibai (alias Jaishribai) and Gunvantabai
Siddhi Hilaal	Shivaji's brave captain; later, his secret agent in Aurangzeb's Darbar
Siddhi Johar	an Abyssinian captain of Adilshah from Kurnool, conferred the title of Salaabat Khan by Ali Adilshah
Siddhi Wah Wah	the first Muslim martyr in the cause of Shivaji
Swami Paramaanand Nevaskar	a holy man visiting Shivaji's Panhala fort. He also became Shivaji's historian
Tanaji Malusare	a valiant associate of Shivaji
Udepuri Begum	Dara Shikoh's Jordanian widow, whom Aurangzeb took for his own

Early Maratha conquests in Shahaji's and Shivaji's time

Map: Charles Joppen (1907)

Source: Wikimedia Commons

1

NETAJI'S ASSAULT ON BIJAPUR

Not too long ago, Bijapur was the most prosperous city of the Deccan. What had happened to it in recent times? Those companies of prancing Arab and Turkish horses, those elephants that carried brocaded caparisons on their backs, those caravans of decked-up camels swinging as they walked—all the pomp and splendour seemed to have leaked out of the city.

It was true, of course, that the invincible warrior Afzal Khan had not yet returned, despite months having rolled by. He had left Bijapur for the Sahyadris after swearing an oath at the durbar that he would bring that renegade Shivaji in chains and parade him through the city streets. He had roared out that he would toss the margatthya in the dungeons of the fort before the monsoons arrived. The monsoons had come and gone, and so had the early-winter festival of Dussehra. Another two months would complete an entire year since he had departed from Bijapur at the head of one of the biggest armies assembled in recent times; yet there was no news of Afzal sahib, nor of his army, nor of the despicable Maavalis, who should, by all reasonable calculations, have been reduced to dust.

For the past few days, dark, ominous clouds had begun to gather in the Bijapur sky. The very air had turned heavy and turgid. City life seemed to have lost its melody and turned cacophonous; its vivacity had vanished. As the days dragged on, the shadow of fear had grown longer and longer.

Badi Begum's face, ordinarily red as a slice of watermelon, had begun to take on a much darker hue. Sultan Ali Adilshah's durbar hours had been reducing steadily, to the point where he would skip it altogether. The grandees and noblemen had begun withdrawing themselves too.

The marketplaces had turned wet with dew. The days of mendicants and beggars had turned bleaker, bringing them perilously close to starvation. The two blind men and the four deaf ones who slept on the open-to-air stone steps of the old mosque in Ibrahimpura, the three skeletal vagrants, the flesh on whose bodies would barely suffice to constitute three separate crows, that cluster of twelve or thirteen beggars, those ragged women with their filthy, matted hair that made them look more like hobgoblins than human beings—all of them brought together made for as dismal an assemblage of *Homo sapiens* as ever blighted the street of a city. Their ragged, grime-laden clothes, their wretched poverty, and the calumny and derision into which they were born had taken them firmly out of association with any religion, Hindu or Muslim.

This gaggle of beggars stayed strictly out of the social circuit that exists among the denizens of a town. Begging wherever they spotted a hope, moving up and down lanes and alleys lost in contemplation, looking for half a square meal a day and two square feet of space for seeing the night through—this was the rut through which their lives crawled.

Suddenly one night, around the hour of midnight, this ragtag bunch of hobos lifted their heads to the sky and began to groan. Hardly a groan, but a blubbering, a clamour, an ululation that jolted awake the honest citizenry of the neighbourhood and set their teeth on edge. Howling as if their revolting tatters were on fire, they ran in terror with their bundles under their arms and the street dogs at their heels. They ran through the front streets and back streets, through the ginnels and tunnels and alleys of the city as if they were being chased, not by mongrels or mutts, but by the hounds of hell.

This tumultuous racket obviously reached the ears of the night-guards, who prodded their horses in the direction of the uproar. It was only when a fair number of these servants of the state had encircled the beggars and blocked their progress that the tumult was dammed. A few well-targeted swishes of the cane, and the noise was reduced to a manageable decibel.

'What are you belly-aching about, you wretched vermin?' shouted the sergeant at the crowd.

When a dozen voices began screeching together in response, the sergeant swung his cane again. He then pointed at a hag and said, 'All right. You, you old crone! What's the hullaballoo about?'

'Havaldar sahib,' the old woman croaked, 'the stuff we saw, it's enough to beat the daylight out of a rusted horseshoe.'

'Stop talking in riddles, hag, else I know how to persuade you,' growled the sergeant, patting his cane on his thigh.

'No persuasion, havaldar sahib, but you'll never believe what we saw. It was no less than Afzal Khan sahib's senior begum Laadli Begum.'

The sergeant looked around at his companions with amusement and anger at being taken for a ride. 'You do need persuasion, don't you?' he said, lifting his cane in the air. 'Stupid woman, Begum sahiba died almost a year ago. She drowned herself along with her sixty fellow wives, and the world knows this!'

'Which is what has agitated us, sahib! I saw her with my own eyes, her hair flying in the air as she went shrieking like a demoness by the side of the Kamal Burz. And she was not alone!'

'So, who did she have for company?'

'It was Khan sahib's entire zenana. They were all beating their chests and pulling their hair and howling with grief as they ran.'

'Makes us fear,' said a skeletal codger, 'that our Khan Sahib and his army could be in trouble!'

'Ah, you do need a beating, all of you bastards!' The sergeant brandished his cane at the old man. 'You live off the crumbs of the city and say such inauspicious things! Shall we herd all these loons and drown them in the Taj Baawadi, Rasool miyaan?' he said, turning towards a colleague.

All of Bijapur seemed to be in a state of perpetual turmoil. Frightening doomsday stories had become rampant. Afzal sahib's preceptor Soofi Hazrat Peer Ameen Chishti Baba had taken to bed. There was a steady trickle of water from the empty sockets of his eyes, some swore. Also, the grand mausoleum that Afzal sahib had constructed to be his final resting place, regarded as a marvel of architecture and the pride of Bijapur by soldiers and citizens alike, was now rumoured to be haunted by lugubrious spirits and occupied by owls that hooted night and day. Guards feared to go anywhere close to it at night, alone or even in pairs.

Barely a couple of days had passed since the sighting of Laadli Begum when the city was shaken up as if caught by a vicious earthquake. The impossible had happened in the Pratapgadh mountains of the Maaval region. That enemy of the people, Siva, had beheaded Afzal Khan as one beheads goats and sheep. The warrior who had fought fifty battles and never known defeat, the man who had laid pipelines of baked tiles across the city to provide the citizens with tap water, the dreamer with his eyes on the distant seas who had assembled a fleet of ships on the waves off the coast of Goa—how could this entrepreneur par excellence, this apple of Bijapur's eye, this Jung Bahadur Afzal Khan have fallen at the hands of the margatthyas? The hearts and hopes of the millions who had expected him to come back leading a victorious army were shattered.

That day, while Ali Adilshah was busy in the durbar with his usual routine, he heard cries of 'Huzoor, huzoor, treachery! Treachery!' coming from outside, as if the enemy had laid siege to the city. A huge crowd of agitated mourners had gathered around the palace, beating their chests and screaming at the top of their lungs, 'Our valorous ghazi Afzal miyaan and our entire army has been decimated in the mountains of Pratapgadh.' It was as if a snowstorm had suddenly hit Bijapur. Loud shrieks and bawls of distress began to resound from all quarters, including the bazaars, the durbar, the Anand Mahal, the Aaina Mahal and the mosques across the city.

Badi Begum was sunk in a pool of grief. Ali Adilshah raised himself from his seat with some difficulty. His head had begun to reel.

As was his custom after durbar work, he walked out into the garden where his royal elephant stood waiting for him decked in golden bells and other lavish ornaments. A jewel-studded canopy rested on its back, all ready to carry the Sultan for a round of the city.

But the agony of the jolt that he had received from the devastating news of Afzal Khan's demise had nowhere near subsided. A five-metal ladder was resting against the royal elephant's back as always, but Ali Adilshah was far too shattered in mind and body to mount it or to seat himself in that gold howdah. Stooping under the weight of his melancholy, he quietly shambled up to a palanquin and had himself carried up to Anand Mahal.

It didn't take much time for the tumult to spread across the market areas, and traders downed their shutters in a hurry. The streets were soon deserted. All one could see there were dogs, donkeys and stray cattle. Even the believers who had gathered in the mosque for their evening prayers were bewildered and disoriented. The desolation that had settled upon the city's fifty-two battlements, the old walls, the palisades and the royal streets was something that hadn't been seen before in living memory.

Wazeer Ikhlaas Khan had passed an order that silenced the kettledrums on the ramparts. The drummers, the policemen and the watchmen sat on their haunches, trying to blunt the pain in their innards. One of them would occasionally look up at the sky and lament, 'Ya Allah, what have You done? How could You grant heaven to the infidel Shivaji and condemn Your beloved Afzal Khan to hell?'

Some of the soldiers who had fled after the defeat in the Pratapgadh mountains had witnessed Afzal Khan's slaughter with their own eyes. When Shivaji had split open Khan's belly, he had come running out of the tent, holding his trailing intestines shouting, 'Treachery! Treachery!' When his palanquin-bearers had tried to whisk him away, the massively built Sambhaji Kavji had waylaid the carriage, pulled Afzal out of it and chopped his head off like one lops off the heads of poultry. These half-a-dozen eyewitnesses had not tarried in the land of their destruction; stirred by the urge of self-preservation, they had whipped their horses and galloped like the wind to reach Bijapur by the evening of the third day.

The huge fortress-like city wall that measured a few miles in length and the formidable battlements atop it seemed to heave sighs of despair. The soldiers mounting guard had turned limp with shock and grief. The citizens of Bijapur who had fawned over their great leader now lay like wounded animals, many of them refusing to partake of their meals. The word was that Badi Begum herself had forsaken both food and water.

The enormous front gate of the Bijapur city wall stood as if frozen. On one end of it was the battlement called Landa Kasab Burz and on the other end was Firangee Burz, both looming fifty feet tall. The guards manning this gate sat in a state of lassitude. Every little while, they would gather in groups to discuss the calamity that had struck their city. They were sure that a disaster of this dimension had not descended upon them in recent memory.

As they sat exchanging notes and local gossip in a sombre mood, a watch-guard on one of the battlements noticed a cloud of dust rising about four miles or so away. 'Look!' he shouted to the others, 'some more of our beaten soldiers seem to have arrived.'

In a little while, five or six horsemen came racing towards them, two of whom shot forward and almost knocked the guards down. They were sweating profusely and had apparently given their horses a rough ride too. Once they were safely inside, they pulled the reins so hard that the horses came to an abrupt halt, tossing their riders into the dust, saddle and all.

The other riders accompanying them rushed forward to help the fallen men up, while one of them shouted loudly, 'Fools! Close the gate immediately. We have an entire enemy army at our heels!'

'But you—'

'Forget us! Close the gates first! Or you will have the margatthyas galloping down our streets!'

The terrifying news exploded like a bomb under the nose of the city. Kettledrums were beaten, and bugles and horns were blown to declare to the citizens that Shivaji's Maavalis had arrived at their gates, and grave danger loomed over their capital. 'Run! Save your skins!' people roared. The lanes resounded with shrieks of 'The Maavalis have come! The enemy has come! Destruction hangs over our heads!'

As Bijapur began to drown in the sweat of terror, the experienced soldiers at their observation-posts on the city walls saw billows of dust rising in the distance and estimated the assailing cavalry to be six to seven thousand strong.

Citizens ran helter-skelter, not knowing where safety lay. Loud cries of 'Har har Mahadev' and 'Shivaji Maharaj ki jai' struck their ears, turning the shelter-seekers on the streets frantic. Those who had any idea of the feat accomplished by the enemy army dropped their jaws in disbelief. 'When our own fleeing soldiers have still not managed to reach the security of the city,' they cried, 'here we have the marauding Maratha army at our door!' They had good reason for their astonishment: these tenacious Marathas had traversed the distance of a hundred and sixty miles in a tad over two days.

'Who is leading this force?' someone stammered.

'Sivaji!' squeaked a voice.

'It's not Sivaji, but Netaji Palkar, whom the Portuguese call Shivaji's alter ego.'

'Oh, that rascal? His horse never stands still, they say, and his sword is never free of blood.'

Inside the huge circle of the outer city wall was another with a circumference of about a mile. Within this inner wall were the Sultan's palace, the large, well-appointed waadas of the rich and mighty princes as well as the city's important offices. This citadel was now overtaken by mayhem, with people running past shops and houses, shouting, 'Netaji Palkar has come, the margatthyas have come. Siva has just dispatched Afzal sahib to Allah. Is it our turn now?'

The seven thousand horses of Palkar began surrounding the city wall. When the Maratha bugles blew into their ears, announcing an assault, the panic-stricken Bijapuris lost all peace of mind. Ikhlaas Khan and the remaining nobles mounted their horses and began moving around to ensure that all the gates were properly bolted from inside. Soldiers armed with missiles climbed up to the balustrades and stood on the alert.

Palkar's strength and spirits were high. His impassioned cavalrymen had done the entire journey in one go, halting only for a few minutes at a time to feed and drink water. As they stood now before the walls of Bijapur, the horses steamed like recently used cannons. The men got off their steeds and glared at the obstacle looming in front of them. These forces had yet to learn the need for rest, relaxation and nourishment!

Running alongside the walls was a trench forty or fifty feet wide, large enough to accommodate four elephants standing shoulder to shoulder. It had pools of water scattered here and there, infested by crocodiles. The Marathas were not intimidated, though. With shouts of 'Jai Malhar!' and 'Rip them apart!', they threw their spears at the crocodiles. The blood gushing out of their reptilian bodies mixed with the slime and formed a strange sludge. Uncaring of the stones and arrows flying at them from the wall, the battle-charged Marathas began descending into the trench. Many of them reached the other side too.

They began assailing the massive doors with big rocks, axes and machetes. Netaji was in a fever. He galloped across, urging his men to apply themselves with more gusto, saying, 'Go on, my brave men! Let's break down this gate and get into the city before the stragglers from Bijapur manage to reach here.'

Some five thousand Adilshahi men had fallen in the jungles of Pratapgadh. The rest of them, numbering about twenty-five thousand, had begun their dismal journey home. There was no knowing when they would reach the precincts of Bijapur.

The Adilshahi army inside the fortified city was less than adequate. Wazeer Ikhlaas Khan had spread them out at the sensitive points. He went around encouraging them to stand firm. 'Keep fighting,' he urged them. 'That demon named Netaji should never be allowed to enter our city.'

'In the name of Allah,' Badi Begum screeched, 'think of our ancestor Ibrahim Khan. Think of the soldiers who were martyred defending Islam. Bijapur has to be saved at all costs.' But these pleas of Badi Begum had the opposite effect, dispiriting the common folk.

Noticing the disorientation, the anxiety and the falling morale of the people, Ali Adilshah shouted in irritation, 'Why are you in such a panic, Ammijaan? We have these impregnable, invincible ramparts that our ancestors built around the city. And what, after all, is this Netaji Palkar but a monkey?'

'What you say is true, son, he is just a monkey. But he is not an ordinary simian, he is Siva's Hanuman. If you remember, Ravana had lit only a tiny fire on that Maruti's tail, but that monkey used it to envelop all of Lanka in flames. May Allah prevent this man from entering the city, otherwise the havoc he can let loose here is frightening beyond imagination.'

Meanwhile, Palkar was applying all his substantial force on the city's fortifications, and his men were responding to his exhortations with great courage. The Marathas had placed all the ladders they had and the ones they could gather from the neighbouring villages against the battlement. The enemy poured boiling oil that fell upon and scalded the Maratha soldiers shimmying up the walls. Ladders broke too, but the effort did not slacken. Gathering whatever bamboo they could find, they were stringing together new ladders and propping them up against the walls.

The battlements, however, were eighteen arms tall, at some places twenty. The width too extended to a dozen arms in some sections. Immeasurable wealth had been poured across the centuries into the building of these bastions.

The battling Maratha braves seemed to have forgotten their hunger and thirst. Their eyes flamed like burning torches. A squad that had been making the rounds of the city walls rode in excitedly. One of them shouted from a distance, 'Commander-in-chief, the enemy had opened the Chand Gate on the other side for a short while. Just for a very short while. They closed it again in a hurry.'

'It couldn't be for no reason!'

'Of course, it couldn't. About five or six hundred Bijapuri horsemen slipped out of it quickly and scampered away!'

Netaji became thoughtful. Slapping the rump of his horse, he said, 'You, perhaps, weren't vigilant enough. They could well have stuffed their costliest jewels and gems in bags and spirited them away.'

'Yes, that's quite possible,' said the senior soldier Morey Mama. 'They would be afraid that the city might fall.' Mama had spent twenty years in the company of Shahajiraje earlier.

It was now well past noon and the skirmish was in full swing. Netaji's soldiers had set fire to the checkposts and the deserted houses next to them. The entire settlement called Shahpur that lay just outside the walls was now alight. When the evening wind fanned the flames, the fire flared up with renewed vigour, sending billows of smoke into the air. The citizens stepped out into their verandahs or the terraces of their houses to see the conflagration that had lit up the fringes of their beautiful city. Ali Adilshah had begun to look wan. Badi Begum too gazed out of the casement of her upper room with a distraught face.

In the evening, sardars like Morey Mama, Rayaji and Suryaji gathered around Netaji. Morey Mama said animatedly, 'Netoba, our boys have thrown their all into battle; uncaring of themselves, they have crossed the trench and ranged themselves against the battlement. But we don't have the adequate weaponry and equipment—'

'Yes—'

'We don't have crowbars, sledgehammers or saws to bring the doors down. And every one of them is stoutly built.'

'Netajidada, if we had a few hundred carpenters and blacksmiths with us to put to work, a miracle could well happen.'

Netaji was flummoxed. He scratched his chin, pulled his hair, and then putting his arm around Rayaji, took him aside. After a while, six hundred of the toughest Maratha horses were gathered on the rear side of the battlement wall. Soon, they turned around and dispersed towards the villages around Bijapur.

As the sun set, there was an unexpected development: a white flag was raised on one of the observation-posts atop a bastion. Looking in that direction, Netaji nodded his head. A little while later, a small wicket door built into the fort's main gate opened and a Bijapuri official named Yahya Khan ducked out of it, followed by a small bunch of soldiers. Approaching Netaji, he told him that he had been sent by Badi Begum Sahiba, 'Netaji sahib, our Queen Mother and the Sultan himself want to know what your demand is.'

'Listen, I worship Shivaji. Although my king is younger than me, he is my life.'

'Yes, so please tell us what you want.'

'Look, my hunger is prodigious; it's not going to be satiated by crumbs.'

'All right, then, what might satiate your hunger?'

'That cannon called Mulukh Maidan which is mounted on your main bastion, it is originally ours. Our gunsmiths at Ahmadnagar dipped their fingers in molten steel and moulded this extraordinary jewel. It was that traitor named Murari Jagdev who had it dragged here. I want to stuff ten or fifteen tons of gunpowder in it and set the wick alight.'

'Why?'

'The little worm that is wriggling inside my head—it wants to see how much of your Bijapur will be devoured by its explosion.'

'Can we speak a little plainer, friend?'

'All right, hand Bijapur over to me by tomorrow morning.'

'Will you then take our Ali Adilshah sahib prisoner?'

'All right, I'll offer him this concession: he can depart from Bijapur tomorrow with the clothes on his back. If he wishes, he can go in the direction of your Bankapur.'

Yahya Khan stared at Netaji open-mouthed, as one looks at a ghost. Evidently considering further conversation fruitless, he silently walked back to the wicket gate and disappeared through it, locking it behind him.

Morey Mama came up from behind him and said, 'Netya, why were you weaving ropes of conversation with that Khan? They are not clean of heart. They simply want to while away time in conversation.'

'What do you think I was doing, Mama? Our Rayaji's squad has gone into the villages around Bijapur. Till he comes back after doing what he has set out to do, I too have to while away time.'

First it had been the eight or ten days of exertion during the battle, and then it was constant riding from Wai to Bijapur for nearly three days at a stretch. Even the short naps that the riders had taken were on horseback. Their feet had stopped only when the animals needed to be given fodder and water. Beyond that, neither man nor animal had known rest of any kind. Every joint in their bodies was screaming with pain.

Shivraya's words were even now ringing in Netaji's ears, 'Netokaka, an assault on Bijapur has to be mounted before the defeated enemy floundering in the Pratapgadh jungles reaches home. Let's see if we can break their spine this way. There's no greater joy than flinging them down and sitting on their chest.'

'Absolutely, Raje. Let traders sit in their markets and talk of success and failure, but this Netaji is in the habit of collecting blood in his cupped hands as he moves from battle to battle. At your order, I offer my head. I am not stopping here for a moment.'

That evening before the walls of Bijapur, the Maratha army dined on whatever dry piece of *bhaakari* was available and spread out some hay to make do as mattresses. After so many days of continuous and intense exertion, Netaji had stretched his back out on this 'mattress' for only a few seconds when exhaustion caught up with him and he simply passed out. His body was able to rest for an unprecedented three hours, before someone shook him awake. He got up with a start to see the braves around him gaping at something in the distance behind his back. He turned around to see that the land there was alight, with fires flaring up at a number of places.

Netaji sprang to his feet and splashed some cold water on his face. The heat of the fire was stinging him even from that distance. It was after a little while that the Maavalis realised these fires were not confined to a spot or two, but spread across a wide area. Pretty much every village around Bijapur was burning.

As dawn broke, the six hundred men who had gone reconnoitering the nearby villages under Rayaji's command returned. In spite of the nippy air, Rayaji himself was bathed in sweat and his face covered in soot. 'Netokaka,' he said in exasperation, 'we scoured the thirty or forty villages around here; we rode to distant places too. Going by your instructions, we searched every settlement of blacksmiths, carpenters, masons and odd-job men with a fine-tooth comb, but not one of them is at their station. They have all vanished.'

'But how can that happen?'

'The answer is that the Bijapuris anticipated our needs. They drove all these people away so that we wouldn't catch them and make them work against their interests.'

Netaji stamped his feet in frustration and indignation.

'Who could have been behind this move?'

'Couldn't have come out of that bratty sultan's head. This move has the stamp of that old coffin-dodger Badi Begum.'

Morning arrived. Impotent wisps of white clouds chased each other through the sky. Netaji and Morey Mama scratched their heads trying to make sense of the untoward events happening around them. The fires, clearly, were not accidental; on the contrary, they seemed to be part of a bigger scheme. And what could the scheme be? Obviously, the stocks of grain and fodder stashed in these villages were being consigned to the flames against the eventuality of the Marathas reaching out for them. If the latter were to dig their heels in and go on with the siege, surely they would need those supplies!

By the time breakfast was finished, the other news-gatherers that Netaji sent out had all drifted back in.

The Bijapuri soldiers who had been killed in the foothills of Pratapgadh could not have been many more than six thousand. The vast majority of their army, numbering about eighteen thousand, had fled after the disastrous defeat and were on their way home. Ali Adilshah had immediately issued a *firman* to Belgaum, Solapur, Indi, Pandharpur, Jamkhandi, Jat, Athni, Miraj and scores of other villages and townships along the route to provide succour in the form of food, clothing, horses and other necessities to these returning soldiers. They were then to be urged to rush back to Bijapur. Among these fleeing soldiers were also chieftains of repute such as Sardar Muse Khan, Afzal's son Faazal Khan and quite a few others.

The enemy that had been so shattered by the passing away of Afzal Khan had begun to gather itself together. Most importantly, the battlements of the city were stronger and more impregnable than even the fortifications of Delhi and Agra. These walls had now come to the rescue of Bijapur with far greater efficacy than all the city's forces put together.

Netaji could see that his leaps at the enemy were not delivering results. But his craving for vengeance was refusing to subside. He muttered to Morey, 'Mamaji, you may withdraw if you want to, but I shall not budge from here. I've given my word to the king, and I won't allow even my dead body to be pulled back before I have lived by it.'

'Netoba, listen to some sane advice. More than fifteen thousand of the returning Bijapuri soldiers are now reassembling—'

'Yes, I know that. So what?'

'So this: all of these soldiers will throw a ring around you when they arrive.'

'So?'

'All right, take a good look at this battlement wall that goes all the way around Bijapur. Now, know that a similar wall about a mile long runs around the crucial hub of the city. When these returning soldiers throw a ring around you, you will be sandwiched between two very hard layers.'

'I see.'

'Also know that there is enough wherewithal stacked inside Bijapur to last them for six months, while our soldiers are hungry and naked.'

'How?' Netaji growled.

'You set off on this enterprise as a knee-jerk response, without bringing any additional provisions for a prolonged stay. And now, the enemy has burnt down the sources from where you could have drawn supplies.'

'So, Mama, what exactly are you driving at?'

'Refusal to withdraw at a prudent time will cause the commander-in-chief's cannon of destiny to blow up.'

For all that Mama tried to make Netaji see sense, the good man remained obstinate. Three hours rolled by. The sun had waxed in strength. In exasperation, Mama prodded his horse next to Netaji's, leaned over, held Netaji's arm and pulled him closer. 'Look, Netoba,' he said, 'there's just this much fodder left for your horse in your bag. If stretched, it will last till Athni-Miraj provided you take that route, or till Pandharpur-Akulja if you take the other. If you don't take timely action, this magnificent beast will collapse on the way because of hunger.'

'No, I cannot withdraw!' Netaji held on like an obdurate boy.

'How the devil will you not!' Mama snapped in suppressed anger. 'If you are Netaji Palkar, I too am Malhari Morey Mama by name! If you refuse, I shall tie you behind my horse and drag you all the way home!'

Still locked in his own idea of valour, Netaji jumped off his horse and stood before Mama's. Like a cobra whose tail has been stepped upon, he glared at Mama, gripped the horse's rein and said, 'Morey Mama, if you were going to get so intransigent, whoever asked you to join my company?'

'He did.'

'Who?'

'The Shivajiraja who dispatched you on this campaign was the person who sent me to give you company.'

'What are you saying?'

'He said, "I am sending Netaji on this enterprise so that the Bijapuris experience the jolt a person suffers when he is rammed in the chest with the force of an elephant. When Netaji rams into them, they will certainly begin seeing stars in daylight."'

'But, Mama, that is exactly what I want to do. Why then do you want to trip me up?'

'Because our king is also aware that once the battle begins to rage, Netaji rages at ten times its intensity. That is why he has sent me—to bring you back to him unharmed and in one piece.'

Netaji's head was spinning like a top. His nostrils were pushing out hot air as if they were a blacksmith's bellows. Every time he turned to look at the battlements, sparks would fly in his head. Mama removed his stole from his shoulder and tossed it on Netaji's, pressing the younger man's arm with affection. Overwrought, Netaji said, 'The king should have tried to forget me on the principle that whoever walks out into battle dies in the effort. Why must he play these twisted games with me?'

Morey Mama responded with the same intensity, 'Arey Netoba, the king took me into confidence and said that this Netaji is not merely another sardar or even a commander-in-chief for him. Netaji is one of Shivajiraja's arms. Many battles must be fought before the spire is placed on the temple of Swarajya. Therefore he believes that he has desperate need for a glowering coal like Netaji in the times to come.'

2

BIJAPUR IN DISARRAY

The sight made the eyes of the night-guards bulge out of their sockets. It was well past midnight when they saw that haughty woman, clad in her flowing ghaagra and ghoongat, walk imperiously up to the door of the Sultan's hall. Nobody remembered ever seeing Badi Begum Sahiba in the palace any time after sunset. She had with her two of Ali Adilshah's most trusted lieutenants, Darya Khan and Ankush Khan, who stood with their heads hanging in shame.

The unexpected news of her arrival at his door made Ali Adilshah break out in a cold sweat. In fact, he had hoped to put this woman in chains and parade her through the city streets the next day. And the same woman now stood courageously in front of his door, without so much as a hair on her head out of place. He quickly tied the laces of his jacket and ran out.

His heart had begun to thump violently. He knew her well. Badi Begum had the stuff in her to bring even the great emperor Aurangzeb to heel. She had compelled him to sign a treaty with the Bijapur Sultanate on her terms and then framed her wazeer Mullah Khan Mohammad for letting Emperor Aurangzeb escape from jail. Subsequently, she had got Afzal Khan to chop the man to pieces in the marketplace for this act of treason.

'Ammijaan, you yourself in person?' Ali Adilshah blubbered.

'Yes, it is I. Forgive me, Sultan sahib, it is with deliberate intent that I have come to pay you a visit on this dark night,' Badi Sahiba said.

'But what could be the reason?'

'The person who is the prime reason for your occupying the throne of the Bijapur Sultanate, this is the benefactor you want to make a state prisoner and parade across the city?'

Ali Adilshah was so flustered that he could do nothing but hang his head in shame.

As she stood there, events of the past flashed through her mind's eye: the old age, illness and passing away of Mohammed Shah sahib, the previous Sultan of Bijapur; the ensuing anxiety about the inheritance of the throne as she had no child of her own. It was she who had taken the initiative of crowning six-year-old Ali as the successor. The grandees of the Bijapur durbar bitterly opposed this move because Ali was the son of Mohammed Shah's concubine and, in their view, no better than the offspring of a slave-woman. But in the end, they were no match for Badi Begum's brilliant manipulation skills and steely temperament. She had brought him up as her own son in Anand Mahal and compelled the royal houses of the Deccan to swear their allegiance to her protégé.

Ali lifted his head with great difficulty. 'What can I say, Ammijaan?' he finally said in a polite but firm voice. 'The Sultanate of Bijapur stands humiliated before the world. Our Afzal Khan sahib, whom we regarded as the ultimate protective wall of our Sultanate—for him to be reduced to dust in the mountains of Pratapgadh by that sinful, dissembling, treacherous Sivaji ...'

'Could you have forgotten, Ali sahib? Don't you remember that we had briefed Afzal Khan most comprehensively about Siva's seductive charm and his sweet, double-dealing tongue? Had we not warned him about the black-magic practices of the margatthyas of those mountains?'

'Yes, but even so, how could we have disintegrated so totally?'

'Can't you see how? It was because our Afzal Miyan, who had the bodily strength of a modern Rustam, fell into the trap of that trickster Siva, quite like a jungle bird falling into the net of a bird-catcher.'

Sultan Ali pointedly disdained Badi Sahiba's parry and riposted, 'Ammijaan, how can we lay the responsibility of this humiliation and destruction of Bijapur on somebody else?'

'What are you trying to say?'

'Ammijaan, who had made the choice of Afzal Khan as leader of the expedition? Who had worked out the battle strategies? Who had appointed the sardars that would go with him and measured out their supplies and rations? Who had taken these decisions other than you?'

'So?'

'So, it's obvious that this defeat is not Afzal bhai's but yours, isn't it?' Ali Adilshah felt suddenly lighter on getting this long-suppurating bile out of his system.

'You are labouring under a misconception.'

'This is no misconception, Ammijaan. It is a fact. While it is true that I sit on the Sultan's throne, all the strings of political and military power have lain in your hands. While the coronation was mine, the real power has always been yours.'

Even in the dim light of the lamps, Badi Begum could sense the changing direction of the winds. She had well understood the resentment that Ali carried in his heart at being denied power; now she quickly perceived that he was using this opportunity to exact his revenge by laying the blame for the disastrous failure of the Pratapgadh expedition entirely at her doorstep.

The impudence of the Sultan was, however, more than a woman of her state was ready to accommodate. 'Sultan salamat,' she said in a tone dripping with sarcasm, 'when a person of your kind asks for profit-and-loss accounts in the matter of politics and warfare, it would be good for him to look into a mirror first.'

Begum Sahiba's barb found its mark and made the Sultan squirm. He had gathered quite a reputation for his philandering and sexual escapades from quite an early age. The city grapevine had it that he had assembled well over three hundred young beauties in his Aaina Mahal. Making a brazen attempt to feign innocence, however, he asked, 'What exactly do you want to say, Ammijaan?'

'Just this: that your useless friends go procuring for you and bring over at least one young girl for your indulgence every fortnight. They sweet-talk the girls into concubinage and deposit them in Aaina Mahal, ruining their lives. Do I understand this to be the cornerstone of Sultanate administration, young man?'

'But, what connection do these things have with the matter of Sivaji and Afzal Khan?'

'They do, my Sultan, they do.' Badi Sahiba's eyes were blazing as she let the Sultan have it. 'Every fortnight you acquire another beautiful damsel for your harem, while that Sivaji there plants his banner of victory on one more of our forts. You hanker after prostitutes while Siva performs feats of valour.'

That frontal assault of Badi Begum's sharp, vicious tongue drained Adilshah of all his bluster. But Badi Begum also knew her responsibility as a senior member of the royal household towards the circumstances prevailing in the durbar. It was important to bring order back into the disrupted state of Sultanate affairs. Reining in her anger, she said, 'The climate these days is quite unhealthy, and when you hear of the true triggers behind the problems that have been brewing out there in the world, it will blow your wits away.' The wrinkles on the old woman's face deepened as she uttered these words.

The Sultan was bemused. But he was beginning to sense that something awful had happened somewhere behind the screen, pushing the ship of the Bijapur Sultanate into a storm that could destroy it forever. Also, something extraordinary had happened at the hands of this woman who had ruled the Sultanate for the past few decades like an empress. How else could this irascible old woman have pushed back the chieftains who had come to arrest her and descended so suddenly here in the middle of the night?

'Every drop of blood that runs through my veins is royal,' Badi Sahiba resumed, preening herself as she did so. 'I was born in a sultan's palace. My father was a sultan; my late husband Mohammed Sahib was a sultan too. The sultan occupying the throne of Golconda—Abdul Qutbshah—is my brother. Not everybody has the kind of lineage that I possess. My heart still beats for the well-being of our Bijapur Sultanate and I continue to do all that I can for its welfare. You don't even know what I have just accomplished.'

'Ammijaan?'

'Without letting it bother you, I have just dispatched a royal regiment of seven thousand horses to suppress a potential revolt at Bankapur. Needless to say, the revolt was not mine. It was someone else's. But I've already made arrangements for dousing this fire of rebellion.'

'What revolt are you talking about?'

'The rebellion was not going to flare up here, but at Bankapur, with ten thousand horsemen all ready to storm out.'

'But, why?'

'To go and join up with your inveterate enemy Sivaji.'

'What???'

'Yes. Those ten thousand from Bankapur and another seven thousand from forts in the neighbourhood of Bijapur were waiting to ride forth.'

'Ya Allah!' exclaimed the Sultan, breaking into a cold sweat. 'Are you sure of what you are saying?'

'Of course, I am. Neither you nor I had got any wind of it.'

'Allah!'

'This combined strength of seventeen thousand soldiers, predominantly margatthya recruits, would have galloped out with a dangerous dream in their heads and hearts. The wicked plot was that Siva would set out from Kolhapur—from the Panhala side—and make a beeline in our direction. On one side would be the intrepid warrior Shahaji and on the other his valorous son; this father-son duo were dreaming the dangerous dream of bringing their two armies together to raze this famous capital city of Bijapur to the ground.'

'Ya parvardigaar!'

'Yes, my lad—'

'Khuda-na-khaasta, if their dreams had materialised, it would have been doomsday for us!'

Even thinking about that prospect made him feel that the earth disintegrated under his feet, and he shivered incontinently. He could be forgiven for it. On the one hand their biggest hero had just been eliminated, and on the other, their nemesis had been waxing with each passing day. And there, far away on the Yamuna bank, sat that predator Aurangzeb with his weapons on the ready, waiting for his prey to drift into sight.

Looking quizzically at Badi Sahiba, the Sultan ventured, 'Forgive me, Ammijaan, I had always considered you as rather a close friend of Shahajiraja.'

'You got it all wrong, Sultan; he was never my friend. If that had been so, I wouldn't have exposed to you the clouds that hover over our Sultanate today. I wouldn't have dispatched our horsemen either, to scotch this incipient rebellion.'

'Ammijaan,' Ali Adilshah turned a little bolder, 'we need to abandon the thought that we owe Shahaji any gratitude for past deeds. This revolt of his gives us cause to put him in chains immediately. All his property in Bengaluru, Kolhapur, Bijapur, Jinji, Tanjavur, Mudgal and other places within our Sultanate should be confiscated. There is nothing wrong in lopping off the branches of his overweening ambition at the earliest!'

Noticing the excitement that danced in the Sultan's eyes, Badi Begum said dryly, 'I can see very well what thoughts are swirling inside your head.'

'Really?' he laughed in embarrassment. 'Tell me, then, what they are.'

'You are eager to pronounce the death sentence on him.'

'No, it's not quite that, but—'

'But you would love to have him killed in an encounter of some kind.'

'Yes, that's true,' he admitted, and added in a sour voice, 'what's wrong with that? It's now two full weeks since Afzal Khan was martyred, and the grief of the common people in Bijapur is such that many of them have not even had a proper meal during this entire period.'

'So, what do you want to do about it?'

'To make that arrogant, tyrannical rebel named Sivaji cry tears of blood. And there's no better way than arresting his beloved father and slaughtering him in the public square.'

Now that the Sultan's heart had been bared, Badi Begum said to him in a soft but firm voice, 'Look Sultan sahib, before he closed his eyes, my husband and your father, Mohammed Sahib, had explained to me with great passion and care that Shahaji has been a friend of the Bijapur state for four years during your grandfather Ibrahim Sahib's time, and for another twenty-four years during your father's reign, adding up to twenty-eight years of loyal service. It was your own ancestors who honoured him with titles and property and made him an important pillar on which the Sultanate has stood. If you decide to ignore this past and decapitate Shahaji only because he is your enemy's father, you will have to pay a heavy price for it in the future.'

'I am not the kind of sultan to tremble at the thought of my ancestors' shadows, Ammijaan. Who would dare cause me harm?'

'You seem to forget, Sultan sahib, that if your army is a hundred thousand strong, forty thousand of them are margatthas. They have come here for employment from the valleys of the Sahyadris and the banks of the rivers Krishna, Bheema and Panchganga. If you know them at all, you will understand that while they may not even care for their gods and goddesses, each man will happily shed his last drop of blood for their dear king Shahaji.'

Badi Begum's words finally found their mark. The Sultan began to see that provoking Shahaji or causing him public harm would invite unwanted repercussions. It did not make sense to throw a stone at a beehive and remain standing under the tree. He also remembered the other enemy that was flexing its muscles on the banks of the Yamuna. Suddenly acquiring a tone of humility, he asked, 'Ammijaan, what do we do about our brother in faith by the Jamuna who is so keen on our welfare? How do we handle the Mughals?'

'Yes, that's a good thought. The fangs and talons of the Mughals are truly poisonous. Keep that in mind always. Suppose, for a moment, that both Shahaji and Sivaji get eliminated. Do you think the Mughals will sit fawning over us? On the contrary, they will find their passage clear for running across Hindustan and swallowing up whatever their eyes fall on, Muslim states included. Nobody has swallowed up more Sultanates than they have.'

The Sultan returned to his bed in a thoughtful frame of mind to find that his favourite wife Khursheed Khanum was still awake. 'What does Badi Sahiba have to say about Sivaji and Shahaji?'

'Begum, whether it is Sivaji or Aurangzeb, it all boils down to politics. Assume, for a moment, that Aurangzeb and I together destroy this Sivaji: will Aurangzeb then think of me as a fellow Muslim and hold me close to his heart? If that man could chop his brothers to bits, what consideration is he likely to have for others?'

The news that the Sultan had been getting from the north was not of the pleasantest kind. It had reached his ears that Aurangzeb would often refer to Ali Adilshah in full durbar as 'that brat of a female cook', the love-child of Mohammed Shah's philandering with his kitchen staff. He had even circulated a firman that the Deccan sultans should not assume the honorific of 'Shah'. At best, they could aspire for the title of 'Khan'.

Sultan Ali Adilshah fiercely resented Aurangzeb's disparaging references to himself as well as to the rulers of Deccan in general. At the same time, he was deeply agitated by the steadily increasing strength of Shahaji's son Shivaji and the consequent growth of this powerful Maratha kingdom right at the border of his own. The one desire that he carried close to his heart was the elimination of Shivaji, and this had robbed him of all peace and contentment.

3

THE KOLHAPUR BATTLEFIELD

Dark clouds had begun to descend lately upon Pawangadh, the twin fort of Panhala, and the extensive plateau of Masai on the far side. Torches and flambeaux began to be lit on the main fort, in the temples and the palaces. Bunches of soldiers and guards were posted at close intervals atop the fort's wide battlements. Torches made of wild grass would occasionally flare up among the flambeaux which, from a distance, looked like the eyes of wild cats.

As soon as Afzal Khan had been killed at the foot of Pratapgadh the previous month, horsemen commanded by Shivraya and Netaji Palkar had galloped off in all directions. Soon the Maratha braves had captured all the Adilshahi stations across the Krishna, the Koyna, the Vaarna, right up to the Ghataprabha.

Shivraya knew no relaxation of mind or body. His sole ambition was to extend the boundaries of his Swarajya, and in this ceaseless strife time had lost all meaning for him. He no longer noticed when the sun would announce the arrival of a new day or the departure of the old one. So overpowering was the passion that drove him that his body had forgotten what it meant to be weary even when his exhausted horses needed to be changed thrice to cover his daily run.

Only eighteen days had passed since the Pratapgadh episode when he mounted his assault on Panhala. He had Shambhuji Jadhav for company during that foray, the same Shambhuji whose grandfather Achaloji Jadhav had been killed in Daulatabad. Jijausahib had brought him up as her own grandson. In Jijau's absence, it was his responsibility to keep a constant eye on Shivraya. That evening, the two of them put the Bijapur soldiery to the sword with such vehemence that, by dinnertime, the Adilshahi fort-keeper had raised the white flag and surrendered the fort.

That night too, the king found no occasion to get off his horse's back. He had millet bhaakari with Kolhapuri jhunka that Siddhi Hilaal had brought, and drank cold water to wash it down while still astride his horse. By his side were the sardars Netaji, Pandhare and Shambhuji Jadhav.

In the orange light of the flambeaux, the king was carefully inspecting the state of the fortifications and battlements he had just captured. The slightest doubt would draw him like a magnet to peer closely at the strength or weakness of a wall and make remarks to the lieutenants around him. It was daybreak by the time he had concluded his microscopic examination of the bulwarks and ramparts of Panhala.

This had become a peculiar practice with Shivraya. While other kingdoms and empires celebrated victories on the battlefield with nights of feasting and revelry, Shivraya, on the contrary, would feel his blood course with redoubled vigour and spend sleepless nights securing the gains he had made. Instead of indulging in hedonistic carousals, he would devote his energy afresh to the service of his dream.

It would be a busy day, anyway, in the Panhala palace. For one thing, an important meeting had been arranged for the Raja with Swami Paramaanand Nevaskar. For another, while no news had arrived from the spies in Hindustan for the past two days, and this was a matter of concern, the information coming in from Bijapur was extremely important and would require a strategic response.

The news of the fall of Panhala had seriously agitated Ali Adilshah. 'That Siva devoured Afzal first and now he has swallowed Panhala. He plucked out one eye first and the second eye next. That hellhound of a margatthya has made us blind!' This despairing remark of the Sultan carried a lot of implications. Shambhuji Jadhavrao had also sent this secret message to the king, 'Shivbadada, there's plenty of bustle happening in the Rangana fort and also in the valley of the river Bhogavati alongside.' The Raja had also got information of enemy troops climbing the Anuskura ghat over the previous two days and arriving at the summit during the night.

In the evening, Swami Paramaanand sat blissfully in lotus-pose on a deerskin spread over the settee in the palace hall. It had been quite a few months since he had arrived in the kingdom. Kavindra Paramaanand Govindbhatt had earned great renown for himself across Hindustan as an accomplished scholar of Sanskrit.

The word going aound was that swamiji was in every way the equal of the great pundit Gaga Bhatt in matters of scholarship as well as religious ritual. He had also traversed the length and breadth of the country on a spiritual quest, starting from Kashmir in the north, past the banks of the Ganga and the Yamuna, all the way to Jagannath Puri in the east, and then down to the Rameshwar temple on the southern coast.

The swami was about sixty-five years of age, but he didn't carry an inch of flab on his body. He was slim as a tamarind fruit. The Raja couldn't take his eyes off him: his eyes, as soulful as they were large and beautiful, his pale skin, with an impressive lustre always playing on his face, head domed like a coconut, a vertical vermilion mark on the broad brow, the deep chest, the Kashi-style dhotar wrapped round his waist, and the garland of rudraksh seeds around his neck.

Swamiji had spent a few months in the Navagazi durbar of Shahajiraja in Bengaluru. It was on the recommendation of Shahaji that he had first arrived at Rajgadh, escorted by a cavalry squad that had been sent especially for him. After a quick chat with Jijausahib, he had set off immediately to meet Shivraya. Those were the days when battle was raging in Pratapgadh, and Swamiji was keen to personally witness the ongoing conflict with Afzal Khan. Soon his retinue of palanquins and a good sixty disciples arrived at Pratapgadh.

Far too tied up in the Afzal Khan imbroglio, Shivraya had entrusted the responsibility of attending to Swamiji's needs to the senior sardar Kanhojibaba. After vanquishing Afzal Khan, he had got sucked into the usual labour of putting things in order. This morning after the conquest of Panhala was the first opportunity he had got to have a relaxed conversation with Swamiji and he was looking forward to it eagerly.

The Raja flashed a pleasant smile in the direction of Swamiji. The latter told the king that he was a native of Nevasha on the banks of the Ghoda and that he had begun his worship of Sarasvati, the goddess of learning, from childhood. Reminding the king that he had just been to Rajgadh, he added, 'Your revered mother looked very worried.'

'Oh?'

'It was during the monsoons that you had set alight the funeral pyre of your Ranisahib. It's been four months now since the great mother has had a glimpse of her son's face.'

'Yes, that's true,' said the king in a regretful voice.

The night air was blowing in through the grand arched windows of the fort. The beloved image of Jijausahib appeared before his mind's eye. Ever since that episode of the slaughter at Kanakgiri, she had only one message for the Raja, 'That hitman of Destiny who goes by the name of Afzal Khan, the person who brought down your elder brother Sambhaji and your cousin Santaji Jadhav—that butcher has to be exterminated at the earliest.'

Now, with the unprecedented victory achieved at Pratapgadh, she would be longing to hold the face of her triumphant son in her hands. Steeped in the memory of his mother, the king said, 'How do I say it, Swamiji? For the past few days I have been so busy galloping across the length and breadth of this Maaval country that I have barely pulled my feet out of the stirrups! It seems that the horse's back has become my throne, and riding night and day is now my administrative routine.'

'Raje, it's the mother's guileless heart, overflowing with love like the pores of a honeycomb.'

'Yes, Swamiji. I had decided to head towards Rajgadh as soon as Panhala was under control, but what can I do? Secret news has arrived of war clouds blowing towards me. And my feet, which had already turned in the direction of my mother, have suddenly turned to lead.'

The conversation between the two would occasionally be punctuated by the arrival of a minion or a spy with some fresh intelligence. Moropant, who was sitting by their side, would also supply some information when required.

Shivraya turned towards Swamiji and said, 'You are a profound scholar of Sanskrit; how did a celebrated person like you think of visiting us in this tiny Swarajya tucked away in the folds of these valleys and mountains?'

Swamiji's immediate impulse was to give the king a detailed account of his conversations with Shahajiraja, but he restricted himself to saying,

'It was Shahajibaba himself who suggested that I should visit the country of Maharashtra.'

'Why would he have done that?'

'The senior Maharaj said that he was no more than a ghost of the past. He said that the present belonged to Shivba who was at this moment fighting in the land of the twelve Maavals to drive out alien powers. He recommended that I should come this way because history was being created here; to experience the forging of history in the furnace of the present … that would bring grace to my style!'

'Waah, Swamiji, you are welcome.'

By now, senior officials had begun gathering in the office for an important meeting. Curious as ever, the king asked, 'Swamiji, what do the common people across the country have to say about our administration and our adventures?'

'The sole topic of conversation everywhere these days is your annihilation of Afzal Khan. There are, of course, a few contrary voices here and there that indulge in nitpicking.'

'What nits could they be picking?'

Swamiji looked embarrassed.

'Please, Swamiji, you must tell me.'

'Well,' Swamiji proceeded hesitantly, 'their only reproach is that … actually they do regard Shivajiraja as valiant, but … that his sword flashes only when under the protective cover of hills and valleys, and from behind trees and bushes …'

'What does that mean?'

'That, unlike other brave warriors, Shivaji does not have the courage to take on a raging enemy in an open battlefield.'

Swamiji soon took his leave, but his parting statement had shaken the king to his core. Was that what the people thought of him? That the mountains and jungles of the Sahyadris marked the limits of his gallantry? That evening, not only Netaji Palkar, Siddhi Hilaal and Moropant Pingale, but even close relatives like Shambhuji Jadhav lost their king's attention. He seemed to be swallowed up by an extraordinary state of unrest.

Two days passed by. On the third night, Netaji and Sardar Pandhare came to meet the king. Netaji gave him the news, 'Maharaj, the regiments of Rustam-e-Zamaan and Faazal Khan moved out of the Rangana fort last night. We have also learned that several cavalry units and thousands of infantrymen marched out of Bijapur a few days ago. Two armies of the enemy moving out at the same time cannot possibly be a coincidence.'

'Oh, really?' the king exclaimed. But the furrows on his brow had disappeared. He snapped his fingers and said, 'The deployment of a fresh army from Bijapur and the effort to scale the ghat of Anuskura here in Konkan: there is only one meaning that can be drawn from this. The enemy is searching for an opportunity to fall deeply in love with us!'

After a little while, the king called Moropant Pingale over to his private quarters and said, 'Tell Siddhi Hilaal that he should stay by my side for a few days.'

From the days when the king had set out to conquer the Adilshahi territories of Kaagal, Kolhapur, Vaarna, Vaalava, Vitey, Bhalwani, Wangi and Nimsod in the Raibagh district as well as the Khatau-Phaltan division, he had taken along with him Siddhi Hilaal and his son Siddhi Wah Wah. Perceiving the trust that Shivraya placed in them, the father-son duo had responded warmly. Along with Shambhuji Jadhav, they would attend to all the personal needs of their king: his clothes, his weapons and the two or three horses he would need for the day's ride, among other matters big and small.

Siddhi Hilaal was an extremely tenacious and intrepid fighter; his short stature, dark complexion, thin moustache, sparse eyebrows and small, blinking eyes made him look like a person of Chinese origin, although of the dark kind. The closeness that had developed between this nimble-footed, enterprising man and his king had begun to discompose quite a few people. That was why Moropant Pingale quietly raised the issue with the king that evening, saying, 'Maharaj, a large number of persons in our army out there are a bit upset with Siddhi Hilaal.'

'Pant,' the Raja said in his direct manner, 'whatever people out there may think, I have seen the spark of faith shine bright in the eyes of our Siddhi here. Won't you ask when and where?'

'Maharaj!'

'After the decimation of the Adilshahi army at Pratapgadh, this man Siddhi and his son Wah Wah were among the four or five thousand prisoners of war that stood shivering in the cold night air. While their compatriots stayed there nursing their wounds, these two, resolved to serve me and began their trudge over and across the Mahabaleshwar mountains. It was on the third day that they met me at the gate of the Chandan-Vandan fort on the banks of the Krishna. Horseless, barefoot, tired and hungry they certainly were, but the eagerness to serve our Swarajya that sparkled in their eyes could not be missed.'

'Waah, Raje! Wonderful!'

The Raja smiled warmly and said, 'Moropant, I don't understand why people should sit discriminating in their heads on account of one man being a Musalman and another being a Christian, a person belonging to this caste or that one. One can easily learn the true meaning of life by observing a gardener. This might be a rose and that a jasmine, the other a champa or a ketaki—does this man who turns the soil ever discriminate between flowers? Fragrance is the only thing that matters to him. My heart too homes in like a bee on the fragrance of a person's character and deeds.'

As he stood listening to his king's loud musings, Moropant thought of Sardar Pandhare, Sardar Jadhavrao and Sardar Kharate who had all arrived at Pratapgadh to fight on the side of Afzal Khan. After they had lost the battle and also their confidence, it was Siddhi Hilaal who had used the magic of his tongue to reach out to these dispirited warriors and turn them around. He had then espoused their cause with the king and got them recruited into the service of the Swarajya.

It was the month of Paush, the turn of the year by the English calendar. Well into the day, the fog that lay over the heath between Kaagal and Kolhapur gave no indication of lifting. But the sun's rays were making valiant efforts to penetrate the screen and had succeeded in piercing through here and there to go frolicking on the earth.

That was where the Adilshahi cavalrymen who had arrived the previous evening had pitched camp. They were joined there the same night by the units of Rustam-e-Zamaan and Faazal Khan who had galloped in from Konkan. Breakfast was still in progress in the various tents scattered over the heath. However, with Rustam-e-Zamaan goading them for an early departure, dismantling had begun from early dawn. The elephant squads, the horsemen, the field-gunners, the camel units—all were busy gathering up their paraphernalia, which, of course, meant that many had to consume their breakfast standing, if not running.

Rustam-e-Zamaan wouldn't let the senior officials eat in peace either. His horse went galloping past their tents, urging them to hurry. 'Wind up, wind up quickly,' he yelled. 'We have to mount our raid on Panhala before night falls. That Sivaji Raja needs to be taught a lesson!'

Army custom required the quartermaster staff to make an early start. Even earlier, the units that went fodder-hunting for the animals had set out. Therefore, these men had made considerable headway and were now riding through the fog with as much speed as they could muster. As they peered through the curtain of haze, what they discerned some distance ahead made their jaws drop.

There, simmering through the thickening and thinning fog in front of them, they saw what they estimated to be an army of thousands of soldiers flaunting ochre pennants on their spears. It was as if an entire mountain of Marathas was closing in upon them. In the lead was a man mounted on a sparkling white horse. He wore a red velvet jacket, and around his neck swung a necklace of emeralds and another of shells. His headgear gleamed like the dome of a temple, topped by an emerald plume. Occasionally the young rays of the sun would filter through the thin wrap of mist, turning everything into gold. In this strange light, the arresting figure of Shivraya radiated a mesmerising force.

The young odd-job men of the quartermaster staff immediately turned their mules around and made a beeline for the Adilshahi camp. 'Go, see what is coming at us!' they yelled, as they came close.

'What's the matter, boys?' some enquired.

'Sivaji has come! There, across the stream, his entire army is waiting for us.'

The shock of Shivaji's sudden appearance drained the assemblage of all their new-found confidence. All the enthusiasm of the morning vaporised within seconds. Those who still hadn't finished their breakfast tossed the remnants of their meal away and threw startled looks at each other as they downed water from bamboo tumblers. The sentinel scouts too came running back, confirming the news beyond any trace of doubt.

Rustam-e-Zamaan pushed away the man tying the string of his cummerbund and strode up to the entrance of his tent. The sun had now climbed quite high in the sky and shredded the curtain of haze at a hundred places. There, barely half a mile in front of them, an entire field was speckled with ochre flags. The sight of this impenetrable wall of frenzied Maratha soldiers turned the Adilshahi hearts to water.

'Ya Allah,' Rustam-e-Zamaan muttered, 'we were planning to encounter this Sivaji at Panhala this evening! And here he stands now at the edge of our camp like a river suddenly rising in flood! Is this a man or a demon?'

'But why did this mountain rat suddenly decide to meet us out here in the open?' Faazal Khan panted.

This powerful jolt administered by Shivaji had stunned Rustam-e-Zamaan. He was the overlord of a big province that extended from the Konkan stretch of Rajapur-Rangana all the way down to Karvar and Raibagh in northern Karnataka. The entire region had been placed under his control. It was not very long ago that Ali Adilshah had sent a sharp missive to him, which read, 'The world knows of your family's intimate relations with that recalcitrant Sivaji. You must now prove that you have not abandoned loyalty to your land, your religion and your sense of honour. All that I can say to a valiant man like you is that blackening the enemy's face always augurs a brighter future than blackening one's own.'

The fear that had seeped into the bones of Afzal Khan's son Faazal Khan since the Pratapgadh battle suddenly resurfaced at the sight of Shivaji's mountain-sized army materialising out of thin air. Seeing his panic, Rustam threw him a sarcastic smile and said, 'Don't you worry, Faazal miyaan, friendship is one thing and loyalty to one's king is another. I have eaten the salt of the Sultanate, so how can I ever betray it?'

The fog had now lifted completely. Those ten thousand swords flashing in the sun, the bright pennants waving in the sturdy hands of the Maratha horsemen, the music of the wind playing upon those fluttering flags—it made for a grand sight.

The Maratha horses had raced all night on subsistence rations of fodder. It was only at around midnight that the animals were given a water break. They had drunk their fill at the Panchganga under the light of the flambeaux. Instead of getting into a long-winded address, Shivraya had come straight to the point with his men. 'My brave men from Maaval, let's show our enemy in the clearest terms that we Marathas are not the mountain rats they think us to be. We are the lions of the open battlefield; we roar. We can grind our enemy into the earth like grass under elephant legs.'

As the bugles and trumpets were made ready for blowing, the king looked to the left and noticed a hermit on a horse a little distance away, waiting excitedly for the battle to begin. Recognising Swami Paramaanand, the king smiled.

The sound of horns, bugles and kettledrums took over, soon to be joined by loud roars of 'Har har Mahadev' and 'Shivaji Maharaj ki jai'. The Maratha battle cries were returned from the other side by loud yells of 'Deen-deen' and 'Allah-o-akbar'.

Weapon clashed against weapon. The incessant hammering of thousands of hooves ground the soil underfoot into powder. Animals rammed against animals, men against men. Pandemonium reigned. The dust kicked up by feet and hooves rose into the air and turned the sky a dirty brown.

The Maavalis had gained dominance of the field from the word go. Soon the Adilshahi forces were on the backfoot and seemed to shrink into themselves. As the day advanced, it appeared that the Bijapuris were becoming more and more defensive in their tactics. Shivaji made a sign to Netaji Palkar, at which Netaji turned around and signalled to Shambhuji Jadhav who was virtually standing in his stirrups as he swung his sword all around him. On receiving Netaji's nod, Shambhuji waved to his archers who immediately let loose hundreds of arrows. The sudden arrival of these flying weapons pushed the dispirited Adilshahi men into further disarray.

As they began retreating with tortured cries of 'Allah, this is the death of me!', Shivraya spurred his horse forth aggressively, inspiring his men to follow with loud roars of 'Jai Bhavani!!!' and 'Jai Shivaji!!!'

Desperate to stem the advancing tide of the Marathas, Rustam-e-Zamaan brought his own archers to the front. Uncaring of the shafts raining down upon him, Shivaji pressed forward relentlessly. In a little while, the Adilshahi archers noticed that after hitting the king on the chest and back, the arrows would fall harmlessly to the ground. The lower edge of his red velvet coat would fly up often, but no harm ever ensued. The Bijapuri archers were at their wits' end. Was there, after all, some truth in the stories that the spirits of the Sahyadris formed a protective ring around this Sivaji?

Accompanying the king's forward thrust, to his right and left were his trusty lieutenants Siddhi Hilaal and Shambhuji Jadhav. Few other than these two knew the secret of the ineffectiveness of the enemy's arrows. Under his velvet coat, the king wore armour plates fashioned out of tortoise shell on his chest and back. These were tough enough to withstand the weight of an elephant. The sleeves that protected Shivraya's arms from harm were made of the skin of wild elephants from the Malabar forests. These gifts sent by Koyajiraja from the south for his Shivajidada had turned out to be magically protective.

With their prime weapon now failing to bring the king down, the piqued archers began to aim at his eyes. But Shivraya was adroit enough to handle that. Like a falcon that flaps its wings and swerves mid-air to avoid projectiles aimed at it, the king's sharp ears would detect the swoosh of a coming dart, enabling him to duck and swerve and let it fly past harmlessly.

Shivaji's sudden and spirited assault flummoxed Rustam-e-Zamaan. He was finding it impossible to corner the Maratha king in any way. Meanwhile, Netaji Palkar's roan horse had begun moving quickly in the direction of Faazal Khan. The latter had not forgotten the man's dash and hauteur during their encounters at Pratapgadh. Seeing the zest with which Netaji was mounting his assault, Khan's men looked for escape routes behind them. Very soon, his flanks were deserted.

The Marathas had whipped themselves into a frenzy. Alongside Shivraya, Waghoji Tupey, Hiroji Ingale, Godaji Jagtap, Bhimaji Wagh and Sidhoji Nimbalkar launched furious attacks on their adversaries. Shambhuji Jadhav's bowmen created mayhem among the ranks of the enemy. Shambhuji himself was like a lion on the hunt. His father Santaji

Jadhav had been martyred along with Sambhaji in the battle of Kanakgiri, and the thought of his father's great achievement would not let the son know any peace. To his mind, there was no greater glory than to be the first in his family's third generation to offer his life for Swarajya.

Shivaji's white stallion was here, there and everywhere on the battlefield; caked with enemy blood and dust, its coat had turned brownish-black. Amidst the fray, an arrow came flying and buried itself in the king's left thigh. It was Rustam-e-Zamaan who had noticed the futility of the arrows raining on Shivaji's body and changed strategy. Though blood began oozing out of the wound and soon soaked the shoe in his left stirrup, it did not arrest the king's forward momentum.

His sardars, however, were enraged at the sight of their Raja's bloodied leg; they swung their swords in the air and went storming into the enemy ranks with greater vigour. When Rustam-e-Zamaan moved into the line of sight of the inflamed Godaji, he was about to dispatch his spear in that direction when Maharaj screamed, 'Stop, Godaji! What are you doing?'

'But … but … Raje?'

'No! Not on your life!'

Frustrated at the loss of this opportunity to send his spear through Rustam's heart, Godaji tossed the weapon away in disgust. As he and Siddhi Hilaal were tying a scarf around the king's wound, Godaji asked in suppressed irritation, 'Why did you stop me, Raje? Who will pay for this wound that has been inflicted on your thigh?'

'Godaji, this wound will heal in due course; don't make much of it. However, if you had done what you had set out to do, the wound of that deed would have remained suppurating in my heart for an entire lifetime. That man Rustam-e-Zamaan, whose chest you would have pierced, is certainly our enemy on the battlefield, but by the ethics of humanity, he is my brother.'

By sunset, the Adilshahi army had been handed a resounding defeat. Nearly a thousand of their soldiers had lost their lives, while several of them had made good their escape down the first lane they espied. Faazal Khan was so scarred by his earlier encounters with the Maavalis that he had abandoned the field even before the battle had truly warmed up. At the end of the day, the Maratha men were richer by two thousand horses and twelve elephants.

At sunset, the Raja could see Rustam-e-Zamaan riding out of the battlefield in the company of a dozen of his fellow warriors. Silhouetted against the red and gold of that evening sky, Rustam turned around and threw a glance at Shivaji. Slim of build and sharp featured, he wore an endearing smile under his dark-red Turani headgear.

The distance that separated them could have been covered in a dozen or so leaps. If the king had wanted, he could have pressed the spurs into his horse or simply signalled to Netaji or Godaji, who were eagerly waiting for a nod to take the whole bunch of them under custody. However, he let them go. The could-have-been prisoners ambled into the sunset and beyond.

The next day, the Raja called a meeting of his senior sardars and other grandees at the Panhala fort. Although several battles had been won since Pratapgadh, none of them had had the time to celebrate these victories. This time around, however, the king insisted that everyone in the fort should celebrate the event with some sweetmeats. Noticing the rather crestfallen face of Godaji Jagtap, he remarked, 'Godajirao, it appears that you have taken yesterday's event a little too much to heart.'

'And why not, Maharaj?' responded Godaji grumpily. 'Why did you have to stop me? What did you owe to his father that you simply allowed him to walk away?'

'You don't realise the truth that you have just uttered, Godaji. The debts of gratitude I owe his father cannot be repaid in a lifetime. I do carry that load of gratitude in my heart.'

'Are you serious, Raje?'

'Of course! When my father had gone to Karnataka, it was this Rustam's father, the revered Randullah sahib, who handed over to the senior Maharaj the freshly captured Bengaluru fort as if it were food on a platter. It is god's own truth that this was where Shahajiraje lived with the luxury and grandeur of an independent king. It was inside the precincts of this very fort that our father taught us the fine art of handling weapons and fighting wars, of dodging gunfire and pushing forward in the most adverse of circumstances.'

This was a story that would have melted the hardest of hearts, and so it did. Within the next few days, Rustam-e-Zamaan sent a secret missive to Shivraya, informing him that he had decided not to return to Bijapur immediately so as to avoid the prospect of getting into arguments with the Sultan. Instead, he had set up camp at a place called Hukkeri in Karnataka; this town was a part of his jagir.

Meanwhile Swami Paramaanand sat in his study at Panhala, jotting down all that he had experienced and observed during the battle he had just witnessed. This material would be part of a biography of Shivraya that he had decided to write. After much contemplation, he picked up his quill, dipped it in the inkpot and began committing to paper the following words which, translated from the Sanskrit, would mean:

> Bereft of confidence, fearful, tense,
> Rustam-e-Zamaan walked out of the battlefield.
> Taking him prisoner was the easiest of tasks,
> But Shiva let him walk away.
> Could a high-born king ever think of using the sword
> On one who had surrendered himself?

Swamiji had engraved in his mind's eye each of the singular and unprecedented events that he had been witness to. Now he sat immersed in the exercise of transforming those images into words and weaving them together with rhyme and rhythm.

4

MAY DOROJI PHAAKADE WIN!

That evening in the Pratapgadh valley, laden with dust and smoke; the felling of the massive Afzal Khan like the trunk of a giant tree; the merciless shredding of the Bijapur army in the dense jungles of Jawali at the foot of Pratapgadh; those few Adilshahi soldiers who, despite the scorching defeat, swung their swords once more in a desperate bid to salvage their future; the spirited Maratha swords that came flashing down on them; the entire countryside soaked in blood and sweat; the stormy night that descended on the forest; horses rubbing flanks in hot pursuit of the broken, fleeing army of the great Khan; the breathless horror and adventure of it all; the spine-chilling experience of standing at the very brink of death!

Every one of those episodes was as fresh in Shivajiraje's memory as if it had happened only moments ago. He had reached his palace atop Pratapgadh, his hands still soaked in Afzal Khan's blood. He was about to take a cleansing bath before offering a thanksgiving prayer when he remembered the three ships that Afzal Khan had docked in the harbour at Dabhol.

Afzal Khan had planned it all meticulously even before the battle had begun. As soon as Pratapgadh was vanquished, he would put Shivajiraje in chains and whisk him off to Bijapur. However, if he dragged Shivaji along the Chaphal-Karad route or across the plateau lands of Indapur and Pandharpur, he would be traversing Maratha territory. Everywhere on this red-hot trail, his people would gather in their thousands, sword in hand and willing to shed their last drop of blood to free their king. Hence

Afzal Khan had put in place a much smarter plan: even before he left Wai for Pratapgadh via Mahabaleshwar, he had moved three of his personal ships from the Vengurla harbour northward past Rajapur and anchored them at Dabhol on the Konkan coast.

The idea was that as soon as Shivaji was taken prisoner, they would hit the track that came down the ghat from Rankadesar that very night. They would then race across the hills and valleys, entering Konkan from the Poladpur side. Their dangerous royal prisoner would be put in fetters and dragged to the port at Dabhol in a day and a half at the most, thrown on board a ship and taken down the waterway to Vengurla.

At the Vengurla bay the party would disembark, ride through the night and arrive at Bijapur early the next morning. As the captor of such a formidable enemy, Afzal Khan would be taken in a victory procession along the streets of his beloved Bjiapur, with people dancing around him in a frenzy. Such were the dreams that Afzal Khan had been dreaming for a long time, but alas! All these dreams as well as his devious plans for fulfilling them were duly reported to Shivaji from time to time.

Sardar Doroji Phaakade, a well-built and immensely courageous man, was standing close by that night at Pratapgadh when Shivaji signalled to him and said, 'Set off for Dabhol right now, Dorojirao, just as you are. Capture the three warships and all the soldiers aboard.'

'Absolutely, Raje, at once!' Doroji responded with a smart bow.

'Take charge of the enemy's boats and strip them of their cargo, from gunpowder to grain to the last thread you may find. The ethics of war clearly stipulate that the victor has legal rights to everything that belongs to a defeated enemy.'

'Yes, Raje, I shall be on my way immediately.'

As he turned to leave, the king added with a smile, 'Aho, hear this out too: both wiles and weaponry have to change according to changing circumstances.'

'As you command, Raje.'

'It is easy to rout the enemy's guns and animals from a battlefield on land, but when this game is played on water, it can be as dangerous as it is fascinating. Battles fought on water need method as much as they need courage. You may set sail believing that you have crocodile skin on you, but you must prepare to be scorched by gunpowder too.'

Sharp-witted Doroji immediately caught the king's drift and laughed as he said, 'Stop, Raje. Life spent under your tutelage has taught me to gather that you mean "curd and rice" the moment you utter "cur..." No need to say another word. I've understood everything.'

'Really? All right, then, what was I hinting at?'

'When ships of the sea are in the mix, you need the help of accomplished boatmen ... people like the Tandels who've spent all their lives grappling with water.'

'Arey waah, Dorojirao! You've hit the nail on the head. All right, then. Set out in the name of Goddess Bhawani, and may success be with you.'

That very night, Doroji Phaakade's horses went galloping through the dense Pratapgadh forests down the steep slope leading to Konkan. Scorning thirst and hunger, he and his men reached the coconut and betelnut groves on the outskirts of Dabhol the next afternoon. Despite their haste, however, precious time was lost in gathering skilled boatmen, sea-hardened fishermen and Malabari youngsters at short notice for the task in hand. Consequently, by the time they arrived at the port, the ships that had lain in anchor there had disappeared along with their crew. All that a deeply agitated Doroji Phaakade encountered was a silent, peaceful harbour, not to mention the occasional seabirds squawking and wheeling in the sky.

Doroji immediately got busy gathering as much information as he could from the townspeople. News of the battle at Pratapgadh had reached the Konkan coast quite a few hours ahead of them. Even before that, Afzal Khan's soldiers and the Tandel oarsmen on board the three ships had been under instructions to leave at very short notice. They were primed to sail out of the port within minutes of the chained and bound Shivaji being brought on board. Much to their dismay, however, what had transpired was just the opposite. The Khan's horsemen had galloped in without their royal prisoner and wailed, 'Ya Allah, we are ruined! That treacherous Siva tore out Khan sahib's bowels and dispatched him to Allah's house. The entire army has been ripped apart!'

'Let's vanish from here while it's still possible,' the soldiers clamoured as they clambered onto the ships. Mahmood Shareef, the Adilshahi subedar of Dabhol, ensured that no time was wasted in dispatching the ships southwards.

Doroji Phaakade knew no rest. Shivaji's instructions kept ringing in his ears. He regarded it as no less than a sacred duty to give chase to the fleeing ships and capture them at any cost. While a squad of four hundred horsemen began racing southward along the coast under his command, a fleet of sturdy fishing boats that he had gathered in Dabhol and Guhaghar followed him along the water route, loaded with seasoned sailors and hardy boatmen who were armed to the teeth.

Neither the stormy winds nor the waves lashing at the shore could deter the rapid advance of the Maratha men. If anything, these forces of nature accompanied the rhythm of their hoof-beats, spurring Doroji and his squad to gallop on ceaselessly.

When he reached the Rajapur coast, Doroji was informed of Mahmood's nimble movements. He and his men rode up to the imposing red sandstone building of the English warehouse where they ran into its governor, Henry Revington. Doroji came straight to the point, 'Where are the three ships of Afzal Khan?'

'Mr. Doroji,' came the insolent reply, 'we hear that the battle is taking place in the mountains of Pratapgadh. What, then, could Adilshahi ships be doing here in Rajapur?'

'Henry sahib,' growled Doroji, 'you may be the great governor of the English warehouse here, but don't take me for a milk-suckling infant.'

'I don't know what you are talking about.'

'Stop playing these games with me. I'm aware of everything that's been going on. At daybreak you let that fellow Mahmood sneak out of the harbour with two ships and sail off in the direction of Vengurla. And look at the inland river bank down there: there stands the third of Afzulya's ships. By law it belongs to us now. I demand that it be handed over to me immediately.'

'Sorry, my good man, but do have a look at the flag that's fluttering atop the mast.'

Without bothering to respond to Revington's remark, Doroji immediately took his men down to the riverbank and took charge of the ship. As his men were unloading the cargo, an officer by the name of Philip Gifford came charging at Doroji, pistol in hand. Doroji swiftly aimed a kick at the pistol and sent it flying into the water. Before Gifford even knew what was happening, he was overpowered and manacled. The

Englishman was then marched out of Rajapur along with all the loot that Doroji and his men had collected from the ship. All that Revington could do was to stand at the gate of the warehouse and glower at the Maratha men with flaming eyes.

Meanwhile, Shivraya had been waiting eagerly for the postbag to arrive from Rajapur. As soon as it did, Gomajibaba undid the silk string in a hurry and the Raja's secretary read it out for all to hear. Shivaji's men had achieved greater success at Rajapur-Kharepatna than he had expected. Doroji Phaakade had compelled the Englishman named Revington to prepare a draft for a treaty. The terms and conditions that those hat-wearers had been forced to agree to were quite interesting.

The king then remained thoughtful for a good while, after which he sat in a circle with his associates and advisers discussing the matter at hand in detail. Finally, he began dictating a letter for Doroji Phaakade. The secretary, sitting at his sloping desk, picked up a quill and began committing the following words to paper in a neat hand:

> Dorojirao,
>
> You appear to have taught that hatted English official named Revington a lesson. I consider it my privilege to praise you for this act of heroism. The other important thing is this: there is this thorn called Janjira that has settled in the heel of our Swarajya. If it isn't pulled out at the earliest, I will have to live with its painful throb for the rest of my life.
>
> There's no need to hurry, though. We propose to mount a raid on the Siddhis of Janjira in a few months. When this happens, I expect Revington Sahib to be by our side with his English guns and ammunition. Going by the promises we have received from him, the English are bound even, if need arises, to shed blood for our cause. These promises, of course, have not yet been committed to stamp and paper, and it will be good if this happens at the earliest.
>
> One thing, however, always needs to be kept in mind. Their fancy hats may appear as attractive as mountains seen from a distance, but if you look closely beneath this headgear, you will find nothing but the scum of crafty selfishness. We, therefore, need to make sure that Revington lives by the promise of aid that he has made for our imminent conflict at Janjira.

Keep a sharp eye on these white traders till such time as everything is put in order. Firangi, by definition, means deviousness and reneging on promises.

Nothing more to say, except a final word of advice: Observe the mantra of alertness at all times.

5

AURANGZEB AND SHAISTA: THE UNCLE-NEPHEW FRIENDSHIP

'Emperor Aurangzeb has departed for the house of Allah. But internal squabbles, fear of enemy attack and other such worries have tied the hands of the administrators. Which is why the passing away of Alamgir after his illness is not being made public.' This gossip doing the rounds, along with the other drops of secret news leaking out, had robbed the denizens of the Yamuna bank of their sleep.

However, Aurangzeb gave them all a rude shock by presenting himself in the flesh in a durbar organised specially for the occasion. Bearing all the marks of wear and tear that his long illness had wrought upon his person, he declared in the Deewaan-e-Aam, the hall of public audience, 'All those who were celebrating the news of my passing away will doubtless be grieved to see me here in flesh and blood. I am one with them in their grief; but the point is, why should I be in a hurry to cross over to the other world? I have already sent three of my dear brothers there with all due honour, while my ailing Abba Huzoor is conveniently living out his worldly days in incarceration at the Agra palace. Indeed, it is rightly said that there is no early relief from this world for evil people like me.'

Muhi-ud-din Mohammad Aurangzeb, who had assumed the regnal title of Alamgir, was forty-four years of age. His huge empire stretched from Afghanistan in the north to Burma in the east. His durbar was bustling with envoys from Bukhara, Persia and the Arab lands, standing before him in abject servility. Aurangzeb's strict and tyrannical rule had created an atmosphere of terror across the realm.

Courtesans and dancers had fled Delhi and Agra in fear of their lives. The slightest sound of music or merrymaking emerging from any locality in these cities would immediately invite a raid by the emperor's police force. Artists were belaboured like thieves, and singers had been reduced to beggary. There was strict prohibition throughout the empire and imbibers ran the risk of having their limbs chopped off.

The lamp of religious tolerance and freedom of belief that Akbar had lit a generation earlier was ruthlessly snuffed out. Most of the Hindu grandees, particularly the Rajputs whom the Great Mughal had bound close to his heart, had now become objects of hate and derision. Equal hate and derision was mandated for the Shi'a, the dissident sect that had broken away from the main body of orthodox Sunni Muslims. As pious as he was fanatical, Aurangzeb would lead the recitation of the Qur'an immediately after the fast was broken in the evenings during the holy month of Ramzan, and continue with the recitation for nine hours at a stretch.

A few months back, he had fallen seriously ill and would often sink into delirium. But he was alert enough to register that his beloved sister Roshanara had begun to look for a successor to his throne and had immediately tossed her out of his affections.

Aurangzeb was the fourth son of emperor Shah Jahan and his wife Mumtaz Mahal. His subjects would often express astonishment in private, of course—that a person born to the most beautiful (and presumably kind) woman in the world should have turned out to be so hard-hearted and bigoted.

When Aurangzeb was still a boy, a soothsayer had alerted Shah Jahan, 'The most renegade of all your princes is this Aurangzeb. One day he is going to be the cause not only of your destruction, but that of your entire lineage.' The emperor had taken this warning to heart. This boy Aurang was the fairest in complexion among the Mughal princes. The emperor would often tell his eldest son Dara Shikoh, 'Never show any mercy to this rascal. He is a white snake that has sprung from my loins. One of these days he is going to bite you and spread his poison in your blood.'

The soothsayer's prophecy came true. Aurangzeb had not only enthusiastically hounded, imprisoned, tortured and finally slaughtered all three of his elder brothers, but even celebrated the event as Shab-e-baaraat, the evening of joy. He had not even spared his own father, a person of no less eminence than Shah Jahan. He had disrupted the water supply to the palace in the Agra fort where he held him prisoner. He had even schemed to have him secretly eliminated.

These blood-curdling deeds had created a dark aura around him and made him a dreaded figure, in whose presence the stoutest hearted quaked with fear. In spite of all this, his maternal uncle Shaista Khan had managed to acquire for himself the privilege of being the emperor's close friend and confidante. Obviously, it was a colourful series of events that had earned him this entitlement.

It was Uncle Shaista who had conveyed verbatim to Aurangzeb his father's message, 'Don't you ever forget, boy, that your old age will bring you more misery than you have brought into mine. Despite being a prince of the realm, you have converted the last days of your old father and king into hell on earth. This act of yours can never find favour with Allah-ta'ala. Even while you have the throne of the empire under your buttocks, you will wander through jungle and heath like the bears that the dervishes drag behind them by their nose-rings.'

'This is wonderful, Maamoojaan,' Aurangzeb happily confessed. 'Whenever I hear my father cursing in bitterness and frustration, when he tears his hair in anger and desperation, I swear, I feel that my day is made.' To ensure that he would not be obliged to visit his incarcerated father every now and then, he had ensconced himself at Red Fort in Delhi, far enough away from Agra.

A pleasant, cool wind was blowing through the palace in the fort on the banks of the Yamuna. The reddish rays of the setting sun had bathed the garden behind the palace in surreal hues. The trees were laden with flowers and fruit. Deer and peacock leapt and strutted everywhere. Skillfully constructed waterfalls and gushing fountains created little streams and rivulets that gurgled pleasantly as they flowed by. The evening air was a heady mix of colour, sound and fragrance. Uncle and nephew were soaking in the atmosphere as they sat chatting under a bower.

'Shall I tell you something, Maamoojaan?'

'By all means, Alam-panaah.'

'A good four or five years have passed since I took over the reins of the empire. The heaven on earth that people call Kashmir is very much a part of our empire, but I have not been able to pay a visit to that land of roses. I have not even been able to indulge in the little bit of hunting that I enjoy so much.'

'Without a doubt, my liege, Kashmir is our own land.'

For Shaista Khan, this growing intimacy with the emperor was nothing less than a blessing from Allah. When the battle for succession had flared up in Delhi during Shah Jahan's reign, it was Shaista Khan who had sent this nephew of his an urgent message, advising him to rush to the capital and jump into the fray, manoeuvre his way past his older siblings by hook or by crook, and snatch the crown for himself.

Quite against character, Aurangzeb had lately been taken over by a strange whim to rebuild his bond with his old father. Not liking what he saw, Shaista Khan sidled up to his nephew and said, 'In my last meeting with Shahjahan sahib, I had told him that trying to snap the bond between father and son is like trying to bisect flowing water with a word. It can never happen.'

'So, what did Abbajaan say?'

'He said that he didn't care that Aurangzeb had caused rivers of blood to flow, but he couldn't forgive him for that one demoniacal deed—'

'Which one?'

'The sheer viciousness of sending to him, wrapped in a kerchief, the severed head of his darling son Dara Shikoh. The humiliation to which the young prince's body had been subjected, and the wicked, black-hearted joke that had been played upon a loving father! He said he would have been eternally thankful if, instead, you had blown him up with a cannon.'

As Shaista spoke on, Aurangzeb's annoyance waxed. The very utterance of his father's name was now sending him into a paroxysm of rage. He had always detested the old man for his philandering nature. Jahaanara Begum, his sister who had inherited the fabled beauty of their mother

Mumtaz Mahal, had remained unmarried despite being the daughter of the most powerful person of his time. Aurangzeb's grouse was that it was their father who had scuttled her prospects of marriage. The gossip doing the rounds in Delhi and other cities along the Yamuna was that the father himself had been preying upon his daughter's beauty like a wild beast.

Such rumours would incense Aurangzeb beyond endurance. 'Lecherous old bastard,' he raged, 'smutty old goat! I've been seeing him from my earliest days. Who did he appoint to guard his palace? Strong, robust young soldiers? No! He had these long-legged beauties specially imported from Iran and Turan orbiting around him, so that he could lust after them. Wanton, filthy man of the first water!'

'Yes, well, there are other things I could say, but I had better hold my tongue,' Shaista muttered.

'No, no, Maamoojaan, come out with it. There's little that can shock me!'

'Well, Alam-panaah, I want to thank you.'

'What for?'

'For not missing a single opportunity to seek your revenge.'

'Why do you say that?'

'I hear that you had once tried to get a firangi doctor to administer poison to the emperor?'

'Yes, I did, but did it help? The old sinner wanted to place that apostate Dara Shikoh on the throne of Hindustan—the dream scenario of our foolish subjects, these infidel Hindus and my senile father! How could a god-fearing Muslim like me let such a catastrophe come to pass? It was my mission to exterminate my heretic brothers, eliminate my wretched father and save the empire from disaster.'

Aurangzeb had proceeded to do exactly that. He had brought peace of a sort upon his empire. All internal squabbles, intrigues and rebellion had been put down with an iron hand. Across the realm, he had whipped the administration into shape and improved security arrangements. In the cities, the old narrow lanes and arches of the cities had been demolished while new battlements and gates were constructed. Protective boundary walls were built on the emperor's orders around the city of Lahore.

Shaking his head as if trying to shake off a bad dream, Aurangzeb said, 'Let's forget all these unpleasant things and talk about a certain unfulfilled desire of mine before I depart for Kashmir.'

'Another unfulfilled desire? You have slaughtered that useless Dara Shikoh like a stray dog and conquered the throne of Delhi!'

'But I haven't savoured the fragrance of his widow, the beautiful Udepuri Begum! And I burn day and night from desire for her!'

'Could Jahaan-panaah be talking about that firangi wife of your late brother?' Shaista responded in a startled voice.

'Yes, Maamoojaan, that's the affliction that keeps me awake nights.'

'Ah, I see!'

'Without her, Kashmir is a wasteland. I in Kashmir, and this ravishing, tormenting beauty in Delhi—does it make any sense?'

Shaista Khan let out a hearty laugh. It was true that Udepuri Begum, a native of Georgia, possessed mesmerising beauty. Turmoil had raged in Aurangzeb's heart ever since he had first set his lecherous eyes upon the unsurpassed loveliness of his brother's wife at the time of their marriage. In that very moment he had decided that once he had succeeded in winning the throne, he would take possession of this intoxicating young beauty too.

Never mind that she was his elder brother's bedmate, or that by the laws of his religion she was his sister-in-law; one day he would certainly make her his consort and the empress of Hindustan. Since the day he ascended the throne, he had found it difficult to stop thinking about bringing this other dream to fruition.

It was true, of course, that unlike most of the grandees and princes who sat in his court, Aurangzeb was not a womanizer by temperament. On the contrary, since he had taken over the reins of the empire, he had placed a ban upon all singing and dancing, parlours and houses of merry-making and indulgence in the city. He had issued a firman ordering the courtesans and prostitutes to settle down into marriage. He had sent into exile all the dancing girls, the musicians, the beautiful temptresses and their touts. In the five years that had passed since his reign began, Aurangzeb had brought the flesh trade and all kinds of hedonistic activities to a grinding halt.

But for all that he was a sworn enemy of vulgarity and self-indulgence, he was a lover of a high order. He was a keen admirer of feminine beauty, Shaista Khan knew. It had come as no surprise to him, therefore, when he learned of his emperor's infatuation for the rare flower that had bloomed in the silver sand of Georgia and was currently living out her life as Dara Shikoh's widow. Like a sharp and shiny rapier, Udepuri Begum had sliced through Aurangzeb's heart and rendered him incapable of retrieving his peace of mind. He wanted her desperately, but the woman herself would spring out of her bed in terror at the very utterance of the name 'Aurangzeb'.

'Maamoojaan, go speak to that foolish woman, tell her that the emperor of Hindustan is standing like a beggar at the door of her heart. Please arrange for this painful cry of mine to reach the ears of my beloved.'

So distraught was Aurangzeb that Shaista Khan was stirred to sympathy. He knew well what force passion for a woman could carry. He began in a solicitous voice, 'Jahaan-panaah, aren't you forgetting something? Since the time her husband was slaughtered, this Udepuri has taken to drinking in a big way. She is under the influence, day in and day out. The emperor Aurangzeb I know detests intoxicants of all kind. If a person even dares to drift into your presence in an inebriated state, you never hesitate to have him tossed into boiling oil.'

'These are two different things, Maamoojaan. Don't you see that for me Udepuri is herself a potent intoxicant? Indeed, when the thought of her beautiful body floats into my head, my senses go into a spin and my legs buckle under me!'

'But your firman ordering that drunkards be flogged in the public square—'

'Those punishments are for others, Maamoojaan, don't you see? Udepuri is my ultimate intoxicant, and I must drink of her at all costs!'

'Subhaan-Allah! If Badshah-salaamat's desire for her has reached such heights, then it is certainly my duty to make sure that it is fulfilled. I am sure I shall not fail in my effort.' With that, Shaista Khan got up from his seat and walked away with determined steps.

6

'IF YOU ARE THE EMPEROR, I AM THE QUEEN OF BEAUTY'

That morning, it appeared as if the Red Fort had caught fire. Cries of alarm rose from every corner of the palace and from the battlements close by. Slaves and minions ran distractedly from one room to the other. All the emperor's wives, the resident guests and the guards had turned white-faced with fear. However hard they tried to keep it under wraps, the news of what had happened at daybreak did finally reach the emperor's ears.

When Aurangzeb heard of how Udepuri Begum had failed by a hair's breadth in her attempt to commit suicide, he was badly rattled. Conscious of his stature as emperor of the realm, he could not create a scene by openly howling or beating his breast. He could not let it out to the world that he had lost all sense of balance because of a 'mere woman', or that he had reached a state where life without Udepuri seemed worse than death.

His inordinately forbidding nature and the iron discipline that he had imposed these past few years had put the fear of god in the very walls of the Red Fort. Thus it was that not a whisper was heard about the episode of the failed suicide, after the initial alarm. However, Uncle Shaista hustled himself into the emperor's presence and said, 'My lord, it was only by the mercy of Allah that her life was saved, by a mere whisker, really. A hundred thousand thanks to You, ya Parvardigaar! At daybreak, this woman was on the point of plunging into the Yamuna once and for all. By a stroke of luck, a guard on the battlement spotted her and pulled her back in the nick of time.'

Noticing that Aurangzeb's face was contorted with grief, Shaista Khan placed a consoling hand on his shoulder and said, 'Please get a hold on yourself, my lord.'

He then told the emperor about how he had managed to avert a catastrophe by rushing to the spot along with his wife on hearing of the incident. He described at length how the two of them tried to bring her out of her grief-stricken state. 'I asked that mad woman point-blank,' he said, 'why she had resorted to this extreme step when no less a person than the emperor of Hindustan sat pining for her.'

Fresh spasms of pain racked the emperor's face. Allowing his distress free play before his uncle, he reiterated his passion for Udepuri. Shaista thought it worthwhile to give him the details. 'I told that foolish, suicidal girl in the clearest of terms, told her that Emperor Aurangzeb was ready to become her slave—'

'And what did the pitiless beauty say to that?'

'She said that my emperor was a murderous demon, the knot of a noose, the tip of a sharpened spear; how could he be anybody's slave?'

'And then?'

'I agreed that you were, indeed, the emperor of Hindustan, but then, she was the queen of beauty! And Aurangzeb was ready to lay his crown at the feet of an enchantress like her. Then, she told me in no uncertain terms to inform you that she would be willing to slake your thirst and become your queen, on one condition—that she would never be asked to give up the bottle. I tried to reason with her, told her that her beauty alone was for the emperor finer than the finest bottle of wine, and that he was willing to lay down his life for her—'

'Arey waah! Looks like my prize is won. Now, I don't care if the rest of the world breaks out in flames.' Aurangzeb smirked with a mad man's delight.

The first night that Aurangzeb spent with Udepuri in his bedroom overlooking the fog-wrapped banks of the Yamuna was straight out of a dream. He simply could not tear his eyes away from the extraordinary beauty of the woman. The Georgian had legs as long and graceful as those of a gazelle. Those beautiful almond-shaped eyes, those pupils of the purest blue flickering like topaz on a ring, her heavy lips red as the petals of a rose—as Aurangzeb lay drinking in the beauty of Udepuri, he refused even to rein in his senses. Many beautiful women had graced the beds of earlier Mughal emperors, Noor Jahaan and Mumtaz Mahal among them, but none had the comeliness to match this dazzler from Georgia. It was as if a throne of ethereal delicacy had been placed next to his imperial seat. A wave of contentment welled up inside him.

As he closed in to taste the nectar of her lips, a faint whiff of alcohol floated into his nostrils, but it was subdued well enough by the fragrance of paan that accompanied it. He had taken the precaution of making her eat a few before leading her to bed. The sweetness of those lips was heady enough for him to disregard such trivial inconveniences, however much he was wont to abhor them. All his conceit, all his fanaticism, all his moral arrogance had melted like butter in the warmth of those kisses.

'Try to be a little generous, Jahaan-panaah,' Shaista Khan pleaded with Aurangzeb. 'It is true that Shahjahan ill-treated you and persecuted you, but history sees him as a magnificent emperor, a lover of art, a great builder. In the Taj Mahal, he created a mausoleum of which the entire world is proud. If you ask around, you will find that people have only good things to say about him.'

'I don't care. Let the rest of the ignorant world admire him as much as it wants to, but I have seen my father since the time I was a naked child crawling around the palace. The world is under the delusion that he fawned over my mother, his wife, but the grim fact is that he treated her as nothing more than a factory for producing children. My mother did not meet her death in the comfort of a luxurious bed in Burhanpur ... she passed away in the agony of delivering her fourteenth baby! And here is this fraud telling the world of the affection he bore for her, singing mournful songs of eternal love in the name of Taj Mahal. The fact, Maamoojaan, is that my father Shahjahan is the most duplicitous, contemptible and unprincipled person the world has ever seen.'

'Put all this bitterness behind you, son Aurang, try forgetting the past,' Shaista Khan said, addressing him with all the avuncular affection he could summon.

'It truly surprises me, Maamoojaan,' replied Aurangzeb with a touch of asperity, 'that you should have forgotten the humiliation the wretched man inflicted upon a nobleman like you, his wife's brother, to boot!'

Shaista Khan first stiffened at these words and then went limp. His shoulders drooped and his head sank into his neck, as tears trickled down his cheeks into his dense black beard. Aurangzeb himself had become overwrought at the memory of the event he had witnessed as a very young boy.

'Maamoojaan,' he resumed in a hoarse voice, 'I can never forget that horrible afternoon at our Delhi fort. Although I was still a child, I was old enough to perceive the utter bestiality of my father's nature. Taking advantage of my mother's absence, he sent my elder sister Jahaanara over to your mansion and got your wife, my aunt, invited over to the palace in Mumtaz Mahal's name. When the poor, unsuspecting Rukhsaar Begum arrived at the palace, this wicked man pounced like a hungry wolf and forced himself upon her. You well know how this shock devastated that simple, god-fearing lady who loved and revered her husband as next only to Allah.

'She staggered back to her mansion in a stunned state. She did not change her clothes, did not wash herself, forgot all about all her meals, and eventually turned into a block of wood. Despite all your efforts to bring her back to life, despite everything the physicians did to revive her, she turned into a corpse where she lay and wasted away like a rootless vine. She was so pious, so clean-hearted, so beautiful and so innocent! The question that still haunts me, Maamoojaan, is: how could you have swallowed this outrage and not voiced even a weak protest?'

The scab of an old wound had been torn off and Shaista Khan was finding it impossible to stanch its bleeding. However, Aurangzeb went on relentlessly, 'The memory of that day remains fresh in my mind, Maamoojaan. As she put us to sleep, our mother would often gather us in her embrace and say, 'You are the children not of an emperor, but of a veritable demon. He violently ravished your aunt and brought about her death. He is a murderer.'

'Stop, nephew, please stop,' Shaista Khan wailed. 'Don't rake it up all over again!'

All these memories, however, hadn't needed much raking up for the old man. He had never forgotten that gruesome episode and always thought of his brother-in-law as the murderer of his beloved wife. That was why, during the battle of succession, he had openly stood by his nephew Aurangzeb, the fire in his heart unquenched. 'Shahjahan,' he had muttered to himself when Aurangzeb had triumphed, 'I have dreamed of this day when I would pull you down from the throne and reduce you to the state of a ghost haunting the graveyard.'

The day had waned. Uncle Shaista tried to distract his beloved nephew from this rather unpleasant topic. 'Forget all this, son,' he said. 'Forget the griefs and misdeeds of the past. Forget, too, these political strategies, these moves and countermoves. Think now of the snow that has begun to melt on the white peaks of Kashmir, those tall peaks; think of the velvet greenery that is breaking out of its white shroud! Think of nothing else.'

'Maamoojaan, despite all that you say, I will have to suspend my Kashmir dream for a while.'

'Huh? Why?'

'Pleasure trips can wait. There's this landmine named Sivaji in the Deccan that needs defusing in a hurry.'

'Can I be of any help?' Shaista ventured, half wondering whether he was biting off more than he could chew.

'Maamoojaan, I am already groaning under the burden of favours you have done for me, but yes, this additional kindness I do seek. If you can do this, I shall happily rip out the strings of diamond and pearl on my crown and have them grace your Turani cap.'

'My lord, your smallest wish is my command.'

'My wish, then, is to hold in my hands the severed head of that Sivaji from the Deccan. If he can be caught alive, bring him to me in chains. If he dies, bring his body like that of a wild animal stuffed with straw.' Aurangzeb was rocking his head slowly, as if watching the pantomime with his mind's eye. 'The heady pleasure I derived from holding my sinful brother Dara's head … it's the same heavenly delight my hands will know by holding this margatthya's head.'

Registering the passion in Aurangzeb's voice, Shaista Khan laughed lightly and said, 'My dear nephew, I think you are seriously overrating this insignificant brigand named Sivaji Bhosale.'

'Look, Maamoojaan, I am not addicted to consulting charlatan soothsayers on matters of state, but there are two persons who do enjoy my confidence in this regard. I consult them now and then, and spend a great deal on their upkeep.'

'Where do they live?'

'Right here, in the palace complex, but in the guise of ordinary minions. If they so much as dream of letting out that they are the emperor's astrologers, they know that their bloated bodies will be fished out of the Yamuna a couple of days later.'

An uneasy Shaista Khan asked, 'Forgive me, huzoor, but please tell me—'

'Whatever you wish to know, Maamoojaan.'

'What, exactly, have these two wise astrologers told you about Sivaji?'

'First, that this rat from the Deccan and his margattha caste may cause the destruction of half my life.'

'Ya Allah!'

'Secondly, my venturing into the Deccan will be nothing short of a deliberate leap into a river of fire. These rogues also prophesy that if I do make my way into the region, I shall spend the next twenty-five or thirty years merely running after my enemies in the hills and valleys of the Sahyadris. And most frightening of all, they fear that once I am sucked into the Deccan, even my corpse has little chance of finding its way to a final resting place on the banks of the Yamuna.'

Aurangzeb suddenly stopped and looked around, as if suspecting even the air around him of eavesdropping on this candid conversation with his uncle. Shaista was well aware that any calamity falling upon Aurangzeb would undoubtedly spell his own doom. Gathering himself together, therefore, he said, 'Qibla-e-alam, if you so desire, I shall be happy to go to Siva's land and bring him to heel. Serving you is the sole purpose of my life.'

A few days later, Shivaji received a letter from no less a person than Henry Revington Sahib himself. In this missive, Revington railed about how Doroji had pointlessly arrested an English official named Philip Gifford and whisked him away to a faraway, narrow gorge in the Kharepatna range; how he had kept the man in solitary confinement in a frightful fortress on the slope of a hill; and how the poor fellow's health had been imperiled by the terror of having to listen to the howls of wolves and the hoots of owls at all times of day and night.

Revington added that this imprisonment of a British official by one of the king's subedars was having a deleterious effect on the confidence of all foreign traders, brokers and agents stationed in the harbour. If Gifford were not set at liberty immediately, the English would suffer serious loss of face and their trade would decline too. Pleading for his immediate release, Revington said that he could help the king to capture the invincible fort on the Konkan coast that he so fervently desired. 'You only have to say the word,' he wrote, 'and I shall present myself personally with our English ammunition and long-range cannon at the Janjira fort.'

The fanciful picture that Revington painted had the king perplexed for a while. He consulted Moropant, 'What do you think about it, Pant?'

'Maharaj,' he responded, 'just yesterday we received another letter from Dorojirao, in which he anticipated that this dissembler would come and roll at your feet to win your heart. But he is of the opinion that it is better to let a poisonous viper go free than to release this English backslider.'

The king laughed aloud at this colourful description, but soon got lost in thought. He surfaced from his reverie in a little while and said, 'You know, Pant, in public life there are occasions when one needs to experiment with trusting people. I am strongly inclined to trust this English fellow Revington and see what comes of it.'

Doroji turned white, his throat drying up, when he received the king's order. But he was left with no choice except to bring his prisoner out of the dark cave in Kharepatna and let him go free. Persuading himself that this was, perhaps, the first step towards a new alliance between the English and the Maavalis, he not only released the man, but also returned the goods he had confiscated.

He let two days pass and then set off for the Rajapur harbour to get Revington's signature on the agreement that the sahib himself had drafted. Riding through tracts of coconut and areca palms, Doroji crossed the Godi, a tributary of the river Arjuna that sprang from the innards of the Rajapur creek, and began climbing the slope. There, he could see before him the expansive red building of the English warehouse. When he reached the compound wall, a guard posted at the gate stopped him and refused him entry into the precincts on horseback. As if this were not humiliation enough, he kept the proud dismounted sardar waiting while he went inside to get clearance.

Doroji finally walked past the gate with a heavy heart. Revington sahib was not in the least happy to see him and he let this unhappiness show on his face. In other words, there was no courtesy in the manner in which he addressed Doroji, but there was little that the sardar could do about it. Keeping his king's welfare in mind, he swallowed his pride and sat before the white man. Pulling out the document detailing the terms of the proposed agreement between the English and the Marathas, he said, 'Huzoor, these are the articles of the agreement drafted by you. All it needs now is your signature.'

A furrow appeared on the fair brow of Henry Revington, but just for a fraction of a second, like a tremor on water when a fish surfaces only to sink immediately. He pinched the red tip of his nose with his fingers and growled, 'What reasons do you think we English could have for shoving our noses into your Janjira problems?'

'You had promised to stand by the king's side with your army at Janjira, that too in writing! The signature is all that is required now!'

'Mr. Doroji, just turn around and have a look. The water in the Rajapur creek hasn't yet dried up.'

'What do you mean?'

'You may toss that document in the water there.'

Seeing the Englishman's unrestrained impudence, Doroji sprang to his feet and said, 'Revington sahib, arrogance of this order is not wise.'

'Well, yes, tell this to your Sivaji: we are arrogant people of the highest order. Which is why valiant men like us cross the seven seas and walk onto your shores—and, yes, live there in our own style.'

An intense conflagration had flared up between the two men. The warehouse clerks as well as sailors and agents from several shores began gathering around. Noticing that these spectators looked at him expectantly, Revington felt strangely uplifted. 'Go, go tell your Sivaji,' he bellowed again. 'Tell him that we shall certainly meet, but not at a table for discussions. Nay, but I should love to cross swords with him on the battlefield.'

Shivaji heard about what had transpired and let it sink into him. He gave no indication of this, but inside, he had exploded like a store of sulphur catching fire. Doroji looked into the king's eyes, and saw there a raging ocean of flames.

7

BADI BEGUM SAHIB AND SHAHAJIRAJE

On the evening that Badi Begum had invited Shahajiraje over to her sitting room in Anand Mahal for a meeting, the latter was in a sombre mood. The bitter battle at Pratapgadh, the subsequent killing of Afzal Khan and the unrest it had sparked in Bijapur had made him both alert and cautious. He had been expecting this summons, either to appear at the durbar or in a private audience such as this.

Badi Begum went through the pretence of a casual stocktaking to begin with, but she couldn't keep the turmoil and anger in her heart bottled up for too long. 'I have often advised you before, Raje,' she broke out, 'to keep an instinctively rebellious boy like Shivaji under control.'

'Aapajaan, I have made this humble submission to Mohammad Sultan sahib: that that boy of mine has a very independent mind. The matter has been out of my hands for quite a long time now. You may take whatever action you wish against him, punish him in whichever way you see fit.'

'Shahajiraje, his earlier acts of insubordination like whisking away a fort or two, or banditry in the mountains, were still within limits of our tolerance until a couple of days ago. But the slaughter of Afzal Khan? He was the darling of Bijapur. Now, my people are boiling over with the desire to seek vengeance on your rebellious son and on you! How do I now dam this river in flood?'

'Aapajaan, ten years have passed since the episode near Jinji. It was under similar suspicions that Mustafa Khan had arrested me. That Afzal miyaan had then put manacles on my wrists and dragged me along for months, humiliating and parading me as an ordinary prisoner, on the road that lay between Jinji and Bijapur. How I managed to swallow the poison of that ignominy, this body alone knows. Was that indignity inadequate that you now want to hold me responsible for the Pratapgadh calamity?'

Badi Begum signalled with her eyes to the officials and clerks working at their desks to disperse. Once she had confirmed that there was no servant or minion left in the hall, she said, 'Keeping in mind the long years of our association, you may, perhaps, come out with an open confession, Raje—'

'Confession? Confession of what?'

'Immediately after the assassination of Afzal Khan, why and for whom were armies of around seventeen thousand soldiers assembled at Bankapur and in the neighbouring forts here? Who was the mastermind behind this rebellion?'

'Look, Aapajaan, whenever I have embarked on a military campaign as a general and a jaageerdar of the state of Bijapur, I have always taken with me this stalwart personal army which consists predominantly of boys from Maaval. These soldiers have served the Adilshahi Sultanate with unstinting loyalty for many years now.'

'But wasn't it your intention to support Sivaji in his act of rebellion a couple of months back?'

'Sultana sahiba, what you call rebellion is known to the people of the twelve Maavals by another name—war of independence.'

'We consider that as rebellion and betrayal, Raje.'

Shahajiraje permitted himself a laconic smile. 'Why do caged birds keep knocking at the bars of their prison?' he asked. 'They, too, thirst for the freedom that other birds enjoy of swinging on the branches of trees.'

'Therefore you have risen up in revolt?'

'What evidence do you have for this accusation, Aapajaan?'

'When I hear of unrestrained horses galloping out of their stables with the passion of war, without due permission or even an intimation, can I consider this as anything but revolt?'

When Shahajiraje chose to stay silent, Badi Begum held him in her razor-sharp gaze and handed him a postbag, saying, 'You want evidence, don't you? Open this bag, then, and read for yourself this copy of a letter sent by a British official named Revington.'

'Revington? Who's this Revington? And what have I to do with him?'

'Raje, he is a senior British official who dispatched this letter to the Company sarkaar in England. It is dated December 10, 1659, according to the English calendar. Our spy managed to intercept it at the Vengurla harbour, copied it down word for word and sent us this translation. It is your good fortune that this document did not fall into the hands of the Sultan.'

'But how am I connected with this entire episode?' Shahajiraje said in exasperation. 'This baseless allegation makes my head ache.'

Badi Begum lifted up her fair nose and began reading out the document through the slant of her eyes, 'Taking the matter of Pratapgadh into consideration, it is evident that Shahaji's son Sivaji has succeeded in dispatching Afzal Khan and his army to the next world. Meanwhile, in Karnataka, Shahaji is so thrilled at this development that he is preparing to announce his own independence. With his army of seventeen thousand, he is ready to come to Sivaji's aid. This rebellious father-son duo is now all set to turn the muzzles of their horses towards the city of Bijapur and take over the Sultanate.'

Shahajiraje froze upon hearing these words from Badi Begum's mouth. The Begum smiled and said, 'So, Rajasaab, if you desire evidence, many such pieces can be produced. But will you answer me one question, please?'

'Yes, Sultana sahiba?'

'How did your Netaji Palkar manage to reach the doorstep of Bijapur merely four days after the battle at Pratapgadh? How did his army manage to race across that distance at the speed of lightning that flashes across the sky?'

Begum sahiba had a veritable hoard of similar jibes. Shahajiraje did not utter a single word. Finally, Badi Begum took a deep breath and released it slowly. 'There is one thing that you will have to admit,' she continued in a sombre tone. 'that history and the pages of destiny did not support your father-son rebellion. It was Allah's mercy that time was our ally and we escaped by a hair's breadth.'

To which Shahaji replied in a calm voice, 'Sultana sahiba, there is no need for you to conduct further investigations. I admit that I am culpable. We Marathas have indeed committed this offence to shake off alien suzerainty and gain our independence.'

Begum sahiba laughed aloud, once more locked eyes with Shahajiraje and said, 'As a mother let me also make a confession, my brother. If a son like Shivaji had been born from my womb, then I too would have followed the trail of his rebellion as if it were a tour of heaven. But where do I have this good fortune?'

Shahajiraje expressed his deepest gratitude to Badi Begum. As she was bidding him goodbye, she said, 'Ah, brother, what's happened has happened. The battle of Pratapgadh has altered destiny, changed history, and whisked the reins of power away from my hands. What, then, shall I do sitting here?'

'What do you mean?'

'I am leaving very soon on a pilgrimage to Makka-Madeena. Sultan sahib has arranged for a ship for me. I take your leave and request you to take care of yourself.'

'My deepest gratitude to you, Begum Sahiba. If I hadn't had a foster-sister like you, then, after the assassination of Afzal Khan, it would have been impossible for a rebellious Maratha like Shahajiraje, in your own words, to stay alive in Bijapur.'

'Another thing, Rajasaab.'

'Yes, Begum sahiba.'

'Never take your eyes off your brother in faith, that Bajiraje Ghorpade.'

'Begum sahiba?'

'I'll tell you this, Rajasaab. A time may come when your great foes, Adilshah and Mughalshah, tire of fighting and stop to catch their breaths. But these insane, twisted enemies from your Maratha brotherhood will never rest. This is the mission of their otherwise useless and barren lives.'

'A million thanks, Begum sahiba,' Shahajiraje said. He was stunned at this information about his Maratha enemies coming out of the old Sultana's mouth.

'Rajaji, the days that have passed were good, but who can say what tomorrow will bring? I can't be sure whether my ship will return safely after my tour of Makka and Madeena. Please be vigilant, brother; know that the air of Bijapur is not very healthful for you.'

8

A CONFLAGRATION IN THE DURBAR

The reputation of the Bijapur Sultanate was getting shredded at the same lightning speed with which the rebel Shivaji was moving from one victory to another. There was nothing left in the control of Adilshah, and the Bijapuris reeled back with less and less energy after each humiliating defeat. The durbar had been shaken to its very foundations. Not a single event was happening anywhere in the realm that gave them reason to feel an iota of pride or joy.

The massively built Khawaas Khan the Second soft-footed up to the Sultan who was sitting in his durbar. After the beheading of Ikhlaas Khan in the market square, the mantle of wazeer had fallen upon Khawaas Khan's shoulders. This second of the Khawaas Khans of the Bijapur Sultanate began in a hoarse, trembling voice, 'Zill-e-Subhaani …'

'Yes, Khan miyaan, the news on your lips is going to be bad,' Ali Adilshah responded in a bitter voice. 'I know it from the shrunken furrows on your face.'

'That Shiva Bhosale has captured the Panhala fort.'

This dreadful piece of information sent a shudder through the cane-slim body of the Sultan. Till very recently, even though Badi Begum had nurtured him with that intention, he had never dreamt that the Sultan's crown would one day rest upon his head. Now that he was realising that this crown could be as painful as the hangman's noose.

How long would the rebellious acts of this son of a servant of his realm continue to meet with success? Panhala was very dear to the Bijapuri heart. For the past hundred years, the fortress had stood sentinel at the northernmost tip of the Sultanate. Since the reign of Ibrahim Adilshah, it had been the summer residence of the Bijapur sultans, who would spend well over a month there in the hot season, finding relief in its salubrious air. The Sultan's palace there, its rose gardens—they were the pride of Bijapur. Now that Sivaji had snatched them too!

Ali had begun feeling abashed at thought of visiting his own durbar. He knew no restful sleep in his bedchamber either. The very idea of taking a tour around the city atop his bedecked elephant made him cringe; there was little doubt that the citizens of Bijapur would look at him with scorn and suspicion, quite convinced that their impotent sultan could no longer offer them either peace or protection. What ill fortune had suddenly wrapped itself around his prosperous city? On its thoroughfares the bugles of victory had stopped blowing, and the war drums had long since ceased to beat, replaced by the keening of broken-hearted women who had lost their husbands on the battlefield.

Ali Adilshah finally arrived at a decision. For how many days, how many months could he sit suffering this disintegration of his Sultanate? The defeat in Pratapgadh, followed by the humiliation of his army near Kolhapur—when was it all going to stop? Sultan Ali decided that he should trust nobody; the time had come for him to put on armour and march out to battle. He had already issued a firman declaring that the first halt of his campaign would be in Murtizabad, also known as Miraj.

'What kind of demon is this Siva,' he roared, 'at the mere utterance of whose name our sardars begin to shiver? Each time I invite one of them to lead a campaign against that margatthya, what do I see? They hide immediately behind the stoles of their wives!'

In a little while Narsinhrao, a Tamilian official who was a part of Adilshah's personal retinue, walked into the durbar. The happy smile playing upon his dark face seemed out of place on this occasion. He announced that he had brought with him an urgent message from a sardar of the Kurnool province, a man named Siddhi Johar. At which the Sultan snapped, 'This Siddhi Johar, I don't like his behaviour one bit.'

It was only very recently that Johar had taken charge of the Kurnool administration. Not long ago, he was a nondescript slave who had grown up in the house of the Bijapuri sardar Malik Abdul. Flat-nosed and bubble-eyed, he lived at the mercy of his master. But on the very night Malik Abdul died, this vile man audaciously pounced upon his master's son and choked him to death. He then occupied the throne of Kurnool, and soon afterwards sent appeals to the Bijapur court asking to be acknowledged as the chief administrator of the province.

However, the Sultan was having second thoughts. In these troubled times, perhaps it would be unwise to shoo a vassal away so peremptorily. This ambitious man too could be tested for the courage he carried in his veins. After reading the letter a second time, Ali sent him an invitation to come and see him immediately.

Johar presented himself at the Bijapur durbar three days later, bringing with him gold boxes loaded with pearls and diamonds. Placing these gifts at the Sultan's feet, Johar bowed obsequiously several times and pleaded, 'How can I forget, huzoor, that up there is Allah, and down here, the Sultan? This slave of yours admits to having committed many crimes and indiscretions. Greed may have pushed me to stage a small rebellion, but I swear by Allah that I am all shattered inside. There's just one single thought that burns me now: the Sultanate in which I have climbed these little hillocks of success, shouldn't I be paying back to it some debt of gratitude?'

'Well said,' responded the Sultan. 'The work I have in mind for you carries a big responsibility. Will you do it?'

'Sarkar, just give this slave of yours one single chance, and see how he seizes this golden opportunity to reduce the enemy to dust!'

'Have you heard the name of that rebel Siva Bhosale?'

'Er … that margattha?' Siddhi Johar, who had been prattling on like a parrot, suddenly seemed to have swallowed his tongue.

Adilshah looked at Johar and smiled gloomily. 'Forget it, Khan sahib,' he said, 'the fault is not yours. The tongues of all our sardars get stuck in their throats upon hearing the name of that demon.'

'It's not that, sire—'

'What, then?' the Sultan roared in anger. 'Looking at my terrified subjects, my disintegrating army and self-interested sardars like you, looking at this parade of corpses, I feel that I will have to unsheathe my own sword to settle accounts with this menace Siva.'

Seeing the Sultan fly into a rage, Siddhi Johar was flustered for a moment. He then rebounded with vigour. 'Please hold on, huzoor, I'd rather die than listen to such words from the mouth of a sultan whom I hold dearer than life. Zill-e-Subhaani,' he announced, sweeping his gaze haughtily over the assembled sardars, 'I give you my word. This sharp axe of Kurnool shall gallop into Siva's land, kill him and grind his body into the slime of his own soil.'

Registering the passion that seemed to flood Johar's body and the quickened pace of his breath, Adilshah was reassured that if anyone had it in him to take on this near-impossible mission, it was this man. Once the decision to dispatch Johar on the campaign had been taken, the Sultan pulled up his sleeves and brought out one firman after another to lift the morale of his army and its generals.

Around the same time, Bajirao of Mudhol had also sent an appeal to the Sultan which said, 'Huzoor, no one can match the fire that runs in my veins to destroy Shivaji. Kindly bestow the reins of this campaign on my hands.' It had surprised many that an eminent Maratha sardar should be so hell-bent on destroying his compatriot.

The Sultan soon announced the appointment of Siddhi Johar as deewaan of the Wai province. A special durbar was assembled to honour Johar, in which the title of 'Salaabat' Khan was conferred on him, meaning a brave, tough warrior with the heart of a rock. The Sultan handed over blank, signed documents called doley to Johar. With these invaluable papers, Johar could raise loans, promote or dismiss sardars, and virtually exercise the authority of the Sultan in campaign matters.

The durbar on this day had acquired the dimension of a victory celebration. Outside the hall stood thirty thousand mounted men and hundreds of camels. Present in the gathering were grandees such as Saadat Khan, Bajirao Ghorpade, Bhai Khan, Siddhi Masood, Badey Khan and Peednaik. Amid the rejoicings a scroll arrived from the south, which the Sultan flourished at the assemblage, asking jubilantly, 'Can anyone guess who has sent this?'

When nobody could hazard even a wild surmise, the Sultan laughed aloud and announced with great satisfaction, 'This piece of paper that fills my heart and mind with joy comes from none other than Siva's half-brother Vyankojiraje who writes to us from Tanjavur. He does not commit himself openly, but he does not conceal where his loyalties lie either. Shahaji's younger prince is telling us, "Khavind, the destruction of evil can happen only at your hands!"'

'What do I say, Khavind?' Baji Ghorpade piped up, drawing attention towards himself, 'Even though that rebel Shahaji and his wicked son Shivaji are rogues, both of them, this younger boy Vyankoji is a good lad.'

Ali Adilshah came down from his raised platform and began walking between the rows of sardars and other grandees standing in the hall. He halted next to Faazal Khan, placed a hand upon his shoulder and said with feeling, 'Look at this prince of Afzal Khan; thrice he has fought that wild Siva, and yet he continues to stand firm in the battlefield. Don't ever overlook him.'

Before the durbar came to a close, Ali Adilshah presented Siddhi Johar with a ceremonial dress and a diamond necklace. Embracing Johar afterwards, he was overcome with emotion; hot tears began to trickle down his fair cheeks. In an overwrought voice, he said, 'I remember so distinctly the day when thousands of soldiers stood behind Afzal sahib, and those rows of horses and hordes of elephants, all ready to ride out of Bijapur to settle accounts with that Siva. What hopes raced inside our veins that day! But, ya Allah, what was the outcome of it all?'

'It was the worst thing that could happen, Sultan sahib!' Even an old, experienced sardar like Khawaas Khan was shaken as he said: 'Neither the flag of victory returned, nor did our beloved Afzal Khan. At the very least, his body should have been interred in his own soil! The thought makes the very walls of Bijapur weep!'

Wiping warm tears from his own eyes, the Sultan said, 'Where Rajgadh, where Pune, and where our Bijapur? Where does this audacity spring from in the hearts of our enemies? In these margatthyas and their steeds? How did Palkar's horses, whipped into a gallop on the banks of the Krishna, manage to reach Bijapur in merely a day and a half?'

The entire durbar stood still. Running his hand over his grief-stricken face, Ali Adilshah continued, 'These disgraceful episodes of the recent past, and the defeat and humiliation attached to them, have filled me with utter shame. All that I can say while sending you off on this campaign is this: the soil of our Sultanate is desperate to hear two phrases only. "Siva's destruction" and "Bijapur's victory"!' Then, looking straight into Siddhi

Johar's eyes, the Sultan asked, 'What do you want in return? If you come back here with that Siva's severed head in your hands, you may even ask for the Bijapur throne and you shall be rewarded. Siva's death—just fulfil this last desire of mine, my warrior!'

9

DARK SHADOWS OVER PANHALA

The Raja was quite certain that horsemen and infantrymen from Bijapur would descend upon them in large numbers any time now. En route to Panhala, the Adilshahi forces would always make a halt at Miraj, where they had a strong fort. Before that, they would stop at Athani, which also was a strong station.

The earthen fort at Miraj was massive. Its walls could be seen from a long distance. From the outside, it gave the impression of being easy to demolish, but the Bijapuris had stacked the fort with such heavy arsenal that the size of the assailing force hardly mattered. When Shivraya laid siege to this fort in the company of Phulaji Prabhu, Bandal, Morey and others, the spirits of the Maratha soldiers were sky high. In the morning, they were certain that they would pocket the fort before the day's shadows had even lengthened. It was simply a matter of pressing the wood-apple fruit hard, the king thought, and the seeds would pop out.

But when the cannons, big and small, the guns and the muzzle-loading devices placed along the ramparts began belching fire, they did not allow the Maratha men to come anywhere close. Shivaji's army took a severe thrashing and the entire day turned out to be fruitless. That evening, a conference was held by the Maratha generals to discuss their strategy going forward. It was during this discussion that Shivaji pointed out to them a peculiarity which he had noticed in the enemy's defences. Above the huge, at least fifteen hands tall, main gate of the fort was a small minaret with the Adilshahi flag fluttering atop. This had made it impossible for the fort-keeper to plant cannon on the battlement there.

Keeping the structure of the gate in mind, the king instructed his men, 'We'll have to try our hardest, but we must capture that fort tomorrow under any circumstance.'

'Why this hurry, Raje?'

'Tomorrow is Paadawa, our New Year's day. I want that fort in our hands first thing tomorrow, so that we may set off by evening, playing our kettledrums, to feast on pooran-poli at Panhala.'

The main gate identified by the Raja had nails the size of human wrists embedded on the front surface; therefore, ramming into it was out of the question. It did appear, too, that firing guns from either side of the gate would be an extremely difficult enterprise. Even if the effort was made, it would be difficult to get the aim right. The plan, therefore, was to place tall ladders against the gate for carefully selected Maratha braves to climb. These men would then saw off the cross-beam on top and bring the entire gate crashing down.

When the Bijapuri soldiers inside the fort saw the long ladders being placed against the gate and carpenters moving up them, they knew what was coming. They tried their utmost to counter this assault, but they were working under severe limitations. Firing cannon at the ladders from the inside would serve no purpose, because that would blow up the gate and allow free entry to the Maratha army.

The Maavali braves began climbing rapidly up the ladder. The guns and arrows aimed at them from left and right were turning out to be quite inefficacious, as had been anticipated. Soon, saws were applied to both ends of the cross-beam and the cutting began. The Maratha soldiers on the ground lined up, and readied themselves to apply pressure to the horizontal beams below in order to bring the gate down. When the gate began to rock, the Bijapuri soldiers inside made desperate attempts to hammer new beams in the futile hope of preventing its collapse.

'Tighten your belts, my brave men,' Shivraya roared. 'Gather your courage. Come what may, even if a few lives are lost, our soldiers must get inside the fort.'

The gate had now begun to creak and swing, outward from the pressure applied by the resisting Adilshahi troops, and inward from the Maratha forces attempting to push it open. Presently, the creak suddenly picked up an ominous note, the decibel level soared frighteningly, and then the crossbeam snapped. Before the Maratha men could move out of the way, both the beam and the minaret above came crashing down, interring twenty-five soldiers and ten horses.

A large rock came rolling out of this rubble, and despite Shivraya's quick leap sideways, it hit his foot with such ferocity that it tore away the nail of the big toe on his right foot. Seeing the badly squashed toe, sergeant Shiva Kashid sprang forward and tightly bandaged the heavily bleeding wound. By the time they reached the camp at night, the foot had begun to throb frightfully. Shiva Kashid rubbed oil around the wound and massaged the king's leg from the knee downwards, but the pain did not quite subside.

As had been planned, at the break of dawn on the following day, the king laid siege to the fort. In a matter of minutes the wicks of the light cannon would be set alight. The cavalry would rush in immediately after the cannonballs had landed. Every move had been neatly planned out.

The assembled soldiers looked expectantly at the king for the signal. The eastern sky was turning brighter by the minute. That was when four men came galloping from the rear, yelling, 'Raja! Raja!!' As they jumped off their horses and strode towards the king, their tense faces revealed that trouble was afoot. 'Sarkar,' one of them panted in the king's ear, 'an army of eight thousand foot soldiers and thirty thousand horsemen has set out at express pace to swallow up our Swarajya.'

'From Bijapur?'

'What Bijapur, Maharaj? The enemy is already at Athani. They would have begun marching in this direction at daybreak today. Their horsemen may very well catch us here at Miraj by noon.'

The king was silent for a little while. This day, barely begun, had brought with it an unusual series of events. He opened his eyes wide, looking up at the sky and then towards the horizon. Then he spoke slowly, 'Panhala is already in our possession. It doesn't make sense to let go of what is in our hands and chase a fleeing enemy. There's no point in lingering here. Let's rush back to Panhala.'

'As you command, Raje,' his generals responded.

The badly injured big toe made riding extremely painful for Shivraya. Shiva Kashid was detailed to ride alongside the king. On the banks of a stream, the sharp-eyed sergeant spotted a kurdu plant. He crushed a leaf, extracted its juice and applied it to the wound. That brought some relief.

They had soon left the Krishna basin behind. Arrangements had been made for the horses to be fed near the inn at Shirola. The king and his retinue lunched in a mango orchard nearby. The Raja had asked Shiva Kashid and his friend Chauhan to sit beside him. Such close proximity with the king made both young men rather tense. Shivraya suddenly lifted his eyes and began looking at Shiva with intense curiosity. He chuckled to himself, ran his fingers over his beard, looked down at his own chest and biceps, and resumed staring at the other man. The latter's beard too was jet-black like the king's, tapering downwards. His eyes were similarly soulful. It came as a jolt to the king: how could two men look so much alike? Almost as if they were twins?

The king then instructed a servant to fetch some ashtagandha paste and had him paint a crescent moon in the middle of Shiva's wide forehead. Loud exclamations and bursts of laughter rose among the men sitting under the mango trees. All shifted their surprised gazes from the face of the king to Shiva's face over and over again. Once lunch was over, the men got back on their horses, galloping towards Panhala. During the ride, Shivraya addressed Shiva Kashid and said, 'Friend Kashid, I give you my word today.'

'Maharaj?'

'When the time comes, you will climb the ladder of honour to a rung so high that you will occupy my place.'

'Please don't say this, Maharaj. For me, there is no better fate than finding some space to sit at your feet.'

'What if I ask you to wear my headgear and my silk jacket?'

'If that ever happens, Maharaj, it will be for that one single day.'

'Why do you say that?'

'Because, Maharaj, from the next day onwards those objects will occupy the highest place of worship in my shrine at home.'

Shivraya reached Panhala on the day of Gudi Paadawa. Cool winds blew over the ramparts of the fort. As the rays of the setting sun turned to orange the miles upon miles of mountains and the dense jungles that spread across them, the residents of the fort were bringing down the gudi, the dolls they had hung at the entrance of their houses, for welcoming the new year.

Soyrabai, who had been waiting for Shivraya's arrival in the verandah of the waada, saw his horse turn towards the palace and quickly walked across the courtyard. As the king entered the waada, she noticed with a jolt of her heart that he was limping in the right foot. When the Raja had seated himself on the couch, Shiva Kashid undid the oil-soaked bandage on his big toe. The royal physician soon arrived, checked the king's pulse, cleaned up the wound and applied a poultice of herbs to it. He also got the Raja to drink some herbal decoction to relieve the pain.

Both the physician and Soyrabai strongly advised the king to take adequate rest and get a full night's sleep, to which he responded with a wan smile. After a quick bath and offering of flowers at the shrine, he started a conversation with Soyrabai. 'Forgive me,' he said, 'I know all of you would have been waiting for me so excitedly with the dolls, but despite the keen desire to make it in time for the festival, I simply could not.'

'What could be done, Raje?' Soyrabai said, a touch sullenly. 'Not wanting the auspicious moment to slip away, I got a priest to set up the doll here.'

'What do I see?' the Raja said, staring at her, 'Why does your mien resemble a shrivelled flower?'

'Please don't bother about all that.'

'How can I not bother, seeing such despondency on your face? You haven't even eaten all day, what's this? It's Paadawa today!'

'If the lord of the house is absent, what joy can Paadawa bring?'

'Soyra, what can I say to an intelligent, capable girl born in the Mohite clan? These shoulders carry plenty of duties and anxieties. A common man's life is bound by his four walls, but a king is called the protector of his subjects. In a manner of speaking, the Raja's palace has no walls. It's his destiny to quell the waves of adversity, battle with mountains of problems and walk on the edge of a sword, day in and day out.'

In fact, the king had wanted to leave in a hurry, but because he wished to avoid gloom on a festive day, he sat and partook of meals with Soyrabai. In the meantime, he also sent a message to his officer Tryambakpant to come and meet him. He then informed Soyrabai softly, 'Ranisahib, the palanquins will be ready before sunrise tomorrow.'

'Palanquins?'

'Yes, the forest road from here to Rajgadh is very long.'

Tears sprang in Soyrabai's eyes. 'Raje,' she cried, 'your words wound me. It's not even four days since I came here, and you want to push me away again?'

'Please go to Shivapattan and take care of Maasahib.'

'What's this, Raje? It was Aaisahib who sent me here to Panhalgadh out of worry for you. She said that you have been away from home and family for so many months now; no home-made food, no loved ones around. But what's happening here is quite the opposite! If the king doesn't like my presence here—'

'Please don't misunderstand, Soyra—'

'And who will see to your well-being here, Raje? What do I say to Maasahib?'

'Tell her that there have been many who became kings and emperors on the strength of their swords. But when the poor, not only of our Maratha realm but of the world, have given her Shivba the kingship of their heart … should he not then live up to their faith?'

Soyrabai could think of no response. She stood there despondently.

'Soyra, please don't look so crestfallen. Wipe those tears that rest in the corners of your eyes. Ausahib has no idea that the thirty thousand soldiers who have set out from Bijapur to take a bite of our land are closing in on us even as we speak.'

'Ago bai! I did not have the slightest inkling of this development.'

'Ranisahib, under these circumstances, what would happen if our women and children were to fall into enemy hands? They wouldn't think twice before etching out the terms of surrender on our hearts with the tip of a sharp knife. Do you, then, expect that I should allow my beloved queen to be exposed to such a gruesome calamity?'

Soyrabai reined in her turbulent emotions and turned away, disappointed. Shivraya too moved away with sad steps and leapt on his horse. Loping out of the waada, he rode on to inspect the preparedness of his army.

Shambhuji Jadhav, Phulaji Prabhu and Bahirji Naik rode alongside the Raja as he scrutinised the entire length of the tall walls of Panhala's vast fortifications from the inside. He looked closely at the battlements and stations placed at regular intervals, the pill-boxes of the soldiers and the state of the infantrymen posted there. It was well past midnight when the king's inspection came to a close. Only then did he finally place his head upon a pillow.

The winds blowing through the bamboo groves created a frightful row all through the night, changing direction at will. The Raja knew that the impassioned enemy was not likely to exercise patience, and might strike at any moment. He wanted to make sure that he was ready when the assault came. Furnaces were blazing everywhere, with swordsmiths firming up the hilts and tempering the blades of the men's weapons. All over the fort, metal was being melted and new weaponry forged.

The morning air had a keen edge to it. Soyrabai's palanquin set out early and began moving rapidly in the direction of Rajgadh. The elephants and horses that had been resting for the night at strategic spots stood up to shake the stiffness of sleep off their limbs. Four horsemen came galloping in, among whom was Bahirji Naik.

Commotion broke out among the soldiers guarding the entrance of the palace. Knowing that Naik had some urgent message for the king, the white-whiskered Ramoshi Bahirji folded his hands in a plea, 'Whatever the message, Naiksaab, please hold your horses. It's just a little while ago that the king has finally fallen asleep.'

'Piryababa, the message I carry cannot wait.'

Ramoji was in a dilemma. After a day of hectic activity, the king desperately needed his rest, but Bahirji was refusing to withdraw. That was when he heard the Raja's voice floating down from an upper window: 'Who's come, Piryadada?'

'Our Bahirji Naik—'

'Please bring him in and seat him in the front hall.'

10

THE SIEGE

The army of Salaabat Khan Siddhi Johar could arrive at the foot of the Panhala fort any time now. Going by the information provided by the spies as well as the gossip in the marketplace, one thing was certain: this time around, the force that Sultan Ali Adilshah had dispatched was not the size of a scouting team—it comprised twenty thousand cavalry and twenty thousand infantry.

The state of the faint-hearted in the Panhala fort was pitiable. Shivraya's strength was barely seven thousand men, and nearly all of them infantry. Whichever way you counted, his cavalry would not add up to more than two hundred horsemen. How would they withstand the impact of the Bijapuri assault?

The palace was in turmoil. The Paadawa dolls had been strung up three days ago; but the new year, instead bringing in of its traditional sweetmeats, had brought in winds of conflict. The opinion being exchanged in undertones was that the maharaj had done a wise thing by dispatching the palanquins and dollies along with Soyrabai Ranisahiba to Rajgadh a couple of days earlier.

Pressing matters were being discussed in the private office of the king. The Raja's brother-in-law and close friend Shambhuji Jadhav, along with Phulaji Prabhu, was constantly circumambulating the fort walls. Panhala's experienced fort-keeper Tryambakpant Kulkarni accompanied them on these rounds. The work to be done was urgent and imperative: assigning squads at all the gates, mounting the cannon on the mounds, posting guards on the battlements, and taking measures to block the enemy's passage towards the fort.

Sitting on his throne at the office, the king said in a firm voice, 'We have to keep the fight going all the time. No matter whether the Adilshahi army is forty thousand strong or four hundred thousand, our duty here is to keep punching back and keeping every single stone—'

'Forgive me, Raje, but we are of the senior Raja's generation and we are worried—' Sardar Tryambak Ingale began falteringly.

'Yes, Tryambakmama, speak on.'

'Raje, can't you work out some other plan? I am worried about your safety, so—'

'Please stop worrying about me. I have no intention of moving out of this fort. On the contrary, I believe that Panhala is our most prestigious seat in the entire region. I am determined to hit back at the enemy with my feet firmly planted here.'

'As you command.'

'If I had moved out of Panhala before the arrival of the enemy, they would have come chasing after us. We do not want them to make inroads into our Swarajya. If I must learn to speak the language of the enemy, then I must make Panhala my field of battle. What, Phulaji and Shambhuji, have you understood?'

'Yes, Maharaj.'

'If the conflict shifts elsewhere, it will mean the devastation of the settlements and farms of our subjects in those parts. I have placed myself here to prevent such ruination.'

The fort of Panhala had been constructed during the reign of the Shilhara king Bhoj about four hundred years earlier. An ancient but sturdy mountain fort, it was sizeable and notoriously difficult to vanquish. Except for the Pawangadh slope to the east, in all other directions it was secured by huge walls and battlements. It was a near-impossible task to plant armies around it or lay mines at its base. The entry point at the foot of the fort fell neatly within the line of vision of the gunners stationed on the battlements above. The result was that no invading force could move up undetected, let alone find a toehold on its stone walls.

After the Shilharas, the Panhala fort was taken over by the Yadavas. After the Yadavas, it was the Bahmani sultans who hoisted their green banners on its flag-post. Later, when the Adilshahs of Bijapur seized it, they didn't let their hold on it relax for a long, long time.

Panhalgadh had always been a unique asset in wartime manoeuvres; it was a strategically located, impenetrable and hard-wearing fort. Whether it was the Mughals coming down from the north, or some firangi army that had marched up from the sea coast beyond Rajapur and hacked its way through the gut-wrenching Anuskura ghat, this fort had only offered them death and destruction. Every one of its formidable walls, those massive gates, and the sinuous battlements built along the mountain's brow—together, they had taught trespassers the bitter lesson that Panhala was more than competent to withstand any kind of aggression. It was without a doubt the pride and treasure of the Adilshahi Sultanate. Shivraya had shredded their heart by snatching it away.

In the king's office, strategies were being worked out on how best to deploy the fort's resources for taking on the enemy. Animated discussions were being held, and while the fort-keeper Tryambak Kulkarni was always ready with his wisdom, others like Shambhuji Jadhav, Kanhojibaba's protege Baji Prabhu Deshpande and his younger brother Phulaji, along with stalwarts such as Rayaji Bandal and Siddhi Hilaal, were straining every nerve in the service of the Swarajya. Baji Prabhu was absent from today's sitting; he had been dispatched on some secret assignment by the king in the direction of Talegaon-Chaakan.

The Raja took stock of the grains and fodder stored in the fort. He instructed his men to secure the stables and to keep their weapons battle-sharp, emphasising the need for frequent unsheathing and polishing. 'The fort has to be in a perfect state of preparedness,' he told them in a firm voice. 'No shoddiness, and absolutely no laxity.'

'Well said, Raje,' chimed in Paramaanand Swami, who was present in his role as observer.

'Yes, Swamiji. In my opinion, laxity is the blood-sister of accidents and ultimate defeat. My parents' strife-torn life has taught me never to tolerate sloppiness in any form.'

The Raja took his bath at the crack of dawn and finished his prayers in a hurry, without waiting for the priests to arrive. Occupying his seat in the palace office, he looked happy and resplendent in his white tunic. Reports had arrived at midnight on the enemy's movements. They had begun spreading themselves out around the fort.

Shambhuji, Phulaji, Tryambak Kulkarni and Tryambak Ingale dismounted at the palace door and presented themselves before the king along with the dawn wind. Having worked all night at the office, none of them had gone to sleep, and neither had the king.

Bowing before Shivraya, Shambhu Jadhav said, 'Maharaj, the enemy's forces have stationed themselves at the foot of all the major gates like Pawangadh, the Dindi Darwaja and the Wagh Darwaja—'

'That's right, Sire. They have surrounded us,' Phulaji chipped in.

The king smiled joyously at this intelligence and said, 'That Siddhi Johar is villainous by nature, I hear, but excitable as a child by temperament. He must surely be dancing like a monkey at the thought that he now has Shivajiraje firmly in his grip. But that's just fine by me.'

While his officials were under immense strain, Shivraya appeared to be totally relaxed. Not a trace of worry showed on his face. Panning his gaze across his restive generals, he said, 'What are you uneasy about? You may take it from me in writing if you wish, but we will not host these guests at the foot of the fort for longer than three months.'

Their faces lit up at these heartening words.

'Just you watch: this loon who has laid siege to the fort, he will himself be besieged by the mountains and valleys of this land.'

'Waah, Raje, well said,' they responded. They had no idea what was fermenting inside their king's head, but his overflowing enthusiasm and the victorious smile on his face put them at ease. Whatever mountains of crises were about to collapse on their heads, they had with them their intrepid king, and knew that they would make it through unscathed. This tremendous confidence that the king possessed was as impermeable and invincible as the walls of the fort.

Work at the Bijapuri court was carrying on as solemnly as ever. As Ali Adilshah sat on his throne, Narsinhrao came in with an important piece of news, 'Khawind, an urgent message has just arrived from Siddhi Johar.'

At a sign from the Sultan, the head clerk read it out softly in his well-trained voice. As he listened, Ali leaned back joyously on his bolster, chortling at each little detail. When the clerk was done, he growled in triumph and said, 'See how that Siva was jolted by the mere news of the arrival of our army? He abandoned the ladders he had placed against the walls of the Miraj fort and turned on his heel to scurry back to Panhala.'

'Thank you for reading it out to us, Janaab,' cooed the assembled courtiers in joy and pride.

'He now knows that a raging storm is headed in his direction.'

That very day, on March 3, 1660, the Sultan dispatched a happy missive to his friend in Tanjavur, Shivraya's half-brother Vyankojiraje Bhosale:

> The foolish Siva has risen in revolt here. To crush him, we dispatched a massive force to your Maaval land under Siddhi Johar Salaabat Khan. But clearly, this Siva has run out of the courage to stand against our intrepid Bijapuri soldiers. He has abandoned the Miraj battlefield and scampered away to Panhala.
>
> A few days from now, he shall be thrown into our dungeons. He is your brother, but I know that no one will be happier than you on receiving these glad tidings. That is why I send you this uplifting news along with a box of sweets.

11

HORSEMANSHIP AND MONKEYING AROUND

A huge army had set out from Aurangabad in the direction of Pune. Shaista Khan was completely overcome by the trust the emperor had placed in him to put him in charge of such a massive and well-provisioned force.

With seventy-seven thousand horses and a hundred and twenty-five thousand men, six hundred caparisoned elephants and thousands of camels, a treasury of three hundred and twenty million, not to mention the perpetual bustle of a royal entourage rolling past with the gold crest atop its tents—it was as if a magical, mobile city of one's dreams had suddenly descended on the landscape of Deccan. The farmers, the herders and the peasants of the villages en route could do nothing but stare and rub their eyes in disbelief.

The emperor had turned emotional while dispatching Shaista Khan to the Deccan. The desire to eliminate Shivaji had become a running sore. 'Remember! I want that Dakkhani Maratha's severed head,' he had admonished his uncle while bidding him goodbye on the eve of the latter's departure.

After leaving Aurangabad, the gargantuan horde passed Nevasa and began skirting Ahmednagar. When they hit a deserted mountainous patch again, the Khan's spies came up to him with worrisome news. 'Khan sahib,' they said, 'those reprobate margatthas are hatching some villainous plots up ahead. We will have to be careful.'

Later that day, Shaista Khan was feasting in his grand royal tent in the company of his sons, sons-in-law and other loved ones when he suddenly remembered the morning's intelligence. He called Namzada Khan over to his tent and informed him about the Marathas' secret moves. In a low voice reeking with conceit, he said, 'This Sivaji will turn to ashes if he comes anywhere close to the blaze of our great army.'

He awoke sometime during the night and remembered the warning again. It would not be wise to disregard the enemy in this manner, he thought. Always better to exercise caution! The next day he decided to trifurcate his army, spread out and advance in a three-pronged formation.

Bahirji Naik was shown into the king's office immediately. 'Raje,' he said in a worried voice, 'the news is bad.'

'Speak on, Bahirji.'

'Raje, Shaista Khan has—'

'Has he reached Pune?'

'Almost. Within a couple of days, seventy to eighty thousand Mughal soldiers will cross the Bhima. His army is huge, Raje.'

The king was startled. The Bijapuri forces around Panhala were nothing compared to the massive wave that Shaista Khan was bringing with him. 'Shiv Shambho!' he sighed. He then called over the scouts of Bahirji Naik and Vishwasrao Dighe and gathered further details from them.

The invasion of Shaista Khan's army was cause for serious concern. Shivraya turned over in his mind what he knew about this general of Aurangzeb's. Of Persian descent, he was an able chieftain as well as a military leader. He had played a critical role in deposing his brother-in-law Shahjahan and placing Aurangzeb on the throne. He was brother to the late queen Mumtaz Mahal and their father Asad Khan was the chief wazeer at the Delhi court. In the Mughal hierarchy, the man stood next only to the emperor.

A scout was describing to the king what he had seen: 'Raje, this Shaista Khan, Aurangzeb's uncle, has brought with him a mountain-sized army. He has with him seventy thousand well-equipped cavalrymen, four hundred war-elephants, and a hundred more to carry the personal effects of the generals.'

'That's absolutely true, Raje. And he carries a treasury of three hundred and twenty million, they say!'

'And what can one say about the grand style in which he moves, Raje? He travels from Aurangabad towards Pune with two huge royal tents—'

'Two?'

'Yes; while he luxuriates in one, the other is dispatched ahead to be kept in readiness for his arrival at the next halt.'

'And what tents, Raje! Each royal tent is divided into huge segments that serve as separate rooms. When they pitch camp, it is surrounded by seventy to eighty smaller ones. Not to mention the hundreds of flowerpots arranged around it every day! The main tent has an office hall that is sixty arms long and thirty arms wide. It is furnished with hundreds of mattresses and bolsters, and you should see the countless silk curtains brought on elephant-back!'

'And the staff! Market-sergeant, tent-sergeant, elephant-sergeant—they're all sergeants there.'

'The main tent is a veritable palace that moves, Raje. Words are not adequate to describe the luxury in which these Mughals travel.'

The Raja was drinking in all the information that was arriving from Pune. It is always difficult, he mused, to drive a bear out of a cave it has occupied. By the same measure, it would be very difficult to push Shaista Khan out once he had settled himself in Pune, which lay at the very heart of the Swarajya. Keeping this in mind, the king dispatched orders to his general Netaji Palkar and to Bahirji Naik, Vishwasrao Dighe and others: 'Stay on your toes, my brave warriors! Even if the strength of our sworn enemy from Agra runs to hundreds of thousands, don't waste your time counting them. Don't rest, my brave Maavalis! Don't let the enemy gain easy entry into our Swarajya. You will, of course, obstruct him at every jungle trail and stream crossing, but go further and make use of every tree from behind which you may mount assaults on your enemy. Like the floods of Mula and Mutha, wash that Khan's evil intents away.'

The evening sun had begun to set on the vast basin of the Bhima. With summer having arrived, there was no trace of water in some parts. Wide swathes of desert had erupted on both sides of the river. There were groves of cluster-fig and jamun trees on the banks, along with patches of black wild grass reaching up to a man's ears.

On this side of the river, concealed in the dense shrubbery of the silk-cotton bushes, stood Netaji Palkar's little tent. He had stretched himself out on the ground, his head resting on the raised dike of a farm. Suryaji was lying next to him. They would lift their heads occasionally to look at the empty farms on the other side of the water. Suryaji asked, 'What's your view of the current state of affairs, Sardar?'

'Well, our king lies trapped in Panhala right now. It will not help at all if this bear by the name of Shaista Khan is allowed to enter Pune. He will rip our beloved Swarajya apart.'

'Is that so?'

'Yes, pora. It's a mountain of danger that is moving over the chest of our Swarajya. This guest from Delhi, therefore, needs to be given a taste of our vaanar-wada.'

'What does that mean?'

'Vaanar, as you know, means monkey. When crops ripen on the farms, the smell attracts these monkeys in droves. They raid the farms and ruin the produce. They nibble the grain-heads and throw them away half-eaten, causing huge losses for the farmers.'

'All right, so?'

'The farmers then get so incensed that they launch a sudden attack on these vaanar armies with sticks, stones and catapults, causing them to scamper away without daring to look back. This is the kind of treat I am itching to hand out to this Shaista, Suryaji.'

Shaista Khan's first regiment of thirty thousand men came down the mountain and began moving into the river basin. The greater part of the basin being dry, the plan was to raise temporary tents on the sand for the senior officers, see the night through and climb the slope on the other side the next morning.

Netaji had the unquestioning loyalty of his men. Every pore of his body overflowed with zest for victory. He always swung the longest shaasan-kaathis in the Jotiba carnivals. The lezim players of the neighbouring villages would dance around him. They would slide to a side, again raise their lezims and come running back to the centre. That was precisely how Netaji's men, hiding in the dark that night, sprang out from behind the bushes and rushed into Shaista's camp to teach the Mughal men a lesson.

On the other hand, Shaista Khan was no half-baked warrior. He had fought on many battlefields, from Afghanistan all the way to Bengal. It, therefore, took the experienced general hardly any time to organise his men and retaliate. They fell neatly into well-ordered ranks and launched themselves upon the Maratha raiders. So fierce was their defense that the Marathas came close to panicking. As for Shaista Khan, with an impassioned cry of 'Allah-o-akbar!', he pushed his horse right up to the frontline.

The twenty-five thousand cavalrymen who had accompanied Khan along with the quartermaster's staff were warriors of the first water. Looking at the vigour of the Mughal horsemen's onslaught, the Marathas lost heart. Two thousand Maavali men turned around to make good their escape. Disregarding the darkness and the stone-strewn terrain, the Mughals set off in hot pursuit of the retreating Marathas. Shaista Khan was speeding like a fire-tipped arrow. Seeing this, Namzada Khan spurred his horse to ride alongside and asked, 'Khan Sahib, to what distance do we chase them?'

'Even if it means chasing them to the very gates of hell, I shall not let these fiendish margatthyas escape alive.'

'Then, huzoor, I shall give you company.'

The Marathas quickly rode up the slope rising from the riverbank and into the jungles beyond. Shaista Khan's horsemen were hot on their heels. However, these animals had been raised and trained on the soft sand and open banks of the Ganga and the Yamuna. They were now finding it difficult to gallop across the stony ground that met their hooves, sending painful throbs up their legs. The thorny bushes that they were pushing through tore at their skins. In this unfamiliar forest terrain, the Mughal horses soon began losing their vigour and speed. The Marathas had, meanwhile, vanished into the darkness. Their pursuers were soon left with no choice but to turn back.

Meanwhile, down in the Mughal camp, they were celebrating their narrow escape from the Maratha raid. The kitchen boys set their pots and pans on fire to resume cooking the evening meal. Tapers and torches were lit everywhere. A cool evening wind had just begun to blow. Before they could know what was happening, twin hordes of Maratha horsemen descended from the mountain trails, two thousand from the left and two thousand from the right, and broke like colliding waves upon the exposed, helpless Mughal camp.

The magnitude of the storm that hit them so terrified the womenfolk in the camp that they clung to each other, shrieking, 'Please! Please save us!' They were convinced that they would now be carried away and molested, perhaps even killed, by the marauding enemy. But those who had not fainted out of terror began to realise that those Maratha men were not so much as looking in their direction.

Dulari Begum, her daughters and daughters-in-law were frightened out of their wits. Their wealth was being looted right in front of their eyes. The servants and guards who had tried to resist the assailants had been put to the sword. When the newly married Nusrat Begum burrowed into her mother-in-law's arms, weeping, Dulari Begum tried to soothe her by saying, 'Don't be afraid, daughter. These margatthyas are Sivaji's men. They are forbidden to so much as touch a woman.'

'Are you sure, Ammijaan?'

'Yes, girl. Whether it is a mosque or a temple, Siva holds all religious places in equal esteem. Which is why our Allah too is pleased with this infidel. He rushes to his aid at the last moment, people say.'

It was very late in the night when Shaista Khan and his men returned, tired and hungry, from their fruitless chase. Approaching, they could sense that a strange quiet had fallen on the camp. As he drew close, Shaista saw his wife's tear-swollen face by the flickering light of a taper. The black of her *kohl* had made dark trails down both her cheeks. Looking around at the terrible state of his camp, Shaista Khan felt a tremor of fear run down his spine. Confused and flustered, he screamed, 'Nanak Singh!! Rahman!!! Where are you?'

At their master's call, the pair emerged from the darkness. Their faces were serene. Stepping forward, they whispered something in their master's ears. Then they escorted him to a pit that had been dug in the sand outside. When he peered into it, Shaista Khan began to breathe easy again. There lay the boxes and baskets containing most of his fortune, secure and untouched by the enemy. In the middle of all the mayhem, his men had had the equanimity and good sense to ensure the security of the main cache of his treasure.

Now that he was assured of the well-being of his women and his treasure, his physical needs resurfaced. He immediately sent for the head cook Laley miyaan. The man appeared with his head bowed in shame and despair. He said in a low voice, 'Forgive my impertinence, huzoor, but I have nothing left to serve you.'

'What rubbish are you talking, rascal? My intestines are shrieking for food!'

Laley continued in his desperate voice, 'Those brigands' raid was so ferocious that every one of my kitchen boys has disappeared into the darkness.'

Dulari Begum found this opportunity to step forward. 'My lord,' she said, 'the horses of those margatthya demons have toppled every vessel, every basket, every dish that held food and spilled it all into the sand. There's absolutely nothing left to eat. We will have to starve tonight.'

The tent erected for Shaista Khan had also been knocked down by the rampaging horses. It was in no state to be used—now, or ever. The best that the Begum could do was to get hold of a few remaining minions and have them spread the tent cloth on the sand. This, then, would serve as bed for the night for the lord of seventy-seven thousand horses and six hundred elephants! The cold night wind blowing across the Bhima did nothing to ease the lord's rest. His wife and the girls managed as best they could, making do with any piece of cloth they could find to stretch out on the cold sand.

At first, the calls of wild animals floated down from the jungles on either side. That was bad enough, but when the sounds appeared to be coming from close by, it became difficult even to remain lying down.

As she lay tossing and turning on her improvised bed, Dulari Begum asked her husband, 'Khan Saab, do you think this was a deliberate trick played by that Siva … to humiliate and discomfit us like this?'

'It wasn't him.'

'Huh? Then who?'

'A strong-willed, obdurate sardar, Netaji Palkar by name.'

Whichever side she lay on, Dulari Begum could find no comfort; sleep was a distant dream. There were sharp-edged stones plentifully scattered in the sand, not to mention the cold that was seeping through the cloth. Groaning, she told her husband, 'My lord, when you do get hold of this rascal Netaji Palkar, gift him to me. I want to roast his liver for dinner one day.'

12

MURDEROUS ASSAULT ON THE FORT

Shivraya had begun to worry. If this siege of Panhala continued, big losses would accrue. Anxiety about Rajgadh and Pune was eating into him too. If he were to be wrenched away from the Swarajya at this time, many difficulties would spring up.

If strength lay in numbers, his position at this moment was extremely weak. If all the men at Panhala were counted, the figure would not cross seven thousand, which was altogether inadequate for piercing through the wall of the forty-thousand-strong army that encircled them. The Adilshahi army was tightening the noose relentlessly from all sides and at a rapid pace. Tens of thousands of Bijapuri soldiers were dancing around the fort in excitement, vengeance on their minds.

Besides, eminent Maratha landlords and feudal chiefs like Khem Savant of Wadi, Shirkey of Kutara in the Konkan region, and Suryadev Surve of Shringarpur had been sending letters of support to Salaabat Khan. Their messages were identical and clear: muzzle this rebellious brat of Shahajiraja's and nip in the bud his callow pretensions to kingship.

Nevertheless, Siddhi Johar alias Salaabat Khan was moving with great caution. He had put up his grand tent of thick, red aalpaan canvas in Ambwade village. This settlement was to the east of Panhala, tucked into the right wing of Pawangadh. The camp at Ambwadegaon had a large bathroom for the Khan, a spacious office for conferences and several small but strong huts to house the soldiers. A temporary parade ground had been prepared there for occasional drills and ceremonial events.

A hillock stood next to Ambwade, somewhat like a horseman sitting astride his steed. From the top of this mound, one could see the eastern battlement of Panhala and an old structure called Sajja-Koti in front of it. A deep gorge lay between Johar's tent and the fort. A big stream the size of a small river crashed into the gorge with a tremendous roar. To his right were the dense green ravines of the Vaarna river. From the elevation on which the camp stood, one could make out the tiny hamlets on either bank. Also visible on the right was a cart-track heading in the direction of Malkapur and Ratnagiri.

The spot was well chosen. Siddhi Johar's searching gaze could now swivel from the Pawangadh height on the west to the eastern walls of Panhala, scanning half to three-quarters of the fort.

Meanwhile Johar's competent son-in-law Siddhi Masood had set up his massive camp near the village Maley on the bank of the Vaarna. Thousands of Bijapuri soldiers participating in the siege had erected their tents and pavilions there. A mosque had been constructed to meet the needs of namaaz. Soon the village acquired the name of Masjid Maley.

Siddhi Johar stood before his pavilion at Ambwade, watching the progress of his siege. He wanted to tighten the noose around Panhala to the point where Shivajiraja would feel suffocated. He was desperate to fulfil his grand dream of taking the king prisoner.

Running his fingers through his thick beard, he looked up at the sky and sighed. 'If this Sivaji sees the tiniest of openings,' he said through his thick, Nubian lips, 'he will try his utmost to slip out of the siege. It is important, therefore, to increase the number of surveillance teams, subject the villagers to greater scrutiny, bring in more light cannon and stack up the armaments.'

'Rightly said, huzoor.'

'If the people at Bijapur call him the king of magic and deceit, they are not wrong. He is not only a great warrior, but also a consummate trickster. He leads his enemies into traps with the greatest finesse.'

'Traps?'

'Absolutely. He began by snatching away our Maaval forts one by one, while sending messages to Badi Begum Sahiba claiming that he was fighting on her behalf. He then told Afzal miyaan that he was too terrified to come down to Wai and thus lured him into climbing up towards him at Pratapgadh. What was the result? Afzal miyaan and his army have been wiped out.'

Pawangadh was Panhala's twin-fort. 'Pawan' means wind, and indeed this fort was often lashed by storm winds, justifying its name in a way. Rustam-e-Zamaan and Faazal Khan had erected their tents on its slope. In the vicinity of their camp, Badey Khan's army of eight thousand foot soldiers stood in readiness.

The western side of Pawangadh was strategically better located than the eastern side. Beyond was the Rangana fort that lay alongside Panhala. Bordering Panhala stood the enormous Masai plateau, on the other side of which were the jungles of the Sahyadris. Two days of strenuous plodding through deep forest trails, across jungle streams and thickets of wild vegetation would bring the battlements of the Khelana fort into sight. Shivaji had recently renamed this fort, standing amid frightening black gorges, as Vishalgadh. If Shivaji were to slip out from that side, it would be a grievous loss to the enemy.

All the five Muslim Sultanates had arrived at a working principle when it came to fighting the Maavalis. If a Maratha had to be brought to rack and ruin, the most potent strategy would be to locate and weaponise an aggrieved close relative. Operating on this time-tested principle, Johar invited the sardars Baji Ghorpade and Peednaik over. 'Ghorpade raje,' he addressed the distinguished-looking landlord of eighty-three villages around Mudhol, 'what would be the happiest day of your life?'

'What a question to ask, huzoor!' Baji sighed and groaned. 'The day I watch the pyres of this rascal Shivaji and the rest of Shahaji's progeny burning on the cremation ground, that's the day on which the fire inside me will be quenched!'

'Wonderful, Ghorpade raje,' Siddhi Johar said. 'I am therefore posting you and Peednaik to the forested plateau that lies to the west of Panhala.'

Senior sardars like Bhai Khan, Masood Khan and Saadaat Khan were assigned the task of helping the two Maratha sardars.

The Adilshahi army slowly tightened its stranglehold on the Panhala fort. Movement in and out of the fort had been completely proscribed. Although it was now close to ten days since the siege had begun, nothing significant had happened—neither Shivraya nor the Adilshahis had much to celebrate.

Sleep deserted Faazal Khan that night. He stepped out of his plush tent into the dark night outside and stared at the demoniacal walls of the fort that loomed before his eyes. The Sivaji who had torn out the entrails of his valiant father Afzal Khan was resting somewhere up there, he thought, and felt inside his belly a churn of irrepressible, implacable hatred for his sworn enemy.

He jumped on his horse and galloped down the slope in the direction of the big red tent of Siddhi Johar. When the sentries posted there blocked his passage, he yelled at them, 'Move aside, you rascals. We are here to fight a war, not to waste our time in sleep. Go wake up your master!'

Hearing the commotion, Siddhi Johar woke up in a foul temper; but when he learnt who the late night visitor was, he restrained himself and instructed the guards to escort the man in. Faazal Khan entered in a state of agitation and stood before Johar in a dishevelled state—no formal Adilshahi turban on the head, no velvet jacket either. It was as if he had simply staggered out of his tent in a drunken state.

Siddhi Johar asked Faazal Khan to sit beside him on his bed and inquired solicitously, 'Son, have you had too much to drink?'

'I am burning with the fire of vengeance, Chachajaan, why would I need any intoxicant? Whenever I look at that fort, my entire body goes up in flames. We have to do something quickly, Chachajaan, else I'll go mad.' So saying, he burst into tears.

Faazal Khan was a fair-skinned, bearded young man with a wide forehead, longish face and a straight, sharp nose. His antimony-lined eyes looked soulful, suggesting high Islamic grooming. In a voice laden with grief, he continued, 'How do I explain it to you, Chachajaan? I wake up at night and see my father standing in a corner of my tent, soaked in blood.'

'Get a hold of yourself, son.'

'Johar sahib, my father trusted that Sivaji when he set off towards Pratapgadh. We were camping at a place on the way when, one frightful night, I heard my father scream. When I ran to his tent, I found him bathed in sweat. He told me, 'I dreamed of the mausoleum I have built at Afzalpur.' My father had made a tomb for himself in the style of the former Sultan's Gol-gumbaz. When I asked him what the matter was, he said in a terrified voice that he had dreamt his slaughtered body would never be able to find its way back from these mountains to that tomb.'

Siddhi Johar was pleased to see that Faazal Khan was aflame with the desire to avenge his father. He knew that a passion-driven enterprise could sometimes shatter rocks.

'Chachajaan,' Faazal Khan roared, 'give me that Siva. How long can we sit sighing here, looking at those unscalable walls? Let's go up somehow, catch by its tail the snake that lies curled up in its hole there, and yank it out.'

As Siddhi Johar scanned the rugged, sprawling and stubborn walls of Panhalgadh, he was put in mind of the thousands of Bijapuri soldiers who were slaughtered outside the Daulatabad fort. If he were to tarry too long in these mountainous forests, could he meet with a similar fate?

A shudder ran through his frame and he shot up. It made no sense to dally in these ghost-infested jungles of the Sahyadris, Johar decided. Instead, they should muster the courage and determination to somehow clamber up the fort and plant the Adilshahi flag atop it. Afzal Khan had allowed himself to be overawed and trapped by the Pratapgadh forests, leading to the annihilation of his entire army. That mistake should not be repeated. Johar gave a flurry of orders to his men: carpenters, blacksmiths, rope-makers and other artisans in the camp were to gather immediately, and make ladders and frames from the largest bamboo poles they could find. Rustam-e-Zamaan and Faazal Khan got behind Siddhi Johar in excitement.

It was well past midnight now. Phantom shadows were flitting soft-footedly along the base of the mountain walls that formed the foundation of the fort. A number of ladders appeared; they were quickly placed against these walls and the Bijapuri artisans began scampering up, with the soldiers close at their heels. The Panhala fort, however, was not built to be scaled by just a ladder or two. The artisans, therefore, went on to hammer more ladders further up the wall as they climbed.

They encountered goat-trails as they made their slow and arduous ascent, but these were too dangerously narrow to negotiate. When they ran into impossible obstacles, they threw ropes across the branches of trees, drove spikes into the wall or held on to whatever roots and vines they could grasp. Soon, they had left themselves with no option but to keep climbing up towards the fort.

The Bijapuri men had used the massive trees at the base and strung ladders up three different sections of the fort's walls. In the pitch darkness of the night, some six or seven hundred of them had managed to shimmy up quite a distance. The Maratha soldiers above had got no whiff of their furtive movements, it appeared. After climbing up two ladders, Faazal Khan let out a subdued but urgent cry, urging his men to follow. The excited soldiers below began scurrying up at their master's call.

That was when they heard the sound of something rolling down from the jungles overhead. In a matter of seconds, a stream of rocks and huge stones, some weighing around a ton, fell out of the vegetation above and came cascading down upon them. They fell on the ladders and they fell on the bamboo platforms, smashing them to smithereens. They fell on plenty of unfortunate soldiers too, reducing them to pulp on impact. The air soon turned thick with cries of 'Ya Allah! Ya Khuda!' and blood-curdling shrieks of physical agony.

But their misery had just begun. Before they knew what was happening, arrows began flying out of the woods above and into the limbs, the backs and the chests of the soldiers still clinging to the ladders. Shambhuji Jadhav's archers were finding their mark in spite of the darkness of the night. So terrified were many of the Bijapuri men by the carnage they saw around them that their grip on the ladders loosened and they went crashing down like over-ripe fruit off a tree.

War cries of 'Har har Mahadev' and 'Jai Shivraya, Jai Bhavani' came reverberating out of the jungles overhead. Next came fist-sized stones tossed by Maratha soldiers with their slings, hitting the enemy on all parts of their bodies, some smashing their faces and cracking their skulls. One found Faazal Khan's foot, fracturing a bone. His men managed to help him down the ladder and carry him back to the camp.

The Maratha soldiers had exploited the security and cover provided by the dense karvanda bushes to the fullest. In their very first encounter, they had given the Bijapuri generals a taste of all the mischief that the woods of the Sahyadris could play upon them. By dawn all that remained on the upper ledges to mark the enemy's nocturnal visit were some loosely hanging ladders and snapped ropes. The sun was yet to rise above the horizon and the sky was overcast too, but the devastation around the Bijapuri camp was starkly visible. The besieging force had paid a heavy price for the encounter. Four hundred out of the camp's six hundred soldiers had lost their lives.

As the shaken, broken Bijapuri soldiers limped their way back to camp to dress their wounds and foment their aching bodies, Shivraya's victorious squads climbed back up to the safety of the fort. Faazal Khan lay on his stomach on the damp grass like an uprooted tree. Physicians were tying bandages over the herbal paste they had applied to his wounds. The sight of corpses scattered all over the camp seemed to have broken Siddhi Johar's spirit. He ordered the scavengers to dig pits for interring the bodies of the dead. It would not do at all for the rest of his men to set eyes upon this killing field. Nothing would dishearten them more than the sight of their comrades-in-arms lying crushed and broken at the foot of Panhalgadh.

13

THE NOOSE TIGHTENS

The siege had been tightened on the slope of Pawangadh to the east, in the ravine of the Vaarna on the right, and at the border of the Bhogawati ravine on the left. The horses of Baji Ghorpade and Peednaik were patrolling the area to the west of the fort at all times of day and night. The vigil had been unrelenting; not even an ant or a frog could cross over without being noticed. The only place that the Adilshahi cordon didn't control was the sky; the kites, eagles and sparrows flying over the fort could flit from one side to the other unharmed.

A ceremonial ablution of milk, curd and ghee was performed at the Someshwar temple in the fort at least thrice a week. The king was insistent that the ingredients used in the worship of the gods should be of the highest quality, as per the dictates of the Hindu scriptures. This made it imperative to have the products supplied every morning from a cowherds' colony outside the fort. The Adilshahi siege, however, had completely blocked the passage of milkmaids, herdsmen and even the poor grass-weavers of the neighbouring valleys to and from the fort.

Therefore, Shivraya sent a messenger to Siddhi Johar's private tent, seeking the lifting of the cordon at least for these daily deliveries of milk, curd and ghee. After plenty of heated argument, Johar issued a firman, 'Let Siva get his supply of milk from the neighbouring villages. Only, a sharp eye must always be kept on those milkmen's houses.'

Accordingly, the supply began from the colony of cowherds on the outskirts of the village Kale at the foot of the fort, in earthen pots that travelled up to Panhalgadh every day on the back of a milkwoman's colt. Gunvantabai, the milkwoman, was old, but very sturdily built. She owned over a score of cows and well over a dozen milch buffaloes, which made it possible for her single household to meet the needs of the palace.

The king soon developed a strong affection for the milkwoman. Gunvanta was tall, nimble-footed and supple as the branch of a wild tree, her unkempt hair white as cotton freshly bursting out of a pod. Her face was covered with a network of wrinkles as dense as the veins of a dry peepal leaf. Her right cheek carried the welt of a claw wound from some earlier adventure. As a young girl, her arms had been thickly tattooed with patterns of flowers and leaves; the green had now faded considerably.

She wore a red Dharwadi blouse, silver bands on her forearms and a slim silver belt on her waist. Her knee-length saree, typical of herder women, was held in place by a waistband. Despite his advanced age, her husband still took his animals out to graze. She sported a round vermilion mark on her brow, the size of a coin, to celebrate her marital status. Occasionally, one would see long, old-fashioned earrings swinging from Gunvantabai's earlobes, making her face look like the mask of the goddess Gauri worn during festivals.

For the first four days, Gunvanta managed to keep a hold on her tongue. But on the fifth day, she could stay quiet no longer. She went straight to the palace kitchen to deliver her goods, found the clerk there and insisted on an immediate audience with the king. Once permission was granted, she headed for the king's office. As soon as she spotted him, she dashed up and bowed down at his feet, cackling, 'Give me your blessings, Maharaj sarkaar!'

Shivraya stopped her midway through her bow and said graciously, 'You should be the one to offer me blessings, mother!'

'The king's blessings must fall on the heads of us poor people. The harvest then is good. Grain glitters on the farms and the barns overflow with animals.'

'Tell me, maavashi, what's that welt you carry on your cheek?'

'It's been thirty-five years since that episode. A tiger had once half-swallowed my goat in the jungle near our village. I was so enraged that I picked up a long-handled axe and swung it at the demon's head. As it writhed, I pulled my goat out of its jaws. I got this scratch-mark from that scuffle.'

'Arey waah! You appear to me as a tigress of the jungle!'

From that day onwards, Gunvantabai would never return without meeting the king. A few days later, Tryambakpant told the king, 'Raje, there are strong bonds that exist between this milkwoman's house and our Swarajya.'

'How's that?'

'This old lady's elder son Krishna fell in the battle of Pratapgadh. His wife gets the monthly pension that we distribute to martyrs' widows.'

On hearing that she was the mother of a martyr for Swarajya, the king felt an even deeper bond with the old woman.

One morning, Tryambakpant adjusted the stole over his shoulder and came down the fort to Siddhi Johar's camp at Ambwade. As he neared the tent, he was surrounded by armed guards and taken into Johar's presence.

Setting aside his hookah, Johar said, 'Come, come, Pant. Anything special?'

'Our king has been suffering from some pain in the knees.'

'So, shall I send a hakeem up to the fort?'

'A hakeem won't do. He needs the oil of a ghorpad.'

'What's this ghorpad?'

'In your language, some call it godha, while others call it the big wild lizard. The firangis call it iguana.'

'All right, carry on.'

'Some three or four hills away, you come to a village called Arul, where the herders sell ghorpad oil.'

'So, that would mean,' intervened Johar's son-in-law Siddhi Masood, 'that these herders treat ailments of the bones.'

'Absolutely right, Chhote Khan sahib.'

'Please arrange for a herder from Arul to visit us too.'

'Why would you want one, huzoor?'

'What do I say, Pant sahib? About four years ago, a frisky horse threw me off its back. Since then, I've had to suffer this extreme pain in the joints off and on.'

'That's easy to manage. Please allow these herders to make a visit to the fort, then. Once these bottles of oil reach the palace, I shall come over myself to gift a bottle to you.'

'We want the bottles, sure, but not from your hands. When those herders come up, send them over here too.'

A written permit was immediately granted, and within four days a few herders arrived at the fort to attend to the king. The same evening, arrangements were made for a squad of Maavali soldiers to escort the herders to the Adilshahi camp. Ten days later, a box full of sweets was delivered to Tryambak Pandit with the compliments of Siddhi Masood.

'Son,' Siddhi Johar would try to reason with an impassioned Faazal Khan, 'have you ever seen another fort as huge, tall and impregnable as this? If you want to plant the flag of victory on such a fort, you will need a minimum of fifteen thousand warriors of the highest quality who are willing to give their lives for this enterprise.'

'Do what you have to, Chachajaan, but I want to see Siva's corpse.'

'Don't be foolish. It was on account of your fretfulness that we made our soldiers climb those bamboo ladders and platforms on that unfortunate night. And what did we get in return? Four hundred corpses lying in the slime. A hundred more were rendered cripples too.'

'Uncle, I am aware of the risks and dangers posed by this operation, but in spite of all that, we must do something. That Siva has to be buried.'

'Yes, of course, do something; but the question is: what?'

'What can I say? I have lost my head. I can't even sleep during the night! And I'm not the only one suffering like this. The entire army is distraught. The filthy rains here, the animals getting bogged down in the slime, the fungus that covers the barks of the trees … this fungus has begun to grow inside our heads too. There has to be some remedy, Chachajaan!'

A thought flashed through Salaabat Khan's head and a smile lit up his face. He drew Faazal Khan closer and put his arm around his shoulder. 'Don't you worry, son,' he said, in a voice full of encouragement. 'Have a little more patience. At this very moment, there are some mysterious things happening at the foot of the Anuskura ghat in the Konkan region. A firangi friend is advancing to help us.'

'And?'

'And he is bringing a medicine with him that will turn all of Sivaji's pride and impudence to rubble in no time.'

'No matter what the ruse or excuse, when an enemy manages to enter one's house, pushing him out again is impossible.'

'Raje, the arrival of this Shaista Khan in our Swarajya appears to have affected you very deeply.'

'Don't you see? This man is moving towards Pune with an army of almost a hundred thousand men. He intends to choke the city, and here I am, incarcerated in Panhala at just this moment—'

'Don't worry, lord,' Bahirji said. 'We shall obey your orders and work for the fulfilment of your dreams.'

'The tyrant has already left his camp at Baramati and is approaching Pune by way of Shirval, I've been told. Send this message to Netaji Palkar and the others: they must obstruct Shaista's passage at every step. He should be blocked at every brook, every stream, every river, every mountain pass. Every tree along his route should turn into a Maratha soldier.'

'Maharaj, this Khan is a big man. Not just his stature or the strength of his army, but the supplies he carries.'

'How's that?'

'For carrying all the big and small goods that his great force needs, including grain, fodder and clothing, he has deployed seven thousand bullock carts.'

'That comes to fourteen thousand beasts of burden.' The king was thoughtful.

The calamity that Netaji, Suryaji, Bahirji Naik and Vishwasrao Dighe had been trying their utmost to preempt could not be sidestepped. With loud cries of 'Allah-o-akbar', they strode into Pune and were soon breaking into Lal Mahal, home to Shivraya and Jijausahib. Even the cemetery on the other side of the waada trembled. The Aambil brook was swollen with monsoon rains, its mournful notes ringing in the ears of the Mughal horses, elephants, camels and mules as they streamed in. The Mula-Mutha could not contain the flood and began overflowing its banks.

The Maavali soldiers had dispersed on account of this humiliating development. Their beloved king had been forced to leave Pune and go into the hills. Matoshri was in Rajgadh. And now, the enemy had entered Pune with the intention of sitting on its chest. They had ensconced themselves in Lal Mahal! The Maavalis were shaken to their core.

When the Raja received the news at Panhala of the Mula-Mutha breaking its banks, he felt hopeful for a little while. This would delay the imminent scourge from descending for some time, perhaps? The torrential deluge and the biting cold that accompanied it would surely prevent the Mughal men and animals from stirring much. They would not have the courage or the perseverance to make any headway till Dussehra season.

That same evening, it was pouring cats and dogs in Panhala. Braving the wild wind and the intractable rain, disguised as a peasant in a woven-grass raincoat that offered him scant protection from the elements, an officer of Bahirji's squad made his way up to the palace. The news that he brought from Pune was inflammatory enough to set the king's bed on fire.

Shivraya had only lately dispatched his old but sturdily built chieftain Phirangoji with instructions that the infiltration of the Mughals should be stopped at all costs. Their men and animals should be denied even the tiniest scrap of food and fodder. In observance of his king's order, Phirangoji got the people of the eighty-four villages of his region to move out with their livestock into the jungles after setting the villages on fire. All the food and fodder that remained in these settlements had been reduced to ashes.

The hundred-thousand-strong Mughal army would now need to buy their supplies from the market for survival. When news of the deliberate torching of all food reserves in the vicinity of Pune reached Shaista Khan, he was furious. Riding out of Lal Mahal into the downpour and crossing the potters' colony with an army of twenty-five thousand horsemen, he laid siege to the fort of Sangramdurg in Chaakan. Shivraya was duly informed that Phirangoji Narsaala was fighting the besieging force with unflagging defiance.

Beyond Chaakan was Mughal territory. This had guaranteed an efficient supply line from Junnar and Gulshanabad right up to Delhi. Now Phirangoji had broken this lifeline, causing Shaista Khan so much agitation that he even forgot his prayer time. 'I shall return only after I have buried this Phirangoji in the slime,' he vowed.

It sometimes happens, though, that one's foot gets mired in the slime and begins to sink deeper and deeper. The rains had increased substantially. At Chaakan, as the imperial army assailed the fort from all four sides, the incessant deluge pouring down on them, not to mention Netaji's men emerging like phantoms from behind the sheets of falling water and mounting violent raids upon the Mughals, did not help matters at all.

The Mula and the Mutha were now dangerously flooded. As Shaista Khan was taking his elephants and horses across the Indrayani, there was a fresh surge of floodwater and his army of six or seven thousand men got stuck on the banks. However, Shaista regained his equanimity, loaded his men and animals on rafts and boldly transported them across the river. Some of his toughest warriors like Sayyad Khan, Uzbeg Khan, Jadhavrao, Hashab Khan, and his chief of artillery Meer Aatish had joined in the siege of Sangramdurg.

In Panhala, meanwhile, the information coming in from the Sangramdurg front was steadily increasing the king's worries. Although he maintained outward calm, news of these waves of calamity sweeping over his Swarajya had unsettled him deeply.

Phulaji Prabhu queried in a timorous voice, 'Maharaj, what about our fort at Chaakan? Is it important or not?'

'Phulaji, when we place our foot somewhere, the participation of the knee is very slight, but we know that the capability of the foot is completely welded to that slice of bone called the knee-cap. That is the importance of our Sangram fort.'

'Quite true, Raje.'

'Chaakan is on the path that travels up the Konkan. It is the arch through which the Mughal forces have to pass to get anywhere near us. Shaista Khan's assault, therefore, is considerably worrisome.' The Raja's face was sombre. But the next moment, he shrugged the grimness off and turned to the anxious men gathered around him. 'But let it not dishearten us,' he said in an effort to lift their morale. 'Our Phirangoji is my uncle, a tenacious fighter who has trained under my father Shahajibaba. Having anticipated trouble in Chaakan, we have stocked the fort with plenty of armaments. Therefore we shouldn't worry too much.'

14

FIRANGI CANNON ON THE SWARAJYA'S CHEST

JUNE 1660

The siege of Panhala, which had begun three months earlier, was being intensified steadily. None of the king's ruses for relief had borne fruit. Even as the sun rose every day with enthusiasm, the gloom of despair was creeping into the fort. Barren nights followed, one after another

One such evening, the sky had turned murky with clouds and the air was humid. Darkness seemed to be descending from the shoulder of the horizon in a bigger hurry than usual. During a routine inspection of the Teen Darwaza at dusk, the king noticed a line of bullock carts coming up the Konkan path. Narrowing his eyes for greater concentration, he was astounded to see a large number of carts, some pulled by male buffaloes, emerging from the jungle trails in the dim light of the setting sun. What material could it be that was being transported in such quantities from Konkan? Shivraya was caught in a whirlpool of thoughts. As Shambhuji's horse approached, he pointed and asked, 'What can that be?'

'Maharaj, there's a huge Adilshahi army scattered all around the fort. They need their rations, don't they?'

'But in such quantities?'

'Why should it surprise you? Counting their soldiers, other staff and the animals, there would be at least fifty thousand mouths to feed, Raje!'

The king then looked over the parapet of the fort wall. He could now see the bullock carts at a distance of about four miles, all seemingly carrying some kind of green cargo. He asked Phulaji who was riding by his side, 'What do you say, Phulaji? Doesn't it look like those carts are covered in broad leaves?'

'Raje, the monsoons are almost upon us. If the grain they're transporting gets wet, it'll be ruined. Looks like they're covering their carts to ensure that that doesn't happen.'

The next day, when the king was in his office, he was informed of another few thousand carts arriving at the base of the fort. There were reports of many more following them. Well, over fifty thousand mouths would require these enormous food supplies, the Raja reassured himself.

The next day, a little before dawn, the king was awakened by loud cries of 'Raje, please wake up!' He walked out of his bedchamber in his rumpled night-clothes and saw the fort-keeper Tryambak Kulkarni, Shambhuji, Phulaji and others gathered outside, their faces tense.

'Raje,' said Tryambak Ingale, 'step out and see with your own eyes.'

'What's wrong, Tryambakmama?'

'There is a lot of activity going on in the enemy's camp.'

'But I had laid a bet with you that this was bound to happen,' Shivraya responded excitedly. 'With the monsoons due any time, they've begun to roll up their operation.'

'No, it's not like that at all.'

'Well? What then?'

'They're doing just the opposite. They are hammering in stakes with the intention of facing the fury of the monsoons right here.'

'Yes, Raje. The wind is blowing in the opposite direction down there at the foot of the fort.'

Even before it had turned bright, the Raja stood on a battlement to scan the scenario below. The bullock carts had indeed carted over huge quantities of material. The Adilshahi men could be seen constructing hutments everywhere, reinforcing the walls with nails, then raising roofs of thatch and palm leaves atop them. They seemed to have spent the entire night in this activity. The loaded carts were still arriving in never-ending lines from all directions. The scale of the frenetic preparations below left the king flabbergasted.

Never had such frustration been seen on Shivraya's face before. All the images that he had been carrying in his head, of the Sahyadri downpours that would send the enemy scampering for cover, had turned out to be delusional. Indeed, the antagonists had proved themselves to be most astute. Without creating the slightest flutter, they had battened down in preparation for a long monsoon siege. The king turned his flaming eyes on Bahirji Naik, who happened to be among those assembled.

Shivraya belched out his anger at Bahirji in devastating scorn, 'It appears that my espionage department has been receiving far more applause than it deserves. What state have you reduced me to at this critical juncture, Bahirji?'

'But, Raje—'

'No words from you are going to compensate for the immense loss the Swarajya has suffered, Bahirji. I had never in my wildest nightmare imagined that such a day would dawn upon us and I would be dragged so close to extinction!'

'I seek forgiveness, Maharaj. It was a blunder.'

'A blunder? And what a blunder! The enemy at whom I have been laughing all these days is now having the last laugh. Why? Because the king of the Marathas has turned out to be a novice in the games of war!'

'We did not understand the real significance of these armies of bullock carts coming from Konkan. We were deluded into believing that it was food and fodder that they were bringing,' Tryambakmama sputtered.

'But look now, look! Look at the enemy's resourcefulness! He has erected thousands of rain-proof huts all around the fort. The misfortune is ours. While he was toiling away and burning midnight oil, we were sleeping as we had never slept before!'

'Raje, we have erred. Erred badly.'

'Aho, but if you had brought this news to us earlier, we could have planned some countermove! What a terrible slip you have committed, Bahirji!'

Four or five days later, Shivraya stood on a hillock near Teen Darwaza, taking in the grandeur of the Bhogawati valley. That was when Sonopant Dabeer, from a high vantage point nearby, called out, 'Raje, look, look there at the foot of the hill in front, see that big caravan moving in this direction!'

An attendant standing next to the king handed him a pipe-shaped telescope of Portuguese make which he tried to focus in the direction Dabeer was pointing at. As the king adjusted the device, Dabeer continued with his report, 'Raje, raje, there, there! That huge cart coming down the mountain slope! And those hundreds of bullocks, pulling it with a rope! There are a dozen or so bullock carts in front and some behind, and four or five hundred foot soldiers. And those fancy-looking palanquins—they are all moving in the direction of Panhala.'

'They are bringing the huge cannon from Rajapur, those British monkeys, to blow us out of Panhala.'

Just then, two of Bahirji's crack spies rode up at lightning speed. 'What sense do I make of all this?' he asked them.

'It's Siddhi Johar who organised this entire operation by bringing the Englishmen of Rajapur on board. That cannon is so heavy and so powerful that they have yoked four hundred bullocks to drag it here.'

'Four hundred?'

'Yes, Maharaj. Our observers have brought in all the news. As the Englishmen were climbing the sheer crags of the Anuskura ghat on their way here, their chain of bullocks snapped thrice. They suffered three big accidents. Some sixty to seventy bullocks choked to death because their legs slipped and the ropes tied around their necks got tangled in the trees along the track.'

'Who are the others travelling with this unit?'

'Four hundred horsemen in front of and behind the cannon, with their swords unsheathed. There are two hundred foot soldiers marching alongside. They have six palanquins for the English sahibs.'

'The other bullock carts are carrying ammunition for the cannon,' another spy chipped in.

The Maratha chieftains turned their horses around. The king returned to his office at the palace. The siege was becoming more and more punitive every day. Valiants like Baji Prabhu and Netaji Palkar had turned their blood to sweat in an effort to loosen the iron ring it had laid around Panhala. Despite mounting incessant raids on the besieging Bijapuri forces, they had not been able to slacken the grip that the enemy continued to maintain with its crocodile jaws. If the pressure went on increasing, a time would come when the inmates would run out of food and begin to starve.

The audacity of these firangis made the king's head spin. He turned towards the spies and asked tetchily, 'This firangi official who has been luring Hindustani rulers into the folly of buying these cannon—what's this fellow's name?'

'Henry Revington.'

'Ah, it's Revington, is it?' the king exclaimed, immediately remembering the cunning, corrupt white man Doroji had met a couple of months earlier.

Revington was now subedar of the English warehouse at Rajapur. Before this, he was an ordinary clerk in the accounting department of their warehouse in Surat. An epidemic had struck the city four years ago, taking away with it three of the highest officials at the warehouse, one after another. Consequently, it was left with no senior administrator. For a new subedar to be appointed, news of the deaths would first have to reach the London office, followed by the selection of a suitable person, and finally, the arrival of the new appointee to his post. Considering that a one-way journey by boat to England took three months and a half, eight months would easily roll by before a new subedar could take charge.

Henry Revington was a crook by nature, selfish and bellicose. But this sudden disappearance of all the senior officials at the warehouse gave him the opportunity, in spite of his utter incompetence, to sit in the subedar's chair, even if as a stopgap arrangement. It was a textbook case of a monkey in a drunken state holding the reins.

While working for the Company, Revington had begun running a private enterprise too: bringing cannon from overseas and selling them at exorbitant prices to the kings and potentates of India. Now that he had the means to finance a hedonistic lifestyle, his self-indulgence knew no limits. He could hardly go to sleep these days without partaking of expensive alcohol in the company of crowds of new Dutch, Portuguese and native friends, not to mention a host of delicately built, flirtatious young girls of various castes and creeds gathered from all around the world.

The more Shivraya thought about Henry Revington, the more he felt dizzy with anger. Reaching out to a good person does not take much time and effort, but teaching wisdom to a base and twisted person is an uphill task. Shivraya had an instinctive faculty for bringing around difficult people, but getting a man of Revington's order of stupidity and venality to see sense was a tough ask.

Like a lion trapped in a cage, the king was finding it very hard to sit still. The siege had made it impossible for him to march out of the fortress with his army, but it was absolutely imperative to stop the advance of foreign cannon towards Panhala and to bind the hands that operated them. Under the circumstances the only option before the king was to find a sagacious mediator, and he set about choosing his man with alacrity. The aim was to find a way to arrest Revington's advance and make him turn around. He decided to dispatch Sonopant Dabeer, one of his wisest and most experienced officials, for the purpose.

'Pant,' Shivraya exhorted him, 'do not mince your words. Tell those blackguard firangis pretending to be traders not to interfere in the internal politics of this land. They should not commit the cardinal error of mistaking their weighing scales for swords!'

The king was in a state of great agitation. His fevered brow refused to cool down. Tramping from one end of the hall to the other and back, he turned to Sonopant again and said, 'He's making a mistake, a big mistake. Excess leads to disaster, but that king among fools doesn't realise it. Pant, will you do this for me?'

'As you command, Maharaj.'

'Give Revington this message from me. Remind him that he just managed to climb the great Anuskura ghat on his way from Rajapur. Did he make a sharp enough observation of its height? It would have taken much effort to scale the near-vertical slope. What if he were to be thrown down from the top of that cliff? It wouldn't take him any time to reach the base. Only, the pieces of his body would be difficult to gather.'

For a person who was renowned for patience and thoughtfulness, the king was in a particularly disturbed state of mind. Even when he was in the middle of work, at times he would simply stop, as if out of breath. He would tell people like Phulaji and Shambhuji who were close to him, 'In matters of planning and strategising, I have never fallen on my face before as I have today. Is this the reward I get for placing unwarranted trust in my espionage system?'

'Please go easy on yourself, Raje—'

'Bahirji Naik is among those who are closest to my heart. He is second to none in the art of espionage. And yet, the enemy has managed to make great advances surreptitiously and now threatens to annihilate my army. It's on account of Bahirji's ineptitude that I find myself trapped in a tunnel here!'

'Raje, you are taking this a little too much to heart!'

'What else can I do? I had gone to the extent of laying a bet that this Johar would not be our guest for more than three months. And what, finally, has fallen to my lot? The enemy that I had hoped to trap in the snare of nature ... he has turned around and reduced me to the state of an animal caught in a trap! I am suffocating as I have never suffocated before.'

The next morning, the king was out inspecting the Maavali troops arrayed on the battlements of Panhala. From the eastern wall where he now stood, he could clearly see the slope of the twin fort of Pawangadh. There, on a terraced piece of land, a couple of colourful tents had been erected. He then saw the raised platform where the firangi cannon had been placed. Its long muzzle had already been pointed in the direction of the Panhala fort.

Next to the platform stood half a dozen tall, well-built English officers wearing orange tunics and trousers. Henry Revington was among them, as was Philip Gifford, to whom Shivraya had sent the best quality of medicine in the cave at Kharepatna. Next to him were Mingram and the bilinguist Velji. Siddhi Johar was there too, dressed in a fine velvet Bhaganagari tunic that flowed down to his heels after flaring at the waist. Next to him stood Faazal Khan, and behind him, two hundred horsemen. Johar and Revington bustled about like the parents of the bride and bridegroom at a wedding, looking very excited. Behind this gathering, the king could see a flag-post on which fluttered the Union Jack.

'You notice that, Pant?' the Raja growled, barely being able to conceal his ire, 'See how arrogant that firangi fox has become? The cheek of fluttering the flag of his country as he aims his guns at us!'

As they watched, they heard the boom of a massive explosion that was immediately followed by a host of echoes from the neighbouring hills. The cannonball had impacted a high wall near the eastern gate of the fort.

The firangis had finally crossed their limits. The temerity of this act of Revington was so extreme that a tremor ran through Shivraya's entire body. If the circumstances were different, he would have punished such impudence by ensuring that the man was captured and trampled under the feet of an elephant. Unfortunately, at this moment, he was as helpless as a caged lion; all that he could do was to turn his eyes away from the horrible scene.

Deeply agitated, the king returned to his palace and began pacing restlessly in his office. Some officials came over to report the extent of the damage that had been inflicted on the walls of the fort. On first examination, the impact did not appear to have been severe, but on the stone wall next to the main gate, fifteen hands high, was a big hole with a crack running right down to the base.

Lamps were burning in the Adilshahi palace complex on the banks of the Panchganga, their lights reflecting on the surface of the river. Siddhi Johar alias Salaabat Khan was housed in the Mirror Palace of the Adilshahs. Right next to his quarters was a smaller palace where Subedar Revington was housed in official dignity. Sonopant Dabeer had just arrived to meet him as a spokesperson for the Swarajya. The two had met once before on the Konkan route and Pant had tried hard to appease the Englishman's ego. But Henry Sahib was so swollen with conceit that Pant had not been able to make any headway with him. Revington made it amply clear to Shivraya's envoy that he viewed his king as no more than a commonplace rebel chieftain who didn't deserve much attention.

There was a lot of commotion outside Revington's residence the next morning. The people who had come to meet him were drifting in and out, looking quite nervous. Something had upset the Sahib, for sure, and Pant wondered whether it would be wise to deliver the message he was carrying at such a time. Deep inside, Pant had no desire to meet this bellicose man at all, but the king's orders were clear. There was no way he could now shrug off the responsibility that had been placed upon his shoulders.

Just then, he was called in. Revington looked at Pant as if he were a dirty mouse that had just crawled into the house. His face was as red as a stale carrot and his eyes were bloodshot. Sonopant bowed courteously before the Englishman in the Maratha style and handed over to him the letter he had brought from the king. Soon, the man's eyes were dancing across the page which carried the English translation that Shenvi's half-brother had done from the Marathi original. It read:

> Greetings to Revington Sahib.
>
> Gentleman, last afternoon, you committed a serious and contemptible act that is deeply disrespectful of us, the people of Hindustan. You fired a firangi cannon from Pawangadh, to the east of Panhala; moreover, you had the audacity to plant the flag of the English queen next to the platform of the cannon. Who could have given you the authority to commit this outrageous deed?
>
> We also have knowledge that the trafficking you have been indulging in, selling cannons and armaments to the kings and potentates of this land, has nothing at all to do with the British administration. The quarrels and differences between the Bijapuris and us are an internal matter of our own country and you have no business to come poking your nose into it.
>
> Therefore, what we have to say to you is this: do not dream futile dreams of changing roles from a trader to a ruler.

Revington read the entire missive twice over and each time the hue of his skin turned a deeper red. Pant then put to him in a nutshell the purpose for which he had come. He said in a calm voice, 'Please gather your guns and return to your warehouse.'

'Why?'

'Because our Shivaji Raja is extremely displeased at your betrayal and your alliance with the Bijapuris; so much so that he looks like he has just stepped out of a pool of fire.'

Revington stared with great contempt at Sonopant's turban and his flaring tunic. His eyes, resembling those of a kite, shone with sharp derision. Sneering, he snapped at Pant, 'The state of your so-called king Sivaji is that of a rat caught in a hole. Tell him to save himself from the steel trap of the Sultanate first; only after that should he flaunt his arrogance before an officer of Queen Victoria.'

Sonopant rose from his seat in a dejected state of mind. As he was about to step out, he remembered something and turned around. Unfazed by the irritation that was evident on Revington's face, he said, 'Forgive me, gracious Sahib, I forgot to deliver to you one last message that my king has sent.'

'Now what?'

'Our Raja has asked me to remind you that you recently managed to push your big cannon up the vertical walls of the Anuskura ghat. You would certainly have noted how high the sheer cliff rises. But now, while you are on your way down to Rajapur, you must make it a point to carefully observe how sharp and deep the drop is. If a person loses his footing and falls, or if he is thrown down from there, his body breaks into such tiny pieces that they become very difficult—no, impossible—to gather.'

It was not in the king's nature to sit still or relax for long. He leapt onto his horse and went for an inspection round of the fort's inner walls in the company of Phulaji Prabhu and Sonopant Dabeer. They saw that the hole punched in the wall by Revington's cannonball was only big enough to let a human fist through. It was fortunate that for some inexplicable reason the firangis had stopped firing the cannon after a single hit; otherwise the damage could have been considerable. The king's eyes turned towards the Pawangadh terrace where the British flag was still fluttering, with some guards posted nearby. But Revington, the other British officials and Salaabat Khan were nowhere to be seen.

As they were riding back, the king turned to Arjoji who had joined them and said, 'Set the masons to work immediately. I want them to patch up that hole in the wall so skillfully that it should look as if it never existed in the first place.'

The king bounded forward, and then abruptly pulled the reins to bring his horse to a complete stop. Clouds of deep regret and frustration had settled on his brow. 'Pant,' he said to Dabeer, 'the hole in the wall of the fort is quite small, very ordinary. But the hole of humiliation it has left in my mind—by that firangi monkey walking up to my door and committing this sacrilege—is very, very difficult to repair.'

15

THE SECRET MEETING WITH SALAABAT KHAN

By the time the Orion constellation had shifted in the skies, it began to rain heavily in parts of the Sahyadris such as Panhala, Bhogawati, Vishalgadh and Malkapur. Gusts of wind raced past battlements at the speed of a cavalry unit. The downpour was now incessant, but there was no sign of the siege slackening at Panhala. As he sat in his office, the king would let his eyes, keen as a hawk's, roam across all that was visible outside. His men were convinced that there was nothing, near or far, that escaped his notice.

The small thatch-roofed huts that the soldiers had erected in the Bijapuri camp seemed to be weathering the monsoon well; they gave the men some comfort and shelter from the unrelenting rain. In brief intervals when the skies cleared and the mists lifted, the huts became visible with their roofs that had changed hue from a dull yellow-brown to uniformly black due to constant exposure to water and damp air.

One morning, Guna maavashi's colt had climbed up to the fort in the rain along with the old woman as usual and stood shaking its body vigorously to get rid of the moisture on its coat, while the servants got busy carrying the vessels full of milk to the palace kitchen. Guna maavashi was wearing a locally made irali. It was ingeniously fashioned from palaas leaves held in a framework of thinly sliced bamboo slits, and kept the wearer dry and cosy in the heaviest of rains.

The Raja would often be busy in his office when Guna maavashi peeped in. At such times, she would make a respectful bow and move on. Since it was raining heavily that morning, the king called her in. She promptly removed her irali, kept it outside the door and walked in, the lower part of her saree soaking wet. At a distance of a few armspans from the king, she folded her legs and sat down. Extracting a small receptacle from a fold of her saree, she took a pinch of snuff from it and inhaled noisily.

'I didn't see you for three or four days last week, maavashi!' the king began.

'I'd gone up to Poundwadi. I perform the ritual of sangad for the goddess there every year during Mrig time.'

'Sangad?'

'"Sangad" means a cock and a hen. A black-feathered hen and a brown-feathered cock. It is our custom to perform the ritual at this time of the year. How will it do to upset the goddess of my mother's house?'

In the course of their conversation, the king began gathering vital information about the villages located in the jungles to the west of Panhala. At a signal from him, Phulaji Prabhu, Shambhuji Jadhav and Tryambak Kulkarni gathered around too. Now that the Raja's hopes of the Adilshahi forces fearfully withdrawing from the rain-soaked forests of the Sahyadris had been extinguished completely, the question uppermost in all minds was how to escape from the enemy's grasp unharmed.

During this chat with Guna maavashi, the Raja and his associates learned that the milkwoman's extensive network of relatives was spread across at least three or four swathes of forest that lay in the west. A sister had been married off to Pawandewadi, and a large number of her cousins, nephews and nieces were scattered across various cowherds' colonies in these jungles. As soon as maavashi realised that the Raja was seeking strategic information on the hills and valleys of those parts, she asked for two measures of rice and an equal quantity of flour to be brought over to the office.

Using the rice and the flour, maavashi's deft hands began moulding the major tracks, the important gorges, and the tiniest hamlets nestled among these forests. Her fingers created the precise shape of the Panhala fort, its walls wide at the eastern end and tapering in the opposite direction. She then constructed the twin-fort of Pawangadh to the west, after which she outlined the elongated Masai plateau to the east. The slopes on both sides of the mountain range that ran westward were clearly delineated.

While the discussion was going on, the Raja signalled to an officer to summon his espionage team immediately. The palace door was then closed, as though a secret conference were in progress. Shivraya's spies, who prided themselves on being all-seeing eagles that flew over jungle and mountain, were humbled by all the information that Guna maavashi was so casually throwing at them. They pulled out their maps and modified the markings of boundaries, rivers, gorges and other landmarks under the old woman's expert guidance.

The Raja asked maavashi in astonishment, 'How do the people who live in these parts manage to survive these days of intense downpour?'

'Maharaj, around the time of Mrig, markets are held in places like Malkapur, Bajarbhogaon, down at Kadoli and all the way to Rajapur in Konkan on the other side. For the next four months, it is nothing but incessant rain on mountain and on heath. The Sun-God hardly ever shows his face.'

'Tell me this, maavashi, those hamlets of yours, high up in the Sahyadris like Kuwarkhind and Pawandewadi ... do you think that these Bijapuri soldiers sitting at the base of the fort would be able to find their way around those places by themselves?'

'What chance do those rogues have? If ever one of their soldiers got lost in those dense green jungles, he would not be found even after ten days of intense searching.'

The Raja could not stop marvelling at this eighty-year-old woman's energy, enthusiasm and depth of knowledge.

The long shadows brought to life by the flickering torches fell on the cloth walls of the tent, shivering and dancing like spectres. Every now and then, as he read the alluring letter that Shivajiraja had sent to him, Siddhi Johar could not suppress a gasp of delight.

Khansahib,

By falling foul of Adilshahsahib in a moment of misplaced excitement, I have ruined my life. What is there for me to hide now, from a friend like you? The miserable state that I am trapped in at Panhalgadh is like that of a leaky boat caught in a whirlpool. The only person who can help me out of this pitiable situation is you.

If you can assure me that my life would not be in danger, I would gather the courage to pay you a secret visit.

Khansahib, it is important for the two of us to find time to sit together and discuss what we stand to gain or lose in all this. For these rich kings and emperors, these sultans and padishahs, we are nothing more than beasts of burden. But if a competent, courageous person like you should one day become the Sultan of Kurnool-Bhaganagar, it will undoubtedly gladden my heart to see my neighbour in the Deccan reach such a height! It will benefit both of us if an occasion can be found to sit together. The rest is best discussed when we meet.

Salaabat Khan read the letter almost half a dozen times and then handed it to his son. After going through it, the boy said, 'Abbu, this Sivaji of yours seems to be in a panic.'

After a short pause, he continued, 'But Abbu, if you read the letter with care, you will notice rebellious hues in it.'

'Rebellious, yes. Against the Bijapuri Sultanate, though. Doesn't sound like a bad idea; no harm in thinking it through.'

'Wait, Abbu! Remember that the Sultan has declared that if you win this battle, he will happily hand over the throne to you if you ask for it. He did so in open court.'

'Hand over the throne, hand over the royal treasury … it all sounds very alluring, doesn't it?' The father retorted in annoyance. 'If he says he will hand over Allah's heaven to me, is that his father's property?'

Shivajiraja's letter had raised a storm in Siddhi Johar's head. Which of the two should he believe in? This invitation from Shivaji to join hands or the Sultan's promise in open court? What choice should he make? 'Allah, help me!' Johar prayed silently.

The daily routine of the sky splitting apart and disgorging millions of gallons of water, lake-sized pools forming around the pavilions, tents and stables, the knee-deep slush wherever one turned, the unnerving roar of the cataracts descending furiously from the Panhalgadh cliffs day in and day out—it wasn't surprising that the Adilshahi men and animals were becoming nervous wrecks. They were all at the end of their tether. In this bleak and tense atmosphere, Shivaji's offer of friendship had a welcome warmth about it.

Confidential confabulations had begun on when and where this secret meeting should take place. The king had already expressed his inability to present himself at Siddhi Johar's office pavilion. A better option would be for Johar to walk some distance from the base of the fort, he suggested, so that the meeting could happen in full view of armed squads from both sides. It would be eminently practical for the heads of the two armies to meet at a point just outside the perimeters of their respective zones of influence and have a quick interaction.

No situation could be altogether free of danger under these circumstances, of course, but Johar was aware of the golden possibilities that rested in the belly of this risk. His son-in-law Masood, however, was not at all happy with the idea of this proposed meeting. The dangerous game of betraying their Bijapuri master and dancing with the enemy seemed to him a suicidal venture. Finally, it was agreed that a small tent would be erected at a suitable spot for the purpose.

As soon as it started turning dark that evening, under the pretext of going on an inspection round, Johar and Masood headed for the place at the foot of the fort that had been chosen for the rendezvous. Although the intensity of the rain had reduced, a chill wind buffeted him with sharp sprays of water. Climbing to the top of a knoll, they saw in the depression ahead a neat little tent that had a temporary but distinctly cosy air about it. It appeared to be swaying in the light wind, but was held firm by stout ropes staked to the ground. The lamps burning inside illumined the tent with a deep red light.

A couple of dozen steps away from the tent, Johar stopped to look around. The sky was dense with rain clouds which seemed to smother the rays of the dying sun. The cold evening air was soaked in moisture too. The gloom was all-pervading. As Siddhi Johar stood there in the darkening air, an involuntary shiver ran through him. An inspiring thought had taken hold of him. Excitedly placing his arm around his son-in-law's shoulder, he whispered into his ear urgently, 'Son, with Allah's blessing, we can write a new page in the history of courage if we wish.'

'What is it now, Abbujaan?' Siddhi Masood asked patiently. He was not unaware of the strange fits of inspiration that seized his father-in-law occasionally.

'Do you remember how this Sivaji bamboozled our Afzal Khan sahib at the very last moment and tore out his entrails with his steel claws at the foot of Pratapgadh?'

'The entire world remembers it.'

'What if we reduce this Sivaji to the same state? The deed will earn us eternal fame.'

The very thought of it made him feel as if his head was floating in the air. But he was immediately brought down to earth by his son-in-law. In a voice loaded with cactus bristles he said, 'Janaab, look carefully at the sharp slope of the fort!'

Johar lifted his gaze up to the rugged fortifications of Panhala high above them and narrowed his eyes. There, behind some dense trees near the walls of the fort, fires were being lit for warmth. He dipped his hand into the pocket of his loose tunic and pulled out a cylindrical monoscope. In the light of the torches flaming above, he could see the glinting muzzles of the light cannon pointed in the direction of the tent below. He could also see the vague outlines of sharp-shooting Maavalis among the trees, carrying spears, bows, arrows and rifles. A hard lump formed in Johar's stomach. His son-in-law added, 'See, Abbu? Your first false step may be the last one you take. Siva's soldiers will annihilate us.'

Scotching his wayward thoughts, Johar entered the tent. When he saw Shivaji already seated and waiting for him, he felt a sense of satisfaction. Proportionally, his sense of self-importance shot up too. He began straight away in an intimidating tone, 'Sivaji Raje, for how long will you keep hiding in this rain? The most sensible course of action for you will be to hand over the Panhala fort immediately.'

Immediately acknowledging the weakness of his position, Shivraya responded timidly, 'That's true, Khan sahib. As I wrote to you in my letter, my army is in terrible shape. As for the fort, I have come to inform you that I am placing it in your lap.'

'Waah, wonderful!' Johar replied excitedly. 'I shall immediately hand over the charge of the fort to Adilshah.'

'Truth be told, Siddhi sahib, no wise trader commits the folly of handing over the most expensive jewel in his hand to another person.'

'What do you want to say?' Johar's throat went dry.

'Look, Khan sahib, why don't you regard a big, auspicious fort like this as the foundation stone of a new Sultanate?'

'What do you mean?'

'Johar sahib, you should become a sultan yourself! Consider us your allies. We will gather our army and stand behind you.'

Siddhi Johar was once again transported to another world. Each of Shivraya's words was a hive dripping honey by the gallon. On the one hand, he knew all that praise was fanciful and excessive. But on the other, if the vision being painted for him by this margattha could somehow come to pass, if fortune decided to favour him and a sultan's robe was indeed destined to fall upon his shoulders ... the dream was glorious enough to make every pore in his body ooze with joy.

The meeting was short, but fruitful. A decision was taken to strengthen their new-found friendship and do something meaningful together. As they bid each other farewell, the king reassured Johar, 'Our representatives will continue to be in touch and prepare a pact at the earliest. As for surrendering charge of the fort, why, if you so desire, I can do so on the very evening we sign the agreement.'

Despite their efforts to keep it a secret, word of this meeting soon got around. Information about it reached Adilshah's ears before sunset the next evening. It was enough to ruin his sleep for the next few nights.

16

AT SHIVAPATTAN

The torrential rains of the month of Aashaad had begun. Swollen streams were leaping down from the heights of Rajgadh in all directions like horses galloping to battle. Jijausahib was in residence at the Shivapattan palace near the foot of the fort.

All the tyrants of the land, ranging from the empire with its seat at Agra-Delhi to the Sultanate of Bijapur in the south, had risen up against the new-born Swarajya like clouds threatening the sun on all sides, accompanied by lightning and thunder. On the one hand, Siddhi Johar's siege had settled around the Panhala fort like a giant snake and was refusing to slacken; on the other, Shaista Khan had ensconced himself at the very heart of the Swarajya by moving into Lal Mahal in Pune.

'Tatya,' Jijausahib addressed Gomajibaba, the palace caretaker, 'over three months have rolled by, yet there is no release for Shivba from Panhala. How long will this go on?'

'Your worry is justified, Ausahib. Matters look impossible to resolve.'

'The sun of our Swarajya has to be freed from the double grasp of the tyrannical Shaista Khan in Pune and the villainous Siddhi Johar in Panhala. My heart shatters into a thousand pieces at the very thought of the plight we find ourselves in.'

The waada at Shivapattan was enveloped in gloom that night when a squad of fifty horsemen arrived with two or three palanquins. Baji Prabhu Deshpande leapt off the broad back of his horse. The man couldn't be missed in a crowd. Six feet and a half in height and built like the trunk of a massive tree, he had bright, smiling eyes, thick sideburns and moustaches the size of small fists on either cheek. Even his walk reminded one of an elephant in a parade.

Jijausahib looked at him with admiration, and turned her eyes towards the palanquins as his two wives Sonabai and Gautamabai descended from them. They had brought their children along too. Baji advanced with rapid steps towards the verandah of the waada where Jijausahib stood and bowed low with a loud cry of 'Mujra, Aaisahib, my salutations to you.'

'Arey, Baji, such an unannounced visit! Good that you brought your wives and children along.'

As Baji's wives bent down to touch Jijau's feet, she drew the children closer and embraced them, patting them lovingly on their pigtails. 'How come you've descended suddenly like a storm cloud?' she asked again.

'I was on official work for the past few days in the region of Dehu-Alandi and Talegaon. As I was turning towards Panhala, I thought my wives, my children and I should take your blessings. Our Sindh village is not far from here.'

'Good, good that you came.'

Jijau instructed the palace manager to make arrangements for Baji's family to stay in the waada for guests nearby. Signalling to the maids, she then took the women inside to the shrine. As the children relished the jaggery-water served to them, Jijau slipped out and took Baji to a corner of the front hall. 'What's happening, Baji? Why did you turn this way, knowing the king is trapped in the siege at Panhalgadh?'

'Matoshri, the king had sent me on a secret mission to Alandi, which I managed to finish before time. Before I turned towards Panhala, I thought I should take a detour to come and see you. I sent word to my family to join me here.'

'I am glad you created this opportunity to spend time with them. Otherwise, men like you are married to your duties.'

'That is true, Matoshri. Soldiers like us leave our homes with our sword as our mistress, after wiping the vermilion off our wives' brows to mark them out as widows.'

'But why do I see you alone? Where's your younger brother Phulaji?'

'He's the lucky one, Matoshri. These days he's become the king's shadow in Panhala. Goes wherever the king goes.'

Baji Prabhu occupied a very high rung in the king's estimation and affections. Accordingly, Jijau took a personal interest in ensuring that the family's overnight stay was comfortable. She kept an eye on the needs of the young children too. Jijausahib's family had known the Deshpandes of Sindh for two generations. When Shahajiraje had established a Nizamshahi post in Pemgadh, he had appointed Pilajipant Deshpande as its chief administrator. The friendship between his grandson Baji and young Shivba was well known across the valleys.

Pilajipant later moved to the Hirdas Maaval, where the Nizam had conferred upon him the title of Deshpande of fifty-three villages. This made him an important revenue official in the region, which led to a bitter enmity with the Bandals, a powerful landowning family in this Maaval. The feud reached its climax when the two clans clashed with each other on the banks of the river Neera.

Among the many who lost their lives were Pilajipant and his son Annaji, Baji's elder brother. Adilshah then called both families over to Bijapur, and after a great deal of effort, persuaded them to make peace. Adilshah himself appointed Baji Prabhu as commander-in-chief of the landlord Bandal's army. It was fifteen years later that Baji Prabhu enlisted in the service of Shivaji's Swarajya as a seasoned warrior and general.

As they sat together for a meal that night, Baji recounted to Jijausahib an incident that had occurred in Lal Mahal long ago. 'What do I tell you, Matoshri? I was chatting with someone in a corner of the palace and my voice would barely have reached the king's ears. It had been many years since we'd met and spoken, yet he immediately recognised it and called out, 'Bajidada, where are you?' Why wouldn't a person run to serve such a sharp judge of men as he?'

'That's true, Baji. Shivba hardly ever forgets.'

'Indeed, Matoshri! Ordinarily, when a person becomes a king and sits on a caparisoned elephant, when he has thousands of men at his command, it becomes difficult for him to retain his humanity. Why would he want to remember someone who had run wild with him as a boy? Our king, however, is cast in a different mould.'

While Jijau and Baji sat having their meal in the palace at Shivapattan, their minds were hovering over Panhala and the cruel siege in which Shivraya lay trapped. The pain in both their hearts was equally intense.

The next day, even before the rays of the sun had hit the meadows of Shivapattan, the sound of horses neighing fell upon the ears of those who had woken up. Soon enough, the steeds of the generals Netaji Palkar and Siddhi Hilaal galloped up to the waada.

As Netaji walked through the main arch of the palace, his feet stumbled and he froze. A strange tremor ran through his body. He just couldn't fathom how he was going to carry himself into Jijausahib's presence. She was bound to say, 'Arey Netoba, why have you come alone? Where is our Balraje?' Netaji stood still in the quadrangle, his head bowed in guilt. With everything that was going on in the Swarajya these days, how could he face such a venerated, resolute person as Matoshri?

Jijausahib entered the room and took her seat on a high platform. Surprisingly, she sat without uttering a word. She neither scolded nor scowled. Her silence made Netaji feel deeply uncomfortable. With his head bowed, he spoke in a low voice, 'Maasahib, we tried our best. Covered the distance to Bijapur in a day and a half. As we raced along with our Maavali men, our dumb horses too were completely spent, drooling blood along with their saliva. The poor beasts had not been given a moment of rest on the way.'

As Jijau looked at him steadily, Netaji went on, 'The enemy had taken years to forge those steel gates. We tried to break them open, even to melt them down, but the supply of explosives with the enemy was huge. The Bijapur walls refused to yield. In sheer frustration, we burnt down the village of Shahapur that lay outside the city walls. Unfortunately, our strength turned out to be a little inadequate.'

'Netaji, even before this account of yours, stories of your intrepid exploits have been reaching our ears. No praise is adequate to describe your heroic deeds. But a single worry has been giving us sleepless nights.'

'Tell us, Matoshri, what are your orders?'

'Netoba, this question has been gnawing not only at you and me, but at the heart of every true subject of our Swarajya. The very person who has inspired you with this zeal to fight against slavery now lies trapped in the innards of Panhalgadh. If one cannot see the tiniest possibility of extricating him, how does one even sit and eat?'

While Jijausahib and Netaji sat talking, Baji Prabhu arrived and joined in the conversation. They were sharply aware of the gravity of the problem.

Yet, however much they tried, they could bring no relief to the mother's agony. 'No, Netaji, no. If my most precious jewel and the guiding force of our Maavali braves remains incarcerated in Panhalgadh, how will sleep ever descend on my tired eyelids? How and when will my prince find his release?'

Jijausahib was regarded as the very epitome of fortitude; no one had seen her in such a distraught state before. Neither Netaji nor Baji had the courage to say another word in her presence. 'Netaji, Baji,' she wailed, 'how can you understand the agony of a mother's heart? How I have struggled to protect and nurture my dear child!'

'Matoshri, we have been tardy in securing the king's release and we beg your forgiveness. We promise to bring it about immediately,' Netaji and Baji Prabhu vowed to Jijau.

It was getting late. Baji Prabhu's family made ready to leave. Putlabai, Lakshmibai alias Jaishribai and Soyrabai joined Jijausahib in bidding them farewell. Sonabai was all tears as she said, 'Aaisahib, when will your feet bless our humble house?'

'Oh, I shall certainly come, girl. What's to stop me?'

Shivraya's wives then made the customary gesture of gifting sarees, blouses and gold ornaments to Sonabai and Gautamabai, after which the two ladies got into their palanquins and set off in the direction of Hirdas Maaval. Immediately after, the young queens performed the ritual to ward off evil spirits by swirling a lamp around the faces of the warriors Netaji and Baji.

The two Maavali heroes visited the shrine of the goddess Bhawani in the waada before they got astride their horses. Seeing them ready and eager to depart, Jijausahib took a few steps forward and said, 'I swear by the goddess before the two of you, at this moment I feel it would be more fruitful to die at the foot of Panhalgadh than to sit pining here through the monsoon days at Rajgadh.'

'Please don't say this, Ausahib—'

'But when I see the fire of determination that lights up your eyes, I am able to gather myself together. Go. May you be victorious! My boy lies all alone in the wilderness.'

'Please stop worrying, Ausahib,' Baji Prabhu said. 'Our blood shall water the battlefield as we fight for the honour of a king as valiant as Shivraya.'

'That's right, Matoshri,' Netaji chimed in, as he pulled the reins of his horse to make it rear and then swivel. 'May we find death so as to keep Swarajya alive.'

Within moments, the two men and their troops raced away from the palace, leaving only a whirlwind of dust in their wake.

The forces of Baji Prabhu and Netaji Palkar rode hard for a day and a half. Galloping past the foot of the Ajinkya-Tara fort, they moved through the night along the Shirala route and plunged their horses into the Vaarna river near Mangalya. The monsoon rains had swelled the flow of the river, but even from the banks one could espy in the evening gloom the distant outlines of the Panhala's battlements. The valiant warriors gazed at those walls with aching hearts. It was the sheer longing to be there, closer to their king, that spurred them to ride their horses into the raging waters.

The bulk of Netaji's army was camping on the heath around the village Naavali, waiting eagerly for his arrival. Every one of the soldiers was consumed by the same worry. Four months had gone by since the siege had begun and there was no doubt that the situation inside the fort was getting worse with each passing day. While it was true that there was plenty of grain stored inside the fort, the shortage of other essentials like oil and condiments had begun to hurt.

The secret meeting between Shivraya and Siddhi Johar was no longer a secret. Some of Johar's detractors in his own army had created a lot of unpleasant noise with the intention of bringing him a bad name. As a result, Johar had fallen from Adilshah's grace and was now seen as unreliable. This breaking of trust between the Sultan and his commander-in-chief in the middle of a campaign would cause grievous harm in the future.

Adilshah had in fact tweaked Siddhi Johar's ears painfully by ordering him out of the Aaina Mahal on the banks of the Panchganga and back to the barracks built at the foot of Panhalgadh. Since then, Johar had been so furious with Shivraya that he had tightened the siege even further. Not even an ant could crawl out of the fort now. The Bijapuri men had been given free rein to slaughter and feast on any goat or sheep that came straying down. They were under strict instructions to capture any man or horse that was seen descending the slope.

These days, even the eagles, kites and other birds flying down from the fort would invite Johar's ire. How dare these birds disobey his express orders that no living creature be permitted to come down from those heights?

At the Naavali camp, hearths were lit at midnight and whatever was available was cooked and eaten. Baji and Netaji sat together to discuss their battle strategies. That done, the horsemen climbed the elevation in front of the camp. The father-son duo of Siddhi Hilaal and Siddhi Wah Wah was among their number. The idea was to mount a raid on the sleeping Adilshahi soldiers before the sun rose. They were fired up with the thought of slaughtering the enemy while they were half-asleep, penetrating the siege and joining their king on the fort.

Just before dawn, the raiders left the thorny thickets of the heath behind. Horse and man were now treading the grass that had grown knee-high in the month of Aashaad. But what happened next was something they had not expected at all. Before they could spring upon the besieging Bijapuri soldiers, it was the enemy that descended on them with cries of 'Allah-o-akbar' and 'Deen-deen'. Despite their alarm, Baji and Netaji's men rallied themselves and resisted the attack with cries of 'Har har Mahadev'. Sword clanged against sword amidst the dense greenery. Spears were flung and horses ran into each other. The battle had begun

Baji and Netaji had actually been taken by surprise. They were now convinced that the enemy didn't sleep at all. It was evident that the Bijapuris were alert round the clock, patrolling the environs of the fort at all times. Their spies had got wind of the activities at Naavali, and Siddhi Johar was able to prepare his men for the attack. Their vigilance would prove a serious obstacle to the determined efforts of Baji and Netaji to break past the ring of the besiegers.

For two consecutive days Netaji and Baji's men clashed against the enemy, and each time the Bijapuris succeeded in pushing the raiders back. Often, in the intervals between skirmishes, Baji and Netaji would be found standing in the jungle at the foot of the fort and looking wistfully upward. The third day dawned. This time, the Marathas were determined to carry out their mission; no other outcome would be acceptable. The force with which they crashed into the enemy was so strong that they broke through the wall of the Bijapuri patrol in their very first effort. Even their horses were charged with the fervour of battle, ramming straight into the soldiers manning the siege.

This fresh assault shook Faazal Khan and Siddhi Johar out of their sleep. They saw in the outermost ring of the siege flashes of fire and clouds of smoke billowing up. The Marathas had set the thatched huts on fire and were now straining to break through the coils of the serpent that encircled Panhala. The very thought that they might succeed was enough for Faazal Khan to jump on his horse in his night-clothes and gallop in that direction, with Salaabat Khan and his men close behind.

The contingents of Baji Prabhu, Siddhi Hilaal and Netaji were already at the trench, only moments away from crossing the ditch and racing up to the fort to join their supreme leader. Just as the Maratha horsemen spurred their animals forward, a hail of arrows came whizzing towards them and pierced their chests, forearms and thighs. A medley of cries like 'Ah! I'm dead!', 'Ride on!', 'Jai Bhawani' and 'Allah-o-akbar' rose into the morning sky. Very soon, swords were slicing into flesh, spears pierced through ribcages and blood poured out of bodies to mingle with the mud underfoot. For two hours the conflict raged on, with many soldiers on both sides falling never to rise again.

Uncaring of consequences, Siddhi Hilaal's son Wah Wah leapt into the trench. Immediately, a couple of dozen Bijapuri soldiers converged on him with shouts of 'Look! Look at the infidel! Get him!' Wah Wah was left with no choice except to swing his sword expertly and bring down as many of his assailants as possible. Encounters and collisions were happening everywhere. Baji Prabhu's eyes were bloodshot; the muscles on Netaji's arms throbbed, glistening with the sweat that bathed them. Both were dealing out death and destruction to all who came their way, their clothes soaked with the blood of the enemy.

This was when a huge contingent rushed in from the east to join the Bijapuri soldiers. A bunch of them surrounded Wah Wah who was fighting like a man possessed. One of them slashed at the leather belt that held the young man's saddle in place, making him slip off the horse along with the saddle which then got entangled with the horse's legs. They immediately closed in on Wah Wah and caught him alive. Seeing his son being carried away, Siddhi Hilaal dashed towards him, only to be obstructed by another stream of enemy soldiers who were now flowing into the battlefield like flood-water.

When Wah Wah saw his father struggling to break through, he shouted, 'Don't bother about me, Abbu. You take care of the king. I'll handle these rogues.' Just then, a spear pierced his back and he fell forward. All that the father could do was to scream in despair at the sight of his fatally injured son being dragged away. Then, he collapsed on the spot from the shock.

The ground was littered with corpses and wounded men and animals groaning and neighing in agony. The blood spurting out of their bodies had turned the rain-wet earth a deep brownish-red. Netaji scanned the blood-soaked battlefield and saw that among those fallen, there were more than a couple of hundred Maratha boys. He realised that waging a blind war would lead them nowhere. Catching Baji Prabhu's eye, he signalled to him to withdraw. Baji, however, was altogether sucked in by the spirit of battle and was refusing to step back.

Netaji, otherwise notorious for being a passion-driven soldier, was uncharacteristically prudent on this day. He nudged his horse towards Baji and tried to persuade him to back off. In desperation, he bent down and seized Baji's horse's reins, at which the latter flared up and yelled, 'Netoba, what are you doing?'

'Bajipant,' Netaji shouted back, 'if we expend ourselves in this manner, who will be left to help the king with his mission?'

Blood was oozing from the cuts on Baji's brow. Netaji's unanswerable question had put him in a bind. Knowing that he could not win this argument, he pulled back from the battle in frustration and with deep regret. He looked wistfully up at the fort, wiped sweat mingled with blood from his forehead and turned his horse around with a heavy heart.

As Netaji looked up at the walls of Panhala high above him, he could not prevent his eyes from turning moist. As he bent his head to mop the recalcitrant tears, a hand was laid upon his shoulder. 'What do I see, Netajirao, tears in your eyes?' Baji Prabhu asked.

'You can see my eyes, Bajirao,' Netaji smiled wanly, 'but can you turn them around to look at yours?'

As the two stood side by side in the rain-laden air under dense green vegetation, one or the other would sneak a glance upward at the distant ramparts of the fort. Their outline was obscured by dark clouds streaked with strange hues of red and yellow. The walls of Panhalgadh were now almost entirely coated with thick layers of moss, with blotches of the brown-black stone showing here and there. The low-hanging clouds had mopped off the line that separated the sky from the earth. The two veterans stared and stared, as if they would never tire of the sight. But neither of those two pairs of eyes spotted a single ray of hope that they could carry back with them to their tents. The ancient jambhul trees behind their backs seemed to shudder too.

17

A BIRD IN A HURRICANE

The month of Aashaad was now well under way. The rain continued its vigil on the dense green jungles of the Sahyadris. Clouds blew into Panhala from the coast of Konkan. As soon as they were close enough, their wings would turn dark and begin discharging immense loads of water. There were occasions when the clouds would descend so low as to virtually rest on people's heads. At other times, the sky looked bright and cloudless. Even in such inclement, unpredictable weather, the king continued to conduct his inspection rounds.

From the walls of the fort, the thousands of thatched huts that the enemy had built around its base were sometimes visible through the haze or the falling rain. Their cantering horses and patrolling soldiers could also be seen from a distance. Then a sudden shower would descend, sending the king scampering for shelter. There was no certainty now either about the mood of nature or about the movement of the enemy soldiers that stood surrounding them.

By now, not only the enemy, but their thatched huts too had become accustomed to the rains. They stood with the obstinacy of mules with their feet firmly planted in the soggy soil. Their roofs refused to leak and their walls provided the Adilshahi men with all the warmth and comfort that they needed.

Gunvantabai and her colt travelled up to the fort that morning. As always, she handed over the containers of milk and ghee to the kitchen help, but refused to part with the wide-mouthed earthen pot that carried the curd. 'This I shall give directly to the king,' she declared. 'Move aside, you.'

Everyone in the fort was aware of the intimacy that had developed between the old woman and the king. This morning, he spotted her from a distance and called out, 'Come, Gunvantamaavashi, come inside.'

The king rose from his seat and signalled to the old woman to follow him into an inner hall where a meeting was in progress. A servant boy emptied the curd into a vessel and left. The king's attention was drawn towards a few palaas leaves at the bottom of the pot. He laughed and asked, 'maavashi, didn't those Bijapuri rascals at foot of the fort frisk you?'

'What do you think? They made me open the pot, ran their fingers around its neck, even sampled the curd. Only then did they give me permission to come up to the fort!'

The king pulled a wax-paper bundle out from under the leaves and then carefully opened it to retrieve a letter. It was from Phirangoji Narsaala, the fort-keeper of Sangramdurg. It was raining fire all around the Chaakan fort, but the eight or nine hundred Maavali men inside had turned out to be a more than adequate match for the twenty-five thousand Mughal soldiers assailing them from all sides.

The king could easily visualse the appearance of that brave old warrior—the turban twirled around his head, the thick whiskers on his cheeks, the eyelashes turned white with age, the proud aquiline nose and the pendulous rings that swung from his earlobes. Keeping that impressive figure in his mind's eye, he began reading the letter:

> O King, from the very first day of the siege, we nine hundred men have tied not our turbans but our shrouds around our heads and stood tall amid the flames of war. The enemy is very strong, so is his thrust. Some say that the Khan has twenty thousand soldiers, others say thirty thousand. What is certainly true, however, is that these Mughal forces have been striking the walls of our formidable fort day and night like the waves of an agitated sea. But, Raje, let this not be cause for any worry. The courage that sits in our hearts can counter a thousand such waves and not crack.
>
> You please take care of the kingdom; this old man shall take care of the fort of Chaakan. Do not worry. Till such time as we hold weapons in our fists and breath in our ribcages, we shall keep fighting.

The king's associate Tryambakrao Ingale was with him. When he heard the contents of Phirangoji's letter, he said, 'Raje, all things considered, our Phirangoji is a tough old veteran. The revered Shahaji Maharaj himself had appointed him keeper of the Chaakan fort. Your father's judgment cannot err.'

'Quite right, Tryambakrao. Whenever my father's perceptive eyes fall on a man, his life gets transformed.'

'Phirangoji is an absolute champion.'

'Indeed! That was why, when we raised the banner of revolt against Adilshah, he immediately severed relations with Bijapur and joined us openly along with the Chaakan fort under his charge.'

For all the courage that raced through Phirangoji's veins, however, the news from Chaakan was grave. The situation at Sangramdurg would need constant attention and monitoring.

As the meeting progressed, Shambhuji Jadhav placed another point for consideration before the king and his associates: 'According to the news that our spies from the north have provided, Aurangzeb is extremely annoyed with his uncle—'

'Why?'

'Padishah Aurangzeb's mandate had been for Shaista to move past Pune before the monsoons arrived, then traverse Satara and reach the base of Panhala. The Mughal and Adilshahi armies could then jointly finish off this nightmare called Shivaji once and for all.'

'Which means,' the king said with a smile, 'that the emperor's mind ran a hundred times faster than a real horse could.'

'Exactly. What happened was quite the opposite. By the time the Mughal army with its seven or eight thousand carts loaded with goods could reach Pune, it had broken into perspiration.'

'But why did the Khan suddenly decide to launch this attack on Chaakan?'

'The spies say that the Khan thought long and deep. On the way from Pune to Satara, he knew he would be meeting rivers like Neera, Krishna and Koyna, all swollen by the raging monsoons. That would make crossing impossible even for the gods. Twiddling his thumbs in Pune was not a viable option either. Instead of becoming the target of the emperor's abuses sitting there in Lal Mahal, he thought it wiser to mount this assault on the neighbouring fort of Sangramdurg.'

There was another issue that caused serious concern in the meeting. In line with the ideas of his Emperor, Shaista Khan had also started implementing a policy of religious intolerance and persecution. He had begun demolishing the spires of the temples in the precincts of Pune and desecrating holy places on the river banks. Blacksmiths, masons and other artisans who had accompanied the Mughal army were reducing the statues of gods and goddesses to molten metal or mere rubble.

Shivraya said to his associates: 'This conflict is going to drag on and on, but we cannot allow Uncle Shaista to carry on with this religious insanity. Hence, it is important to accost the Khan in Chaakan and put a muzzle on him.' But as soon as he had uttered these words, the king snorted in frustration and said almost to himself, 'But, for performing that deed, one first needs to get free of the crocodile-jaws of Panhala.'

Baajappa Dighe, fort-keeper of the neighbouring Pawangadh, had paid a flying visit to Shivraya the previous evening. Bringing his arms together from the elbow to the palms and fingertips, he had pleaded, 'Raje, the danger has increased substantially. Pawangadh may succumb at any moment to the powerful assaults of the enemy.'

'Any particular reason why you should be so panic-stricken?'

'They are now hustling to repair those English cannons that have been lying unused. What if they begin spitting out those demoniacal fireballs at us again? The noise alone can wake the dead!'

'Look, when people are anxious, they will mouth the first thought that comes into their heads. A person like you who holds the responsible office of a fort-keeper should take particular care to disregard such fearmongering gossip. Keep your courage up and go on fighting. We are with you.' Baajappa was comforted by the king's words and returned to his post invigorated.

Restless, the king let his horse amble along as he made his daily round of the fort. His head had now begun to throb from perpetual worries. There were gaps here and there in the procession of clouds drifting past the fort. The monsoon rains were taking a break. The horse took the king to the temple of Someshwar within the fort. Balabhatt Shastri quickly arranged for white champa flowers and some long-stemmed, green-leafed, red lotuses from a nearby pond to be brought there for the king's prayers.

The king placed the flowers on the pind of Someshwar and the priest distributed the sanctified sweets. Shivraya sat for a little while in front of the grand statue of Vishwanath. He meditated on Someshwar, Ghruneshwar, Bhuleshwar, Rohideshwar and Shambhu Mahadev of Shingnapur. He recited the various names by which Lord Shankara was worshipped—Lord Shankara, under whose benediction the Bhosale lineage had flourished. 'Deva, Mahadeva,' he mumbled as he left the temple, 'we are under your care.'

The populace assembled outside bowed to him in respect. The king never allowed his flower-like smile to disappear from his face, but his eyes were betraying him all along. He was racked by the thought of the stranglehold in which the fort and all its inhabitants had been caught, not to mention his other worries. The peasants, who were ready to give their lives at the tiniest signal from him, did not miss the red tinge of anxiety in his expressive eyes.

A number of Bhois, the community of palanquin-bearers, were sitting listlessly around the temple. Ordinarily, these hard-working people were in their element while carrying palanquins, chairs, doolies and all kinds of loads on their shoulders up and down the fort. Now they had been rendered utterly jobless. At this stage of the siege, Siddhi Johar had brought all movement of men and animals in and out of the fort to a complete halt, not only along the regular paths but through the jungle trails too.

The Raja had made arrangements for allowances to be given to the Bhois, the fishermen and other labourers whose livelihood had been hit. His concern was that they should at least be able to light their hearths every day. His heart ached as he accepted the greetings of his subjects and looked at their faces ridden with worry for their king.

He had hardly settled himself down in his office when two spies presented themselves before him, looking quite distraught. 'Yes,' said the king, looking at them, 'what news have you brought?'

'Last morning, the troops of Netaji Palkar, Baji Prabhu and Siddhi Hilaal launched a major raid on the Adilshahi forces, but in the battle that followed, Raje, two hundred and fifty of our men were either martyred or seriously injured.'

'Whose troops?'

'Mostly from Netaji's army.'

The king closed his eyes and somehow managed to suppress the pain that was threatening to explode in his innards. He ran his fingers over his rosary of shells to calm his nerves.

'What you are saying, therefore,' he said to the spies in a melancholy voice, 'is that our valiant warrior Netoba, who has been making life miserable for the besieging enemy through his relentless raids upon them, has had to face defeat.'

'That is exactly the misfortune that's come to pass, Raje.'

It rained right through the day. The king had turned extremely grave. The news that the fort-keeper of Pawangadh had brought of the developments on that side, and now this inconceivable defeat in battle of Netaji Palkar, these two events sat like a heavy weight upon his chest.

News had reached Panhala that Shaista Khan was accelerating his efforts to bring Shivaji to his knees. Towards this end, he was now trying to infiltrate and weaken the king's innermost circle by luring or prising away his closest friends and advisers. Secret letters had been dispatched to a number of prominent Maratha families and chieftains, warning them of dire consequences if they continued to keep company with Shivaji. They would be much better off accepting the posts of sardars and fort-keepers under the Mughal administration. If the disease of dissension were to spread unchecked, it foretold a dark future for the Swarajya, the king could see.

One day, Phulaji came to the palace and stood with fear writ large on his face. 'Why do you look so agitated, Phulaji?' the king asked.

'It's bad news, Maharaj. I'm afraid even your patience, unrivalled though it is, will snap at hearing this. It's treachery.'

'Tell me exactly what happened.'

'If you remember, Maharaj, Bajidada had informed us about turncoats like Babaji Honap and Krishnaji Kalbhor of Pune meeting Shaista Khan even while he was still in Burhanpur.'

'Yes, that's true.'

'Those traitors have given loyalty a bad name, Maharaj.'

'Yes, Phulaji, I am aware of all these backstabbers, but why don't you divulge the information that is choking you and get rid of it, once and for all? My heart turns numb at the thought of news so bad that its very enunciation can lacerate your tongue. Out with it, then!'

'Raje, gold has turned to filth. Sambhaji Kavji, the hero of your battle at Pratapgadh, has turned traitor.'

A storm cloud seemed to have descended upon the king's head. It was a seismic jolt that passed through his entire body. All through the day, Shivraya could not shake off the image of that powerfully built man who had the strength to carry a horse in his arms in the manner of a shepherd holding a lamb close to his chest. It was with unconditional trust that the king had dispatched him on the Jawali campaign, and how, with a single stroke, the man had sent Hanumant Morey rolling to the ground!

The siege around Panhalgadh had begun to choke the breath out of all who were trapped inside, with no remedy in immediate sight. Under these circumstances, the news of the defection of a front-rank warrior like Sambhaji Kavji was impossible to keep under wraps. This duplicitous act had sent a tremor of sorrow and fear through the hearts of the soldiers in the fort.

'The Sambhaji who pulled the bleeding Afzal Khan out of his palanquin and decapitated him, the man who had gone dancing up the steps of Pratapgadh in a frenzy of victory with that severed, bleeding head in his hands—where could that man have disappeared? And who could this man be,' the king wondered aloud, 'who had tossed a lifetime of merit away and sold the cause of Hindvi swarajya for a few gold coins?'

The king's wounded heart refused to heal. As he got up from his meal, he froze for a moment in mid-stride. Seeing the despair that had overcome their leader, Sardar Ingale, Tryambakpant and others tried to reason with him. 'Please, Raje, please put this misfortune behind you. We have never seen such distress on your face before.'

'Where? Where did I fall short in showering my love and admiration on this Sambhaji Kavji? After Pratapgadh, I had him promoted as Master of the Stables at Chaakan; very soon he would have become the keeper of a major fort. When the sparkling-white honour of such a soldier begins to show smears of faithlessness, the heart is bound to grieve.'

'All that is true, Raje, but even so, it's best forgotten.'

'I'm trying, I'm trying. If I had lost a fort or two, I could have come to terms with it; but if the enemy begins plucking gems like Kavji from my crown, it portends dark days ahead.'

It should never have come to this. The zest and confidence with which Salaabat Khan was sustaining the siege surprised him. Even more shocking had been the tenacity with which the man had withstood the raging Sahyadri monsoons. But what had given him the biggest jolt, no less than Kavji's betrayal, was the recent defeat suffered by the greatest of his warriors, Netaji Palkar. Furthermore, the insolent behaviour of the firangis of Rajapur, the lining up of heavy-calibre cannon in the precincts of Panhala, and the cheap, discourteous comments of Revington had deeply maimed his native pride.

Once the king retired to his bedroom, the only person who had authority to peep in was Shambhuji Jadhav. Since he was the younger man by four years, he would address the king as Shivajidada. If ever the king felt the need for anything, if there was some discomfort to attend to, in the absence of the queens, it was Shambhuji who played the role with care and affection.

The king had been running a mild fever for the past few days. Shambhuji had therefore made it a point to get up twice or thrice during the night, softly approach the king's bed, rearrange the sheet that covered him and creep back silently. Occasionally he would hear the king call out after him, 'Shambhu, how long will you stay up? Don't you need some sleep too?'

'No, dada, no. I have strict instructions from Jijau aaji: "Take care of the protector of millions!"'

By now, supplies in the fort had begun to dwindle, and the animals had turned stiff from lack of exercise. It was now common knowledge among soldier and peasant that the state of their king was that of a bird caught in a hurricane. When the Raja began to sense the presence of an undefined fear even in the speech and demeanor of his household staff, he was deeply grieved.

Each morning, once the king had got out of bed, bathed and put on a fresh set of clothes, all his anxiety, weariness and grief would be left behind. One such day, as he sat in the office looking into matters at hand, a clerk came up to him and said softly in his ear, 'Raje, shoulder-loads of sweets have just arrived from Siddhi Johar's camp.'

A faint furrow appeared upon the king's brow. 'Any note or message accompanying it?' he asked.

'The Bhois who brought the load say Khan sahib sent no message or note. Just sweets from Bhaganagar.'

'But how can this be possible?' Shivraya asked Phulaji. 'If these sweets have been sent by Johar himself, shouldn't they be carrying his official seal, or at least be accompanied by a clerk of some kind?'

'Raje, these Bhois have a ruffianly look about them. They turn abusive the moment we ask them to identify themselves,' complained a clerk.

'They are impertinent and crass,' another piped up. 'They stick their tongues out and tell us about how they hanged an Adilshahi official from a tree on the way.'

The matter was turning stranger by the minute. After exchanging glances with Phulaji, Shivraya snapped at a guard, 'Who are these audacious roughnecks? Why haven't they been dragged to the royal court here?'

'Those rascals threaten us with violence. They say they will not meet this person or that; they want an audience with the king.'

Shivraya said to Phulaji, 'Go and see who these people are. Bring them over after a proper frisking.'

Phulaji departed in a hurry; but within a short while, roars of laughter could be heard from the direction of the staircase outside. The king stepped out to see what was happening. Red kerchief tied around the head, skeins of yarn wound trader-style around the body, a short muslin dhotar ending well above the knees, side-whiskers thick as wrists—a Maavali Bhoi stood before him. Within the next fraction of a second, Shivraya had rushed forward excitedly and gathered the man in his embrace with a loud cry, 'Come, Baji Prabhu, come. You have arrived at the most appropriate time. I have been waiting for you.'

'Raje, it was with great difficulty that I managed to overcome this mountain of calamities. If I have succeeded in reaching on time, it is entirely due to the blessings of Ma Bhawani, nothing else.'

'I was quite certain of your arrival. I knew that even if it meant turning day into night, you would certainly take this leap. But before anything else, tell me what the state of affairs is at the foot of the fort.'

'It is difficult to gauge this from the top, but down there, Raje, the enemy does not rest even for a moment. He is perpetually on the alert. His horses make rounds of the base of the fort at all times, through rain, mist and slime.' Baji Prabhu's voice was heavy with anxiety as he spoke.

'Then, Bajiba,' the king said in a delighted voice, 'your exploit of managing to enter the fort today will now become a new hallmark for bravery, do you understand?'

The king's attention then shifted to a person who stood behind Baji Prabhu. It was Siddhi Hilaal, standing still as a leafless tree. Flashing a bright smile of satisfaction at finding Hilaal too in this brave company, Shivraya said, 'Hilaalbaba, why alone? Why isn't your son Wah Wah with you?'

The question brought that scene of the battlefield, in all its vividness and horror, back into Baji Prabhu's mind. With tears in his eyes, he related to Shivraya how the Adilshahi soldiers had surrounded the valorous man, how his spine was broken with a spear that pierced his back, and how he was carried away by the enemy. Despite hearing this narration of the details of the tragedy that had befallen his son, Siddhi Hilaal stood there unflustered. There was impressive restraint in his face and in his voice, a formidable discipline in his demeanour. He resembled an open, dry river bed. Looking at this man who had invited such sorrow upon himself in the service of the second generation of Bhosales, the king asked, 'Hilaalbaba, how is it that there is no outburst of sorrow from you?'

Hilaal replied, 'What do I cry over, Rajaji? A few years back, I rubbed my nose at Allah's threshold and begged: 'Ya Allah, give me a score of children to put into the service of Shahaji and the Bhosale lineage. And

Allah accepted my plea. What if one has gone? I have five living still, to do service!' As he was uttering these words, his voice lost control and he began sobbing. The sobs soon turned into wails.

The king rose from his seat and, walking up to the shaking, weeping Hilaal, gathered him in his embrace.

There wasn't sufficient manpower in the fort to put up a successful resistance if the need arose. By now, it was evident that Netaji Palkar's men had found it impossible to climb up to the fort to strengthen their defense. There was no saying when the cannons of the firangis would begin belching fire.

Such were the misfortunes in which the king found himself trapped. He couldn't sneak out of the fort; nor could anyone come running to answer his call for help. What could be done? Where could he go? How much longer could he sit doing nothing, gathering monsoon fungus as if he were the bark of a tree?

It was midnight, and the king was twisting and turning in bed. Finally, the cold monsoon wind that was blowing in from the open window did the trick, perhaps. He drifted into sleep, and began to dream. He was atop the Pemgadh fort now, next to Baji Prabhu, astride a horse that stood bathed in sweat and panting in the courtyard, just back from a long and hard ride. His elder brother Shambhuraja's horse stood in front of his in an identical state of breathlessness. And, surprise of surprises, it was one of those rare days when Abasahib, Shahajiraje himself, was present in the fort. Whenever he found the boys idle or unoccupied, Abasahib would call them close and tell or teach them something.

That day, memories of the Bhatwadi battle had come flooding into his head, and with them the image of Malikbaba. The king was telling young Shambhu, 'Son, it's not as if guerilla wars are fought only on the battlefield. If you can cripple the enemy's mind by launching mental assaults on him, the wounds you can inflict will be far more lethal than those of the battlefield.'

When the king stepped out of bed after tossing away the coverlet of the dream, his face glowed with the joy of a fruitful search. Sleep was now as far away as the coverlet he had sent flying. In front of his eyes rose the dark, Habshi face of Siddhi Johar. That man was valiant on the battlefield and crooked of heart; but when the fumes of arrogance filled his head, he could be amazingly foolish. This understanding of Salaabat Khan was good enough for Shivraya.

The clerks arrived at the office at daybreak. The draft for the letter was ready in the king's head, and he got it transcribed on paper. Well before the skies had turned bright, Gangadharpant swifty descended from the fort with an escort of handpicked soldiers for the express purpose of an interview with Siddhi Johar.

The general was in the midst of his breakfast in the company of his officers. He had already polished off two well-roasted chickens and was about to sink his teeth into the third one when a guard informed him of the arrival of an urgent message from the fort. Johar signalled to a clerk to read Shivajiraja's letter aloud.

> Treasure of the Deccan, Light of Kurnool,
> Supreme Khan, Salaabat Khan, Jung-bahadur,
>
> In light of the valorous personality that you possess, these titles are far too inadequate. I wait for the day when I shall have the honour of addressing you as Sultan-e-Bhaganagar-Dakkhan. By the blessings of our goddess Jagdamba and the grace of your Allah-ta'ala, that day is not too far away—'

'Maasha-Allah! Wonderful!' Thrilled at the adulation, Siddhi Johar put his chicken leg back on the plate and mopped his lips with a silk serviette. 'How beautifully this boy of Shahajiraje writes!' he remarked to the clerk.

An official sitting at the table couldn't restrain himself from blurting out, 'These are all false praises, huzoor.'

'Of course they are false, moron, but they are beautiful, nevertheless. And keep this other point in mind, donkey: it requires intelligence to be able to write such ornate phrases for creating delusions in the enemy's head.'

The official turned red and hung his head in humiliation. Not wanting to invite the ire of the general upon himself, the clerk reading the letter resumed with greater animation.

Khan sahib, may a large-hearted personage like yourself deign to give ear to my entreaty. How long should I lie rusting here in Panhala, huzoor? I have already met you and confessed my misdeeds. I shall even be happy to surrender the fort to you the moment you instruct me to do so. Please have mercy on me and help me as you would a younger brother.

I place my supplication before you with all the humility I possess. Please take charge of this fort of Panhala. As to whether you wish to retain it for yourself or hand it over to Adilshah, you are the master of your will. Keeping the welfare of of us both in mind, kindly allow me to depart from the fort.

Please let the umbrella of your indulgence shelter my head. Once I come down from the fort, I shall look neither left nor right, but follow my nose and cross the Vaarna river. Beyond that, I will take the route via Shirala fort and then the jungle trail straight to Rajgadh. Such is my decision.

Siddhi Johar was lifted into a mood of unadulterated joy and gratification by the language of surrender that embellished the letter. That evening, he confided to his son-in-law Masood, 'If I do become the Sultan, I shall appoint this Sivaji as my deewaan or wazeer. What do you say?'

Masood, of course, had nothing to say. He had begun to suspect that his father-in-law's mad dreams, spurred on by this man Shivaji's honeyed words, would land their army in a serious calamity.

Siddhi Johar's self-confidence was so contagious that it soon infected his deputies, his sardars and the other grandees in the Bijapuri camp. However, he did sound a note of caution: 'This Siva is a cunning man, a rascal. We must stay wide awake. Even if you permit him to reach up to you, the crafty man will try to slip out somehow.'

'Once, and if, he lands in our hands, you may forget all your worries, Abbu,' young Masood said, running his fingers over his lately sprouted moustache. 'Only his soul will slip out of your pavilion; his corpse will not.'

18

A PALANQUIN IN THE RAINS

The Prabhu brothers stood chatting on the verandah outside the office at the palace that morning. 'Why does your face look so tense, dada?' Phulaji asked.

'What does one do, boy? Whenever I look at the king, I feel the sting of a scorpion in my heart. How much longer can a bare handful of people fight on? In how many different directions? There you have Shaista Khan, sitting with the Pune jaageer stuck in his gullet, and here we have this Adilshahi noose thrown around the Panhala fort. How much pain can a person withstand, even if he is a warrior-king?'

'Those perfidious rats like the Siddhis of Janjira have been working against us from quite early on. But now we also have serpents rising from our own houses like the Savants of Wadi, the Surves of Shrungapur, the Shirkeys of Kutara and that Baji Ghorpade from Mudhol.'

'Fortunes change and earthworms turn into full-blown snakes, the wretches.'

'Their tongues have become vitriolic too. The kind of cheap shots they've been taking—"the sun has begun to set", "the days of your Shivaji Incarnate are over", and so on.'

It was raining cats and dogs the day the king sent for Shiva Kashid. It was as if the sky had decided to split apart and release all that it had been gathering for weeks together. Sunlight had virtually vanished.

'Look, Shiva,' the king said to Kashid, 'the two of us may have to leave on a mission to a faraway place this very night.'

'I await your command, Raje.'

'An important assignment may spring up in the vicinity of Siddhi Johar's camp too.'

'Issue the order, Raje.'

'That friend of yours, that Chauhan from Nebapur, where has he disappeared today?'

'Right here, Raje,' said Chauhan Patil, emerging from behind.

'What's this I hear, boys? You are accomplished mimics who perform during the festivals in the villages, they say! And this Shiva here, he once stuck a beard and moustaches on his face and impersonated me, I'm told!'

'Yes, Raje,' the two said with embarrassed titters.

The rain was coming down in buckets on the Khan's camp. The clouds were so dense that the entire Panhala range was enveloped in darkness. A thick fog had muscled in too. Neither the rains nor the fog cared a dime for either Adilshahi or Marathashahi.

Breaking the monotony of this festival of gloom, an astute spy whispered some sensational intelligence into Faazal Khan's ear: 'Khan sahib, spread your people around and filter all this fog through a fine sieve.'

'Why? What's happening?'

'Siva is going to take advantage of this thick haze. Our information is that he might make the leap any time now.'

The news stunned both Faazal Khan and Siddhi Masood. Already, several small bands of young soldiers, trained to move around without being spotted by the Maratha guards from the battlements above, were on surveillance duty despite the weather. These boys were accustomed to galloping through the Sahyadri mists with their swords slicing through the air.

This evening, Faazal Khan himself goaded the other officers into action and had them ride their horses into the blinding fog, shouting 'Alert! Alert!' Siddhi Masood joined him, trotting around the jungle at the foot of the fort with a naked sword in hand, letting out cries of 'Deen deen!'

A grey-white vapour, dense and cottony, had spread all around the base of Panhalgadh, which the ever-vigilant Faazal Khan, Rustam-e-Zamaan and their men were crisscrossing, leaving not a patch unattended. Sentinels had been posted everywhere to make sure that nobody could pass unquestioned. The Adilshahi surveillance that night was utterly impeccable.

By evening, a moist, biting wind began to blow about the ramparts of the fort, allowing no rest to door-hinges or window-panes. It turned extremely dark, as rain clouds took complete charge of the atmosphere. The king's closest associates gathered around him. Every official of note was in attendance at the meeting in the office hall of the palace, including Shambhuji Jadhav, Rayaji Bandal, Siddhi Hilaal, Baji Prabhu and Phulaji. In the rapidly changing scenario, it was difficult to say what the king's final decision would be.

Tryambakrao Ingale advised, 'Raje, there's no point in your remaining stuck here any further.'

'I agree,' Rayaji Bandal said. 'The rains don't show any signs of relenting. You must make good your escape at the very earliest.'

'We can leave behind only five or six thousand men to defend the fort,' the king informed Tryambakpant. 'The remaining seven hundred foot soldiers will travel with me.'

'Yes, Raje.'

'Exercise extreme caution. Be vigilant at all times. The enemy that besieges us is over thirty-five thousand strong. From this point on, the responsibility of the fort lies on the shoulders of you two Tryambaks—Tryambakrao Ingale and Tryambakrao Kulkarni.'

The two old-timers stepped forward and lowered their heads before the king. Tryambakpant Kulkarni said, 'Abandon worry! Whatever strength we are left with, we shall wage war on the enemy with hundred-fold intensity.'

After a hundred and thirty-three days of forced residence at the Panhala fort, Shivraya was setting out to meet the challenge of a wondrously wild and stormy night. The escape route that beckoned to him ran through ten impossible miles of dense, pitch-dark forest, across countless freshets, along streams descending in terrifying cataracts from the tops of mountains, and past rock faces ascending to formidable precipices.

In the presence of his trusted courtiers, Shivraya placed fistfuls of flowers at the feet of Ma Bhawani's idol and the priest applied ash to the king's forehead. His soulful eyes had an extraordinary glow, like those of a hero of legend who descends into a dark valley to destroy a demon. Everyone waited with bated breath, ears cocked, to gather every single word that would emerge from those firm, determined lips.

'Eight months have rolled by since the day that Afzal Khan was annihilated at Pratapgadh,' the king began with gravity, 'and we have not known any rest during this entire period, you and I. We have forgotten the meaning of a full night's sleep. And now, for the last four months and a quarter, the enemy has incarcerated us in Panhala to suffer the vagaries of the scorching summer and then the relentless monsoon rains.

'Months have gone by since we began living our life far away from our households, our farmyards, our children. I am human too, and it is natural that I should be missing my revered mother and others in the family. It has been months now since I have seen the smiling face of my little boy Shambhu. This separation causes my heart to ache, but there is no remedy for it. This is life, where man dreams of one thing and destiny has other things in store for him.

'At this juncture, all our armies are engaged in fighting for the defence of our Swarajya at several different places at the same time. Our own status here is that of being under house arrest, with thirty-five thousand swords and spears keeping watch day and night over our slightest movements.

'Despite the mere handful of soldiers at our disposal, we have managed to obstruct the enemy hordes from climbing even a few steps closer to the fort. But the enemy too has succeeded in blocking all our exit routes and locking us up in our own bastion.'

'Even so, you shouldn't worry, Maharaj,' several of the sardars spoke out. 'Even after being skinned and beheaded, we shall keep fighting.'

'The fort's stock of food and fodder has been depleting rapidly,' the king continued, 'but an even bigger concern is the situation in Pune. That

Shaista Khan should not be allowed the comfort of camping permanently in the city. If that happens, there is every danger of the prized jaageer falling permanently into the lap of the Padishah in Delhi. This is why, at all costs, a hole has to be bored through the ring of steel in which the enemy has encircled us. We must suffer the consequences that follow, and advance towards Pune at the earliest possible opportunity.'

Shivraya called the two Tryambaks aside and entrusted to them a piece of sculpture from his shrine. It had been worshipped in Panhala since ancient times. In an overwrought voice, he said, 'As I bid goodbye to the soil of Panhala, there is one knife that cuts and makes my heart bleed: after a hundred and thirty-three nights of being confined, I am leaving you here in the enemy's stranglehold.'

'Please stop worrying, Maharaj. The walls of this fort are made of hard stuff, tough enough to break the enemy's teeth if he grapples too hard with us,' the others declared.

'Raje, in all of Deccan, there is nobody else who has had the pluck to stand up against, and actually humble, the mighty Mughal war machine. Please abandon all anxiety; you will succeed in these endeavours.' Baji, Phulaji, Shambhuji, both the Tryambaks, Manaji and all the others gathered around the king to shore up his faltering spirits.

Two palanquins had been ready since the afternoon. One of them was dispatched at sunset through a secret passage to a colony called Waada within the precincts of the fort.

Baji Prabhu had hired a squad of well-built Bhois for carrying the king's palanquin, men who were not only strong but also experienced in walking jungle tracks and crossing flooded streams. Noticing the vehicle that had been chosen for their journey, Shivraya said to Baji Prabhu with a smile, 'Bajidada, we are going to travel through forests so dense with thorny vegetation that even a tiger would think twice about venturing through it. Of what use can a palanquin be there?'

'You mean we shouldn't take the palanquin? Are we going to do it on foot, all that distance?'

'That's right, Bajida. In the jungles that we are about to traverse, even the tigers don't peep out of their caves during the three months of the monsoons. Snakes slither out of their holes and wrap themselves around the branches of trees for a bit of warmth to survive the rainy season.'

'How many horses do we take, then?'

'Horses? Why? And for whom? Shambhuji, where's our Guna maavashi?'

The crowd gathered in front of the king parted, to allow the white-haired, eighty-year-old matriarch to step forward. Lean and resilient as the branch of a babool tree, she held in her hand a cane reaching up to her ears. Around her waist was a rope which she ordinarily used to tie her calves to the stake. As planned, she was dressed and ready to travel with the king. Addressing her, the king said, 'maavashi, please talk to our Bajidada here. He wants to take horses along the path we shall be walking.'

'Whatever for, boys? This dread trail is so full of sudden twists and turns! Even otherwise, the trails in these jungles have awfully narrow mouths. They keep hopping from one valley into another like girls playing phugadi during the festivals. One sharp turn, and you are in the next set of hills and gorges!'

The old crone's colourful description of the forest paths had everybody in splits, including the king. She went on, 'And if you're asking about the current season, every single track is flooded with streams, as if the sea itself has spilled over into these mountains. All that slime and sludge! Your leg can get buried in it, sink right up to your thigh. While pulling your limbs out, you will break into a sweat even in a bone-drenching shower! Then, there are those places in the jungle where you have to chop the overhanging thorny vines with a scythe before you can inch forward. This is a jungle that does not want you to move ahead.'

Her lively narration had begun to give the travellers some idea of the challenges the journey was going to throw up. Shivraya said, 'As a medicine man tears open the belly of a dead animal and examines its innards, so have I been studying the complexities of this terrain systematically for the past hundred days and more. As Guna maavashi has been telling you, the journey is going to test your skills, patience and tenacity to the hilt.'

'You will run into such intricately tangled vines and bamboos that you will have to go crawling under them at many places. Where, then, would you tie your horses?' Guna maavashi said, casting a scornful look at Shambhuji, Phulaji and the others.

Inside the palace, arrangements were being made for the king's farewell. As always, the servants had brought over the his velvet clothing, his ornaments and his glittering mandeel, neatly arranged on a tray. Shivraya cast a glance at Shambhuji Jadhav, who immediately brought over another tray covered with a kerchief. The king then got up and went with him to the inner hall. In a short while he returned, and the assembly stared at him in disbelief.

He was dressed in a long, loose tunic made of the rough wool of Bidali sheep. It would help him stay warm inside while keeping the rainwater out. On his head he had wound a turban in the style of saint Tukaram, under which lay concealed his steel skull-cap. Bowl-shaped like a large coconut half-shell, this was the protection he had used in his Pratapgadh encounter with Afzal Khan. He had thrown a capacious shawl around his shoulders, below which his calf-hugging trousers were visible.

Tryambakpant stepped forward and said with feeling, 'What's going on here, Maharaj? You propose to step out in this clumsy garb of a farm labourer?'

'This is the kind of coarse clothing that best—'

'But you should wear your mandeel, at the very least!

'Pant, didn't you hear what Guna maavashi had been saying? Traversing that dense jungle means hacking our way through all those wild, thorny bushes with axes and scythes. There'll be constant stooping, bending and crawling for large parts of the journey. How will a mandeel help in these circumstances?'

'But Raje, that's your mark of royalty—'

'Don't worry. When the occasion demands it, even a king should forget his splendour and put aside his regalia. He should grapple with the circumstances that are before him. First comes the mission, next comes the body, and finally, wealth. It is important to recognise the order of these priorities.'

This unprecedented escape plan had sent tremors through the spines of all the king's associates. The only people who had been privy to this mission from the beginning were Guna maavashi, a few herders who would guide them through the trails, Shambhuji and Phulaji. Even Baji

Prabhu and Siddhi Hilaal, having arrived only a couple of days earlier, were relatively uninformed and confused.

Using the authority of his fatherly status, Baji Prabhu threw a volley of straight questions at his king: 'What mad enterprise have you got into? Why are you risking your invaluable life in this venture? Why frolic with death? What is the pressing need that compels a person of your vital importance to take a walk down such a treacherous, torturous, horrific trail?'

The king responded to Baji Prabhu's volley with great calmness. 'This jungle trail is the one path which can get me past the whirlpool of calamities I am caught in, and enable me to move towards the east without fear. Within a single night, I shall reach the desired destination.'

As everyone absorbed the king's words with great attention, he spoke on with confidence, 'Another reason I've fallen in love with this route is that not merely the Adilshahi forces, but no army in the world can chase me through it in the darkness of the night; nor can the bravest and most resolute of warriors appear on this path before me with a sword in hand.'

'You mean there's no possibility of an encounter with the enemy?'

'Impossible, absolutely impossible. They would have to cross four major forests with impenetrable walls of trees and impassable undergrowth before they can intercept us on our route. It will be daylight by the time they can traverse these jungles. By then, of course, forget humans ... even the birds of the forest will not be able to tell them how and where we went. Journeying past those deep gorges, turbulent streams and fearsome crags, by daybreak we shall enter the jungles of Gajapur. After that, there will be just one half-hour interlude during which we may encounter man or animal under the open sky. After that, we will be back in the dense woods outside the purview of the human eye. There will be no chance for anyone to spot us.'

'Rajaji, I will consider it my good fortune if I may have this opportunity to walk the jungle trail with you,' Siddhi Hilaal said.

'Forgive me, Raje,' said a completely mollified Baji Prabhu. 'Now that I have grasped the situation, I too wish to travel with you down this punishing path and participate in this extraordinary expedition.'

A shadow of hesitation seemed to flicker across the king's face for a moment or two. He then looked around at the gathering and said in a worried tone, 'But my brave friends, even in this marvellously conceived plan, a sliver of danger still remains.'

'What's that, Raje?'

'There are seven gruelling trails from different directions that pierce through the heart of these impossible jungles and ravines, but they all emerge further ahead to meet at one single crossing.'

'So, what is the danger there?'

'Once we set off down this trail, we are going to be out of reach of everyone. The enemy will not be able to sleep or eat for the next five to seven days; he will simply wander in a maze searching for us.'

Baji Prabhu's confusion was nowhere near resolved. 'Raje, it seems to me that you have tied all the knots neatly together. So, where is the danger that you fear?'

Shivraya turned serious again. Again there was that flash of hesitation, as if he was not sure whether he should speak his mind. His eyes fell on a wooden plank in front of him where a relief map of the land they would be traversing had been laid out. Gunvantabai, with the help of the jungle guides and some native lads who knew the terrain, had used rice and flour to prepare the three-dimensional reproduction.

One could see a series of mountains rising like the spines of tall horses. This segment of the route would be covered after eight or nine hours of vigorous walking through the night. Next came a flat patch in a hollow, which would be reached around daybreak. Beyond this spot was another jungle. Placing his finger there, the king said, 'This is the spot which we shall hit at daybreak. It's only during this half-hour that the rising sun will be able to see us.'

Letting out a deep sigh, Shivraya looked at the trusted men gathered around him in the light of the flambeaux. The pupils of every eye reflected the flames of the torches that surrounded them. Throwing a piercing look at them, the king said, 'Before the sun shows itself, with darkness and the jungle enveloping us completely, we shall not be visible even to the sky. But as the sun is lighting up this patch of land that we shall meet at daybreak, if we find that even half a dozen horses belonging to the enemy have already reached the place by any route whatsoever, we may happily assume that one of us has betrayed us all.'

Shiva Kashid and Chauhan Patil came down from the fort to their houses in Nebapur village. On the outskirts of the village was the thatch-and-mud hut of Shiva. Despite being poor, these were people with rich hearts.

Shiva was in a raging hurry today. He had to finish his meals, take the blessings of the gods in his household shrine and set off on the mission assigned to him by the king. By sunset, he couldn't hold himself back any longer. The kitchen and the inner room in his hut were separated by a curtain, behind which was an alcove containing a tiny shrine. Brass masks of Jyotiba and Ambabai were placed there with great reverence, alongside ancient icons covered with yellow rust and coated with layers of vermilion and gulaal. In the twinkle of the earthen lamp flickering there, Shiva found the faces of his gods illuminated with a new kind of resolution.

Rising to his feet, Shiva swiftly undid the knot of the big silk bundle he had brought tucked in his armpit from the palace. Pulling out a velvet tunic and a pair of close-fitting trousers, he put them on in a hurry. Being a barber by profession, Shiva kept the appliances of his trade in a bag that was always at hand. He pulled a mirror out of this pouch and examined himself critically. That tapering cut of the face, the wide brow, the lovely, lustrous eyes and the shapely beard: he was delighted at reconfirming his uncanny resemblance to his master. As he was preening himself, he saw another face appear in the mirror looking over his shoulder—the face of his mother Gajarabai. She seemed both entranced and aghast at the noble appearance of her handsome son.

'Oh Shiva, you stupid worm, what have you gone and done?' she cried.

'What? What have I done?'

'This imitation, you have done it to perfection, but why did you have to steal the king's clothing?

'No, Maavale, this is not stealing. Shivaji Maharaj hugged your boy and gave him these clothes. And now he is sending this lackey of his to do an important job.'

As he spoke, he picked up the cask of vermilion from the shrine, applied some wax to his forehead and drew a perfect crescent moon on his broad brow. He slipped a shell necklace over his head and turned to his mother with an expectant smile. Overawed, Gajarabai asked, 'So, you've been asked to put these clothes on for doing the king's job?'

'Yes, Maavale, I can only call it my good fortune that he picked me out from a thousand and held me to his chest.'

'Then, boy, live like a king, behave like one, fight like one, and if the need arises, die like one, but don't ever fall from a king's stature.'

Shiva quickly bowed before the shrine, placed his head at the feet of his parents, and suddenly remembering something, went back to the bundle. Extracting a necklace of jewels, he handed it over to his mother.

'Arey deva! This ornament is loaded with precious jewels, boy!'

'Yes, the Raja gave it to me with instructions to hand it over to you. He said: "Shiva, if there's an earthquake tomorrow, if you and I do not return, your children should not die of starvation."' Shiva's voice turned hoarse as he said this, his head grew heavy and the rims of his eyes glittered like the jewels on the necklace.

Just as he was setting out, the rice cooking on the hearth came to a boil. His mother quickly scooped out a few spoons into a bowl. Just then, Shiva's wife Lakshmi arrived with a pailful of fresh milk. She poured some on the rice, which Shiva ate hurriedly.

Just as he was about to step out of the hut, Shiva turned around to address his wife, 'Take care of my calves, Lakshey.'

'Avo, but whither are you blowing, like a gust of wind?'

'Our king is on this pilgrimage called Swarajya. I'm joining the procession.'

Saying that, Shiva walked out into the rain. Lakshmi turned her head over her shoulder and watched him till he disappeared into the darkness. The rain refused to let up.

The king of the Marathas walked out of his palace into the rain that evening, dressed like a common farmer. His head was protected from the downpour by a double layer of blankets, tied down with a silk kerchief. His usual velvet tunic and gold waistband were noticeably missing; so were the gold necklace around his neck and the jewelled rings on his fingers. He did wear his tight leggings, though, on the insistence of his companions that leeches that would be aplenty in the slime.

Tryambak Kulkarni held the king's hand and said in a tearful voice, 'Raje, the state you have been reduced to!'

A look of satisfaction flashed through the king's face. Baji Prabhu said, 'Pant, he is the king of the Marathas as well as of the impecunious farmers. When in the tiger's cave, one should move like a tiger. The glitter of your false ornaments pale beside the king's sharp elegance today.'

Old Gunvantabai was there, willow cane in hand. She was surrounded by some relatives, a few shepherds of the jungle hamlets, grazers and fishermen, all of whom knew the jungle like the back of their hand.

Into the rain descending in torrents and the strong winds making it dance in all directions, the king and his unusual retinue emerged from the palace. They were joined by the foot soldiers who had been assigned to the expedition. Shivraya himself walked in front, with a speed that forced the others to scurry along. In a little while, they had left the walls of the fort behind, and then—far behind.

The rain refused to part company with the walkers. After so many days of ceaseless soaking, the jungle had become one massive sponge. The trails had turned into little rivulets, each singing their small note of 'glug glug' that fused with a bigger symphony: the wind's duet with the falling rain, the subdued roar of the distant waterfalls and the ripples of the water flooding the farms along their route.

Shivraya's contingent moved rapidly down the slope. In the darkness intensified by the presence of giant trees, descending that slippery incline was a dangerous and demanding task. But the urgency of the mission had sharpened the men's eyesight and quickened the movement of their blood, enabling them to make progress at a smart pace. Occasionally the clouds would turn thin here and there, allowing the intimidated moon to peek wanly through a curtain of haze. In this ghostly light, the walkers could sense the wispy presence of the huts far below. Even from that distance, and in this inadequate light, it was evident that the enemy was wide awake and alert. The flambeaux in the Adilshahi camp blinked, horses neighed, and the exchange of greetings among the patrolmen reached them in incomprehensible murmurs of sound.

Escaping from the circle of the blockade that the enemy had laid around the base of the fort was a near-impossible task. Surveillance squads roved the entire area through the night and covered every patch of land in their overlapping movements. To dodge this night patrol, Shivraya's men made a tangential crossing at a tricky angle to the fort. It was through this narrowest of slivers that they planned to emerge into the wilderness they were to traverse on that dark night.

An acquaintance of Guna maavashi named Bandoba Gawade was accompanying the group as a guide. He had spent his entire life in these forests, hunting wild boar, sambar, rabbits and other wild animals. He walked confidently, taking long strides on his lanky legs, while Shambhuji Jadhav and Phulaji Prabhu trotted along beside him as best they could.

'May this rain burn in hell!' cursed Guna maavashi. 'It's been going on and on for the past four days like a brat with dysentery.'

'Maavashey,' drawled Bandoba, 'if you look at it another way, the sky has actually come to our aid. Consider it a blessing from the lord.'

'Gawade, any possibility of a crack somewhere?' the king asked.

'Maharaj, only if this violent rain has slit open a river bank or caused the earth to slip somewhere, otherwise none. The enemy encircles the fort as tightly as a rope around the neck of a calf.'

'Aho, but Gawade, for how long do we keep walking like this?' Shambhuji Jadhav asked.

'Look, Guna maavashi,' Bandoba replied obliquely, 'we just keep moving on westward through this rain and fog for some time. On the upper side here, in a nook on the side of Turukwadi, we will come to a big waterfall. Its pool is deep as two elephants. There's a stream there at the mouth of the base. The rain has been heavy today, so its flow will be heavy too. If the gods help us, we shall be victorious today.'

'Keep moving, Bandopant,' came the stern voice of the king from behind.

Soon the travellers reached a stream in a dense patch of the wood and saw the water that came roaring down from the top of the mountain. Crossing here was impossible. Even if they managed to brave the speed of the flow, there was the danger of huge, sharp rocks injuring their limbs.

They began climbing carefully down the wet slope along the bank of the freshet.

Leading this unsteady descent was Guna maavashi. At each step, she would test the wet ground in front with her long stick before setting her foot down. Alongside her were Shambhuji and Phulaji, with Shivraya, Baji Prabhu and the other senior officials following. Of the hundreds of soldiers who walked with them, twenty carried loads on their heads that contained precious jewels and ornaments—in other words, the mobile treasury of the king. As for swords, scimitars, cutlasses, daggers and spears, each one carried his weapon of choice with sufficient caution.

In very little time, it had become obvious to everyone that this trail was meant only for wild goats and other beasts of the jungle. The couple of dozen horses that had been taken along carried neither rider nor any load on their backs. Despite the absence of these burdens, they stumbled down the steep, slimy slopes with frothing muzzles, arching and twisting their bodies to ensure that their hooves found some dependable footing in the sludge underfoot.

Once they had descended the ledge, they arrived at a flat, grassy patch of the jungle. The flow of the mighty stream issuing from the falls continued its journey on their right, but the flatness of the land here had slowed its movement and made it swerve like a lethargic python. Finding some shelter in the thickets along the bank, the men tried to catch their breath and rest their stretched muscles. The information was that both the banks were under the surveillance of the Adilshahi patrol. But luck was with the travellers. The growl of the stream muffled their sounds and the fog concealed their presence.

Bandu Gawade and two other guides hopped into the stream like frogs to test its depth and velocity. The water rose up to their waists. They walked some distance downstream to check whether the enemy was around. After a while, they returned to report that they could sense movement not very far from the banks.

'Arey, but rascals, are you absolutely sure?'

'Yes.'

'How wide is the crossing downstream?'

'Say, sixty to seventy steps.'

'Well then, boys, what does it mean?'

'No need to worry, maavashi. It has rained heavily in the mountains above, causing the banks to overflow here. That has forced the patrolling soldiers to withdraw quite some distance from both banks. Which means that the area on either side of the stream is relatively unwatched. And we have the fog on our side.'

This was a golden opportunity for Shivraya and his men to make the crossing. Guna maavashi went up to the king and said, 'Raje, let's move fast. Make full use of the fog!'

A silent relay of signals brought all the men out of the trees to the bank. They began wading through the stream with as little noise as possible. The water clung to the men and horses with the affection of a mother, while the fog protected them like a father.

As they waded downstream and across, they tried to peer cautiously into the gloom beyond the banks, but the fog yielded no answers. It was quite clear, however, that the Adilshahi surveillance men in this neck of the woods had let nature have her way and retired for the night, sitting around the braziers in their huts and pulling at clay-pipes loaded with pleasurable marijuana.

Nevertheless, the men in charge of the horses in the king's company were still in in fear of an animal letting out an unexpected neigh or snort. They held the muzzles of the animals as close as possible to preempt such an eventuality. Fortunately, the animals created no such crisis and soon emerged on the eastern bank along with the men.

After walking a few more miles, the king called for a small halt and took a headcount to ensure that everyone was keeping up. It turned out that five men who had been carrying bundles of bhaakari and chutney were no longer among them. 'What now?' somebody asked in a low voice. 'How long do we wait for them?'

The king and his advisers held a quick discussion. There could be some grave reason why the five had lagged behind. There was no point in waiting for them and thus endangering the king's life. The decision was unanimous and immediate: keep moving forward.

The bell of the Maruti temple near Sajjakoti began ringing wildly. A palanquin had been set down near the waada. It was festooned with ribbons of brocade. Young boys danced around it, swinging ornamented umbrellas and ochre pennants. Inside the palanquin sat Shivraya. There was no mistaking his handsome, radiant face with its peculiar grace and dignity, or those deep, expressive, mesmerising eyes and the crescent moon drawn upon the wide forehead. As was his wont, the king held in his hand a tassel that hung from the roof of the palanquin.

The palanquin began to move despite the pouring rain. The boys had spread a waterproof cover of irali across the top and held it high as they walked briskly along. The villagers saw the dancing lamps and torches go rapidly past their doors, followed by the royal palanquin. They ran out of their houses to pay obeisance to their king. A well-built, important-looking man walked beside the palanquin, wearing a fancy barabandi tunic and an impressive turban on his head. Big earrings dangled from his lobes. He was obviously a senior official of the king's court. Some of the villagers, however, found in his overall appearance and demeanour a striking resemblance to Chauhan Patil of Nebapur.

As the palanquin proceeded through the rain and the darkening air, carrying a Shivraya apparently lost in contemplation, it was suddenly accosted by a voice ordering them to stop. 'Who are you? And where are you going?' a Maratha man in Adilshahi uniform asked, sticking his head out of his irali rain cover. Next to him stood Siddhi Masood, surveying the whole scene with curiosity. The Bhois brought the palanquin down from their shoulders and rested it on its four legs.

'First tell us, who you are,' the dignitary escorting the palanquin asked. 'How dare you obstruct the king's palanquin? Have you abandoned all social etiquette?'

'Aho, Pant, what are you saying?'

'You unlettered boor, can't you recognise the king of the Marathas? Bow down before His Majesty and show your respect.'

'Wait!' Siddhi Masood said, walking over. 'If this gentleman in the palanquin is Shivaji, where do you think you are going with him?'

'That we shall explain directly to Siddhi Johar sahib. You get out of our way.' The Bhois were becoming restive.

At that, Masood drew his sword and said, 'Johar sahib is not here. His pavilion is up there on top of the Ambwade hillock, on the other side of the stream.'

'Son Masood, will you come here, please?' The voice was so hypnotic that Masood was drawn towards it irresistibly. 'Why do you stand here arguing like an ignoramus in the middle of the road?'

Masood was so taken aback that he instantly bowed low to offer his respects. 'But why are you going in this direction, Rajaji? The pavilion is on the other—'

'Son, Masood, as the sun was setting, a herald came on horseback with the message that I should meet Johar sahib urgently at the village of Maley. And by the way, what's going on here?' the king said in a stern voice. 'Does it behove a responsible senior officer like you to accost me in the middle of the road?'

Masood was rattled. Obviously, the clerk in charge of dispatches had made a serious error, he assumed. It did not occur to him that the matter needed any further investigation. He tried to pacify the king by saying, 'But Raja sahib, not in this direction. Abbu is waiting for you on top of that other hillock.'

'All right, then, that's where we go,' the king said.

In a little while, the king's palanquin reached Siddhi Johar's camp. It was pandemonium at the camp that evening. Hordes of animated soldiers were gathering around with feverish calls of 'Sivaji is coming! Sivaji is coming!'

Siddhi Johar stepped out of his pavilion to welcome the king. He held the king respectfully by the hand and led him to his office. As he was being escorted, the king said, 'All right, let's not waste time. As agreed earlier, you must send a squad to accompany us to the bank of the river.' Siddhi Johar, quite overcome by the personality and bearing of the king, was eager to please him.

However, there were some renegade Marathas in the camp who had joined the Adilshahi army. They whispered into Siddhi Johar's ear, 'Huzoor, this person looks exactly like our erstwhile leader, but our hearts tell us this is not the real Shivaji.' Siddhi Johar was perplexed. He took Masood aside and said, 'I met him only a few days ago. The same voice, the same eyes!'

However, the whispers in the camp refused to stop. An unprecedented situation had suddenly emerged. Neither Siddhi Johar nor Masood could decide what they should do. That dignified personage sitting there, popping grapes and belting out Sanskrit verses—who could he be but the king himself?

They could, of course, resort to the extreme solution of having the man beheaded, but if he did turn out to be Shivaji, a mountain of problems would come crashing down on their heads. One person who could settle the issue for them was Rustam-e-Zamaan; soldiers were dispatched immediately to locate him and call him over to the pavilion.

Fortunately for them, Rustam-e-Zamaan was in the vicinity, inspecting some guard posts. Within no time his horse came galloping over to Siddhi Johar's pavilion. As he entered, he saw Shivaji seated there with great calm and dignity. He also noticed that the people assembled there were in the grip of some great confusion. As soon as Siddhi Johar saw Rustam enter, he held him by the arm and took him aside. 'Bhai,' he said, 'after Allah, it is you alone who can say whether the person who sits there is King Sivaji or not.'

'Miyaan, that's settled in a moment. He looks like the king, all right.' With that, he advanced towards Shivaji, bowed low and offered his salutations: 'Mujra, Rajan.'

'Come, friend, Rustam-e-Zamaan, please sit here next to me.'

Once he had gone really close to the man, Rustam started. He immediately turned around and walked away. Siddhi Johar went after him and said, 'All right, now, what do you think?'

Rustam-e-Zamaan was sweating as he stood, mumbling to himself, 'How dare this person—'

'Rustam, tell me this instant, is this man Shivaji or not?'

'This man? Shivaji? Ya Allah, I have never before seen an impersonator like him!'

As soon as these words were out of Rustam-e-Zamaan's mouth, a couple of dozen swords were drawn out of their sheaths. Shiva Kashid too jumped up, swiftly grasped the shaft of a spear that was close at hand and stood in a defensive stance. Soldiers brandishing swords immediately surrounded him like a pack of wild dogs encircling a tiger.

'You bastard, you!' screamed Siddhi Johar in anger, 'What kind of a Shivaji are you? Chop this man to bits!'

When the men began closing in, Kashid planted the shaft in the ground at an angle, threw all his weight over it and leaped like an acrobat to one side. Then he ran out of the pavilion, with hundreds of Bijapuri soldiers converging on him now from all sides. Gathering all his strength and courage, Shiva Kashid did all that he could with the shaft in his hand to bring a few of the enemy down. He began shouting disjointed phrases in praise of his master: 'Victory to Shivba! My life for you! Everything at your feet, my master! I shall blow away the cannon, empty the arsenal! … I shall lift my razor to hoist the ochre flag …'

For a while, it was as if he had miraculously erected a fortress around himself. He fought valiantly, injured as many as he could, but finally he was outnumbered. With a wound on the arm, another on the leg, a third on his shoulder, and then on his back, he was slowly but surely brought down. On that full moon night Shiva Kashid was chopped to pieces in the service of his master, his dismembered body scattered all over the wet grass.

As he neared his end, he would certainly have exhaled a few breaths of joy and contentment. He had promised his king, 'Raje, for your sake, I shall put up such a performance and eat up so much of the enemy's time that by the time I'm finished, you will have covered at least half the distance to your destination.'

19

THROUGH THE CAVE OF DARKNESS

The night wind was whistling through the moisture-laden valleys. The giant trees were rustling and crackling. The huge streams to the east of the fort, cascading down in waterfalls, filled the air with their reverberations. The stream that ran between Pawangadh and Panhala fell off a stark precipice in a cataract of immense momentum.

The king's contingent had arrived at a paddy field near Turukwadi. What looked like a vast, flat-topped mountain rose in the darkness before them like an all-pervading shadow. This was the magnificent plateau of Masai. Before beginning that stiff climb, the group rested awhile in the field. A small conference ensued. At Baji Prabhu's signal, twenty-five of his men got astride the horses that had accompanied them. Some of them had bundles tied around their chests and stomachs. These riders carried a serious responsibility upon their shoulders or, rather, wrapped about their torsos.

They had to get to the narrow cart road that descended into Konkan along the Bambwade-Malkapur route. As they rode, they also were tasked with keeping a sharp eye on the surroundings. Even before the king's party reached their appointed spot on the mountains at daybreak, this cohort had been instructed to take the turn past Malkapur. By dawn they were required to reach a post called Pandharpani. The responsibility of this cohort was to ensure that the king's jewels, clothing and horses were available to him for the next leg of his journey.

Soundlessly, this small squad of riders took a trail going downwards and soon disappeared into the darkness and the rain. The remaining foot-soldiers got busy grappling with the Turukwadi rise. Moving diagonally up the face of the precipice, they made good time and soon reached the top. This place was a part of the king's territory. There, in the fork of Mahalung, was a patrol post of the Marathas where many had gathered, awaiting the king and his companions. Guna maavashi and Bandoba had sent messages in advance to the hamlets in these parts; accordingly, a fresh batch of guides had arrived there with their blankets tightly wound around them. Shambhuji Jadhav informed the king that all was going as planned.

For the next segment of the journey, they were going to walk across a few miles of plateau land—a small patch of that vast, flat or gently rolling terrain. The Maavalis who belonged to other regions had never seen such a landscape before. The earth was clothed in soaking-wet, knee-high grass, which made a squelching sound as they stepped on it. They found this wetness very soothing and moved rapidly over the level ground, finishing half the distance within three-quarters of an hour.

A small, ancient temple stood on a rise amid this deserted upland, littered with the trunks and branches of trees. It was the shrine of Ma Masai Devi, the patron goddess of the plateau who sat there through the ages, offering protection to herders and their animals as well as the birds and beasts of the wild.

When they reached the entrance to the temple, everyone sat down to give their legs a few moments' rest. Guna maavashi touched the stone brow of the idol that had turned moist with the monsoon wind. Dipping her fingers in vermilion and turmeric pastes, she applied them to the forehead of the goddess. 'Maibai,' maavashi began her supplication, 'hey mother of my calves and kids! The lord of Rajgadh, my king Shivba has come to your feet. I have reached my farthest limit. It is you, mother, who must travel with him the rest of the way. Grant victory to this king of the poor and the destitute, O mother mine.'

The greater part of their journey was over. Shivraya was nearly out of danger now. However, Baji Prabhu and Rayaji Bandal had begun to look a bit edgy for a while now. Noticing their restlessness, the king said with a smile, 'All right, Bajida, what is it that you want?'

'Raje, both Rayaji and I reached Panhala late. The two of us are full of curiosity. So why don't you give us the details?'

'Of what?'

'When we were setting out last night, you had told us that there are seven trails, known to the native boys of these parts, that traverse these mountains and jungles, coming together at cusp of the village Pandharpani.'

The king gave a delighted laugh at Baji Prabhu's question. Rayaji Bandal also chimed in, 'Yes, Maharaj, tell us about those seven mysterious paths.'

There was no reason left now for the king to conceal anything from his brave associates. In fact, they would be reaching Pandharpani in the next three or four hours, around daybreak. Pleased at the thought of finally being able to share with his companions the information he possessed on this extraordinary network of jungle trails, he asked one of the guides for a few fistfuls of rice from his bag. Laying the rice-grains out in lines, he started mapping the terrain for them in words.

'Look,' he said, 'the route that we took eastwards from Panhala crosses the Masai plateau, and then moves past Khotwadi and Ringeywadi to reach Pandharpani. The second trail goes down from the other side, traverses the Manparal gorge and comes up to meet the same point. Now look at this third trail that runs along the side of the Anuskura ghat and ascends to Pandharpani. Then there's this fourth one which moves through extremely difficult terrain via Pavadaiwadi to arrive at Pandharpani. The fifth, here, travels around the far side of Malkapur, then goes straight to the Paleshwar cataract, and from there climbs up Thanewadi, culminating at Pandharpani. This sixth one comes from behind Vishalgadh, goes past Kemburnewadi and crosses this jungle patch to reach the same place. As for the seventh and final trail, it originates from the Anuskura ghat too, takes you via Yerdon to Yelvanjugai and then up to Pandharpani. These seven trails are known only to the very best hunters and gatherers of these jungles, those who roam the wilds in search of the earth's produce. And, of course, to the tigers to whom these jungles belong. There is absolutely no possibility of anyone else getting wind of these passages.'

Hearing this remarkable explication of the mystery of the seven trails from the mouth of their king, the listeners gaped at him in awe. Guna maavashi was to part company with them here. As soon as it was light, she would set off in the direction of the herder's colony towards the east. But when the time came to say goodbye, she was overcome by anxiety for her king. 'Raja, shall I come along with you to the end?' she asked.

'No, maavashi, no, the enemy is quite strong here,' the king replied, holding her wrinkled hands in his. 'Yet, for you to possess this courage at the age of eighty is astounding. You carried the sky on your back and travelled through the night for the sake of our Hindvi swarajya. This service has been stupendous. Please turn back from here. A few of our men will accompany you home.'

'No, Raja, there's no need for that. Come, I'll come along with you a little distance further. All this land I have roamed as a young girl in my mother's house.'

'But what of your animals?'

'Oh, I've got plenty of relatives here to take care of them.'

'You have done enough and more. You sacrificed the son of your womb in the battle of Pratapgadh. How much more can you give? Listen, maavashi, you must stop here.'

Guna maavashi was left with no choice but to listen to the king. She strictly instructed the boys going further with the king, most of whom she knew at least by face, to take great care of their master. As she bid Shivraya farewell, there were tears in her eyes. Placing her gnarled hands on his temples, she said, 'Maharaj, you are truly a fearless son of my Jija maavali. Please take care of yourself and of our Swarajya.'

As soon as they resumed their journey, stormy winds broke out at the eastern end of that gigantic plateau, accompanied by frequent flashes of lightning. Soon, the descent from the plateau began. The wet, biting wind seemed to be travelling with them. Villages were left behind in quick succession. Ghumti, Khadakkhol, Ijol, Chaphewadi and many such small hamlets slipped past.

20

THE ROYAL GUEST

After wiping Shiva Kashid's blood from their blades, the Adilshahi soldiers set off immediately in pursuit of the real Shivaji. Siddhi Masood led the squad, fuming with anger and frustration. He had hand-picked three thousand and five hundred horsemen for the task—the finest of his army of thirty-five thousand, rigorously trained for crucial operations like these.

It was almost midnight now. He was utterly furious at the thought that Shivaji had managed to pierce the steel ring they had placed around the fort. And all that he could do in response was to dance in impotent rage like a juggler's bear! Not only had Shivaji given the slip to the Adilshahi forces raging around the base of the fort like a sea in high tide, but he had tricked them into wasting at least two precious hours dealing with an imposter.

Masood and his men were galloping at breakneck speed. He spurred his horse with more than his usual ferocity as he shouted, 'Gone! That Shiva has gone! The demon has disappeared, and we are left wallowing in shame.'

'We shall find him, Sarkar. Where can he go, after all?'

'If we don't find him, how shall we present ourselves to the Sultan? My father-in-law Johar miyaan has lost his marbles, so he doesn't have a future anyway. But what of our future? With this shame on our heads, forget the Adilshahi durbar, nobody will give us an inch of ground to stand on even in a graveyard!'

The strong-limbed steeds were speeding like cannonballs through the slime and the dark. They crossed the heath around the base of the fort and arrived at an Adilshahi checkpost on the eastern periphery of the siege-ring. As Masood directed his horse towards the post, he saw a strapping Maratha man emerge from the shadows leading a squad of about a dozen horsemen.

'Arey, this looks like a senior commander from Shivaji's army!'

'Yes, Khan sahib. I am exactly that: a Maratha from one of the best families, directly descended from the lineage of the Sun God.'

Even in the darkness, every pore of his being exuded treachery. The lackeys riding with Siddhi Masood, however, decided to tease him. 'And yet, you bastard, you continue to serve Shiva's army!'

'Yes, and I shall continue to do so.'

'Catch hold of the rascal and chop his head off!' came an angry cry from behind.

Raising cries of 'Enemy's man!' and 'Shiva's servant!', the soldiers encircled him. Some caught his arms from behind and held him firmly in their grip. Instead of resisting these aggressive moves, the man merely stood with an amused smile on his face. Looking at his supercilious face, Masood placed the edge of his sword under the man's chin and said, 'Rascal, with your master putting us in these dire straits, what do you mean by standing here and throwing those roguish smiles at us?'

'Because, Masood Khan, you yourselves have dug the hole in which you stand now.'

'Why do you say that?'

'Shivaji is ten times cleverer than your Birbal and craftier than all your princes. Where will you search for him? And for how long? He has vanished down such an impossible route that even the moon and the stars can have no inkling of it.'

'Can no one give us a clue?'

'Yes, of course, I can. He has taken narrow jungle tracks that your horses cannot penetrate because of the monsoon vegetation. All you will find there are thorns, moss, mud and slime.'

'How do you know all this?'

'Khan sahib, I am a hunter and chasing prey is my profession. I alone can lead you to your man.'

The point was well taken. Masood knew that the hills and gorges surrounding them were no less than a playground of demons on this dark monsoon night. Even if he were to send for a guide from the nearest village, it would mean waiting till daybreak for the man to arrive, assuming that a suitable person could be found.

The Maratha went on, 'I alone am aware of where the rivers and hills and valleys lie in this impenetrable jungle, where the tracks come from and where they can lead you.'

'All right, Tukajirao—'

'Let's not drop names here, Khan sahib. This work is of an extremely delicate and confidential nature. You may call me Mehmanji, if you wish.'

Siddhi Masood saw sense in what the man was saying. He had also noticed the peculiar viciousness with which he spat out Shivaji's name, as if he had some ancient score to settle with the man. Sensing the volcano of hate that rumbled inside him, he said, 'All right, Mehmanji, we must set off immediately.'

'Tell me what you want.'

'That's quite clear. I want that hellhound Siva, and that too, alive!'

'Let's get started, then. The bird that has flown out of your hand for now ... but where it is going to perch by daybreak only this Mehmanrao knows.'

Although Mehmanrao spoke with great self-assurance, there were many among Masood's squad who were not altogether convinced. What if he turned out to be another Kashid, planted by Sivaji to lead them away from their quarry? What if he were to eat up the precious hours of the night that remained?

That was when a loud voice rose from behind, saying, 'Go on, men, this Maratha is certainly speaking the truth. He too, like me, belongs to these jungles. And he has sworn to bring Shivaji to his destruction, as I have.'

Siddhi Masood turned around to see that the familiar voice belonged to Bajiraje Ghorpade, a handsome and distinguished-looking Maratha sardar. Ghorpade then announced that he too wanted to join the hunt, but Siddhi Masood protested, 'But Chachajaan, show some consideration for your age!'

'Don't you worry about that, boy. I have been burning with a single desire all my life, and that is to set alight the pyre of this renegade Shivaji, the son of my lifelong enemy Shahaji.'

'That's wonderful, Chachajaan,' Siddhi Masood said with a smile, 'but you have done enough by vouching for this man. We are grateful.'

'That's good, but I too want to come with you.'

'No, no, Chachajaan, it's not fair to put you through such discomfort at your age. This man will do nicely.'

Finally, an agreement was reached and Ghorpade decided to stay behind. Mehmanrao and Masood applied the spur to their animals and plunged into the dark, wet night at the head of their three thousand five hundred horses.

As those seven- or eight-hundred hardy warriors moved along the spine of the mountain, they could have been just so many ants crawling along. The dark silhouettes of massive boulders could be seen dimly outlined against a marginally lighter sky. One such rock climbed straight into the sky like a tapering pillar. Standing around it were big blocks of stone, some of which had been chiselled by sun, wind and rain into near-human shapes.

As they walked, the guides told the king, 'This place is known as Kunwarkhambi's mountain-pass. That tall pillar there is a beautiful young maiden of some ancient era who was on her way to her wedding. The rocks around it are members of the marriage procession. It was summer-time when they set off. There were musicians in the group too, the story goes. But she came under a curse and the entire wedding party is said to have vanished. They all turned to stone. The girl remained a virgin. When the wind blows through these parts, the villagers who live close by hear a melodious whistle quite distinctly. The eerie strings of that unfortunate girl's marriage procession and of her unfulfilled dreams still haunt this wilderness, it is said.'

As they were walking through the stone-strewn path bordered by thickets and and pockmarked with puddles, Baji Prabhu's mind knew no rest. His eyes scoured the landscape around him like those of an alert hawk. He would sometimes take it into his head to race ahead of the others, and at other times suddenly decide to tarry behind, to peer behind every bush and boulder or squint into the darkness to check whether there was the slightest hint of enemy movement anywhere.

They ascended two more mountains and made the descents too. The streams and brooks of these deep valleys flowed in the other direction—towards Konkan. On the way, they heard the rush and tumble of a torrent leaping over a steep edge. As it came thundering down, this fall gave the impression of horses jumping over the cliff. The precipitation of the previous four days had been so unceasing and copious that it had bequeathed unprecedented muscle and heft to these waters of the wild.

The men reached the banks of a river in the semi-darkness. But when the jungle guides and herders saw the force of the current and heard its ferocious roar, they froze where they stood. It was terrifying enough to drill holes in the stoutest heart. What was to be done now? That was when Shivraya emerged from the scrub behind them and called out, 'Move on! Why are you waiting?'

'Look at this, Raje,' Baji Prabhu shouted. 'This water is flowing with the force of five elephants, at the very least.'

Shambhuji said in a deeply worried voice, 'Shivajidada, trying to cross a surge of this might will be hazardous in the extreme.'

As Shivraya moved closer to the water, his companions gathered around him. 'But the equipment we carry for such eventualities, the ropes, the stakes, the—'

'We have all that, Raje, but look at the strength of the current!' Bandoba Gawade groaned, 'Entering the river here is nothing short of flirting with disaster.'

'Very well,' the king said, 'so, how about turning back and climbing up the slope we just came down? Perhaps, if we were to find a point upstream, the crossing may be narrower there!'

'Well, maybe. But have a look at the track going up the banks of the river. It's so slippery and strewn with broken rock that even a mountain goat would not want to take chances there. Besides, climbing that steep mountain all over again, taking a detour and traversing the plateau to look for a better crossing will consume precious hours.'

'How many?'

After a quick consultation with the guides, Shambhuji and Phulaji came back with some rough calculations. 'It's going to take a minimum of four hours; that could eat up half a day.'

'The kind of delay we simply cannot afford! In that case,' the king said with unshakeable decision, 'we have no choice but to take the plunge. Whatever must happen will happen; we have no choice except to face the danger head on.'

The young guides waded into the water with stout ropes, looping them around the few trees they met on the way. They sank and then surfaced, struggling against the savage flow. Baji Prabhu gathered his courage and stepped into the current. Then he extended his hand to Shivraya. Baji was a well-built man who was considerably taller than the king. His intention was to carry his leader on his broad shoulders, but the king turned down the offer immediately and moved into the water. Some of the younger men immediately placed themselves before and behind him to secure his crossing.

Not only was the water rushing with overwhelming force, it was bitingly cold too. The pull of the torrent drained the strength of some of the young men leading the way and they floundered. But they managed to gather all their strength into their shoulders by sheer force of will and somehow managed to reach the far shore. Baji Prabhu was leading the king by one hand, while Phulaji followed close behind. As they approached the bank, Phulaji suddenly sank. He had encountered a depression on the river bed, perhaps. While all the others scrambled onto the shore, Phulaji seemed to have disappeared. Shambhuji called out loudly, 'Phulaji, where are you?'

The jungle guides immediately jumped back into the water and began searching for the missing man. Very soon they located him close to the bank, his arms entangled in some vine which had prevented him from throwing his shoulders forward to push through the current. With great skill and courage, the boys disentangled his limbs and brought him ashore.

Once again they began plodding through the sludge and climbed up yet another steep incline. Baji Prabhu moved closer to his younger brother and said, 'Phulaji, stay a little more alert. Death seems to be waiting for you at every turn.'

'Dada, I shall consider it my good fortune to die for the sake of our king.'

'Don't blabber like a fool, Phulaji. Whatever calamities lie ahead, we shall push the god of death aside and move on. But meanwhile, boy, till the king reaches his destination, what right do you and I have to die?'

The alternating sequence of tall hills and deeper gorges refused to end. The wind came chasing the rain and the rain went tailing the wind. All the elements in that vast wilderness seemed to be playing a similar game.

They reached Ringewadi, after which they came abreast of the Patewadi rise. The mountain-pass of Paavadai made them break into a sweat in spite of the rains. Close by was a wood of densely packed trees, so dense that the rainwater was obstructed by leaves and branches, allowing the forest floor to remain relatively dry. Underneath that bower was an ancient open-air temple of Paavadai Mata.

The three-foot-tall stone statue of the goddess was sheltered by jungle vines interlocking to form a roof of sorts. As was the custom in these parts, for centuries together, devotees had applied oil-based pastes of ground turmeric and vermilion to the idol. With the elements contributing their inimitable touches to her image through wind, water and temperature variation, the goddess presented a bellicose visage to the world.

Shivraya and his company had been walking now for nine hours without rest, through heavy, incessant rain, rough trails and sharply undulating terrain. The king went down on his aching knees to place his head at the feet of the goddess, then finally rested his own feet by seating himself on a grassy mound next to the idol. After this gruelling all-night journey, the joints of the travellers were overheated like the parts of a machine and their breath came in heavy gasps.

As they lay resting, a girl in her twenties came rushing up to them and bowed before Shivraya. In the dim light of the moon, the king looked closely at the young woman and remembered that she was Lakshmi, Gunvantabai's daughter-in-law. She had taken the jungle trail a day earlier so as to make arrangements for the king's arrival. This was the village of maavashi's sister.

Lakshmi was accompanied by the womenfolk of her own village and from other hamlets close by. Braving the extreme weather and the long, arduous walk through those jungles rife with thorns and poisonous reptiles, they had brought with them bhaakari made of naachani millet, onions and red-pepper chutney for the king's men. When Baji Prabhu saw the fare, he shouted out to the men, 'Bring out the bhaakari you are carrying in your waist-pouches.'

Unanticipated delays could spring up in difficult journeys like this one; to guard against such contingencies, the king had ordered his men to carry bhaakari and jhunka, tied up in bundles around their waists. But heavy rainfall through the night, as well as their adventures in the streams, had reduced these emergency rations to pulp.

It was, therefore, a godsend that Lakshmi and her companions had brought over this fresh food. Nothing could have delighted the palates of these tired, hungry men more than the freshly cooked food that these women served to them with genuine affection. As his companions sat hungrily wolfing it all down, the king was overcome with thankfulness for Guna maavashi, and for Lakshmi and her friends. He asked the young woman solicitously, 'Girl, how did you manage to cover this long distance yesterday?'

'Maharaj, it's familiar territory for us.'

'Who else came with you?'

'Aatyabai was to travel with you, and the others had to stay behind to look after the cattle, so I came all by myself.'

'Didn't you feel frightened?'

'Frightened? Of what? During the monsoon, even the tigers don't step out of their caves for four months at a stretch. As for the bisons and boars, they roam around only in the mornings to forage among the crops. So I had nothing to fear at all. I simply flew with the wind and crossed over in no time.'

The king's heart swelled with pride. He looked at Lakshmi a little more carefully and noticed that there was no vermilion in the parting of her hair, which obviously meant that she was a widow. So, it was her husband who had sacrificed his life for the Hindvi swarajya in the battle of Pratapgadh. And here she was now, offering her own services after the husband had given his all.

Shambhuji got busy fussing over his king. He pulled a shawl out of his bundle and insisted that the king throw it around his shoulders for warmth. When the king stretched himself out, Shambhu noticed that the soles of his feet had turned white with all the water they had absorbed.

They were also covered with cracks and gashes inflicted by the difficult terrain they had crossed. Shambhu dipped into his bag, brought out some mustard oil and gave the king's feet a soothing massage.

The manner in which Lakshmibai, Shambhuji and all the others were indulging him and looking after his every little need brought tears of gratitude to the king's eyes. Noticing this, Baji Prabhu knelt on the soft grass, held his hand and said, 'Maharaj, why tears in your eyes while we are still alive?'

'Bajida, these tears are not an outpouring of grief, but an acknowledgment of the success we have achieved.'

'How do you explain this?'

The king ran his eyes over his companions who lay in various postures of rest around him in the semi-darkness. Despite the moist grass beneath them, the flame of hope burnt bright and warm in their hearts. Shivraya said to them, 'My friends, you consider me as some kind of god, but the fact is that I am no different from the flesh-and-blood human beings that you are. Only, by the grace of Ma Bhawani, I saw the sufferings of the common people, as I saw the injustice heaped upon them either by the sultans of men or by the agencies of nature. As I witnessed and suffered these calamities by their side, I was accosted by a goddess named Humanity. She taught me the obligations of a king. It is the awareness of this duty that holds me by my finger and puts me to work. The love I receive from these simple folk, the affection you shower upon me, the endurance of the mountains, the limitlessness of the ocean, the velocity of the wind, the stars in the sky—from all these I have derived a vision of the future. My true strength, my true wealth, lies in the love of all of you for me and for Hindvi swarajya. How will I ever free myself of the debt I owe these simple people, Bajida?'

The king mopped his eyes. He called over one of the men entrusted with carrying the treasury. Dipping his hand into a bag, Shivraya pulled out a fistful of gold coins. Much though they hesitated and demurred, the king compelled his associates to accept a gold coin each as a token of his appreciation for their service. He gave Lakshmi two fistfuls of jewellery and conveyed his respectful regards for Guna maavashi.

'Jai Paavadai Mata!' somebody called out in a low voice, which became a signal for the resting men to get back on their feet and ready themselves for moving on. The dawn wind had just picked up. The king spoke about the remaining leg of the journey to Baji Prabhu, loud enough for all to hear, 'Bajida, we have nearly two hours of travel left before we reach the village called Pandharpani.'

'Let's get started immediately.'

'We shall tarry there to form an estimate of the winds and of the enemy's movements, after which we shall leave for Vishalgadh.'

'The king, therefore, plans for us to have our breakfast at the Vishalgadh fort,' Phulaji said, drawing a laugh from the rest.

The small flag atop the stone temple of Paavadai Mata had just caught the first wisp of the morning wind and begun to flutter. The downy trace of hair on eighteen-year-old Phulaji Prabhu's upper lip shone with the first glimmer of morning light.

It was a tiny little hamlet of about three dozen houses nestled in a dense green jungle of the Sahyadris. Since it was exposed to the fury of four months of intense rainfall, the roofs were woven of long grasses and had a sharp slope to them, ensuring that even a handful of water poured on top came racing down in no time. Some sixteen or seventeen horsemen had arrived there at the crack of dawn after having travelled through the night. These were the horsemen who had parted company with the king the previous evening at the stream near Panhalgadh.

In the open meadow next to the stream, the water flowing over rough stones produced a constant rustle, not very different from the sound of distant hooves of horses galloping at full speed. The riders climbed down from their horses and stretched their limbs to release the stiffness that had settled in their joints. They cast casual glances over a landscape that was completely covered by thorny scrub and bushes. They could see small patches of farmland close to the village called Pandharpani.

In every direction they turned, they saw tall, forbidding mountains. The tired little trail that came from Konkan after crossing the Anuskura ghat passed through this village and picked up speed from here on its way to Malkapur. Eight miles to the west, well concealed in that green wilderness, stood the fort of Vishalgadh.

One of the horsemen pulled out a silken bundle that contained the king's clothing. All of them had their eyes fixed on the eastern horizon. It was only a little while ago that the sustained drizzle had decided to take some rest. The dark clouds above had split here and there to reveal a dark blue morning sky. The trees in the jungle were scattering the raindrops that remained on them like birds giving themselves a vigorous shake to get rid of the moisture in their feathers.

The men took their horses to the stream where, after slaking their thirst, the animals began to graze on the grass that grew on the banks. When the men raised their expectant eyes to the east again, they saw their companions of the previous evening emerge from the jungle and move towards them across the heath. The horsemen exchanged happy smiles and said, 'We arrived here in good time.'

The king walked up, looking tired and grimy after his night-long odyssey through the jungles. He walked straight into the stream and gave himself a vigorous scrub. Then he went behind a tree and changed out of his soiled clothes into the fresh set that befitted his stature. Having put on his elegant silk tunic and his gold waistband, he finally placed the royal mandeel back on his head and looked down at his reflection in the water. Hearing the screech of a jungle bird, he looked up with a start. From there his eyes travelled downstream. What he saw at a distance made his eyes widen and his jaw drop in amazement. Noticing the expression on the king's face, Baji Prabhu came up and asked, 'Is something the matter, Raje?'

For a moment or two the king stood like a pillar of stone. Then he drew Baji's attention to the top of a rather stunted-looking hillock far away. There, on the distant horizon, they could see horsemen materialising as though out of thin air.

'Arey deva! It looks like the enemy. So early in the morning! How did they manage to get here?'

All along their perilous path, Shivraya's companions had been moving in the conviction that nobody could possibly get wind of their movements. Indeed, the king himself had assured them of it in no uncertain terms. Now they could see with their own eyes that their complacency had been misplaced.

'Bajida,' the king finally found words, 'how could the impossible have happened? How could the enemy's horses have taken a roundabout route, and yet reached this exact spot at the same time?'

'Betrayal?'

'Yes, of course. One among us has betrayed the rest.'

'Well, so be it, then. This is the occasion for us Maavalis to show the world the place our king occupies in our hearts. Have no fear, Raje. However, your security is all-important. Please move on, while the rest of us stay behind to grapple with the enemy.' Baji's blood had begun to race and his temples had turned hot.

Three among the horsemen of the previous night had slowed down to detect enemy movements to the rear, if any. Now they came galloping down the Malkapur route via the Paral pass. Despite the nip in the morning air, they were bathed in perspiration. Jumping down, they quickly presented themselves before the king. 'Raje,' they panted, 'there's been treason. The enemy is almost here. Right at our tail.'

'How many horses?'

'Close to four thousand.'

'Any indication of who they could be?'

'Johar's son-in-law is leading them. There are five or six other sardars with him.'

'And one of our own?'

'Of course! Wearing hoods of sackcloth over their heads to conceal their sinful faces, there are two or three Marathas riding with them, showing Masood Khan the way.'

The king was overcome with emotion. He did not fear death, but the thought of his dream of the Swarajya ending here, destroyed by treason, was unendurable. It was on this dream that he and his brave men had staked their lives during the night's crossing. There was no time now for careful evaluation. For Swarajya to endure, it was now critically important for the king to survive.

On the other side of the stream was the mouth of the Ghodkhind mountain pass, a narrow tunnel of a passage that stretched for almost a mile. Shivaji and fifteen of his chosen men leapt on their horses. He had split his forces in two. Most of them would stay behind and prevent the enemy troops from advancing through the pass. The rest would move with the king and protect him during the one hour it would take to reach Vishalgadh fort.

'Shambhuji, you come along with me,' Shivraya said.

Shambhuji, however, dug his heels in. He saw the three-hundred-odd Maavali men taking their positions at the mouth of the pass; he then turned his eyes towards the valley behind them, into which the enemy horde was already pouring in their thousands. To give his king a fighting chance to reach the security of the fort, the enemy would need to be blocked right there at the narrow pass. Jijausahib had said to him countless times: 'Shambhu, my boy, I do not worry much about my Shivba because you are there with him. Always be ready to protect this protector of millions!'

Remembering both his promises and his hopes, Shambhuji replied in a firm voice, 'Shivajidada, I belong to the house of the Jadhavs of Sindkhed. Whenever calamity threatens to descend on the Swarajya, our blood races to jump into the fray. You proceed towards safety, Raje; I propose to stay here at the mouth of the pass.' Shivraya saw that Shambhuji could not be shaken.

'What about you, Bajida? Are you coming with us?'

'Maharaj, you are known for your wisdom. How can you indulge in such frivolous talk? I have the reputation among my fellow Maavalis of carrying an elephant calf on my back like a sack of jowar. Why would I choose to accompany you when I can stay here and make a heap of the enemy's heads at the mouth of this pass?'

'Now, please don't even ask me to come, Raje,' Rayaji Bandal added. 'I too propose to stay behind with my three hundred Bandal men to offer our blood as an oblation to the gods of this pass. Please make haste and move on!'

'Raje,' Baji, Phulaji and Shambhuji chorused, 'please don't tarry here. Get away, go instantly!'

Shivraya's face turned dark as a rain cloud at this moment of departure. 'Aho, Bajida,' he groaned, 'the enemy is a bit excessive in number!'

'That needn't be your worry or mine,' Baji Prabhu responded. 'The weapons we carry will take care of all that. Besides, these men who surround me here are all offspring of the Maavali soil, and each one of us can outweigh ten or fifteen of the enemy soldiers. You must depart immediately.'

The enemy troops had now begun to scream and shout as they came rolling down the slope. They could, perhaps, now see the king's men standing at the mouth of that treacherous pass. Hence the excited battle cry of 'Deen deen!' The minutes were slipping by. The king could not rid himself of the weight on his chest as he bid Baji Prabhu goodbye. He patted his horse and called out, 'I go now, Bajidada. Give them a tough fight. As soon as we reach the fort, we shall give the wick to the cannon. Keep fighting till you hear the cannon boom five times. Block the enemy. Keep them in the pass.'

'Raje, please leave!! The lips of this Baji of yours have been quivering to plant a kiss on the mouth of death for the sake of Swarajya.'

'Baajee!'

'Maharaj, please don't worry about me! Aho, it doesn't matter even if my children are exposed to the vagaries of fate by my passing away. Your living on will end the misery of a hundred generations of Marathas from here on. Why should my death count?'

The king's horse shot forward, then halted mid-stride and spun around, as if it too wanted to take one last look at the hero. Baji Prabhu ran forward and took the horse's muzzle in his arms. As he held it lovingly against his chest, the king bent down and hugged Baji. Then the three hundred and fifty braves escorting the king began moving rapidly into the bushes ahead.

Baji turned to face the enemy. Fishing out a small receptacle from his waist-pouch, he took a pinch of tobacco. As he ground it with his thumb against the palm of the other hand, he added to it a few leaves of the ghuee plant that he had noticed growing on a flat stone. He tucked into his left cheek the potent mix of tobacco and ghuee that was known to heighten excitement and pulled his sword out of its sheath.

A strange intoxication seeped into Baji's consciousness. He was ready and eager to meet the enemy.

Siddhi Johar sat in an agitated state in the gloom of his pavilion. The rains had stopped, but the wind was still chilly. His colleagues too were caught in a similar state of anxious inactivity. Till yesterday that Sivaji had been sending conciliatory notes, letting them slip into a state of careless jubilation. The shock that his sudden disappearance had caused continued to throb in their nerves.

A company of about two hundred horsemen rode in from the darkness. Slightly overweight but still handsome, wearing a smartly cut beard, Bajiraje Ghorpade dismounted from his horse. Seeing him arrive, Siddhi Johar rose from his seat and said in a mournful voice, 'Come, Bajiraje. Our boat has well and truly sunk. How will we show our face to the Sultan now?'

'Arey, Khan sahib, this is what I have been drumming into the ears of everybody in Bijapur and elsewhere: this Shivaji, the renegade son of Shahaji, is a very shrewd bluffer.'

'With Siva gone, everything is lost. The water has risen above our heads.'

'But Khan miyaan, this isn't the kind of earthquake that you think it is. Fortunately, your Allah has given you a very capable son-in-law. He has gone down the right track chasing Shiva. There is every chance that he may be able to capture him.'

'What are you saying? Let's hope for Allah's blessing then, and for luck to favour this Johar,' Siddhi said with a quiver of hope in his voice. Then he asked point-blank, 'But why didn't you go along with them? Were you worried about saving your own skin?'

'Khan sahib, I must ask you to take your words back. If there is an opportunity for plucking this Shivaji and his lineage out root and branch, this Ghorpade will not be found wanting in enthusiasm! What do you take me for?'

'But then, why didn't you go with Masood?'

'I have provided Masood with the best possible guides. They will take him to the exact spot in good time. After all, we Mudholkars spend a couple of months every year in your "Adilshahi Manzil", hunting in the environs of Panhalgadh. Nobody knows the trails, passes and jungles of this region better than we do.'

'That's why, if you had gone along—'

'What could I do? Your son-in-law was drunk with the desire of garnering the entire credit for chasing down and capturing Shivaji; he, therefore, left me behind and sped off—'

'But Ghorpade dada is he going to succeed?'

'He may fail too.'

'Fail? Ya Allah! How can that be?'

'It is that fear which has brought me here in the middle of the night.'

'Tell me what I can do.'

'Masood has barely three thousand and five hundred horsemen with him. I doubt whether this number will be enough to bring Shivaji down.'

'How many, then?'

'You will need at least that many more to help Masood succeed. This boy of Shahaji's is valiant, of course, but more importantly, he has a head that's sharper than any sword ever made. With that alone, he can blow your men away. I recommend that you send reinforcements for Masood. I shall provide you with guides to help them reach the spot.'

Siddhi Johar was thrilled at this prospect of sending another regiment to hunt Shivaji down. Noticing Faazal Khan standing close by, he growled, 'What are you waiting for, boy? It was your father's entrails that the man had torn out, not mine. You should be burning with the desire for revenge, not I.'

21

WHITE WATER, RED PASS

The sun had begun to climb. The three thousand five hundred horsemen under the leadership of Siddhi Masood came racing down towards the open space in front of the pass. Fully intending to chase the enemy down, they tore across the stream and were soon at the mouth of the pass.

But now they stood gaping at the mountain walls rising high on both sides of a very narrow opening. The pass was barely wide enough to allow the passage of three horses shoulder to shoulder, four at a crawl, perhaps. This natural tunnel stretched for almost a mile between the mountains.

Baji and Phulaji Prabhu, Rayaji Bandal, Shambhuji Jadhav and the other gallants stood guarding the mouth of the pass with their weapons unsheathed. They saw Siddhi Masood prancing at the head of his army, all hot and excited at the thought that he had succeeded in trapping Shivaji's forces in the jungle. Thrilled at this achievement, neither he nor his men had second thoughts about launching a frontal assault. The Maavali men, however, were ready and waiting to receive this onslaught.

They responded with extreme violence to the Adilshahi men who had, literally, leapt before looking at what was in front of them. Masood quickly realised the folly of his precipitate action and withdrew his men. He now began to work out strategies for better results against Baji's men. The Marathas knew they had to keep the enemy at bay until such time as they heard the boom of the cannon at Vishalgadh. Defence, therefore, was to be their chief mode of operation.

The men carefully assessed the opportunities that the pass offered and began to settle into secure nooks from which they could counter the enemy offensive. Rayaji Bandal said, 'Amazing, isn't it, Bajidada? The enemy must have started quite late last night and yet managed to travel all this distance! That too, with thousands of horses!'

'That's right, Raya; they are nearly four thousand and we are barely three hundred and fifty. Which means that each one of us will have to account for ten enemy men to have any chance of surviving this unequal battle.'

'Yes, dada,' the young hot-bloods Phulaji and Shambhuji responded. 'At all costs, we must beat the living daylights out of these sons of Adilshah and make the survivors flee homewards.'

Both sides had journeyed all night through dense jungles; both sides were keen to drag victory to their side in this encounter. From the banks of the stream came the roars of the Adilshahi battle cry, 'Deen deen!' and 'Slaughter Siva's men!' Back came the spirited response of the Maratha men, 'Har har Mahadev!', 'Jai Bhawani!' and 'Jai Shivaji!'

Weapons began to clash and clang again. With each stroke, the soldiers were testing the worth of their opponents. Siddhi Masood had rightly estimated that the Marathas were outnumbered, and he fought with the intention of annihilating them. But Baji Prabhu was counting on the extreme narrowness of the pass, the dense vegetation all around him and the advantage that nature had just granted them by sending the rains in again. Using these natural defences, they were able to respond with force and venom to every fresh surge of the Adilshahi assault.

Compared to Baji Prabhu and Rayaji Bandal, Phulaji and Shambhuji were callow youngsters, higher on excitement than on wisdom. In the thick of battle, Shambhuji declared to Baji, 'Dada, you see to the rear. Phulaji and I shall take seventy or eighty of our Bandal men and leap upon the enemy like lions. In another age, Shareefji Bhosale had thus barged into the ranks of the Mughal army in the battle of Bhatwadi. We want to repeat that miracle here!'

'No, most certainly not!' retorted Baji Prabhu. 'That will not work at all.' Then, noticing the scornful smile playing upon the young men's faces, he said, 'Don't you snort, boy. Please keep in mind that not one of us here in this pass hopes to return alive. We stand at the cusp of death and soon our blood will become one with the earth here, all for the sake of Swarajya and Shivba. But before the king reaches safety of the fort, how can we afford to perish in the opening bout of the conflict?'

'So, what do you suggest we do, dada?'

'Every one of our brave men must be used with great discretion and frugality.'

After a while, the enemy launched another foray at the mouth of the pass. While the Maratha men resisted the onslaught and slaughtered many, they were pushed back into the narrow passage by a few steps. Seeing the entrance to the pass look less populated than before, another wave of Adilshahi soldiers pushed themselves forward. They had enough men and more to spare. The Marathas rushed into the bushes bordering the path and found there both concealment and security. Using tree trunks as shields, they began shooting arrows at the advancing enemy. The advantage had shifted to the Marathas again.

The Adilshahi men were getting flustered at not being able to advance as they had hoped. Animated cries of 'Har har Mahadev' were only adding salt to their wounds. Every time they saw a large crowd of Marathas at the mouth, they would come rushing in, but before they had fully closed in, the place would suddenly empty out, confusing them thoroughly. Then, inexplicably, they would find the enemy attacking them from all sides—from the tops of trees and from behind the trunks—and exacting a heavy toll. Rayaji, Shambhuji, Baji, and Phulaji were all on fire. Their swords smoked as they fought. A distraught Siddhi Masood wondered what it was that had given his enemy such skill and daring.

The pass itself was a miracle of nature; it was a thin passage, twenty-five hands high and barely six hands in width, gouged out of the earth. In appearance, it was not unlike a jungle trail. Starting from the village of Pandharpani, it took some turns during its journey of a few miles and ended at the source of the Kasari river. The water that flowed through the passage, the huge stones that had rolled down on either side of the trail, the exposed roots of massive trees that sprawled over the floor of the pass—together, all these factors made Ghodkhind a virtual deathtrap.

As part of their defensive strategy, the Marathas would allow the enemy to enter and advance some distance into the pass, then release a barrage of stones upon them with their slingshots. The fist-sized stones were catapulted with such velocity and accuracy that most of them found their mark on the foreheads of the Adilshahi soldiers, leaving them seriously injured. No battle of earlier times had put mere slings and stones to such effective use as this one.

Adilshahi and Mughal generals had often ridiculed the Maratha forces as an army of monkeys; on this day, however, using the Ghodkhind pass to their tactical advantage, the Marathas really made the enemy suffer from their monkey tricks. Any time a Bijapuri soldier walked into his range, a Maratha man would pounce upon him from a branch above, or come sliding down a groove and make short work of him.

Baji Prabhu was by far the most feisty among the warriors when the battle began. He wielded his gauntlet-sword with such dexterity and speed that anyone who came too close suffered grievously. In the sheer violence of close combat, his turban was soon drenched in blood which began to drip into his thick side-whiskers. Uncaring of sweat, blood, wounds and his own life, he swung the sword for which he was famed and dealt death with a generous hand. The ground around the raging Baji Prabhu was soon littered with the heads of Bijapuri men. Seeing his valour, the simmering warrior in Masood had come to a boil too and he was trying to get close to the veteran to engage him in direct combat.

There is a game that people of the jungle play with sticks, which gets truly exciting only when the ground is slushy. The players slide, even fall, and then swiftly recover their balance to outwit their rivals. This was the kind of game that the Adilshahi and Maratha armies were playing in the sludge of the Ghodkhind pass that day.

In another section of the pass, young Phulaji and Shambhuji were exulting in their swordsmanship. They had slaughtered a number of enemy soldiers, but there always seemed to be more, striving to push them further back into the tunnel. As a result, their clothes were slashed in many places; often, the enemy blades had come closer still and left cuts on their flesh. Eventually, they took shelter under an old tree to recover their breaths. Their spirits were still high, but after so many hours of fasting, their stomachs rumbled for nourishment.

Shambhuji said, 'What do you say, Phula? Do we continue to squeeze our limbs, as your dada has advised?'

'Why are you stuck on that? That was his age and temperament talking! He said what he had to say; that doesn't mean we shouldn't do what our youth and strength are prompting us to do!'

'Well said, Phula! I think we should abandon all thoughts of survival now. Let your corpse and mine fall in this pass. Dada can have the privilege of carrying our salutations to the king at Vishalgadh.'

Before the conflict in the pass had begun, Siddhi Masood had made his calculations. As Shivaji didn't have a large force in the Panhala fort to begin with, Masood was reasonably sure that the king could not have had more than four- or five hundred men with him when he made his escape. With the vastly superior force that he had brought with him, Masood had imagined it would take him less than an hour to slaughter them at the stream.

What had transpired now was quite contrary to his expectations. Time was slipping away and the Marathas were refusing to slacken. They were certainly not going to run for their lives; that much was evident. After observing their skilful guerilla tactics for a while, he told himself, 'These satanic margatthyas are playing a game of life and death now. They can be overwhelmed only by the sheer force of numbers.'

Siddhi Masood then modified his strategy. He divided his men into groups of three hundred which made several consecutive assaults on the Marathas. The enemy began advancing in waves, and to counter this the Marathas intensified their tricks, disappearing and reappearing like murderous wraiths. As time went by, Masood's tunic was soaked in blood and his frustration mounted. These Maavali monkeys were neither dying nor withdrawing from the battle!

Four hours had gone by since the weapons had begun tasting blood. The men on both sides had been drained out by the previous night's nightmarish journey and suffered the pangs of starvation. The Marathas had consumed all the food that they had carried in the bundles at their waists. The Bijapuris had not taken their kitchen unit with them. Hunger was gnawing at their insides. No food and no water meant that, as the battle progressed, their bouts of energy were increasingly short-lived. They took more frequent breaks and rested wherever they could find secure cover.

Wherever one turned to look, one saw the dead and the dying strewn on the floor of the pass. By then, news of the bloody battle at the mouth of Ghodkhind had spread, sending shivers up the spines of the peasants and herders who lived in the nearby villages and jungle hamlets. A few of their number had seen Shivraya's horses travel towards Gajapur early in the morning.

A villager from Gajapur named Mahadu had brought his goats to graze in these parts. From the safety of a treetop, he watched the fray and heard the dreadful war cries of 'Kill! Kill!' and 'Har har Mahadev'. It seemed to him that the native red soil of Konkan was deepened a shade or two by this great smattering of blood.

Goatherd Mahadu moved furtively from one bush to another till he reached a ledge overlooking the trench where the battle was raging. Peeping down, he saw a strongly built Maratha sardar in his sixties who was brandishing a gauntlet-sword, his tunic red as that of a butcher.

Frustrated at not being able to make any headway, the Adilshahi men were losing heart and had begun to retreat. Frantic with hunger, they would take turns to move to the rear of the company and dip into bags of horse-feed, trying to chew on it as they stood.

Bone-tired from the incessant fighting, Baji had paused for a while. The hole that hunger had gouged inside his stomach had begun to whir and hum. He bent like a goat at a stream nearby and drank straight from it. That was when Mahadu, who had been hiding behind a bush directly above Baji, jumped down. He undid the bundle tied to his waist and brought out some naachani bhaakari along with red-pepper paste, which he placed in the warrior's hand. The old man tried to hand it back to Mahadu, saying, 'Don't do this, boy; you'll have to go hungry.'

'Don't worry about me. You've been fighting all through the day for our Shivajiraja. For the sake of Khandobaraya, dada, eat.'

Baji Prabhu immediately took two or three massive bites of the bhaakari and swallowed it like a hungry wolf. Suddenly he remembered the youngsters Phulaji and Shambhuji, and tucked the rest of the bhaakari in an unsoiled fold of his dress. But when he looked up, he was amazed at the miracle that was unfolding around him.

Dozens of men and women from the neighbouring villages had materialised from the bushes and begun distributing a bizarre meal among the starved Maratha soldiers. They had obviously gathered whatever was immediately available in their kitchens—a motley mixture of bhaakari, vegetables, grams, curd and milk—and rushed to the edge of the battlefield to serve it to the fighting men. Every soldier got at least a bite or two of nourishment. They washed it down with water and were ready for battle again.

Suddenly they heard yells of 'Deen deen' coming from the entrance of the pass and lifted their swords again. The skirmish resumed. The sound of the enemy's battle cries, however, had turned distinctly louder. Rayaji Bandal gathered some intelligence and returned with a worried face. 'Bajida,' he said, 'it looks like bad news.'

'Why? What has happened?'

'A fresh lot of soldiers has come to the aid of Masood's forces. That Afzulya's boy, Faazal Khan, seems to have arrived with a company of three or four thousand men.'

'So?'

'They have begun to replace their tired soldiers with these fresh arrivals, all eager to do battle.'

'Arey, Rayaji, who's afraid of reinforcements anymore? We'll just fight twice as hard as before. Once I hear the booms of the cannon at Vishalgadh, I don't care even if the bull of Yama, the god of death, comes over to trample me.'

It was late afternoon. Bajiraje Ghorpade had played his hand well. He had suggested the route and supplied the jungle guides that Siddhi Johar had used to dispatch a fresh regiment of four thousand men. The battle was now completely lopsided. The highly charged enemy was advancing aggressively. The evening wind had just begun to blow. The jungle surrounding the battlefield was dense, which meant that the shadows had begun to fall well before dusk. While the Maavalis continued to fight bravely, they had begun to fall one after the other.

When Rayaji brought news of the reinforcement for the enemy, Shambhuji and Phulaji were so incensed that they instantly dashed towards the mouth of the pass. The increase in the volume and intensity of war cries emanating from the entrance suggested that mayhem had descended there. Baji Prabhu had also begun moving in that direction as he fought.

As Baji approached the mouth of the pass, he saw the corpses of sixty or seventy Maratha men scattered around. In the vicinity was the body of a heavily-built Khan who had collapsed into a squatting position. His tunic was ripped apart and the intestines had spilled out. A sword had entered the man's stomach, pierced a thick mass of flesh and penetrated deep into the ribcage. It was a particularly hideous sight.

Baji's eyes then fell on the gold-plated, fish-shaped hilt of the sword and his heart gave a massive thump. Just the previous month, Shivraya had gifted two such beautiful swords from his personal armoury—one to Phulaji and the other to Shambhuji. Although he was shaken, he knew he could not afford to tarry there, but he was sure that the sword stuck in the innards of that Khan belonged to one of the two valiant boys.

When they noticed Baji Prabhu, a bunch of enemy soldiers came racing towards him. As he readied himself to confront them, his foot touched the body of a man writhing in the final throes of death. He looked down to see Shambhuji Jadhav—the king's intimate friend and brother to his queen Kashibai. As Baji bent down towards him, Shambhu made one last desperate effort and lifted his flailing arm to point towards the right.

There, on a flat, wet rock in the stream, another man lay twitching in terminal agony. His body was pitted with wounds; his chest and his arms were punctured by spearheads. The blood bubbling out of his injuries was turning the water under him red. Phulaji's body was thrashing about like a fish thrown out of water; but in that state of semi-consciousness, he was looking at the blue sky like an innocent boy.

When Baji saw his boy writhing in insupportable pain, he rushed towards him, but just then he was surrounded by a horde of Adilshahi soldiers crying 'Deen deen' and 'Allah-o-akbar'. The battleground was taken over by such a fever that there was no time for ascertaining who was alive and who dead. Baji was left with no alternative but to abandon all tenderness and compassion, and dash forward with his sword swinging.

As the enemy converged upon him, a fellow soldier quickly handed Baji his favourite weapon: a gauntlet-sword. Raising the sword in his formidable hand, Baji began swinging it with such wild ferocity that his opponents fell like sugarcane stalks sliced by a hundred scythes. It was enough to make the very battlefield break into a sweat, and heads began rolling at his feet.

The battle in the tunnel of the Ghodkhind pass had been going on incessantly for upwards of five hours. The air was rent by the screams of mortally wounded soldiers and the agitated neighing of horses. The time was close to nightfall. Baji Prabhu's entire body had turned red—his back, his chest, his face, even the tuft of hair on his head. His barabandi tunic was soaked and dripping. His dhotar was so caked in blood that it stuck to his skin. The blade of his gauntlet-sword had broken. He brought the shield on his back against his chest, but soon, that too was smashed by the spears of the enemy.

He was not worried about dying, but the ears of this doughty champion had been scouring the air for some distant sound. The wait refused to end. He was surrounded by three hundred of Adilshah's soldiers. But the flame of anxiety that consumed his entire being like a dry sheaf of millet stalks had nothing to do with his own predicament. With a sharp Khurasani sword and his turban cloth wrapped around his shield-arm, the hero fought on like a character in the Puranas.

Just then, a loud boom reverberated over the pass from somewhere far away. Insane with joy, Baji Prabhu wiped the blood off his face and cocked his ears. And sure enough, four other booms followed. In a state of complete elation, he cried out, 'Raje! Raje!!!' At that moment, Masood's grenade came whizzing through the darkening air and knocked the dauntless warrior's head off. His body collapsed in the pass like an ancient tree and became hallowed forever.

22

A GUN SALUTE AND HEARTBREAK

Around eleven o'clock in the forenoon, the king crossed Gajapur, with Siddhi Hilaal riding alongside him. Through the downpour they could see the distant battlements of Vishalgadh. Judging by the movement of the rain clouds, the wind was moving in that direction too. The main bastion of the Vishalgadh fort and the steep drop to its left, known as the Varaatkada, would disappear suddenly behind floating bales of black-and-red clouds. Again, when the wind parted the clouds, the outline of the fort would re-emerge against the backdrop of the lurid sky.

As they approached the fort, the Maavali men let out loud war cries of 'Har har Mahadev' and 'Shivaji Maharaj ki jai.' When they took a sharp turn after crossing a hillock, they heard cries of 'Deen-deen' and 'Stop those men!' from the path ahead of them. The company that stood there to block their passage presented a confusing mix of faces. While some of them looked like Adilshahi soldiers, most of the others seemed to have been recruited from the Konkan region.

The king pulled the reins of his horse to bring it to a halt next to some villagers and a few officials who had come down from the fort. Shivraya asked them in a stern voice, 'Who are those men in front?'

'It's Raje Jasvantrao Dalvi Palankar of Konkan and Suryarao Surve of Shringarpur who stand in your path, Maharaj. Our—'

On hearing the names of the two Marathas, the king gave a scornful smile and said, 'Is this an army? It looks more like a ragtag crowd of scarecrows brought out on hire. How long could it take for us to drive them out of the way?'

'Let's move forward,' came a call from behind. 'Har har Mahadev!'

The three hundred soldiers of the king's company descended upon the men blocking their way. Behind the enemy, the land was sloping downwards. It had rained incessantly for the past two months, converting the red earth into mud and slime. When Shivraya's men mounted their assault, the enemy's horses could not find any purchase for their hooves as they moved backwards. Consequently, the riders lost balance and began toppling one by one.

Both Surve and Dalvi were wealthy, hedonistic landlords, accustomed to lives of luxury. In sharp contrast, Shivraya's men and animals were lean and tough, having just traversed fifty hills and valleys. They were quite used to untoward circumstances and uncertain landscapes. Quite like their masters, Surve and Dalvi's horses were idle, luxury-loving creatures that had spent their entire lives chewing the finest variety of oats in the comfort of their stables. They stood no chance at all against Shivraya's hardier steeds.

Just then, a series of explosions were heard from the base of the fort. Surve and Dalvi had known that they would not be able to prevent the king and his men from advancing towards the fort. Hence, they had a contingency plan in place.

The base of the Vishalgadh fort and the flat top of the mountain in front were separated by a narrow ravine which was about a thousand feet deep and five or six armspans wide. A bridge of wood and bamboo had been built over it for men and animals to cross this natural trench to the fort. Despite the rain, Shivajiraje could see smoke and flames rising out of the ravine. The landlords' devious plan was this: if Shivajiraje could not be stopped in his tracks, he should at the very least be denied straight passage up to his fort. Accordingly, various obstructions had been created. Even the wooden bridge had been blown up with dynamite.

The king saw his enervated, cowardly enemies make good their escape through the green woods nearby. However, his rapid movement towards the security of the fort had been stalled. It would be impossible to repair the bridge within the time they had at their disposal, particularly with the rain still pouring down. The only option available to them was to descend into that dangerous trench and come up on the other side.

The trench was steep; it would almost be like climbing down into a well. The horsemen dismounted and manoeuvred their animals as best they could over the moss-covered stones that paved the steep downward slope. If the descent tested their patience and skill, so did the ascent on the other side. Though they managed to cross over without serious injury or setbacks, they lost a precious couple of hours.

Once they had entered the walls of Vishalgadh, the fort-keeper Sabnis and other officials rushed up to welcome the king. Although the king had the satisfaction of finally planting his feet inside the fort, his mind was still hovering over the pass where his men were in perilous conflict with the enemy. He was keenly aware that even as they were risking their lives to keep the Adilshahi forces at bay, their ears were waiting anxiously for the promised boom that would signal to them the safe arrival of their king. How could they be faring, his valiant men? Baji, Phulaji, Rayaji, Shambhu … how many of them would make it back?

Shivraya instantly issued the order for five cannons to be fired. Within minutes the wicks were lit one after the other, and their boom reverberated through the mountains, echoing back to hit the eardrums of the men in the fort.

The king's stay was arranged in the fort-keeper's waada. Siddhi Hilaal and the other generals pleaded with the king to take a bath, and then a proper meal. After seventeen unbroken hours of walking through the forests of the Sahyadris, and another three of hard riding from the mouth of the Ghodkhind pass, every bone and joint in the king's body was groaning from unfair use. A vigorous bath was certainly in order, after which he would bow at the feet of the gods for having brought him this far.

He used up three large pots of hot water to bring relief to his aching limbs, then wrapped himself in a sheet of cloth and visited the shrine which had been temporarily set up with the idols of a few of the king's regular deities. Supper was served immediately after that. Whenever he was in the Konkan belt, Shivraya would partake of the distinct cuisine of that region. Accordingly, the table had been loaded with bhaakari of naachani millet, a paste of red chillies, and roasted gram flour mixed with curd and powdered groundnuts. But the king was so preoccupied with the events being enacted in the Ghodkhind pass at that very moment that he lingered at the shrine, hardly noticing that the meal had been served.

For a long time he stayed with his brow touching the floor in front of the deities. He finally raised himself and turned around. Siddhi Hilaal had just returned from praying at the shrine of the holy man Malik Ultazar that was behind the waada. Knowing the respect in which he was held, the other officials pushed him forward to plead with the king. Hilaal stepped forward, plate in hand, and said, 'Rajaji, whoever the person may be, Rustom or Iskandar or your Rama or Kishan Bhagwan, even when a god incarnates himself in the shape of a human being, he has to eat—'

'Siddhi sahib, you cannot imagine the state I am in. My body might be here but my breath is there. With my valiant warriors Phulaji, Baji, Shambhuji and Rayaji, who have still not returned.'

'But lord—'

'Do you not know how a person's heart rises up and chokes the throat when his dearest ones are caught in the turbulence of the battlefield?'

'My boy Wah Wah was just twenty-eight years old. I could only stand and watch when the enemy dragged my boy away. We have walked across these mountains and valleys of distress, Rajaji, to help you succeed in your mission—'

When Siddhi Hilaal extended the bowl of milk in his hand, the king found it impossible to refuse the offering at the hands of a martyr's father. He shut his eyes tight and downed a mouthful. That was all the nectar that went in. The next moment, he heard a movement behind him and turned around.

Four of Bandal's boys stood there in the company of two spies, motionless like blocks of ice. Their clothes were painted a dirty reddish brown by water, slime and the ruddy earth of the region. Six pairs of moist red eyes were staring numbly at the king. Perceiving their tearful, petrified state, the king knew they were bearers of bad news. He leapt forward, took Suryaji Bandal in his arms and asked frantically, 'Tell me, boy, who all fell?'

'Shambhudada Jadhavrao and Phulaji in the late afternoon … and just when the boom of the cannons sounded, around dusk, Bajida's head fell as an offering at the feet of Swarajya. It was a bloodbath, Raje. Over a hundred of the Bandal men were ground to death.'

The king sat motionless for a long while in his seat. Nobody had the courage to approach him. When he enquired about the corpses of his martyrs, Suryaji's response brought some relief, albeit of a bitter sort:

Rayaji Bandal was alive, and the men of all the villages within a radius of ten miles had come forward to gather the bodies of the slain soldiers. Rayaji would arrive with them at the fort in due course.

The wheel of the kingdom has to turn on. It has no regard for who lives and who dies. The king began to put his affairs in order. The soldiers of Siddhi Masood and of Faazal Khan who had followed him with reinforcements had been deeply scarred by the dark, frightful shadows that had descended upon them from the trees and leapt at them from behind boulders. Despite having won the battle, they did not return with the thrill of victory. On the contrary, the Bijapuri army could not wait to make good their escape from the dark, desolate jungles of the Sahyadris. They turned back and rapidly came down the Malkapur mountain-pass, camping awhile on the bank of the river Kasari.

Shivraya, however, was alert and full of vigour. He began taking steps to increase manpower at the fort, sending word to his companies posted across the region to turn towards Vishalgadh.

It was the day after the battle at Ghodkhind pass. The rains had stopped altogether. A swarm of three to four hundred villagers emerged from the dense vegetation at the foot of the hill. The news of the martyrdom of Shivraya's valorous men had reached ten neighbourhood villages and they had decided to help the king in any way they could. They brought down the palanquins used during carnivals for carrying images of the gods and goddesses, and left for Ghodkhind.

With reverence, they placed the bodies of Baji, Phulaji, Shambhuji and others in the palanquins and began their walk towards Vishalgadh a little after midnight. They reached their destination just as the sun had begun to rise. The dead bodies were covered with palaas leaves and anointed with turmeric paste. When the king saw the calm, sage-like faces of his lion-hearted colleagues embalmed in eternal sleep, he could not hold back his sobs.

That afternoon, the king came down to Paataaldari with his close associates to perform the last rites of the martyrs. Rayaji Bandal and the others walked rapidly with him through the wet grass. Although the downpour of the previous day had abated, the sky was still overcast and there was a mild wind blowing, making the waist-high grass sway ever so gently. The sound of the countless rivulets, brooks and cataracts around Vishalgadh pervaded the air. When the corpses of Baji, Shambhuji and Phulaji were placed upon the funeral pyre, the king removed the shawl he was wearing on his shoulder and spread it lightly upon them. As he did so, the dam burst and he wept like a child.

After the mortal remains of the heroes were consigned to the flames, the king ordered the fort-keeper to begin making a garden in memory of the martyrs of Ghodkhind.

Within the next few days, the king identified the urgent work that needed to be done in the Panhala-Vishalgadh region and arranged for its immediate commencement. He then set off on the jungle trail along the Malkapur-Ameni route, crossed the Vaarna river and headed for Ajinkyatara, past the Ladoba mountain. He had to reach Rajgadh in three days' time.

Before Shivraya reached his capital, he was determined to pay a visit to Baji Prabhu's village, Sindh. When he came upon the road that led to the village, he was overwhelmed with emotion. Rayaji Bandal was riding alongside him.

It was only a few months since Baji had finished his work at Dehu-Alandi and visited Rajgadh along with his wives Sonabai and Gautamabai. When he spoke about this visit to the king, Baji had said with great feeling, 'I've to place a request at your feet; please don't turn it down. Please pay my mother Bayobai a visit at our village Sindh.'

'I'll do that, Bajida, I'll certainly visit your mother in Sindh.'

'Raje, she remembers you from your childhood days. That boy from Pemgadh called Shivba, he was just a piece of moon in the sky, she says, and now people say he's become as big as the sky. She would dearly love to see you before she dies.'

As Shivraya entered the valley, he felt a tremor pass through his body. He said to Yesaji, 'Gadya, I have no fear of jumping into a raging battlefield astride my horse, but how do I stand in the presence of the mother after both her sons Baji Prabhu and Phulaji Prabhu have gone? My heart beats violently.'

The king dismounted in a tamarind grove outside the village. The entire region around Sindh had been plunged in gloom at the passing away of the heroes and sons of its soil, Baji and Phulaji. Turning down the offer of a palanquin, the king walked barefoot in the company of the villagers who had gathered there to welcome him. The men and women, the barebacked horses and other animals, even the tiny tamarind leaves of Sindh looked mournful.

They arrived at the old waada of Pilajipant. His grandchildren Baji and Phulaji had, as it were, added a golden spire to the honour of the house. The king was first received by the two surviving brothers Volhoji and Annaji. As soon as the king recognised them, he stepped forward and pulled them into his embrace. There was no stanching the flow of tears after that. The brothers were immediately followed by Baji Prabhu's two widows, Gautamabai and Sonabai. They broke into loud wails at the sight of the king and lamented, 'You have come all by yourself, Maharaj. Where have you left our man behind?'

Last of all, a woman in her eighties hobbled in, leaning heavily on a staff. Bayobai was like a dry peepul leaf, skeletal and tired, but her eyes were bright and alert. She was in no physical state to give expression to her grief.

She had Shivraya sit beside her on a rug that had been spread out in her courtyard. The entire village had gathered around, waiting anxiously to hear what the king would say. Courageous Sonabai came forward and said spiritedly, 'Maharaj, please inform the enemy that has brought us to widowhood, tell him that the sword of the house of Prabhus has not turned blunt. Tell him we still have eight sons who will fight alongside the king.'

The king felicitated the eight boys by tying ceremonial red scarfs around their waists. He announced the induction of Baji's son Babaji as a sardar in the royal court and took the other seven sons into his service as well. He also assigned other members of the Prabhu community to various posts according to their competencies. The most eligible men among them were appointed as petty officers in the forts.

Keeping in mind that several Bandals had also sacrificed their lives at Ghodkhind, the king paid his respects to a Bandal matriarch by the name of Dipaaoo Bandal. With Rayaji by his side to help him, the king bestowed favours on a number of Bandal men and women.

As the king recounted the heroic deeds of Baji and Phulaji to the assembled villagers, his voice often grew hoarse and the tip of his fair nose would turn red. 'The brothers Baji and Phulaji, sons of our village, sacrificed themselves for Swarajya on the night of the full moon. Stars like these find a permanent place in the constellations you see in the sky above. They turn luminous to defeat the darkness of the moonless night. Brothers, till yesterday, your Baji and Phulaji belonged to this village of Sindh. Now they have become the shining beacons of not merely the Swarajya but of the entire world. Till such time as the ballads of Maratha valour are sung far into the future, the victory pennants of Baji-Phulaji, Shiva Kashid, Shambhuji Jadhav and Siddhi Wah Wah will keep flying high.'

As the king was about to mount his horse after taking leave of the villagers, he noticed a member of his espionage squad waiting for him expectantly. He took the man aside and received the latest intelligence on enemy positions, including information on Shaista Khan at Pune and also the developments at Burhanpur and Agra. That done, he jumped on to his horse and was off.

23

THE ROYAL COURT AT RAJGADH

It was after a gap of almost a year that the king's feet had turned in the direction of Rajgadh. Jijausahib and his seven queens had been waiting for this day with the eagerness of chaataka birds. When the king arrived, the air in the upper fort rang with the sound of auspicious musical instruments.

At the threshold of the royal palace, he was greeted with aukshan, the circling of the holy lamp before the face and chest. Jijausahib rushed forward. This meeting between mother and son had come about after a long, long time, against the backdrop of countless events, both good and bad, and it churned up deep emotions. They held each other in a tight embrace, both breathing heavily, the king's chin resting on Jijau's shoulder.

He lifted his eyes to see fair, chubby-cheeked, bright-eyed Sambhaji, alias Shambhuraje, cuddled in the arms of one of the wet nurses. The king beckoned the woman and took the prince in his arms. For a short while, the citizens of Rajgadh were treated to the uncommon, delightful, sight of Shivraya gathered in his mother's arms, holding his own gurgling baby close to his chest.

They walked together into the palace to the thunderous accompaniment of horns, trumpets and drums. Jijau first guided Shivraya's steps towards the main shrine. Her face glowed with the joy of her son returning to her unscathed. Outside, the cannons of Rajgadh boomed to formally welcome the king.

The royal family spent a long time at the shrine. Shivraya, seated in his chair, watched little Sambhajiraje toddling in every direction. The baby would sometimes waddle up to his father and fall into his arms to be lifted up and cuddled immediately, much to the delight of both. Jijausahib sat drinking in the sight of her son unblinkingly. Suddenly, she was overcome by another thought and her eyes welled up. Some of her beloved sardars—Baji Prabhu and Phulaji Prabhu, Shambhuji, the grandson of her dear brother Achalojirao, and so many others who had left for the campaign with the king—had not been able to make it back. It was a grief that did not allow her to experience unalloyed joy.

There was an important issue that had been causing the king great anxiety, and it needed immediate consideration: Phirangoji Narsaala's superhuman struggle to keep the Sangram fort in Chakaan from falling into the enemy's clutches. In the meeting that was held at Rajgadh the same evening, senior sardars like Moropant, Sonopant, Mohite, Ghatge and others spoke of the conflict at Sangramdurg: 'Maharaj, barely seven or eight hundred Maavalis inside the fort, and close to thirty thousand Mughal crows besieging them from all sides! The battle is unimaginably uneven. Phirangoji baba is fighting at Chaakan under unendurable pressure.'

'Yes, I am aware of it. Wherever I happen to be, I insist on receiving reports on the developments at Chaakan at least thrice a day.'

'But, Raje, more than forty days have passed since the assault has been at its horrendous worst. The situation there has been worsening every day since. Phirangoji has pledged his life to protect the enormous arsenal that we have stored in the fort. If it were to explode, there is every likelihood that seven or eight hundred Maavali men will be reduced to cinders. It is a terrifying thought.'

'You think I don't know all this? Phirangoji has been one of my father's most esteemed colleagues. Anxieties about the situation at the fort have been agitating my heart and mind for a long while now. What do I say, Matoshri, and how?' he said, turning a sorrowful look towards his mother. 'I had not wished at all to take the Satara route from Vishalgadh to come to Rajgadh. I had wanted to go over the Purandar ghat, past the Karhe plateau, and descend straight into the Bhima valley. I had wanted to reach Chaakan quickly.'

The king's words stunned everyone present. His sincerity, however, radiated from every pore of his being. 'I had wanted to jump into the mighty Chaakan conflict at the earliest, but—' Shivraya caught his breath for a moment before he resumed in a helpless, frustrated voice, 'I believe that no god or goddess can stop me from taking that leap towards Sangramdurg, but it is the infuriated incarnation of nature that stands in my way. The river Bhima is in such tremendous flood that people say this kind of overflow on the banks has not been witnessed in the past fifty years. It was the flood alone that blocked my path; else, I would not have come to Rajgadh at all.'

This clarification from the king changed the tone of the meeting. Discussion began on how a campaign could be launched to cross the Bhima as soon as the flood showed signs of abating. Moropant came up with some information on all the efforts that had been made. 'After your orders were received, Raje, Netajirao Palkar threw himself heart and soul into the campaign. He even tried to lower boats into the roaring flood, but the obstacles were too many. One can load a maximum of forty men on a boat made of wooden planks. The force of the flow was frighteningly strong, and there was also the problem of carrying horses, guns, cannon and other war equipment on wildly heaving vessels.'

'But for all that, the man's name is Netajirao Palkar; he is not the kind who would ever sit contented after encountering defeat. He will heap effort upon valiant effort, but somehow reach out to help Phirangoji.'

'Maharaj, it is contrary to his nature to wait on the bank. Despite the enormous risks, he actually managed to launch a boat on the massive current and attempted the impossible feat of trying to reach the far shore—'

'What are you saying?'

'How can one stop a born warrior like Netaji? He went slicing through the raging waters along with his men. But wily uncle Shaista was anticipating some such wild adventure against impossible odds. He had planted cannon on the other bank in preparation for such an eventuality, loaded and ready for the torch. When the cannonballs started thundering across the river, it became impractical even for a person such as Netajirao to press on. He had to turn back with all the war equipment he had lowered into the water.'

'Oh, really?' exclaimed Shivraya and added with a sigh, 'This Shaista is getting quite adventurous.'

'Well, it is his destiny that is making him tread the path of adventure. The Emperor had issued a firman two or three months ago decreeing that he should not tarry in Pune but set off immediately for Panhala via Satara. Evidently, even though such a move would ultimately benefit Adilshah and Siddhi Johar, Padishah Aurangzeb doesn't mind, as long as he can feast his eyes on your dead body.'

'Well, then?'

'It's obvious, then, isn't it, that this charade at Chaakan was only to help Shaista save his face! And now, he's trapped there like an elephant in the sludge.'

The various military campaigns, the combat with the enemy on five fronts at the same time, all these were expensive adventures. Add to that Shaista Khan's prolonged encampment in Pune, and the Maratha kingdom's finances were bound to stretch to the very limit. Shaista's gargantuan entourage was placing insupportable stress upon the city, the green fields around it and the farming community that tended to them.

The traders in the city's markets were having serious doubts about financing Shivraya's ventures. Their genuine fear was that if Lakshmi, the goddess of wealth, were sent in that direction, she might not return at all. As a consequence, the supply of funds for fresh campaigns had shrunk alarmingly. It was imperative therefore that Uncle Shaista, who was sitting atop it all like an incubus, be dislodged and tossed as far away from the body of Swarajya as possible.

The king met Swami Paramaanand Nevaskar that evening after a gap of many days. After listening to the king's monetary woes, the sage pronounced a Sanskrit sloka:

Yasyaarthaastasya suhado asyaarthaastasya paurusham
Yasyaarthaastasya sarvey pi sahaayah sambhavati hi

'Swamiji, it will be a great kindness if you can elaborate on your priceless words for the edification of our men here.'

'Whosoever possesses plenty of wealth attracts friends. The wealthy man is the conqueror. Everyone rushes to help the person who has money. Who will ever throw a glance at the poor man?'

This bitter but eminently practical message emanating from Swamiji made the king thoughtful. The mountain of financial worries facing them was considerable. The king said, 'When enemies from the Ganga-Yamuna plains come galloping down to our Swarajya, we need adequate armies and weapons to counter them. And without a doubt, money is needed to organise men and material.'

'Yes, Raje,' said Jijausahib, who was present in the gathering along with Kanhojibaba and other senior sardars. 'There's no success without a well-stocked treasury.' The others nodded vehemently in agreement.

'If securing funds is the goal, there is no alternative to imposing taxes and going on money-collecting expeditions,' Swamiji said, his glance taking in the entire assembly. 'Such measures are in agreement with the prescribed tenets of running a kingdom. This royal court would do well to give sanction to such ventures.'

'We concur, Raje, we concur,' was the response from all corners of the hall.

'Running a kingdom is not the same as looting one's subjects,' the king said thoughtfully. 'Placing public welfare and a commitment to the poor and helpless above all else: this is the meaning of true kingship. If there must be taxation and gathering of funds for expansion of the kingdom, it has to be done by ethical means. Otherwise, what is the difference between this royal court and a congregation of dacoits?'

The king, however, had begun to think quite proactively about replenishing the treasury, transactions with moneylenders, and military expenditure. The manner in which he was now trying to balance revenue and spending alerted some of his more perceptive colleagues to the possibility that their shrewd leader was in search of a large treasure trove somewhere. Or, perhaps, he was mulling over a major campaign.

It was after an age that the entire royal family had assembled in Soyarabai's bedroom. Jijau sat there with all her daughters-in-law: Soyarabai, Jaishribai, Sagunabai, Putlabai, Sakvarabai and Kashibai. Her little granddaughters Balibai, Nanibai and Kamalabai were frolicking around too.

Next to Jijausahib sat a tranquil Shivraya, leaning against a bolster. The mother's hand would sometimes rest affectionately on his shoulder, or run lightly up and down his back. The young queens were keenly aware that their husband was the maker of the destiny of Hindvi swarajya. Every breath he took was laden with value. It was at his glance that the winds of destiny blew through these mountains and valleys. The murmurs of his voice determined the direction in which the chariot of the kingdom should move. It was inevitable, therefore, that his formidable personality would leave an impact upon the minds of his queens. Even in their most intimate moments and candid conversations with the king, each one of them was acutely conscious of his greatness and his capabilities. Sometimes this presented an insurmountable barrier, making them nervous in his presence.

If Matoshri Jijausahib happened to be present at such private meetings, the daughters-in-law would use her as a crutch and become far more expressive. They would bring into play their big and small opinions, their indulgences, obstinacies and insistences with great skill. It was after many months that such a family gathering had become possible, a rare, golden opportunity in those days of continuous strife.

While a happy, intimate conversation was in progress among the members of the family, a servant arrived, bowed respectfully and stood in a corner. He then sought the king's eyes and said, 'My reverence, Maharaj. The office superintendent has sent me to you with an urgent message. Shilimkar has arrived.'

'Who? Haibatrao?'

'Yes, Raje. The superintendent dispatched me to inform you of his visit immediately. Haibatrao, standing outside, seems to be in a big hurry. It might not be proper to let him go away without meeting the king.'

'Haibatrao is a close associate of ours, and our mutual affection stretches across generations. How can I let him go without meeting me? Tell the superintendent that I shall be there in a minute.'

There was an occasion long ago when Bajiraje Ghorpade of Mudhol had made a bid to arrest Shahajiraje in the jungles of Jinji. It was Haibatrao's father Balaji who had taken him under his protection then. Such was the background to the relationship between the Shilimkars and the Bhosales. The king always had a special place in his heart for young, intrepid, straightforward and loyal warriors like him.

During the Pratapgadh battle, Khandoji Khopade of Utrali had fought on the side of the enemy. This turncoat who sold his soul for the sake of a small piece of land was Haibatrao's father-in-law. While the father-in-law had found advantage in changing sides, the son-in-law had never allowed his genuine fealty to Shivraya to falter under any kind of pressure.

Shivraya accepted the young man's salutation and said, 'Yes, Haibatrao, what brings you here so early in the morning?'

'Maharaj, I once again beg forgiveness for the behaviour of my father-in-law Khandoji Khopade in the battle of Pratapgadh. It does not behove a respectable Maratha to act in that manner. I completely concede that his conduct was shameful.'

'Yes, all right. What more?'

'But he happens to be the father of my wife. Every single day, she laments the fate of her father. Our children too are worried about the security of their grandfather's life.'

'Haibatrao, even if they happen to be close relatives, why continue relationships with people who are determined to turn to dust our dream of Hindvi swarajya?'

'That's quite true, Raje, but—'

'I hold that there is a limit to how treacherous a person can be. We slaughtered Afzal Khan at Pratapgadh, demolished his army and caused them to flee. Do you know what wonderful exploits your revered father-in-law then got into? Any idea at all?'

'Raje?'

'This menace to our Swarajya, your father-in-law, came forward to help Afzal's son Faazal Khan. Treating him as one would a dear relative, the scoundrel helped the man slip out along the jungles on bank of the Koyna river and reach Karad.'

'Raje, I am well aware of the man's wretched, self-centred deeds, but even so, I request forgiveness.'

'These self-serving rats nibble away at the kingdom so quietly that you will know only when the roof of the Swarajya crashes on your head. Why should a person of your integrity support the cause of a rogue like him?'

Haibatrao was startled at the intense dislike that the king harboured for Khandoji. Instead of pressing his case at this juncture, he deemed it prudent to quietly withdraw.

When the king returned to his private quarters, the queens were worried by the sudden change in their husband's demeanour. He was usually the very epitome of patience and strength, hence it was unsettling to see signs of stress and restlessness on his face.

In an effort to get him to speak frankly, Ausahib said to him half in jest, 'Balraje, most people consider your nature to be as soft and malleable as freshly made butter. Why has this butter suddenly melted in a steel furnace?'

'My apologies, Matoshri, but have I been remiss in any way?'

'Prince, I can find ways to ignore the worry lines on the countenances of my daughters-in-law, but please look at the faces of my tiny grandchildren. See how tense they are because of the anxiety that shows on their father's face!'

The king then informed his mother about the visit of Shilimkar pleading for forgiveness for his father-in-law. It took no time for Jijausahib to flare up.

'No, out of the question!' she said in a steely voice. 'Whether it's Khandoji Khopade or that Patil of Ranjha or Sultanji Jagdale of Masoor, any communication with these ungrateful wretches can only invite adversity and misfortune for the Swarajya.'

'But Ausahib, it is all a bit awkward. After all, he is the father of our Shilimkar's wife.'

'Send him my message: Haibat, boy, the integrity that runs through your veins makes the heads of even elders like us bow in respect; but the blackguard named Khandoji in whose advocacy you have entangled yourself, that wicked ingrate is not at all deserving of our affection.'

The conference room at Rajgadh had become a beehive of activity. It was now close to three weeks since the king had returned to his capital. Morning and evening, he would pose to his officials only one question: What was happening on the banks of the Bhima? Had the waters begun to recede? When was that likely to happen?

The king's anxiety and restlessness would not abate. When he asked about Netaji Palkar, he was informed that the warrior had retreated to a hideout somewhere in the vicinity of the riverbank, waiting for the waters to subside. Meanwhile a force of four thousand soldiers was camped in front of the Shivapattan palace, awaiting the king's orders to move towards Sangramdurg. He would groan in the presence of his closest colleagues, 'Look at the ripe age at which Phirangoji Narsaala is battling at Chaakan with such passion! I consider it a crime to be hanging behind here in the palace these days.'

'But Raje,' Jijausahib would remind him, 'if Bhima Mai has decided to obstruct your way in her most violent manifestation, what can you do?'

'But Maasahib, barely seven hundred men are keeping an army of twenty-five thousand at bay in Chaakan. It is my duty as king to somehow rush to their aid at the earliest.'

One evening, four spies climbed up to the fort in pouring rain and were granted an immediate audience with the king. The news they brought sent tremors through all of Rajgadh. 'Maharaj,' they said, 'last night, a series of terrible explosions took place in Chaakan, so powerful that the peasants of the region mistook it for a massive cloudburst.'

'What are you saying? Has the enemy finally blown up our arsenal?'

'No, Maharaj, the story is quite different. Seeing the success of our spirited defence of Sangramdurg despite our small numbers, they were so annoyed that they dug a tunnel alongside the northeastern wall of the fort and stuffed it with explosives. The explosions were so loud and violent that many people in the neighbouring villages are complaining of damage to their eardrums.'

The king's brow turned dark. 'I fear that a terrible disaster has struck us. What news of Phirangojibaba? And our seven hundred men?'

'Doesn't look like a disaster at all, Raje. Although the fortifications have suffered some damage, the Mughals keep receiving gifts of sling-stones, arrows and gunshots from the other side. Even after blowing up a part of the wall, the enemy has not been able to find a way in. Which clearly shows, Maharaj, that our Maavalis have not relaxed their guard the slightest bit. They are fighting on.'

Nobody slept at Rajgadh that night. Bhima Mai showed no signs of relenting either. All ears were cocked in the direction of Chaakan. Heralds arrived two days later with news. Despite the massive explosion outside their walls, the soldiers inside the fort had continued to fight fiercely for fourteen hours. Some seven hundred Mughals were grievously injured and close to three hundred lost their lives in an effort to snatch the flag from Maavali hands. An utterly thwarted Shaista Khan finally appointed a Rajput sardar to start negotiations with the defenders. When he received assurance of safe passage for the surviving Maratha soldiers, a beleaguered Phirangoji finally handed over charge of the fort to the Mughals.

Continuing with his narration, the herald said, 'What do I say, Maharaj? Aurangzeb's uncle Shaista Khan was completely overawed by the unshrinking resistance that Phirangoji had put up. He sent messages to our sardar, offering him a place of honour in the Mughal army. He promised to shower wealth, power and privileges on Phirangoji if he abandoned Shivaji's insignificant principality and shifted allegiance to the mighty Mughal empire. Phirangoji sent a message back saying that he was quite prepared to give Shaista more battle if he so desired, till such time as there was life left in him. The Khan sahib was being given the house, but he should not dream of owning the temple that resided in Phirangoji's heart.'

The story of Phirangoji's valour dazzled not only Shivraya and Jijausahib, but all of Rajgadh. The battle of Chaakan was not seen as a defeat of this veteran warrior, but as the glorious culmination of his career as a soldier. Shivraya publicly declared that the daredevilry of Phirangoji and his men should be given due honour; accordingly, five cannons were fired from the fort of Rajgadh to offer salutations to the heroes of Sangramdurg.

Two days later, the king was informed that Kanhoji Jedhe had arrived at the Shivapattan waada. The word was that Haibatrao and Khandoji Khopade were with him. Kanhoji had sent a message to the fort that stated, 'Tomorrow I shall be coming up to Rajgadh to meet the king. Maharaj is not going to like my coming with a recommendation for a certain person, but when it is a matter of life and death, who should a subject appeal to for mercy and forgiveness if not to the king? As of now, I want to say just this much: Khandoji is writhing in the throes of repentance. The rest I shall discuss in person tomorrow. I request an audience with the king.'

Shivraya was in a terrible dilemma. But Kanhoji Jedhe was an eminent and charismatic personality, undoubtedly a foundation stone of the Swarajya. His eldest son Bajirao was barely a few months older than the king. Shivraya had seen Kanhojikaka move around in his father's company starting from Pemgadh and Mahuli right up to Bijapur. Evidently, Haibatrao Shilimkar had roped in a powerful advocate to plead Khandoji Khopade's case. It was absolutely unthinkable to keep Kanhoji waiting at the base of the fort.

The next day the king held an urgent consultation with the queen mother in his office. He thought again and again of those days when the Afzal Khan menace was at its peak. He reminded Matoshri, 'Kanhoji Jedhe got all the Deshmukhs of Maaval to rally behind us. He told them in no uncertain language that Afzal Khan was a rogue, and that one day he would destroy us all; that for the sake of Maharashtra, they should all come together in support of the king. Who else can match Kanhoji's integrity and patronage of our cause?'

Jijausahib finally said, 'This is undeniable, Balraje. A gem like Kanhoji is far dearer to us than inconsequential people like Khopade. We must grant his request.'

Khandoji was the kind of sardar who had brought respectability to terms like 'backstabber' and 'turncoat'. After having 'served' the enemy so well, a self-respecting person would have been ashamed to present himself at Rajgadh, but Khandoji was nothing if not utterly shameless.

After the battle of Pratapgadh, he had been consumed by the fear that his fiefdom would be taken away from him. Finding that there was nobody in the Swarajya who was willing to assist him, he had gone to his son-in-law for help. 'Son,' he had beseeched, 'the king of Rajgadh is so well disposed towards you that if you demand it, he will happily send you on elephant-back in a procession from Pune to Bijapur.'

At the fort, Khandoji was first made to sit in another room when Kanhoji and Haibatrao presented themselves before the king. Excitability was a shortcoming that the king had never allowed to come close to him. On the contrary, he had always kept intimate company with patience and forbearance. But when his eyes fell on the long-faced, long-nosed, beady-eyed Khandoji from a distance, he lost his cool. It became impossible for him to keep his temper under control.

'That treacherous Khopade,' he snarled, 'he was little more than a destitute in his own land. Yet, we overlooked his offences and made him landlord ten years ago. And after all that we had done for him, he betrayed us. Began licking that Afzulya's boots. Went and joined the Adilshahi Sultanate.'

Haibatrao could only hang his head in shame. He looked towards Kanhojikaka for help. Much as the old man held Khandoji in contempt, his affection for Haibatrao was ten times stronger. It was a delicate situation. Kanhoji cleared his throat, ran a tentative hand over his thick whiskers and said in an apologetic voice, 'Please listen, Raje, out of consideration for my white hair.'

'Jedhekaka, what are you trying to say?'

'Let Khandoji's offences be marked against my name. I'll take the penalty too, if desired. But please grant protection to his life and fiefdom.'

Seeing a person of his age, seniority and dignity beseeching him thus, the king's heart melted and he decided to pardon the traitor. When the servants took the message to the next room, Shivraya added a note of warning, telling Kanhoji, 'Please tell him to live within the limits of decency from here on. If he falls back into crooked ways again and brings indignities upon us, he shall certainly lose his life. Please make sure he is aware of this.'

Kanhoji went to the next room and brought Khandoji along to make his obeisance to the king. He had already told him to simply bow and leave the room, without saying a word. As they were coming down the fort, Kanhoji told Khandoji sternly, with Haibatrao as witness, 'Your life was saved only on account of the merits of your ancestors. Behave with grace and dignity now. The king's anger doesn't seem to have cooled at all. Don't get into any kind of mischief behind his back.'

But living with grace and dignity was alien to Khandoji's essential nature. Barely eight days had passed by when he began making the rounds of the fort as though there had never been a black mark against his name. Soon his beat began to include the upper fort and the palace, from there to the lake temple and the office, and from there to the stables and the quarters of the cavalrymen. Presenting himself as a loyal sardar of the Swarajya, he was soon sitting with the gunners and cannoneers, partaking of the gossip and tobacco. Finally, without making any appointments whatsoever, he began paying casual visits to the office, wanting to meet the king. Soon he was imposing himself on petty officials and on the guards.

One day the king expressed his irritation to his mother, saying, 'Matoshri, I think I shouldn't have succumbed to the pleadings of Kanhoji, even though he is a good man.'

'What do you mean?'

'Despite his open collusion with Afzal Khan, this traitor Khandoji did not get the punishment he thoroughly deserved. Quite the opposite! Now he moves around the fort cockily and throws his weight around. People have begun to complain that while the chief defector of Pratapgadh gets honoured, the king has no time to attend to the martyrs of the Swarajya and their families.'

Jijausahib was nonplussed. Perceiving Shivraya's agitation, she said, 'If the man believes that his earlier association with the Bijapuris and his shifting of allegiance are matters to be proud of, he is being extremely foolish.'

'If a lump of coal deludes himself into believing that he is a piece of diamond, it may be treated as a misfortune. But if this man, despite being a traitor, struts around the fort like a bridegroom, shouldn't we be concerned that his behaviour might be warping the minds of our loyal soldiers?'

'All right, Shivba, you are the king and you should acquit yourself like a king. In this case, there is no reason why even my recommendations or wishes should be honoured more than they need to be.'

One day, there was a great commotion in Rajgadh. By the king's orders, an arm and a leg of Khandoji's had been amputated. The news soon reached Kanhoji's waada at his village Kaari. The relatives of Jedhe and Shilimkar were incensed. They began throwing oil on the fire, crying, 'Of what worth are Jedhe and Shilimkar? Who cares for them at Rajgadh?'

One afternoon, Kanhojibaba came and stood outside the waada at Rajgadh. He had for company Haibatrao, his son Baji and a few other relatives of both houses. When Kanhoji began voicing his distress at the development, the king said, 'It was because of you alone, Jedhekaka, that I did not have that Khandoji executed.'

'Why wait for him to die now? He has already lost a leg and an arm. Why should the master shame a loyal servant thus?'

'Kaka, you may take it to mean that I have pulled a poisonous thorn out of the Swarajya's foot and tossed it away.'

'But Maharaj, you had given me an assurance and granted Khandoji his life. If the king begins reneging on his promise, our lives will turn to dust.'

'After having pardoned the offender once, I could not turn a blind eye to the fact that he had slipped back into his old brazen ways. His arm was hacked off for the offence of having taken up arms against us at Pratapgadh at the prompting of Afzal Khan. The leg that was chopped off was the one with which he had walked away from his motherland in the direction of Bijapur. That is all there is to it.'

'But why did you go back on your promise after granting him exoneration?'

'Forgive me, kaka. You have been a loyal companion of my parents. For me, there can be no bigger misfortune than having to break a promise that was given to you. But please think this over a little carefully: if I go around granting pardon to traitors against the Swarajya, and if that traitor takes to strutting around the capital, twirling his moustaches, and if this behaviour leads to a breakdown of discipline in barracks and among the citizenry, who will then be accountable?'

24

THE FORT IN THE SEA

The rains had still not withdrawn from Rajgadh; nor had the clouds of the crises that beset the kingdom.

One stormy midnight, a guest from Goa came up the fort to meet the king. He wore a hooded cloak that looked like it was made of wax paper. Underneath was another hooded cloak that was woven of a thick woollen material. While his five servants stood outside, the gentleman held a swift consultation with the king and left soon after.

The king returned to his private chamber at dawn. He carried in his hand a wicker basket which contained a consecrated sweetmeat on a small plate, carrying the blessing of the goddess Shanta-Durga. He took a reverential bite of the sweet, bowed his head and turned towards his bed.

The rain stopped at daybreak. The guards posted around its outhouses noticed that the lamps in the palace seemed to have been burning through the night. Did their king retire at all? What was going on?

Two attendants hurried out of the palace with the information that the king was about to set out for a round of the fort. Within minutes, Shivraya stepped out. Grooms and footmen were waiting with the king's horse, but as the prospects of a downpour were strong, the palace staff had arranged for rain-cover for the king.

Situated at a considerable altitude, the upper fort in Rajgadh was visited by strong, whistling winds all the year round. During the monsoon months, the wind's fury was of quite another order. This morning, it also had mist for company. As the king walked through the haze, from a distance appeared to be floating over the clouds. The lines etched deep on his face revealed that there was a storm of restless thoughts whirling in his head. That was also why, perhaps, he had spent a sleepless night.

Despite the strong drizzle, Shivraya continued his promenade along the battlements of the upper fort for a long time. Worried onlookers sent a quiet message to the queens, which brought them scurrying out of their beds. It was only when the rain stopped that the king was jolted out of his deep reverie. Seeing that his clothes were dripping wet, he returned to the palace.

When he reached his bedchamber, Soyrabai was standing in the doorway with a towel and a set of dry clothes for him to change into. She set about vigorously drying the king's dense head of hair, grumbling, 'Maharaj, is this the age to go prancing about in the rains?'

Shivraya smiled.

Jijausahib's official residence was the Shivapattan palace at the foot of Rajgadh, but because she had been deprived of her dear son's company for so long, and as there was no saying when he would disappear again and for how long, she had stayed on in the Rajgadh palace. When the king noticed Ausahib's presence that morning, he felt a tad embarrassed.

Quickly finishing his bath, Shivraya threw a shawl over his shoulder and went to the shrine to pay his obeisance to the gods. When he returned, he saw his mother sitting peacefully on a couch in the outer room. The king avoided looking into her eyes. She looked quite content, but the bemusement in her eyes was quite markedly visible. For quite a while she did not utter a word.

Soyrabai stood next to Ausahib. But her eyes travelled to the lampstand near which the priest had placed a dish of sacramental sweets in the late hours of the night. A folded piece of paper lay next to it. Soyrabai picked it up and unfolded the sheet, to see a roughly sketched map. She carried it to her mother-in-law and the two began scrutinising it eagerly. At first glance it appeared to depict a coastline with swirls alongside, indicating a sea. On closer examination, this stretch of coast seemed to have two huge bodies of water on either side, suggesting the presence of two creeks to the experienced eye.

The king noticed the two ladies examining the piece of paper. Before he could even say a word, Jijausahib asked in an authoritarian voice,

'Soyra, there was some visitor last night, I hear! Stayed till a very late hour, it seems!'

'He looked like a great explorer or a scholar to me, Ausahib,' Soyrabai replied, keeping her eyes fixed on the king.

'Well, Ranisahib,' the king asked Soyrabai, 'who do you think it could have been?'

'Either Vishwasrao Dighe or Bahirji Naik.'

The king laughed loudly at Soyrabai's conjecture. Matoshri's face, however, looked quite grim. Adopting an anxious tone, Soyrabai turned to her mother-in-law and said, 'Matoshri, please grant me permission to present a complaint against the king in your court.'

'What complaint can this be, Ranisahib?' the king enquired.

'Matoshri, you too should pay attention in this matter. Look, I believe that Maharaj should get at least a few hours of undisturbed sleep at night, but is it happening at all? He has not only forfeited his own sleep, but denies people working under him a decent night's rest too.'

Jijausahib couldn't hold back any longer. She said in a stern voice, 'There is a limit to all this, Shivba. Nothing that you say can convince me otherwise. You may consider my daughter-in-law's complaint as my complaint too. What's going on? It's only lately that you have escaped the mountain of calamity that was Panhala, and your feet have finally found rest in Rajgadh just about four days ago. After having survived such enormous ordeals, how will it do if you continue with these endless worries, these political intrigues, campaign plans and so forth?'

'Matoshri, as the saint Tukaram has said, I have only battles to think of day and night.'

'Shivba, I am well aware of the troubles that you are grappling with, and I know the reasons for your unceasing worries. But what happened last night that has taken away your sleep? What is causing the blood to race so feverishly through your veins?'

'Honestly speaking, Ausahib, my entire being has been in a state of conflagration since last afternoon.'

'What exactly happened?'

'A delegation of well-respected citizens from Thane, Panvel and Vasai, including fishermen, traders and community leaders came to see me last afternoon. Their complaint was this: "This land is ours, the soil is ours; the coast and its waters have come down to us from our ancestors. This being so, by what right do these Portuguese block our boats and our vessels while plying the creeks of Thane, Panvel and Vasai? Why should we pay taxes to move in and out of our own waters? And that too to the Portuguese?"'

'Shivba, what they say is the unadulterated truth.'

'Ausahib, these firangis sail across the seven seas, suffer six months of excruciating travel across rough waters. But the moment they arrive here, they begin to treat our coasts and our creeks as if it was their ancestral property. Why should we tolerate this bother, this humiliation, this merciless browbeating? But on the other hand, do we have any dominance over the waves? The harbours, the sea forts, the coastal waters, do we have ownership over them?'

The king often discussed political matters, military strategies and future plans with his queens Soyrabai and Jayashribai. In the same vein, he continued, 'What do I say? These thoughts and questions are hardly new; they have rendered me sleepless for nearly half a dozen years now. Even when my eyes are closed, these ideas keep racing through my mind. There is this dream that god has planted in my head.'

'What's that?'

'Janjira. That sea fort of ours that the Siddhis have poached.'

'Ours?'

'Yes, it belongs to our people. A proud, daring young man of the fishing community, named Rama Koli Patil, laid the foundation. He was the first person with the enterprise to build a fort over water on this coast. And that holiest of holy places is known as Janjira.'

The two women listened with rapt attention.

'The Siddhis swallowed it up like a python swallows a precious jewel. Hundreds of soldiers have choked on gallons of seawater in an effort to pull it out of the jaws of those Habshis. A number of them drowned in the effort. We have been trying to capture it for years now, but that dream fort remains out of our grasp.'

'Balraje, I know that for about five years now you have been making efforts in this direction. I know of the wonderful shipbuilding ventures that you started in the regions of Panvel, Durgadi near Kalyan as well as the Dharamtar creek near Pen.'

'For our kingdom to survive and flourish in these days of wild ups and downs, Ausahib, it is important that we gain mastery over the weapons of these modern times. Every time that I think of the Janjira fort, my blood begins to boil. It is our fort. It was our man Rama Koli Patil who constructed it.

'But how did this wretched Siddhi arrive at our Kulaba coast in the first place?'

The king then narrated the hundred-and-fifty-year-old story related to the Ahmadnagar Sultanate: 'Rama Koli was a son of the sea, born and brought up in a coastal fishing village of Rajpuri. On his intiative, an ingenious fort of wooden planks was raised on a rock in the sea. The officers of the Nizam were deeply agitated. They made many attempts to destroy the settlements of the Kolis in Murud and Rajpuri. Rama, however, used the security of his wooden fort to roast the Nizam's soldiers with cannon-fire. When the Nizam saw that open war was not helping his cause at all, he resorted to subterfuge.

'One evening, three boats suddenly arrived from Surat and dropped anchor off the coast close to Janjira. The boats belonged to some silk merchants who made a beeline for Rama Koli and wailed that their boat had been attacked by pirates. The sailors, who claimed to have been hung upside down and whipped, begged for a couple of days' shelter at the Janjira fort to recover from their injuries. They also had in their boats bales of silk worth thousands of rupees, which they wanted to unload at Janjira for safety. Rama Koli, who was otherwise quite alert to danger, saw the arrival of these uninvited guests as an opportunity for getting into the silk trade and gave in to their plea.

'He welcomed the traders to his sea fort, helped unload their cargo and treated them to an evening of generous hospitality. There was song, dance, conversation and quite a bit of alcohol too. Among the sailors, in the garb of a trader, was a Habshi adventurer named Pir Khan. He ensured that Rama Koli was served more drinks than he could handle and got him thoroughly intoxicated. Their ruse had succeeded. The valorous Rama Koli was arrested, tied to a post and whipped. Meanwhile, the hundred-odd soldiers that had been brought over concealed in the bales of cloth sprang out, slaughtered Koli's men and tossed them into the sea for the fish to feast on. Rama Koli was then forcibly converted to Islam. An important lesson here is that one should never lower one's guard even in sleep; enemies are always waiting for a chance to pounce.'

Once the fort had passed into enemy hands, it never returned to its rightful owners, the king said. Murtuza Nizamshah later demolished Rama Koli's wooden fortification and erected strong stone walls in its place.

Shivraya sat for a long time in a contemplative mood. Doroji Phaakade, who had joined them later, asked the king after a little while, 'Raje, five years back, when we won Kalyan and Bhiwandi, didn't our Shyamjipant Peshve and Baji Gholap mount a ferocious attack on Janjira?'

'Yes, of course, they did.' The episode was still fresh in the king's mind. The Siddhis, who belonged to the Habshi tribe of African descent, had established a principality called Habshan along an estuary of the Murud-Rajapur coast. They had also built a beautiful palace in the township of Tala which they called Aarasey Mahal, the palace of mirrors, and peopled it with a harem of fifty beautiful women. They would often go there to regale themselves.

Both Shyamrao Peshve and Baji Gholap were warriors of great repute. When Shyamjipant launched an offensive on Janjira, two prominent Habshi commanders named Siddhi Khairiyat and Siddhi Kasim had come over to Habshan to block the progress of the Marathas. Shyamjipant mounted a major assault on Tala with a company of two thousand men, frightening the pair enough to send them scurrying into the safety of Aarasey Mahal, which Shyamji instantly blockaded. All that he had to do now was to infiltrate the palace and drag the two Siddhis out. But these Habshi warriors were as inventive as they were brave. They shaved off their beards and slipped into women's clothing. The palanquin of a high-born lady left the mahal at midnight, accompanied by a gaggle of maids, among whom the two Siddhis had disguised themselves. Thus, they managed to make it back to Janjira.

Shyamjipant, however, was a veteran soldier who had trained under Shahaji at Bengaluru. He took the entire coastal area of Dandrajpuri opposite Janjira under his control and surrounded the fort with boats loaded with cannon to suffocate the Siddhi forces inside.

The Siddhis, however, had been equally determined not to let the fort go to the Marathas. To loosen the noose that Shyamji's blockade had thrown around them, the wily Khairiyat resorted to trickery again. He waved the white flag and invited Shyamjipant and Baji Gholap for a meeting to discuss terms of surrender, lacing the invitation with the prospect of creating bonds of friendship over an evening spent together. He even sent his musicians over to escort the guests to the fort in style.

Four or five days passed before the two returned to the Dandrajpuri coast on a boat, looking ragged and bruised. When Shyamjipant presented himself before Shivraya at Rajgadh, the king had asked in a stern voice, 'Peshvekaka, you had gone to the Siddhis at Janjira to seal a victory agreement. Why does your face look as woebegone as a broken mirror?'

'What do I tell you, Raje, and how? The Siddhis broke faith with us. They actually tied us to a post and whipped us!'

The king had rearranged the silk shawl over his shoulder with a flourish and said, 'The humiliation of an elder like you is a personal insult to me. I shall give you a fresh company of soldiers, as many as you want. Prepare to attack Janjira again. All those who tied you to the post, I want you to tie them up in a bundle and toss them into the sea before you return.'

These words coming from the king seemed to dampen the old man's spirit still further. His advanced age showing in his demeanor as well as his voice, he had said, 'Raje, you may send me on any campaign and I shall not say no, but the oath that I have sworn on my religion, I shall not be able break it.'

'What oath are you talking about that stands against the goal of Hindvi swarajya?'.

'The Habshis have a golden statue of Ganesha at their shrine in the fort. Those rascals got us to offer prayers there, after which they banged our heads against the feet of the idol and made us take an oath in the name of our children.'

'What oath?'

'That we shall not so much as glance in the direction of Janjira as long as we live.'

For a while, Shivraya hadn't known how to respond to this strange admission. Finally he said, 'You will have to break this oath of yours. Get on your horse and head back to the coast. Take boats and ships with you, and mount an assault on the fort. I want Janjira at any cost.'

'I seek your forgiveness, Raje, but at least during this lifetime, for me there is no returning to Janjira. I shall lay down my life, if you so desire, but I shall not break a sacred oath.'

'Kaka, I consider it my misfortune that a veteran like you should not understand what true religion is. The song and dance you have spun around the Ganesha statue of those Habshis doesn't behove your dignity at all.'

The entire episode had left Shivraya bemused and deeply disheartened. Every time he made an effort to reclaim the Janjira fort, he met with failure and disappointment. What auspicious moment had the Siddhis chosen to capture the fort, he wondered, that made it so unattainable?

His eyes drifted towards the map of the South Konkan region of Vengurla and Savantwadi. It depicted a spot on the coast where two huge creeks met the sea from both sides of a tongue of land. The map had revived fresh hopes in the heart of the king.

As Jijausahib watched him with admiration, Shivraya let out a deep sigh and said, 'Ausahib, Janjira has been eluding me all my life, but that doesn't mean I should abandon my dream of owning a fort in the sea. We shall certainly build a Janjira of our own, so mighty and invincible that the Janjira of the Siddhis will look like a toy in comparison.'

'It appears to me, Shivba, that you have already located a suitable place for such a venture.'

Shivraya looked into his mother's hopeful eyes with a smile and said, 'I don't know why, Matoshri, but lately I've begun to hope that things will fall into place sooner rather than later.'

25

RAIGADH AND RAIBAGAN

Shivaji Raja had placed a big responsibility on Sonopant's shoulders: to somehow find a way to persuade Emperor Aurangzeb to alleviate the hardships that Shaista Khan had imposed upon the Swarajya. It was essential to lighten the burdens that the peasantry of the region were suffering. Even Shaista was inclined towards it, but without an express nod from the Emperor himself, he was not willing to take any initiative in that direction.

On the very day that Shaista had gained control of the Chaakan fort, he sent for Sonopant, who was a resident there. 'Shahenshah Aurangzeb lives in Agra,' he said to him, 'and papers have to be sent to him for final approval. It's only after the signal arrives from him that peace talks can move forward.'

'Khan sahib, why not resolve it at your level? Why send a camel-post all the way to Agra?'

'Pandit, our Shahenshah looks at his own shadow with suspicion. However, stop worrying. My heralds will be on the road to Agra in the next three or four days.'

True to his word, he had dispatched the papers to Agra a couple of days later. Aurangzeb's response arrived in due course, which left Shaista Khan feeling like a child who had received a stinging slap on the face from his father. For Shaista, there were only two things that mattered: Allah in his heaven and Emperor Aurangzeb on earth. No wonder, then, that the Emperor's missive had made his spirits plummet.

Dear Maamoojaan,

When I was informed by the daroga-e-daak about the arrival of a post-bag from you, I was sure that my dear Maamoo would have sent his lately anointed nephew a gift that would tickle the cockles of his heart, but what happened was quite the opposite. The foolish, worthless proposal you have outlined in your letter has only served to increase my choler. The sheer audacity of suggesting that the Emperor of Hindustan should sit for conciliation with a traitorous rebel! A curse on such proposals!

When I entrusted you with the responsibility of annihilating Sivaji, I had asked you to give me an estimate of the expenditure the enterprise would involve. I could see you break into a sweat even while suggesting 120,000,000 rupees, but I did not blink an eye while sanctioning 320,000,000 for the campaign, because I had seen the fire in your eyes.

But now, instead of rattling your sword, you talk carelessly about accommodating that uncouth Siva, and my head hangs in shame. That god's own soldier should abase himself by suggesting we appease that hellhound leaves me mortified.

Know that I shall have no sympathy for such irresponsible talk from you in the future. Your job is to go boring through the wild jungles of the Sahyadris, flush out that mountain rat, and have him squashed under the feet of elephants. Keep this in mind, Maamoojaan, from this moment on I shall have no tolerance at all for empty words other than your sword and the severed head of Siva. There shall be no third topic for conversation.

After a sleepless night of tossing and turning in bed, with his beloved wife trying to pacify him, Shaista Khan decided to stir himself and his men into action. He called an emergency meeting of his most high-ranking officials, generals and sardars, including his three sons and his sons-in-law. He had assigned some of his cartographers to prepare maps of Rajgadh and the region around it, while another group got busy making wax images of the mountains and hills around the fort. Once the men had assembled, he looked at them sharply and declared, 'We shall mount an assault on Rajgadh in ten days' time.'

The announcement left his audience stunned. Shaista noticed that not one among those gathered was willing to look him in the eye. 'Hello, my brave men,' he said in a voice loaded with scorn, 'what has happened? Why has the thought of marching on Rajgadh paralysed your tongues? Yes, Naseeb Khan, you are a veteran of fifty such conflicts! Why do you refuse to meet my eyes?'

Old Naseeb Khan let out a deep sigh and said, 'Huzoor, dreaming fanciful dreams does give us the joy of paradise, but if we pursue these dreams and they turn out to be nothing more than momentary bubbles, we shall become the laughing stock of our people.'

'What rubbish are you talking, Naseeb miyaan! Is this Siva more formidable than a mountain?'

'Huzoor, at an ordinary fort like Chaakan, less than a thousand margatthyas kept a Mughal force of twenty-five thousand hopping in agony for well over two months. And we have heard that the great forts of Siva at Rajgadh, Torana and Raigadh are even more invulnerable.'

'What can we say about Rajgadh, huzoor?' Namzad Khan piped in. 'It is surrounded by huge mountains and impenetrable, uninhabited jungles, where you may not get drinking water for ten miles at a stretch.'

'You may manage to reach there, but there is no saying whether you will return alive.'

'And how will our seventy thousand horses survive if they don't have water to drink?'

Everybody had broken into a cold sweat, not excluding Shaista Khan himself. If men and animals began dying of thirst in those desolate mountains, the precincts of Rajgadh would turn into a massive Mughal graveyard. Even as he sat there, Shaista began imagining a forest full, not of trees, but of tombstones.

Shaista Khan was in a terrible state. Not that he lacked in material comforts at all. His harem included, in addition to dutiful wives like Dulari Begum, a large number of beautiful young women from Iran and Turan as concubines to indulge his every desire. But now, just as the choicest dishes had lost their flavour, even the most agreeable of his bedmates had lost her charm.

Dulari Begum too was deeply concerned about her husband's state of mind. The sun had reached its zenith and a listless Shaista still lay in bed, disdaining not just his morning bath, but even so much as a change of clothes. Dulari asked anxiously, 'Are you feeling unwell, my lord? Shall I send for the hakeem?'

'Begum, why talk of health? I have become home to all kinds of fears.'

'Ya Allah! Fear? And you?'

'This Lal Mahal of Pune is teeming with the Shahenshah's spies.'

'True. I've been carrying this fear too.'

'Those flies on the wall! They see and hear everything happening here, and send immediate reports to Alamgir in Agra every single day.'

'But why should that surprise you?

'Three months have passed since I received that vitriolic letter from the Emperor, and he continues to believe that I have been wallowing in a life of comfort and ease; not grappling with Shivaji, not besieging any fort.'

'But Khan Sahib, you did blow up the walls of the Chaakan fort!'

'Begum, Chaakan is not the same as Konkan. However frighteningly located atop the Sahyadris it may be, there are no dense, brambly forests around it. It is on the level land of the plateau.'

'Then, my lord, why don't you stir yourself and mount an attack on Rajgadh straight away? Why linger in Lal Mahal and ruin your reputation?'

Shaista Khan smiled bitterly and said, 'Are you mad, woman? Or do you think I am a hedonistic fool to prefer luxuriating in the comforts of Lal Mahal? But what do I do? The moment I utter the name of Rajgadh, the bravest of my sardars begin to tremble at the thought of the infernal mountains around it.'

Shaista had begun to wonder who the hunter was and who the game. He had come here to lay a trap for Shivaji and capture him dead or alive; but here he he was, caught in a prison from which there was no escape in sight. As he was in conversation with his wife, one of his trusted officers came over and bowed in respect. 'Huzoor,' he said softly, 'there's a missive from the Emperor.'

Shaista caught his breath for a moment. Noticing his master's discomfiture, the officer came closer and said, 'Huzoor, though the missive is from the Emperor, I don't think it likely that its contents will be distressing. It has been delivered by Rai Bagan.'

'Who's this Rai Bagan?'

'The Shahenshah's favourite lady chieftain from Mahur.'

'Is she alone, or has she come with her forces?'

'Huzoor, the news came last evening, but we were informed that you had retired for the day. We received word of Rai Bagan crossing the river at Lohgaon with an army of seven thousand men. Right now, her men are resting on the other side of the stream at Ambil inside the border of Malkapur. But the Sardarin sahib has arrived with her officers and is waiting for an audience with huzoor.'

'Arrange for some fruits to be served to her. I'll be with her in a little while.'

As Shaista Khan hurried towards his spacious bathroom for his ablutions, he recollected all that he had heard of this astonishing woman. Udoji Kulkarni of Mahur in the Vidarbha region was a Persian scholar. Through the good offices of a friend in the imperial army, he went to Delhi where he joined the Mughal force and earned a name for himself. As a reward, he was gifted the Deshmukhi of the towns Washim and Mahur. Later, his son Jagjeevan went to Delhi and was killed in battle while marching with Aurangzeb.

His mother, a woman named Lakshmibai, took over the fiefdom and put down a rebellion against Aurangzeb. The Emperor was so impressed with this brahmin woman's intrepidity that he honoured her with the title of 'Rai Bagan', the royal tigress. Her skill in horsemanship and agility on the battlefield won for her the robe of a sardarin, a lady chieftain.

When Shaista entered the office, she bowed to pay him respect. A tall and handsome woman of about fifty, Rai Bagan wore a hooded cloak that covered her upper body and loose trousers which accentuated her robust body. She wore nothing around her neck except a rosary of black basil seeds. The absence of vermilion on her wide brow not only indicated her state of widowhood but also amplified the masculinity of her carriage. She wore a jewel-studded belt around her waist, in which was stuck an impressive-looking sword.

The women of the Deccan rarely stepped out of their confinement to hearth and home. In such a milieu, the sardarin Rai Bagan exuded enough dignity and authority to make heads turn and eyes widen. Shaista Khan welcomed her, had her seated in the front hall and kept drinking her in for a few moments.

The post-bag that she had brought was presented to Shaista Khan on a platter. The Khan's attention was immediately arrested by a sentence of the Emperor's that read, 'Maamoojaan, I have been told that your soldiers start to tremble if they so much as look in the direction of the Sahyadri jungles. Brave men turn into snivelling women, I'm told. To get your spirits back up and to help you in your enterprise, I am sending to you a tigress who is known by the title of Rai Bagan.'

Shaista Khan threw admiring looks at Rai Bagan. It wouldn't be easy to find a man who could challenge this woman in horse riding, spear throwing or swordsmanship. As they chatted, Shivaji came up as a natural topic for discussion. 'Days and months have been rolling by, sister,' Shaista groaned, 'but success against Shivaji has remained a pipe dream.'

'Bhaisahib, from the man on the street to the mighty emperor himself, everyone has a painful throb somewhere. If it is located and pressed, the agony shoots straight to the heart and brain.'

'Quite true, but unfortunately, this reprobate Shiva seems to have no human failings—no luxurious tastes, no womanising, none of the pleasures that we Khans value so much. So, does he have painful throbs anywhere at all?'

For a little while, Rai Bagan looked down at her toes. Then she looked up and said, 'Bhaisahib, Shivaji has fallen victim to a different kind of obsession.'

'Really? What could that be?'

'He wants to rule over the waves. He wants his own naval force with battleships and gunboats ...'

'Yes, but how does that help us?'

'Don't you see, Bhaisahib? This is his painful throb, and this is what we must exploit. At the Durgadi harbour near Kalyan in Konkan, at the Dharamtar creek beyond and in a few other places, he has begun building ships. He has employed Portuguese shipwrights at ten times their usual rate and set hundreds of labourers to work in his factories there.'

'How does it help us?'

'Bhaisahib, once we begin raiding these places, confiscating the ships and taking over the factories, you can be sure that it won't take any time for Shivaji to come roaring out of his mountain stronghold. When the tiger is lured out of its cave, hunting it becomes so much easier.'

'Waah, sister, waah! This is brilliant.' Shaista Khan's eyes glittered with uninhibited admiration for the woman. 'I had been wondering till this moment: our Emperor has never deigned to honour any man by addressing him as a tiger; so, why would he want to honour a woman by conferring such a title? Now I have the answer.'

After Rai Bagan's visit that morning, Shaista Khan suddenly began to see rays of hope. Kartalab Khan had lately won the fort at Paranda. The Nizam's fort-keeper had handed the fort over to the Mughals without any resistance, but Kartalab had been strutting around Pune with his chest stuck out, in the manner of a soldier who had shed blood for acquiring it.

Struck by a bright idea, Shaista snapped his fingers. He decided to seat the preening Kartalab on his horse and send him into a proper battle. That would show where he truly stood as a warrior. He called the man over and explained the circumstances to him. 'Miyaan Kartalab, one of the reasons this Sivaji has become so conceited is the dominance he now exercises over the coast, with all his gunboats and ships.'

'Simply tell us what we should do, huzoor. Whether it is Nagothane or the Chaul coast, the Panvel creek or Kalyan or the coast along Bhiwandi, you point to it and we shall win it.'

'That's wonderful, Miyaan Kartalab. If you can spell things out in such detail before I have opened my mouth, half the war is already won.'

'Shukriya, huzoor.'

'Kartalab, this is not so much your duty as a challenge.'

'Give me four or five days, huzoor. I shall set off from Pune with a force of thousands of men and animals in the direction of Konkan.'

Seeing Kartalab Khan's overflowing enthusiasm, Shaista Khan felt a tremendous sense of relief. Soon, preparations for Kartalab Khan's campaign were in full swing. Care was taken to ensure that he did not want for anything by way of resources. Twenty thousand of the best horses were picked out, the kind that would be able to gallop through the dense gorges of those parts. There would be ten thousand foot soldiers too.

A number of sardars like Jaivantrao Kokate and Jadhavrao who were setting out on the campaign along with Rai Bagan were veterans who had fought many a battle in the jungles and heaths of the Sahyadris. Even so, as a precaution, Shaista Khan called over old hands like Sardar Chauhan, Amar Singh, Mitrasen and Kachchhap to Lal Mahal and said to them in a grim voice, 'Whether it is Kokate, Jadhavrao or Rai Bagan, remember that they are people affiliated to this soil.'

'What are you suggesting, huzoor? Don't you have faith in these people who have come with you from the north?'

'Who can say what may happen? Often, it is not mere men, but even nature and time that lay the foundation for treachery. If ever you find these people turning sympathetic towards Siva, consider it your duty to leap forward. Hazard your lives if you have to, but this time that wretched enemy Siva should not be allowed any avenue of escape. The longer he eludes our grasp, the more our prestige is shredded to tatters.'

26

AT UMBARKHIND

FEBRUARY 2, 1661

As the grand, picturesque army with twenty-two thousand horses at its head moved enthusiastically along the banks of the river Indrayani, people from nearby villages, largely women and children of the settlements at the foot of the mountains, would line up on either side to watch the passing carnival in awe. Kartalab Khan, seated on his canopy atop an elephant, noticed two high-rising forts on the left. 'These are Shivaji's forts of Lohgadh and Visapur,' Kokate informed him.

As Kartalab Khan stared open-mouthed at the sturdily built twin forts, he had a vague sensation of dread. He turned a tad anxiously to Jadhavrao and asked, 'Is there any possibility of that Siva bombing us from those heights?'

'What bombing can that Bhosala do?' Jadhavrao replied scornfully. 'He doesn't have the courage to come anywhere close to Khan sahib's forces.'

'Why do you say that?'

'Our Shaista sahib has been ensconced in Pune for three years now. What has that Shivaji done, except scurry from one place to another hiding his face? Has he come anywhere close to us?'

'Sardar Kokate,' Kartalab cautioned, 'don't ever fall into the error of underestimating your enemy. It often becomes an invitation to disaster.'

The army pitched camp a number of times and for a number of days as it marched along the Indrayani. At Lohgaon it left the river to go past small, green Maaval hamlets. Passing a relatively large village called Lanavali, they reached Khandala.

It was afternoon and they had to begin climbing down Borghat. As Kartalab Khan and his associates were about to set out with their troops, they heard a commotion erupt in the patch of vegetation beside the camp. Soon, a bunch of soldiers emerged from the bushes escorting four heavily built traders with two women. It appeared to be a Marwari family and they were wailing as they came forward, 'We are ruined, Khan sahib, we are undone.'

'That wretched Shivaji has wiped us out.'

Kartalab Khan observed the distraught family as they stood in front of him. The seth lamented that his silk dhotar was torn, gold buttons had been plucked out of his jacket, and his two grand horses laden with costly goods had been taken away from him. The looters had also stripped the women of their gold and silver ornaments and expensive clothing. On hearing the racket, Rai Bagan brought her horse close and asked, 'Who were these highwaymen? These robbers?'

'They were not robbers, sister; it was that rascal Shivajiraja.'

'Siva?' Kartalab enquired. 'What can Siva be doing in these parts?'

'That vagabond is sitting down there near Khopoli, at the bank of the river.'

'There's a big Maratha army hiding in the jungle at the foot of the hill. Like you, huzoor, they have thousands of horses and camels.'

Rai Bagan and Jadhavrao pacified the agitated Marwari family as best they could. One of the Marwari men, of slighter build than the others, was still so rattled by the robbery that he bowed before Kartalab Khan and whimpered, 'Huzoor, it's soon going to turn dark, and we've got women with us. This Shivaji has unleashed such terror in these parts that I am afraid of what will happen to us. Please, sarkar, allow us to spend the night behind the shield of your army.'

'Look, old man,' Sardar Kokate said, speaking for Kartalab, 'Our army rules do not allow us to accommodate unknown persons in the tents of the soldiers. But you may seek shelter with one of the traders who are accompanying us.'

Kartalab's army called a halt just ahead of the mouth of Borghat. The evening trumpets were sounded. The elephants were brought down on their haunches. The horses were unburdened and given their oats, the camels their wet fodder.

The quartermaster's men bustled about and raised a temporary dining tent for Kartalab, Rai Bagan and other senior sardars. As they sat popping the grapes that were served to them, they were riddled with doubts and uncertainties. What could be going on at the foot of the ghat? How many soldiers had Shivaji assembled?

As they sat worrying, four hot and perspiring horsemen rode up to the tent. They were the quartermaster's men who generally went a dozen or so miles in advance of the army; one of their important tasks was to reconnoitre the route ahead, detect enemy movement or other disturbances, and report back to the main army. Kartalab utilised this opportunity to get a thorough briefing on the situation at the foot of the hill.

'That village down there ... it is called Khupwali or Khopoli or something ... there are dense woods outside it and a big mango orchard inside. It is difficult to guess how many soldiers could be hiding behind those trees. But our estimate is that at least two thousand horsemen are camped there with their margatthya flags flying high. '

While the other sardars looked perturbed, Kartalab surprisingly broke into an amused chuckle and ran his fingers delightedly through his scanty beard. 'What could it be, huzoor,' Sardar Amar Singh enquired, 'that you find satisfying in this situation? Are you privy to some secret information?'

'All right, then,' Kartalab got up. 'Let that Siva sit waiting for us at the foot of the ghat for as many hours as he wants to. Meanwhile, we shall descend from the ghat on the other side and fly away like free birds.'

'What are you saying, Khan sahib?'

'All the information I need has been provided by my spies. That Siva Bhosala travelled from Rajgadh and descended into Konkan four days ago, down the Telbail ghat on the other side of this very mountain. The river Bhogawati flows past the Pen village there. He has begun to gather his army on the banks, and his entire camp lies open and exposed. While he sits waiting for us to arrive via the usual ghat, we shall take this other route and come down upon him from the other side. Thus we shall demolish the entire army that he has assembled at his main camp near Pen.'

'But, Allah, what a man he is! Flies over forests like a bird and swims through rivers like a fish! Here today and hundreds of miles away on some other mountain tomorrow!' The thought of Shivajiraja's presence in the Sahyadri jungles had given several hearts in the Mughal camp severe palpitations.

Kartalab asked his attendants to bring a sheet of paper and began drawing a rough map of the land with a soft piece of coal. 'Jadhavbhai,' he crowed, 'I know a great deal more about the lay of your land than you do. Look at that rise in front. What is it called? Nagaphani or something?'

Kartalab Khan had hired special guides to travel along with the army, people who knew every undulation of the terrain they would be advancing through. These four loose-limbed, nimble men belonged to the Koli and Thakar jungle tribes of those parts; their traditional occupation was gathering honey, wild fruits, lumber and different varieties of grass. Strong and supple as coir ropes, they had callouses on their feet that looked like small knots on trees. Their thick beards and moustaches on their faces reminded one of sheep's wool.

At a sign from the Khan, a couple of them came forward and pointed at a massive eminence that rose up from the Khandala jungles ahead of them. Called Nagaphani, this high cliff was shaped like a hunchbacked man. Regarding a secret but hazardous path that began there, a guide said, 'An extremely difficult pass descends through the gorge on the other side of Nagaphani, a narrow gorge that is known to almost none. Only the most daring of bandits and dacoits are known to use it, that too on the rarest of occasions.'

'How does it serve the dacoits?'

'Sometimes, when very expensive goods are unloaded at the Konkan ports, they smuggle the stuff through these precarious passages to save on customs duty. They make use of the hardiest khillari bullocks to negotiate these treacherous routes. Four hundred of them on a single trip, sometimes.'

'Which ghat is this?'

One of the guides took a piece of charcoal and drew a rough map of the pass on a plank of wood. 'Look, huzoor,' he said, 'it is called the Kurwanda ghat, named after the tiny village of Kurwande on top. This pass goes straight down the mountain into the jungle and meets the village Chavani here. It takes a man one full prahar, which is about three hours, to reach there—provided he's not carrying any load. See this river Amba. If you move along its bank, your last stop will be a village called Umbare, after which this dreadful pass is called Umbarkhind.'

Kartalab Khan decided that it was no use whiling away time in discussions. Now that the sun was on its way down, moving around indiscreetly in these Sahyadri jungles was inviting death. There was no saying when Siva's Maavalis would spring out of the darkness and rest their swords on one's neck. Hence, the Khan was both impatient and edgy. He had revised his plan in a hurry and now failure was completely unaffordable.

The departure horn was blown, hustling the men to get started. The entire caravan turned around and began moving southwards. They passed a number of big and small lakes in Khandala and particularly in Lanavali. The farms in these parts were surrounded by plenty of shrubbery and groves of trees.

They hit Kurwande at twilight. Tents were already erected on a wide stretch of land called the Holi heath. As always, the traders had gone ahead on their mules, arrived early and set up small shops to get an army market going.

When Kartalab Khan's elephant came to a halt near the Kurwande temple, the village had nearly been swallowed up by the night. The Khan's footman placed a ladder for him to descend. He had enquired about the village deity on entering the settlement, and now here he was, standing before an ancient, waist-high, chiselled stone idol of Korai Mata at the base of a tree. The Khan went near the idol with its tiny, burning earthen lamp and laid his head at the deity's feet. He instructed his sardars to offer an oblation of five coconuts and mumbled fearfully, 'Oh goddess of the Hindus, please take us too into your court!'

All eyes were now riveted on the darkness of the land that lay below. The tremor inside the Khan's heart was refusing to subside. The quartermaster's men had put up a big shamiana on the heath for the Khan, in front of which his twelve elephants stood rocking in the cold evening breeze. He assembled his guides and a few of the better-informed locals in the orange light of torches at the entrance of the shamiana and began discussing his movement with them. Having begun to see the perils in his last-minute choice of the Kurwanda ghat, he listened to the villagers with great attention. The question he asked was: how could he take his thirty thousand men and nearly fifteen thousand animals across and down the ghat the next day at the crack of dawn?

'There is no doubt, Khan sahib,' said the village elders, 'that the shortest route to Pen is through the Kurwanda-Umbarkhind ghat.' This endorsement gave Kartalab Khan the satisfaction that his decision was well taken.

Sitting in the light of the torches in the chill night air, the villagers would often sneak apprehensive glances at the elephants that stood in front of the shamiana. Noticing their anxiety, Kartalab Khan asked, 'Haven't you seen elephants before?'

'Janaab, if an unburdened man can break a sweat while tackling that pass, how do you propose to carry these excellent animals through?'

Kartalab's heart lurched into his throat. 'Are you saying,' he asked, 'that elephants have never travelled down this pass?'

'Khan sahib,' an old man replied, 'I have spent seventy monsoons in these jungles, but I have neither seen nor heard of elephants going down that pass.'

'Allah!' the assembly groaned in chorus.

'Even horses defecate copiously as they climb down,' another villager added. 'How can you talk of elephants?'

'The only animals that have the stomach to carry loads along this route are khillari bullocks and some really tough mules.'

Kartalab Khan's face turned dark with worry. His slave had spread the prayer rug for him inside the tent; for the first time in many decades he forgot his duty to Allah. He exchanged a glance with Rai Bagan, perceiving that she was now fully alert to the danger that confronted them. Her heart had begun to beat rapidly too.

As he sat absorbing the darkness around him, the other thing that struck Kartalab—indeed, shocked him—was the extreme shortage of water. The harsh Sahyadri summer had begun. The stream that flowed past Kurvande had formed some eight or ten puddles close to a place called Ghodekhadak, the horse-rock, and the animals had immediately flocked to this spot. The difficulties of watering fourteen thousand animals became immediately obvious. Huge queues had formed everywhere. The grooms and the villagers brought the information that no more than ten thousand or so animals would be able to just about wet their lips; the rest would have to move on thirsty.

As the night advanced, so did Kartalab's anxiety. He once again assembled the elders of the village and the nearby hamlets, and courteously placed gold bracelets upon their wrists. Joining his palms before them deferentially, he said in a hoarse voice, 'My dear elders, I seek your forgiveness. I've got trapped in this difficult pass because I changed my route at the last moment. Time is running out for me. Come what may, you will have to help me take my army through this ravine.'

'Khan sahib,' Rai Bagan mumbled, 'we may be better off if we retrace our path from here.'

'Sister, going back is simply not an option. Our sworn enemy Shivaji is not likely to waste any time in the meanwhile. It is obvious that he is playing games with the Emperor's army. I shall not let him slip away either, but for that I need time and the help of Allah.'

'What, then, can we do?' came the groan from all directions.

'We will simply have to travel through the pass and confront the hardships that fall on our way. No alternative remains.'

The villagers warned him in grim voices, 'Listen, Khan sahib, half of your men are likely to die on the way crying for water.'

'Please, brothers, don't pronounce such frightful outcomes! Suggest some solutions instead!' Kartalab's voice had begun to break.

'Well, do this, at least. Get half your men to begin descending immediately.'

'Why?'

'Once you are past the first two cliffs on the way down, you will reach the turning of Thakarwadi in an hour's time. You'll find three or four big wells there that have water all the year round. You will be able to slake the thirst of your animals.'

'Thank you, brothers, I thank you from the bottom of my heart!'

'The men that remain can be sent down around the time of daybreak. The passage will be easier and the cold morning wind will prevent them from becoming excessively thirsty.'

'But now, what about my elephants?'

The trail that went down the cliffs was full of twists and turns, hedged in on both sides by dense, thorny vines and bushes. There were thick groves of brambly karvanda and kembal plants too. The branches of some gigantic trees on the path hung so low that they made the passage of elephants and even horses impossible. It was, therefore, essential to send an advance party with axes and machetes to hack those low-hanging branches and clear the meshwork of bracken and vines that lay everywhere impeding the movement of travellers.

Looking at the mountain of problems heaped before him, Kartalab was as close to bursting into tears as a warrior can be. Rai Bagan, however, stepped forward and said, 'Don't worry about the elephants, huzoor. I'll take care of them.' Kartalab gave her a wry smile.

There were about seven hundred artisans of all kinds travelling with the army: masons, blacksmiths, carpenters, basket-makers, and the like. They had with them sharp scythes, knives and hatchets. In addition, the villagers supplied them with their own axes and sickles. Rai Bagan gathered young artisans and peasants along with their tools from the small settlements in and around Kurvande. Khan undid the strings of his purse and the sardarin distributed gold coins freely among all who had assembled to help.

A battalion of around a thousand men went down the narrow trail at midnight and began the arduous job of widening it for the army to follow. Kartalab had even sent a couple of elephants along to help them get the measure of the difficulties posed by the route. Wherever the animals were obstructed by bamboo groves and wild vines, axes and machetes would be swung to create a passage wide enough to let them pass through. The pachyderms trumpeted, snorted and grunted with terror as they negotiated the dangerous edges and the sharply falling terrain. Horses defecated each time their hooves slipped. The sounds of the hacking as well as the distress of the animals reached Kartalab as he tossed and turned in bed, fearing what the morrow held.

When dawn broke over the camp, nobody so much as thought about morning ablutions. Every heart was frozen with the fear of the impending journey along the perilous trail through the gorge. The other fear that asphyxiated them was the likelihood of Shivaji's men descending upon them like kites swooping down on helpless chicks.

The sky had turned relatively brighter by the time they reached a hillock outside a village named Mhardand. It was a stiff climb; they wheezed and panted and groaned, but managed to put the hillock behind them. Before them now was a sharp, rugged, precipitous descent, the likes of which they had never encountered before.

Morning had properly arrived by the time the last contingent of Kartalab Khan's men moved out of Kurvande. The transverse fall of land began from the first crag that they passed. Calling it a mountain trail would be a massive understatement. It was more like a series of footholds one would encounter while descending into a deep well, but on a vastly different scale. A single untested step meant doom. The pressure that this descent exerted upon toes and hooves, ankles, calves and knees was enormous for man and animal alike.

By now a summer day was in full bloom, heralded by an unmistakably dry, warm wind. The first leg of the journey was behind them, and soon they reached Thakarwadi which had a dozen or so stubby earth-and-reed Thakar homes and an equal number of houses belonging to the herder community. There were two or three good-sized wells with plenty of water, but drawing the water up in large vessels was a difficult chore.

The wells had been visited the previous night by a ten-thousand-strong company, converting their vicinity into a morass of slime and muck. Seeing the vast assemblage of men and animals milling around there, a few platoon heads decided to play it smart. Instead of waiting endlessly on the periphery of the crowd, they thought it shrewder to take the track down to the base of the crag where, through the jungle vegetation, they could glimpse the dry banks of the Amba river. If there was a bank, their argument went, there was bound to be a river, and if there was a river, surely there would be a few puddles too at the very least!

Soon after they set off down the path, they were pleasantly surprised at hitting a relatively flat jungle track. The thousand-odd artisans and labourers who had preceded the army had done a commendable job of making the trail navigable. But the undulations of the land were beyond their abilities to repair. A half-hour of pleasurable marching was all that they would get. The crag that appeared next and the sharp drop that immediately followed it sent a tremor down their spines. The fall was nothing if not precipitous. The only way to negotiate the downward journey was by putting all their weight on their toes and moving sideways.

The four-footed creatures suffered the most. The horsemen did all that they could to help their steeds find whatever footing was available. As they walked alongside, they held their muzzles close to their chests to assuage their terror. Inevitably, however, increasing numbers of men and animals lost their footing and went screaming down to their doom.

The elephants in particular, it seemed, were marked out for the toll to be paid to Yama, the god of death. Rai Bagan had volunteered to take on the dreadful responsibility of piloting them down the treacherous trail. As she led her own Turkish horse by the muzzle, she managed to keep an unblinking eye on how the elephants were faring. She had assigned a score of men to help each of the mahauts steer his precious charge.

Whenever the occasion demanded, sturdy ropes were wound around them so that they could be lowered using the leverage of a sturdy tree or root nearby. Stout bamboo poles and logs of wood were tied to the soles of their massive feet for securing a better grip on the earth. The malicious trail seemed to have robbed these proud behemoths of all their confidence and their beady eyes flamed with dread as they grunted and snorted and stumbled their way forward.

Soon it was well past breakfast time, and the stinging, singeing summer heat had begun descending upon the jungle. There was no wind either to mitigate its impact. The hundreds of water-suppliers employed by the army roamed far and wide to fill their water-skins. But all the water they had managed to gather was nowhere near enough to so much as wet the lips of the thousands that screamed for it.

The extreme exhaustion caused by that gruelling descent, together with the sapping heat of the Sahyadri summer, brought horsemen and foot soldiers alike to the edge of despair. They rasped as they wailed for water. They had begun to chew on the leaves of wild plants like blueberries and karvanda in the hope of lubricating their parched throats. It took them no time to realise that their hopes were seriously misplaced.

The abuses and curses uttered by the men went up by several decibels, high enough to reach Kartalab's ears. But, circumstances being what they were, he chose to play deaf and dumb to the persistent question: 'Who was the imbecile that chose this route?'

It was after four excruciating hours that the murderous descent came to an end. Just a little further down, past a gentle decline, they could see the tiny village of Chavani. When they turned around to look up at the ordeal they had just emerged from, they could see the hill atop the mountain lift its head towards the sky like a cobra with its hood extended.

The trail now proceeded along the bed of the river Amba. Although there was plenty of greenery on either side, the river had nothing to show for itself except white sand and dry, reddish rocks. With the hot, molten sky overhead and scorching sand underfoot, every throat was desiccated to a point where the mere passage of air made it sting like a raw wound. Although the thirst was killing them, there was no breath or moisture left in their lungs to call out for water. The horses refused to indulge their masters and responded to any effort at mounting them with rearing and kicking.

On either side were high mountains, and in the middle was this white streak of sand with red-hot boulders which should have been a river. The only comfort that Kartalab and his sardars could offer to their distraught and demoralised men was the hope of some water around the next bend. A couple of anaemic puddles that they did encounter were cleaned out by the first few dozen animals. The passing horses' hooves would, in any case, make whatever was left unpotable.

The wind too seemed to have turned into an ally of the Marathas; it had not stirred since morning. The trees that stood still and mute on the forbidding slopes could be soldiers of the devil's own army. The atmosphere was not merely grave—it was phantasmagorical. The silence that reigned in the mountains had taken on a mortuarial quality. All that the luckless soldiers could do was to crawl on.

27

BATTLE IN THE MOUNTAINS

The army marched on for another mile down the dry river bed and arrived at its half-way point. The sun had begun to explode on the heads of the soldiers in a shower of bright orange orbs. Just when it seemed that their ordeal couldn't possibly get worse, they heard the gut-wrenching sound of battle-horns coming from the mountain on the left—and then, from mountain on the right. Trumpets, kettledrums, bugles and war cries soon coalesced in a nightmarish medley of martial music that tied their intestines in knots.

When the infernal music burst out from behind them and then ahead of them too, their minds began to unhinge in unmitigated terror. Hundreds of soldiers simply turned chalk-white and sat down where they stood, in a pantomime of despair. The echoes that multiplied in the mountains did nothing to restore their equanimity. Then came the wails from behind, the piteous keening of men standing naked and unprotected in the presence of their nemesis: 'Sivaji has come! Run! Run if you can!'

The drums, the horns, the strident cries of 'Har har Mahadev' and 'Shivaji Maharaj ki jai' echoing at them from every tree and every fold of the mountain, the sky raining brimstone—there could be no doubt that they had been trapped in hell's own gulch. As pure instinct compelled them to run, they didn't even know which direction to take. Equally disconcerted, equally confused, but with a reputation to protect, sardars like Kokate, Jadhavrao, Mitrasen and Amar Singh tried to reason with them, 'Where will you run, fools! And for how long? Stop milling around. Let's find some way out of this noose.'

Within minutes, their worst nightmares started playing out: from the stands of trees on the mountain slopes, arrows darted out with fearful whistles and began piercing their arms, thighs, chests, backs and necks. Very soon after, it began raining stones, dispatched expertly in their direction with slings and catapults. As they lay bleeding and groaning in agony, their helplessness was compounded by the realisation that they were yet to sight the enemy. While the option of escape had never existed, launching a counter-attack was equally untenable.

To their right stood the Garnala mountain. Going by the sheer volume of the stones that were being flung from the trees there, there was little doubt that each tree concealed at least a dozen margatthyas. From the direction of Sakhu's Thakurwadi, the sheer din of the hideous orchestra that reached them suggested a gathering of at least twenty-five thousand Maavalis up there. There was this other hill that raised its head from behind the broken ridge on the right. At its foot was a village called Chimurde, and from there too loud rallying cries rang out that would need thousands of throats participating. Kartalab Khan, Rai Bagan and other sardars who stood cowering and confounded on the dry river bed were left with no doubt now that they were hemmed in by at least seventy thousand, if not a hundred thousand, Maratha men on three sides.

A frantic, panic-stricken Amar Singh rode up and screeched, 'Khan Sahib, we are inescapably blocked on three sides. There is only one direction in which we can move now.'

'And which is that?'

'The direction we came from.'

'Have you lost your senses, Amar Singh? Just turn around and look at the wall down which we have descended!'

All heads turned involuntarily to stare at the mountain behind them—hardly a mountain, more a wall that rose a sheer two thousand five hundred feet into the sky to meet the cobra hood. The mere thought of the climb churned the entrails of the observers. Rai Bagan burst out, 'Even if we can climb it, which is doubtful, it will take us at least eight hours of excruciating labour, if a minute. And that's only for the men. As for the animals, it had best not be imagined.'

'Taking this route back is impossible,' Kartalab agreed. 'This Siva has reduced us to the state of stray dogs.'

Their world had turned upside down. And now, the top of the crag whence they had descended was tinted with the ochre flags of the Marathas, scotching any thought of return for good.

Three spies rode in with the latest news. 'Huzoor,' they began excitedly, 'that man has been galloping right and left along the mountainside, fanning his men to a red-hot fury that will consume us all. He is unstoppable.'

'Stop blabbering, you idiot! Who are you talking about?'

'Netaji Palkar—'

'Ah, that fiend!' the sardars groaned. 'The only remedy is to have him crushed under an elephant's feet. If that rogue can be eliminated, Sivaji will be left at least half-paralysed. But how does one catch him, in the first place?'

Upon a rather prominent hillock near the village Umbare on the bank of the Amba river were Netaji, Tanaji and a few other Maratha sardars who had participated in the Umbarkhind adventure. The manner in which they sat on their horses revealed their pride and contentment. Three or four nights of meticulous planning and hard work had brought them this resounding success, exactly as Shivraya would have wanted it.

Shivaji himself sat astride his high-backed Kathiawadi steed, cutting an impressive figure. As he surveyed the narrow river bed flanked by tall mountains that ran for a good five miles, he was finding it difficult to suppress the smile of satisfaction that would keep returning to his face. The enemy had been lured into the slender channel between the mountains exactly as planned. Twenty-five to thirty thousand soldiers had found themselves penned in a space so small that they had absolutely no room for manoeuvre.

The ravaged Marwari trader who had met Kartalab Khan the previous evening at the mouth of Borghat now stood proudly astride his Turkish horse and looked at the king with a sense of accomplishment.

'A job well done, wouldn't you say, Vishwasrao?' the king asked rhetorically as he turned to the trusted chief of his espionage squad.

'Absolutely, Raje. The manner in which we have decimated the Khan's army, it's unprecedented,' responded Vishwasrao Dighe.

'We have been preparing for this eventuality since we were barely twelve or thirteen years old, remember? Once we boys set out from Lal Mahal, even these twelve Maavals and thirteen Ners were not enough to satisfy our greed for adventure, right, Vishwasrao?'

'Perfectly true, Raje. I remember that we had at least two or three of our jungle meals at exactly this spot on the bank of the Amba.'

'Aha!' exclaimed Netaji with joy. 'Now I understand why you chose this spot for the ambush and how you managed everything with such precision!'

Bone-tired, hungry, thirsty and disoriented, Kartalab Khan and his soldiers stood on the dry river bed in a state of complete despair. A few of his spies galloped in from the east and one of them took his horse right up to the Khan. 'I have seen him with my own eyes, huzoor,' he blurted out.

'Seen whom?'

'Shivaji himself! In flesh and blood!'

'What? Shivaji himself? In person?'

'Yes, huzoor.'

'What does he look like?'

'Dressed and ready for battle. Impregnable steel armour, helmet, a quiver of arrows on his back. He wore a necklace of precious stones and a belt of gold around his waist to hold his sword. The lustre that he exuded as he sat on his horse, he could be the sun in human form!'

'What?' Kartalab Khan was so incensed at this glowing description of his enemy from the mouth of his own minion that he sprang down from his steed, lifted his horsewhip and let it fall with all his pent-up frustration on the poor man's back. 'You dog, you! If he is a sun, then what am I, you blackguard? A dung-fly?'

He began belabouring the poor spy with such fury that Rai Bagan had to intervene. 'What are you doing, Khan sahib?' she remonstrated. 'Please get a hold of yourself. It is true that Shivaji has completely outfoxed us and snared us in this gully, but letting off steam on a poor servant will not help us in any way.'

'What do you want me to do then?' Kartalab screeched in exasperation.

'Huzoor, as the commander-in-chief of this army, you will have to take some firm decisions before it is too late. Even if we escape from the Maratha sword, we shall surely die of hunger and thirst if we don't find a way out.'

Kartalab could not fail to notice the tremor of fear that undergirded Rai Bagan's voice. 'So, what are you suggesting?' he said. 'Do you want me to surrender?'

'Well, you may at least examine that alternative carefully.'

'Over my dead body!' he screamed arrogantly, though not altogether convincingly.

'Khan sahib, look at all these parched mountains and gorges that surround us. Already we have no water to drink, let alone cook with. Please use your head, not your heart, while making this decision, and make it quickly! Every moment's delay in this dire situation is costing us the precious lives of our men and animals, and will ultimately lead to the annihilation of the entire army. You will know where to place the responsibility if this happens.'

But it appeared that Kartalab was not willing to accept the gravity of the crisis in which he and his army were caught. 'Sister,' he said obstinately, 'I know that some of our men are trying to slip away, but the majority are quite ready to tighten their belts and launch themselves at the enemy; our real strength is in our numbers.'

'In the first place, huzoor,' Rai Bagan went on doggedly, 'you are grievously mistaken if you believe that our men are in a fit state of body or mind to confront the enemy. Secondly, even if they can be persuaded to fight, in which direction will they shoot their arrows? They can see the weapons of the enemy, and feel their sting. But do they see the enemy at all? Who will they rush upon?'

'Sister, your words are those of a coward.'

'Khan sahib, please open your eyes to the circumstances we are in. Hunger and thirst have already rendered our men and animals incapable even of fleeing.' She looked in the direction of the sun that had begun its journey west and said, 'Once the sun starts descending behind the mountains, we shall almost certainly be doomed; afterwards, the outside world will not even know what happened to us.'

Amar Singh stepped forward to support Rai Bagan's effort and said, 'Huzoor, darkness has always been Siva's ally. These margatthyas are famous for their night raids; this time, it looks like a certainty. In that case, this may well be our last night on earth.'

'The two of you are trying to demoralise me,' was Kartalab's mulish response.

The intrepid warrior and proud leader in Kartalab Khan was finding it impossible to digest the thought of a humiliating defeat. However, as he looked helplessly around, eyes moist and frantic, reality began to sink in, which brought tears of impotence flowing down his cheeks. This mountain pass of the Sahyadris was clearly a playing field of ghosts and demons. The sun, the wind, the water, even destiny, appeared to have committed themselves to the cause of the margatthyas. The noose that this merciless gorge had thrown around their army would certainly tighten as the night set in, and there was no saying how many of them would survive to return to their families. The only way out, however disgraceful, was to capitulate.

Mitrasen, an important chieftain, was assigned the task of negotiating the surrender with Shivaji. He immediately mounted his horse, white flag in hand, and trotted away towards the distant knoll that the Mughal spies had identified as the enemy's lookout. As Mitrasen took the bend of the river, the rise came in sight, where the Maratha king stood as if expecting him. Kartalab's envoy bowed before Shivraya and said in a humble voice, 'Rajaji, you and your mountains here have brought Mughal pride to its knees.'

'Speak on,' Shivraya said with a pleasant smile playing upon his visage. 'Any discomfort?'

'Which discomfort do I start with, huzoor? We haven't even had a proper drink of water for the past two days.'

'So, what do you seek from me?'

'Forgive my impertinence, huzoor, but I come to plead for safe passage out of this valley of death.'

'Well, all right, we are willing to grant you and your men the gift of life. But obviously, there will be conditions.'

'Huzoor?'

'In the simplest of words, you will move out of here with not a stitch more than the clothes on your back.'

In due course, Kartalab Khan, Rai Bagan and the other Mughal sardars presented themselves before the king to pay their respects. They were left speechless by the strategies and skills in mountain warfare displayed by the Marathas under the astute leadership of Shivraya. The king extracted handsome ransoms from each one of them for the privilege of walking away with their breaths intact. Several Maavali soldiers emerged from their hiding places behind trees and rocks, dancing with their bows and spears held high. But a large number of them played their victory drums and blew their horns without revealing themselves, continuing to create the impression that they were present in their tens of thousands.

The Maratha chieftains set about gathering everything that they could use from the defeated men: elephants and horses, weapons and ammunition like guns, grenadess, swords and spears, tent material of the best quality and, of course, several trunks full of treasure. The sardars were also divested of any jewellery that they wore upon their person. A number of the Mughal units had actually fled even before the deal was struck, leaving all their belongings behind.

Shivraya requested Rai Bagan to step forward and gifted her with robes of honour.' We are proud to meet you, daughter-in-law of our Udamrao Deshmukh,' he said with great courtesy. 'Your skill in horse riding and your exploits on the battlefield are as admirable as those of Chand Bibi herself.'

'Thank you, Maharaj,' Rai Bagan said as she bowed before the king.

'We do have one regret, though.'

'What can that be, Maharaj?'

'The sharp-edged sword that glitters in your strong arms … it is a pity that it flashes for the benefit of the outsider, instead of for its own people.'

Kartalab Khan, Rai Bagan, Mitrasen, Amar Singh and the other chieftains walked back to the river bed to gather their men and begin their trudge into the wilderness. The heavy losses incurred by this humiliating defeat had brought their heads low and slowed their steps to a shuffle. They hadn't taken many steps forward when they were arrested by a call from the king, 'Stay, Khan sahib!'

The party turned around, walked back towards the king and stood waiting for his pronouncement. Shivraya had, meanwhile, given some instructions to his fort-keeper. 'Khan sahib,' he said, addressing Kartalab, 'it does not look right to us that princes and chieftains of your eminence should plod your way out of our land like forlorn travellers.'

'No, no, Maharaj, we really have no complaints.'

'How will this do? Even if you have laid down your weapons, you have battled with a king. You cannot be made to walk away like travellers looted by dacoits.'

Kartalab and his sardars were quite taken aback. Meanwhile, the fort-keeper had returned with six of the best horses that had been confiscated and handed them over. Pointing at the two guides who would accompany them, the king continued, 'Don't wander around in the jungle endlessly. These men will take you straight across the two depressions and then you will come to Khalapur, where you will meet a flowing river. To the right you will see Borghat, which offers the straightest route to Pune.'

'A thousand thanks, Raja sahib,' said an overwrought Rai Bagan. 'It is so heartening to see that the large-heartedness that distinguished your revered father Shahajiraje Bhosale courses through your veins too.' With that expression of gratitude, the six of them bowed low before Shivraya and left.

The spoils of victory collected from the Mughal army were brought to the village of Umbare. The king's men set about organising the immense hoard and arranging for its storage with customary discipline. The various items it contained were systematically sorted and marked to be sent to their assigned places in the fort.

A dinner of jhunka and bhaakari was arranged for the twelve hundred or so men present. For the previous three days, Shivaji and his lieutenants Netaji, Tanaji and Vishwasrao had been so engrossed in planning the details of the campaign that they had lost all sensation of hunger or thirst. Now, when Netaji saw his chief finally bite into hot bhaakaris with joy and contentment, he said, 'Raje, now you must return to Rajgadh. How much longer can you keep grinding on?'

'Netokaka,' the king replied, 'I have always held rest, relaxation and recreation in contempt. Our entire life is a razor-sharp sword whose edge I cannot allow to rust or go blunt. It is an ever-expanding flame, a belching furnace whose intensity must not subside even for a moment.'

'What do you have in mind, then, Raje?'

'Netokaka, I am making arrangements to equip you with an army that you will secretly maintain in the jungles that lie between Khalapur and Jambhulpada. If the Mughal armies try to come down the Kasara ghat near Nashik, or move towards Borghat, Telbail or Waghjai from Pune, your task will be to pin them down in those jungles.'

'And where are you headed?'

'I propose to go to Konkan and snatch back from both our local and foreign enemies the coastal lands they have been nibbling away for a long time. I am completely committed to having our victory flags flutter all across Konkan. There is no holding back now.'

Netaji couldn't contain the joy that was bubbling up inside him. He went close to Shivraya, held his hand and said with unconcealed delight, 'Raje, I cannot restrain myself from congratulating you.'

'What for, Netokaka? What new thing has happened?'

'How can you ask me this, king?' Netaji crooned. 'Here's a general who has barely twelve hundred soldiers, but he uses them with such dexterity that he brings a Mughal army of twenty-five thousand to desperate straits. He compels it to surrender abjectly! He strips them of everything but the clothes on their backs and gets them to flee with their tails stuck firmly between their legs. In the annals of war, have you heard of any episode that bears even a close resemblance to this one? Waah, Raje, we have had the good fortune to witness this miracle—indeed, to participate in it—and there's no greater blessing than to have served under this general.'

28

DOWN THE COAST

The king had no time to tarry at Umbarkhind; he set off immediately with an army of seven thousand men. The quartermaster staff were given instructions to turn their horses in the direction of Konkan in the south. The beating of the kettledrums sent currents of excitement coursing through the veins of not just men but even the animals.

Whenever a campaign was announced at short notice, the king would hold his war council in a tent erected on the open ground of a heath. At the outset, Shivraya informed Netaji, 'While I advance, your job will be to keep the rear safe and secure. After the mortification that Shaista has suffered, Delhi is not going to sit idly. There is every danger of Shaista's reserve force descending upon us from the Tikona, Visapur, Lohgadh and Tung, seeking vengeance.'

Netaji was somewhat saddened by the king's decision to leave him behind. He remonstrated, 'Maharaj, both the natives and the firangis of Konkan regard me as your shadow. How can you move ahead without your shadow in tow?'

'Netokaka, my plan is to go quite deep into the south along the coast. After the disgraceful defeat he has suffered, Shaista is quite likely to—'

'If it is revenge we are speaking of, he could mount an assault on Rajgadh too. In such an eventuality, who will rush to defend our capital city?' Netaji queried anxiously.

'The answer is obvious, Netokaka. Do you know of any person who can beat you in the alacrity needed for this enterprise? In brief, if I have the assurance that my capital city, my possessions, my mother and my entire family are safe under the protection of Netaji Palkar, I shall have no anxiety while I roam the south.'

The king's trust in Netaji, displayed so generously and so publicly, moved everyone present. The sardars broke into loud applause, while Netaji's eyes brimmed over.

After the meeting, Shivraya stretched himself out on the rug for a much-needed rest. He had barely slept for a couple of hours when his ears were assailed by the sound of huge waves breaking upon the shore. He woke up with a start to realise that he was only dreaming. As he hurriedly stepped out of the tent, Siddhi Hilaal, who had been sleeping on a rough blanket in the open air, sprang to his feet and bowed in respect.

Netaji, who met them outside, again expressed concern about the king's health. 'It's good, Raje,' he said, 'that you have begun this process of destroying your enemies; but depriving yourself of sleep will not help. The body and the mind need rest.'

'I don't know what to do about it, Kaka,' Shivraya replied. 'The sound of the waves has been churning me up lately. The coast that stretches from Goa and Vengurla down south up to Vasai and Virar in the north … it keeps dancing before my eyes. There is a single cry that keeps reverberating in my ears: take control of it as you would throw a saddle upon a horse! It is the call of Goddess Jagdamba and of Destiny herself. How, then, can I think of food and rest?'

As the king and his commander-in-chief were exchanging these thoughts, Tanaji Malusare quietly put in, 'Maharaj, now that you are leaving Netajidada behind, please cast us in the role of your shadow during this campaign.'

Casting an affectionate look at his diligent lieutenant, the king said, 'You already occupy the front row in the shrine of my heart, Tanaji.'

'Maharaj, if you are heading in the direction of Chiplun anyway, you could make a small halt at this village called Umarath—'

'Your village is not exactly on the way, Tanaji, and I am in a tearing hurry. I have to go past Dabhol right down to Kudaal in the southern region of Konkan, and that too within fifteen days.'

'Please, Maharaj, don't say no. My mother Sarsadevi worships you as she worships the sun and the moon. Please make a small detour for her.'

Tanaji had been at the forefront of several of Shivraya's principal campaigns: the assault on the Moreys of Jawali, the suppression of dacoits like Kallu, Subhanya and Yallya in the Mahad region, and many more. With foresight and acuity, he had inducted the dacoits into the Maratha army and given them important positions. Thus, he had performed the miracle of converting these hard-nosed bandits who had lived by plundering the villages into the service of the Swarajya.

The king had heard much about Sarsabai, the mother of Tanaji and Suryaji Malusare. She was the patlin of the village Godoli near Panchgani. When an Adilshahi official of Wai had deceitfully killed her husband Kaloji, she took her two young sons and crossed the crests and canyons of the Sahyadris to return to her father's village Umarath. But when she came within sight of the village, she was struck by doubt. Would her blood relatives support her happily or would she be an imposition upon them? Not wanting to take a chance, she took shelter in a cave near a waterfall in the jungle close to the village.

When some children of herders from the village came to the jungle to gather twigs, they saw her there and reported the matter to her relatives. Shelaram rushed to the jungle in the company of other villagers and escorted the self-respecting woman home. They built a house with a single sloped roof for her in Umarath, where she brought up her two bold sons by the sweat of her labour.

On February 3, 1660, at daybreak, Shivraya was pressing forward through the jungles on his horse. He had with him Tryambak Bhaskar to manage his administrative affairs and brave warriors like Tanaji and Nilkanth Sarnaik for strength of arms. Tanaji was continuing to insist on a visit to Umarath. The army's route lay along the jungle track to the west of the village, before crossing Poladpur and then traversing the Kashedi ghat. At this stage, time was of the essence.

The king discussed the matter with his associates and found a compromise. It had been planned that he would spend about five or six hours in a mango orchard on the banks of the river Savitri near Poladpur. Some three hundred horsemen would stay with him as a royal guard while the bulk of the king's force plundered the town of Nizampur. Suryaji was assigned the responsibility of bringing his mother over during this interlude.

Accordingly, after cleaning out the market of Nizampur in the morning, the main army moved on towards Mangaon, Mahad and beyond, while a select few stayed behind at the riverbank. Suryaji galloped off in the direction of Umarath. For Tanaji's mother, the mere prospect of this meeting with the king was an overwhelming experience. She was finding it impossible to contain her joy. Having brought along some delicious shevai that she had dried on her rooftop, she presented it to Shivraya soaked in milk and jaggery. The king was visibly delighted as he consumed it with his associates.

In the evening, torches were lit in the orchard. Only two small tents had been erected for the king, to offer him some protection from the wind. Although Sarsabai was in her seventies, she looked a good ten or fifteen years younger. Wrinkles had begun to appear on her face, but the constant hard work of tending to the farm and the animals had kept her muscles taut and her joints supple. Her skin too had a healthy glow. In her early youth, she had got her right arm tattooed with floral patterns from the wrist to the elbow, among which the king saw the word 'Kaloji', her late husband's name.

Shivraya was instantly drawn to Sarsabai's affectionate and expressive nature, and the energy she exuded. The plan had been that he would set off with his men immediately after dinner so that he could cross the sharply rising Kashedi ghat before they made their next halt. But the old woman's simple charm had worked its magic on him. 'Subedar,' he said to Tanaji, 'please inform the administrator that my greed for the company of Tanba's mother does not allow me to part with her. We shall leave only at the crack of dawn tomorrow.'

After instructing his men to start cooking their meal, he turned to Sarsabai and said, 'Mother, will you fulfil a small desire of mine?'

'Ask for anything, Raje. I've already handed over my sons in the service of the Swarajya. If you want this old hag to stand somewhere, stick in hand, and do guard duty, I shall be delighted to obey.'

'The soldiers travelling with me will soon have supper ready. Please stay behind to share it with us. Your son will take you back to your village at daybreak tomorrow.'

Sarsabai's face lit up. However, the next moment, she turned to her son and upbraided him, 'Why didn't you tell me in advance, boy? The king is our guest, and his entire company should be treated to dinner. Go and call the villagers over. All those big vessels used for cooking during the carnivals are easy to retrieve from the temple warehouse. Give us a little time, Raje. It won't take long for the food to be ready.'

The king laughed heartily and then addressed the old woman, 'Tanba's mother, this is our Swarajya, not the caravan of the Mughals. Their armies carry with them a fully equipped kitchen, complete with a battalion of cooks, their minions, huge vessels and tons of raw ingredients to cook and eat. We in our Swarajya need none of that. Even our capital is nothing more than a token presence at Rajgadh. Our palace has no walls. The service of our poor subjects is our sole act of worship. Our real wealth is our twelve Maavals and thirteen Ners.'

Tanaji's mother could see evidence to support the king's words in whichever direction she looked. Every horse carried two bags hanging on either side of their saddle. One bag contained oats, grams and occasionally even green fodder for the animal. The other bag carried millet flour, chutney and salt as well as cooking utensils like skillets and flat, shallow vessels. If ever these men were required to negotiate a jungle trail or a steep ravine, or if they were trapped or encircled by the enemy, they had enough provisions with them to keep starvation at bay. They would simply arrange three stones in a triangular pattern, set alight some twigs and get their hearths going. After a meal hurriedly cooked and consumed steaming hot, they would be ready in very little time to confront the enemy again.

This night too, the soldiers worked in groups of two and three and lit up their makeshift hearths. When Shivraya's cook Subhanya sat down to pat the dough for the bhaakaris on a wooden board, Sarsabai swooped down upon him and pushed him aside. She patted and roasted a couple of naachani bhaakaris and served them to the king with extreme fondness and care. When the king desired her to join him for dinner, she turned the offer down saying, 'You must eat first, king. How can a mother eat before first feeding her child?'

The brothers Tanaji and Suryaji were consuming more with their eyes than with their mouths. A strange contentment had filled their minds so that their desire for food had virtually vanished. Suryaji looked at Tanaji and asked, 'Why do you sit there looking so lost and silent, dada?'

'See for yourself, boy. Like the first showers that fall upon the dry earth and become one with it, so does our king become one with those around him. There's just one thing that I desire from the gods now.'

'What's that?'

'The good fortune to die for a single cause, fighting on the battlefield for this Shivajiraje of ours!'

Sarsabai had heard many stories about Shivraya, stories of the difficult circumstances in which his parents Jijausahib and Shahajiraje had brought him up. Now that she had this opportunity of being in his presence, she asked him how they were doing and when he had met them last. Suddenly, the king's throat clogged and his eyes brimmed with tears.

Baring his heart to the old woman, he said, 'Even the birds on the trees go back to their nests for warmth and togetherness, but I have no such luck. For many months now, I have been riding here and there like a man possessed, running one campaign after another. That makes it impossible for me to get so much as a glimpse of my mother for months on end. But now that you ask, Tanba's mother, here's another painful regret that I must confess to. I have suffered twenty hot, searing summers now, endured twenty years of rain and storms, since the last time I set eyes on my father.'

A lump had formed in his chest; words had become difficult to formulate and pronounce. He was silent for a moment or two, so as to compose himself. 'Why should a person turn to stone in pursuit of one's duty? Why should one turn into a saw and keep lacerating one's own heart? This wretched pain cannot be put on display, but there isn't a moment when it is not felt deep in one's gut.'

Hearing these words, the men in the king's camp stayed awake till late into the night. Shivraya departed from the spot at daybreak, but not before taking the old woman's blessing and arranging for Suryaji to escort her back to Umarath.

The king's horse had settled into its steady trot again. Time was short and the tasks were many. The Konkan coast that was writhing under the firangis' heel had to be set free. For this enterprise and for others that would follow, he would need strong, committed, tenacious, enthusiastic youngsters. The process of identifying and recruiting them had begun, but it required speeding up.

The royal retinue stopped at the river Vasishth near Chiplun. After an elaborate bath, the king climbed up a charming hillock where he visited Lord Parshuram's ancient temple and paid obeisance. He arranged for regular worship to be performed at the temple as well as an annual remittance to be made to the Vedic scholar Govind Bhatt for conducting the rituals.

Ever since he set out on his Konkan campaign, he had been unable to rid his mind of the images of two worthies: Suryarao Surve of Shrungarpur and Jaswantrao Dalvi of Palwan. He could not forget the mischief that this traitorous pair had manufactured during the siege of Panhala. These two had also set Siddhi Johar on Shivraya's trail after he had slipped out of the fort that stormy night. Subsequently, they had done all that they could to prevent the king from reaching the safety of the Vishalgadh fort, but had been roundly belaboured by his men for their effort. Yet, even after being taught so many lessons, the canker of perfidy had refused to depart from their souls.

As they approached the dense green region of Palvan, the excitement among Shivraya's men increased palpably. After the Vishalgadh episode, Jaswant Dalvi had left Tanaji Malusare and the others feeling so bitter that they had decided to give him a thrashing he would never forget. They resolved to lay snares around Palvan as one does to catch a wild jungle cat, hang Dalvi upside down from the tree outside the Dalmeshwar temple and beat him within an inch of his life.

They crossed dark-green groves of coconut and areca palms with Tanaji leading the pack. Shivraya saw him stop at the boundary of Palvan, stand there observing for a while and then come galloping back. 'Maharaj,' he yelled from a distance, mingled pride and disappointment in his voice, 'the jungle cat has fled.'

'Where?'

'A traitor will seek shelter under another traitor's roof, won't he?'

'Ah! So Jaswant Dalvi has found refuge with Suryarao Surve at Shrungarpur, has he?' Shivraya voiced his hunch.

An important thing the king noticed was that not a single native sword was unsheathed to counter his advance against Dalvi in the entire region of Palvan and Dapoli. On the contrary, the common Konkani folk had celebrated the king's arrival by beating drums of joy and tossing gulaal in the air. The king took this opportunity to appoint a fresh set of officers under a new chieftain to replace the one who had fled.

Within the short duration of his reign so far, Shivraya had experienced the many ups and downs of kingship, and suffered assaults delivered by men and by nature. As a result, he had matured in a hurry. The Shivaji who was prone to rush into a battlefield and thrust his chest against blazing cannons only a few years ago had now become a great deal more patient, sensitive and devout. Wherever he went on campaigns now, he would worship at the local temples as well as meet and hold discussions with the scholars and holy men of those parts.

When his regiment reached the coastal town of Kelashi, he went to meet a Muslim holy man by name of Yakootbaba Sarvari. The fakir had arrived on this coast from a faraway Arab land a few years ago and moved around dispensing wisdom to the inhabitants of Dapoli-Ratnagiri. He now had a vast following of disciples belonging to all castes and creeds. Shivraya was deeply affected by the service the fakir was rendering to the unwell and the unhappy.

Seeing the impecunious circumstances in which the man lived, and the fact that the crowds of devotees who came regularly to visit him had no shelter of any kind, the king said, 'Fakir baba, at the very least, a person of your benevolence and piety should have a roof over his head. Please allow me to have a hall built here.'

Despite the fakir's protestations, the king allotted six hundred acres of land and gave orders for the construction of adequate shelter for the holy man and his followers.

As he was moving out of the Kelashi region, the king looked carefully at the placid sea to its west. His experienced eyes immediately told him that if a foreign power ever anchored its ships in these waters, defending the region would be well-nigh impossible. He immediately instructed Tryambak Bhaskar to draft and issue an order for the construction of the Mandangadh fort next to Dapoli. He also started building another fort called Palgadh close by.

The Adilshahi chief of the station at Sangameshvar had got wind of Shivaji's imminent invasion and decamped, fearing for his life. Late that night, the king's cavalry was negotiating a narrow, slippery track that ran along the elevated bank of the river Shastri. The trail wound its way through jungles densely packed with vines and thickets of taru and kalaki. The darkness created by this thick vegetation was so intense that a few horses lost their footing in the slime, which brought the others crashing into them. Since the downward incline was also sharp, their legs twisted and buckled; the spines of two unfortunate animals actually snapped, rendering them immediately useless. The next day, their carcasses were dragged out of the water and abandoned at a distance.

That evening, as they sat in conference, Shivraya brought up the state of disrepair in Sangameshwar and said to Malusare, 'Tanaji, my friend, it looks like you may have to stay behind here.'

'Have I erred in some way, Maharaj?'

'Nothing of the kind. It's just that we need you to work with the plumb-line rather than with the sword for some time. Take charge of building a good road here which is about five miles long. You've seen how we had to lose eight or ten healthy horses because of that wretched track. Other travellers have suffered similar misfortunes, and this should not happen in the future.'

The wounds inflicted by Suryarao Surve's treachery at the foot of Vishalgadh were still raw for many, and they had begun harping on the need to exterminate him. But the king was mulling over other troublemakers as well. There were several ruling families in the Konkan region who were swollen with conceit. After building fortresses for themselves, they had begun fawning at the feet of Adilshah on the one hand, and taking pleasure in persecuting their subjects on the other.

Shivraya had lately been gravitating towards a more moderate stance. Instead of coming down on them with a heavy hand, he was seriously considering the conciliatory approach of winning their hearts. Addressing his agitated associates, the king said with a smile, 'Taking into account the changed circumstances of these times, I believe that we should grant them forgiveness.'

'Who's "them"?' Tanaji asked in a raised voice.

'Suryarao Surve of Shrungarpur and his friends. Let's try to accommodate them in our Swarajya enterprise, offer them friendship, and win them over.'

'No, never, Maharaj!' Tanaji voiced his protest. 'That wriggling, poisonous worm from Shrungarpur is not worthy of being taken into our company.'

But by the time the meeting was over, the king had consulted all his chieftains and found most of them sympathetic to his line of thinking. 'All right, then,' he declared, 'we have resolved to forget the past and offer Surve one more chance to mend his ways.'

When their agent Sonopant returned from Shrungarpur the next evening, he was completely bowled over. 'Surve extended such overweening hospitality,' he chuckled, 'that it was difficult for us to hold him back. He didn't stop at that. He sends the message that Maharaj should consider him as a slave one buys in a market, and that he would offer Maharaj the fealty that is expected of such a minion.'

'But Sonopant, the man's past deeds suggest that his words can't be trusted,' growled Tanaji.

Tanaji's reservations again put the king in a thoughtful mood. After due consideration, he pronounced, 'We have a kingdom to administer and preserve. There are occasions when even the stupidest of persons have to be treated with deference in the interest of public welfare.'

Shivraya then dispatched this message to Surve: 'We are pleased with your declaration of loyalty. As we proceed on our campaign towards lower Konkan, we are leaving behind a small army unit in Sangameshwar under the charge of our Tanaji Malusare. While we are engaged in our enterprises on the southern coast, we hope that you, Tanbaji and the other officials will run a good administration here with a single mind.'

29

ASSAULT ON RAJAPUR

MARCH 10, 1660

'Doroji,' Shivraya said to Doroji Phaakade who was riding alongside him, 'when that Englishman Revington aimed his cannon at the Panhala battlement, I felt that he had actually aimed it at my chest. The very thought of that incident blows my mind to bits.' The king was in a hurry to see that red-faced Henry Revington in person.

While the Maratha army was galloping at breakneck speed towards Rajapur, news of the imminent invasion had preceded them, plunging the English warehouse in a state of turmoil. The harbour town was agog with the rumour that Shivaji's forces could ride in at any moment. The markets were buzzing.

Richard Napier, Samuel Bernard and other English subordinates of Revington stood nervously before their chief officer. Although the river was swollen with water from the creek, the Englishmen had plunged in with their horses to present themselves before their boss, soaking wet, wondering what his reaction would be. Throwing a scornful look at them, Revington snarled, 'Siva? What Siva? Is he a mountain or something? Why are you so perturbed?'

'Mr. Henry, sir, his strength has grown by leaps and bounds. He now controls the entire Kalyan-Bhiwandi coast and its trade—'

'—and he has been building fifty warships of the finest quality near the Chaul harbour—'

'And do you remember, sir, that you had aimed your cannon at his Panhala fort? It did him no harm at all. On the contrary, he has been flying in all directions like an eagle ever since. Let us be sensible, sir, and preempt this calamity. Let us reach out to him and at least pretend to make peace.'

'Stop this nonsense!' Revington barked. His earlobes and the tip of his nose had turned red. 'That ordinary brigand may scare you, but he doesn't scare me.'

'Sir, a little patience—'

'Enough! No more of your blather. Do you think he is some kind of a phantom? A magician?'

His subordinates knew that Revington was too conceited to allow space for any opinion except his own. After usurping power at the Rajapur factory of the East India Company, he had become even more self-seeking, whimsical and irresponsible. And he had never hesitated to promote his interests at the expense of the company.

The warehouse was built on the raised bank of a stream that met the creek that lay between Dhootpapeshwar and Rajapur. While Revington was shouting his subordinates down, a loud uproar emerged from the bank below. A number of villagers had crossed over to the warehouse and were screaming in panic as they jumped out of their boats, 'Run, hurry! Save the warehouse! Shivaji has arrived with an ocean-sized army!'

Three company heralds raced up to the warehouse and stood panting in front of the gate. They seemed to have lost their voices with all the shouting they had done. Wiping the sweat off their white brows, the English officers rushed down to the heralds. Samuel asked, 'Have you seen them with your own eyes?'

'Yes, Saiba, yes! A huge cavalry force is racing in from the west. The horses' hooves have kicked up so much dust that the sky has turned red.'

The firangis were so terrified on hearing this report that they began running down the slope towards the river. Soon, the chief accountant, the guards, and every other Englishman on the premises had fled to the jungles that lay behind the warehouse. As Henry Revington stood and watched, the entire building emptied out.

He stood like a candle flame flickering in a haunted house. The loneliness of his position struck him hard and he broke into a sweat. After making a few futile calls for his servants, he rushed out of the warehouse, sprang on his horse and waded across the slimy creek. Once on the other side, he began the steep climb up the slope, eager to reach the security that only the companionship of his countrymen could give. The fear of loneliness can be truly felt when one is left alone.

Two thousand horsemen and an equal number of foot soldiers were rapidly closing in on Rajapur. The mere name of the town would inflame the king and make him urge his horse faster. The picture of the arrogant Revington would immediately spring to his mind's eye, standing by the long-range cannon on the hill next to Pawangadh. There was also that hateful Union Jack fluttering in the wind beside it. The memory of that scene set his entire being on fire.

Very soon, houses and groves of coconut and areca palms became visible, tucked into the folds of the valley abutting the creek. Wherever Shivraya went, it had become his custom to meet and confer with the elders and other respectable residents of the place. Accordingly, his heralds had reached Rajapur in advance to make arrangements for such a council.

On the outskirts of Rajapur was a stretch of open land where mats had been spread on the red soil for people to sit. All the local worthies were there: the Hindu and Muslim merchants who had business dealings with the warehouse at the Rajapur harbour, the moneylenders, agents and brokers involved in the buying and selling of spices. There were also touts who had lately become rich through their dealings with foreign traders, the spoiled sons of some wealthy families and a few haughty Arabs.

Also in the gathering was a huge crowd of Malabari labourers who transported goods to and from the harbour and adolescent boys from settlements near the creek who drifted around doing whatever odd jobs came to hand. They had all come to feast their eyes on Shivraya. The women too stood leaning against the trunks of mango and jackfruit trees, happy to catch a glimpse of the king from a distance. All these people—men and women, young and old—were totally engrossed in drinking in the pleasant, handsome, magnetic personality of their king; their eyes had been thirsting for this sight for a very long time.

Nothing gave Shivraya greater joy than being in the proximity of his people, giving ear to their problems and woes. He listened to them with rapt attention. When he turned his eyes to the left, he noticed a few carrot-red men in red robes and triangular hats. These were Revington and a few of his colleagues who had evidently thought it a smart move to infiltrate this gathering of ordinary folk, in order to obtain an audience with the king. It was their fond belief, pehaps, that this approach would grant them absolution for their past sins.

Shivraya's eyes slid over the assemblage of poor labourers and clumsily clad traders, and finally came to rest on the firangis. At the sight of those abominable white men, the eyes of this man who was known for his patience and cool temperament hardened. The volcano lying dormant inside him erupted. He pointed his finger at the most conceited-looking personage of the lot and growled, 'You, white man, why are you sitting here? Who invited you?'

The daggers that his looks were throwing at them made the Englishmen squirm. 'How can you come to a meeting without being invited? Have you English people any courtesy left in you or not?' The king made a valiant effort to restrain his anger, but he did not quite succeed. 'Why do you think that you are fit to be tolerated in the company of decent human beings? I have yet to come across a worse set of blood-sucking bandits than you. And idiots, to boot.'

Several of the Maratha chieftains who were present, like Doroji Phaakade, Ragho Ballal Atre, Rahuji Somnath and Moropant, were dumbstruck. They had never imagined that their courteous, soft-spoken, personable king could carry such a streak of anger inside him. An ill-tempered trooper whipping his recalcitrant horse couldn't have done a more merciless job.

The king pointed at the tall, rather horsy-looking Englishman whom he had first addressed and asked Doroji, 'Doroji, is this the king among fools who goes by the name of Revington? He looks quite like the rascal who had aimed his cannon at us in Panhala. Could he be the wayward firangi who has forgotten that he is a trader and become insolent enough to dabble in the politics of our country?'

'Rajaji, please forgive me,' Revington blubbered fearfully. 'It was a grievous error on my part.'

'You, Revington, whose job it is to stand with a measuring scale at the harbour, how could small fry like you gather the temerity to point a cannon at us? Tell me now, once and for all, whose flag were you fluttering next to the cannon that day?'

'Huzoor, that was the Union Jack of Great Britain, the flag of our queen.'

'And who did the cannon belong to?'

'Sorry, sir, but the cannon belonged neither to our country nor to our company,' Revington mumbled, hardly able to meet the king's eyes.

The king glowered at the man. Despite being subjected to such public humiliation, he seemed strangely unrepentant. 'Henry Revington,' he went on, 'I sometimes wonder whether I should admire the impudence of a mere clerk of a trading company who dares not only to fire cannonballs at native forts but also plays traitor to his employer and his own country.'

'Please, Rajaji, I beg for mercy.'

'Silence! I have seen you with my own eyes tamping gunpowder into the cannon at Pawangadh. A person who behaves with such impertinence in a foreign country and commits treason against his own deserves no mercy.'

As the Englishmen looked this way and that, wondering how they could escape this tongue-lashing, the king signalled to a senior official of his army and commanded, 'Sabaji, bring your squad over and arrest this refractory firangi on the spot.'

When Sabaji moved forward with a pony to carry Revington away, the king shouted again, 'No horse for this man! Drag him across the red earth and toss him into the dungeons of the fort.'

When two soldiers held Revington by his arms, he said some words in English that carried a strong strain of pomposity. He was complaining about the injustice of his arrest, perhaps, and seemed to be issuing a threat too. When the king sensed the swagger in Revington's voice, he ordered the soldiers to halt. He then turned to the interpreter who was present and said, 'Tell me, Santosh Shenvi, what lessons in morality is this supercilious firangi trying to teach us?'

'He is saying that if the king does not show restraint, he may invite serious crises upon himself.'

'What kinds of crises?'

'He says that Emperor Aurangzeb is very eager to bring under control the anarchy you have let loose in your own land and in Konkan on the pretext of Swarajya. He intends to move hundreds of thousands of Mughal soldiers from Surat to south Konkan by sea, and for that purpose he has asked the chief of the Surat warehouse for the use of the English fleet. This firangi is warning you that if you misbehave with him—'

'Ah, misbehave! So, what will he do then?'

'He will then recommend to Surat the lending of that fleet. That will mean your certain destruction on the ocean.'

If looks could kill, this one from the king would have reduced Revington to ashes. 'Revington,' he said coldly, 'you expect me to shiver in my shoes on hearing Aurangzeb's name? Know that minnows like you are merely an irritating distraction for me. Ma Bhawani has sent me to earth to smash your emperor and his empire. I will see to that in due course, but in the meantime, let me see what I can do with unrepentant ingrates like you.'

By the king's order, fetters were clapped on Revington's wrists and ankles before he was dragged away. Among the others arrested along with him were Philip Gifford, and Richard and Rudolph Taylor. That very evening, Doroji and Atre's squads were dispatched to the warehouse on the mound across the creek to raze it to the ground. The residents of Rajapur and Dhootpapeshwar heard the sounds of sledgehammers and pickaxes all through the night.

The Marathas did the demolition work with such meticulous glee that they left no brick standing. They also unearthed quantities of treasure that the Englishmen had stashed away. Along with trunks, pots and woks full of bright yellow gold, they found huge quantities of silver, emeralds, rubies, coral, ivory, musk, sandalwood, rose chestnut and other priceless wares.

First, the Englishmen were given a taste of the Rajapur dungeon. Orders were later passed to shift the prisoners to a near-inaccessible fort called Kasota in the jungles on the other side of Karhad. Richard Napier and Samuel Bernard were confined to a prison in the Kharepatna fort for a few days. As the air there didn't suit them at all, they fell ill and swiftly succumbed to their illness. Revington was shifted along with his senior colleagues from Kasota to a fort called Songadh near Mahad in the Konkan region. Since the Konkan prisons began causing considerable damage to the health of these sahibs, they were subsequently moved from one fort to another in the Raigadh region for a change of air. But confinement in these jungle prisons, replete with fungi and leeches, became extremely distressing for the white men.

After the episode at Rajapur, the British, Dutch and other foreign adventurers were jolted at the firmness with which Shivajiraja could come down upon intruders. The whispers that were exchanged in their warehouses underlined an important lesson: it was dangerous to poke one's nose into Shivaji's territory. It wasn't the nose alone that was at risk; lives could be lost too. It was, therefore, much more prudent to stick to their primary enterprise: business.

The entire coastal region stretching from the Karvar harbour to Vasai had begun to attract Shivraya greatly. It had become a benchmark, a vibrant hub for modern ways of trading. But while exploring this coastline, the king also had to negotiate treacherous creeks, formidable fortresses as well as people of strange and variable temperaments.

A spacious tent had been erected on open ground within the fort at Kharepatna, where the king sat in conference with his associates. The ambit of the Swarajya included a large number of narrow-minded, short-sighted zamindars, jaageerdars and noblemen who claimed to be descendants of the sun god. The main question that was being discussed at this council was: how could one bring them in touch with reality? How could their strength and energies be exploited for the welfare of the kingdom?

The king had once believed that Lakham Savant of Kudaal would help him in opening a new front on the western coast, but the current circumstances were very upsetting. He said to Doroji and Tryambakpant, 'It's not even three years since this man had come to me begging for mercy. He had Santosh Shenvi with him. Swaying like a reed in the wind, he bowed to me and said that he too was of the Bhosale lineage. Since he was twenty years younger, I should consider him as a son and hold him close to my heart. What humility, what a dripping display of affection!'

Continuing in the same sarcastic vein, the king said, 'The people of Kudaal are quite skilled at playing the ten incarnations of Vishnu. I am now convinced that before he got into politics, this man was an excellent mimic in some troupe of actors.'

'You are absolutely right, Raje. When Adilshah visited Kudaal last year, this same man used the opportunity to bend like a bow before him and literally rolled at the Sultan's feet.'

'It's quite a riddle, isn't it, how people make such complete turnarounds? How quickly they abandon what they perceive as lost causes and make a beeline for the rising star? This Lakhamrao was bawling before the Sultan in the marketplace of Kudaal, we hear, begging to be saved from the menace called Shivaji.'

As the meeting came to a close, Shivraya said with a sigh of relief, 'Well, at least one good thing has happened. The gods have finally given our Suryarao Surve of Shrungapur the sense to behave well.'

After having taught the sly, red-faced traitors from Britain a bitter lesson, the king made ready to gallop at daybreak in the direction of Kudaal. The quartermaster staff had already gone on ahead to make arrangements for his stay there. Shivraya was absolutely determined to make the turncoat pay a stiff price for the fickleness of his allegiances.

From Nizampur-Chiplun to Dabhol, and then on to Rajapur, the king had been perpetually on the move, riding day and night without a moment of rest. Unusual though it was, the excessive exertion had begun to tell on him. His eyes had turned blood-red, and he felt an irresistible need to lie down, even if for a couple of hours, before the departure at dawn for Kudaal. Siddhi Hilaal rushed forward and laid out some mats and blankets for the king to catch some desperately needed sleep. Hilaal had made it his primary duty these days to attend to his king's comfort.

Shivraya had just about stretched out on his mat when Tryambakpant called anxiously from outside, 'Raje, please forgive me, but the information we have just received is urgent and worrisome.'

'Yes, Pant,' the king said, rising immediately, 'what's happened?'

'That Suryarao Surve of Shrungapur has turned traitor again, and the news is that he has also imprisoned Tanaji.'

'What are you saying?' Shivraya said, as he stepped out of the tent, tying the laces of his vest.

Despite the biting-cold winds blowing in from the mountains on either side of Kharepatna, all the sardars, administrators, clerks and attendants—in effect, the entire camp—had been jolted awake by the news and came rushing out of their tents. Everybody knew that the king would now move like lightning and they began to assemble on open ground just outside the camp. Shivraya looked up at the milky spread of the stars in the sky, heaved a sigh and said, 'Let's get going. There is no way that I will allow a person so dear to my heart and so important to the Swarajya to be placed at any risk. Also, that renegade Surve needs to meet his just deserts immediately. Turn the muzzles of your horses northwards, immediately!'

'You mean right now, lord?'

'Absolutely. Nobody looks for an auspicious moment to respond to a calamity such as this. Wake the soldiers; have them stir their horses. Tell them of my anxiety. Even if they are seared by thirst on the way, they shall not stop at any river bank to quench it!'

The king and his cavalry galloped unceasingly through jungles and hills and gorges. The journey was long and arduous, but the horsemen were irrepressible too. They wrought a miracle by covering the distance to Sangameshwar in barely a day and a half. As soon as they reached the camp on the outskirts, the king leapt off his horse like a young boy and shouted, 'Where's my Tanba?'

As he walked forward he saw, in the orange light of the torches, Tanaji himself—luxuriant side-whiskers and all—rushing out of a tent to meet him. It was only when the king had gathered him in his embrace and squeezed him tight that he felt a sense of relief. 'What happened, Tanba?' he cried. 'I want all the details.'

'Maharaj, the man you had put your trust in turned out to be a rat after all. He has returned to the arms of his former Bijapuri benefactor. The other night he mounted a vicious attack on our camp with a big army. The suddenness of the assault in the dark hours of the night stunned our sleep-addled men, but they soon gathered their wits and hit back ferociously. They have sent the enemy packing, bloody and battered, back to Sangameshwar.'

'It's wonderful, the way our men fought back,' Shivraya replied, as he set off with Tanaji for an inspection of the camp by torchlight. As he kept the conversation going, he was looking around with a sharp eye. All the men were up and about on account of the king's arrival. Suddenly, he asked, 'Why don't I see Pilajipant anywhere?'

'Oh, the skirmish of the other night has made him feel a little unwell. He is resting, perhaps.'

The topic of Pilajipant brought a trace of amusement to a number of faces. Some of the younger boys couldn't suppress their giggles. As they walked on, Shivraya got to hear the entire story. On the night of the attack, while the other soldiers had pulled out their swords and fought back fiercely, Pilaji could not gather the courage to confront the raiders. He sneaked out of the camp and began to run in the other direction. Tanaji noticed the cowardice of his colleague, leapt on his horse and chased Pilaji down. He then had him tied to a big boulder on the stream as punishment.

The next day, the king mounted a raid on nearby Shrungapur, but by then, of course, it was too late. After reducing the good name of his ancestors to dust, abandoning his velvet bed and palatial comforts, Suryarao Surve had decamped.

At one time, Shrungapur had enjoyed the reputation of being a seat of learning for the language and literature of Sanskrit as well as other languages. Shivaji fell in love with the natural beauty of the scenic town. There was the beautiful palace with its arches and windows, and a rippling, limpid stream that ran by. The king's attention then travelled to the imposing mountain that stood just outside the town, proud and erect as if it was the king cobra around Lord Shankar's head with its hood spread out.

The king's eyes fell on the escarpment and then travelled up to the ridge on top. He immediately called Arjoji Yadav and Tanaji over and said to them excitedly, 'Do you see that gorgeous summit reaching up to kiss the white clouds floating in the sky? If someone were to try climbing up to a fort up there, he would be left with no choice but to use ladders all the way up. Arjoji, get started with planning and building an invincible fort there.'

'Yes, Raje.'

'This fort will be an epitome of both beauty and efficiency. Therefore I suggest that we name this fort "Prachitgadh".'

The king's next move would be to bring to heel Khem Savant of Sundarwadi in the south. He also planned to make the arrogant Portuguese in Goa fall into line. At midnight, he had just given orders to the quartermaster squad to set out at dawn when a few spies came running into the camp with urgent news. Tanaji Malusare immediately took them to the king and said, 'Maharaj, there is turbulence in the Kalyan-Bhiwandi area.'

'What turbulence?'

'The Mughal army has entered Kalyan.'

'Oh, I see. Tanba, the message here is clear. The Mughals are trying to retrieve the honour they lost after we put their sardars to such shame in Umbarkhind.'

The chieftains gathered around him waited for the king to pronounce his decision.

'As long as these Mughal vultures do not move away from our Pune region, we will have to be all the more vigilant with regard to our Kalyan-Vasai coast. We have launched our secret shipbuilding activity in so many places on that stretch. We cannot afford to be neglectful of this vital enterprise.'

30

BRING THE FLAMBEAU, PLEASE

Sultan Ali Adilshah looked at Shahaji with pride and said, 'Rajaji, as a close associate and friend of my father Sultan Mohammad sahib and also my great-grandfather Sultan Ibrahim sahib, you have displayed great exploits in Bijapur.'

'Quite true, Sultan sahib. All told, I have been serving this land of Bengaluru-Bijapur for thirty years now.'

'That's right, and you have never defaulted in your service to our Sultanate. But there is one thing you will have to concede.'

'What's that, huzoor?'

'Look, if someone were to call me a rake and a philanderer, I may allow this accusation some space,but when it comes to running the Sultanate, I am a committed and dedicated sultan. As such, I have the duty of keeping a very sharp eye on all my chieftains and generals.'

'Huzoor?'

'Rajaji, you may believe it or not, but I have plenty of information about you, so much that it can rob you of your night's rest! Just tell me this: have you, in your entire life, ever let a single opportunity go by of helping that renegade son of yours, the one named Sivaji?'

'I don't quite understand, huzoor.'

'All right, let me explain. Look at the extremely powerful and able people that Sivaji surrounds himself with in the twelve Maavals—Phirangoji Narsaala, Mankoji Dahatonde, Dadoji Kond'dev, Dadaji Lohkare, Kanhoji Jedhe … the whole lot. Where did Shiva get these valiant men from? At one time, all of them were serving with us here in Bijapur. So, who sent them to "Maharashtra"?'

Shahaji preferred to stay silent.

'Ten years earlier, Mustafa miyaan arrested you near Jinji. You could have tweaked that rebellious boy's ears if you had wanted to and got him under control. He was barely eleven or twelve then.'

'Huzoor?'

'Sivaji and his mother, your queen Jijabai, stayed here in Karnataka for two years and then returned to Pune. Within two or three years of his return, he openly began to raid our mountain forts and indulge in various mutinous activities. This clearly indicates that all of his illegitimate pursuits had your tacit consent, if not your support. How can you even begin to deny it? The royal seal that you gifted to him spoke the language of independence and rebellion. You gave it to him when he was twelve!'

The Sultan was truly taking Shahajiraje to task. Ali Adilshah, with his longish face and beady eyes, was slightly built, almost to the point of looking frail and ill. But he clearly had a strong head for political analysis and intrigue. Once he had taken over complete charge of the Sultanate from Badi Begum, he had begun to display immense confidence in his abilities. His voice too had gained the resonance of power and authority.

Admonishing Shahaji in a firm tone, he said, 'Well, we shall not rake up your past anymore. Let bygones be bygones. But as a wise, intelligent servant of the state of Bijapur, you can certainly improve your ways and take steps that could be beneficial to our Sultanate as well as to your personal fortune.'

'Huzoor?'

'Your prince Sivaji is so inflamed by his unbridled lust for independence that he is quite beyond anybody's wise counsel. You, perhaps, may be the only person who can guide him back to good sense.'

'Forgive me, Sultan sahib, my boy has crossed all limits, and there may not be much point in pinning these hopes on me.'

'In that case, let me put matters before you plainly.' The Sultan looked sharply at Shahajiraje and said, 'If I have to keep my Sultanate going and if your Siva doesn't mend his ways, there can only be death and destruction in his destiny.'

Shahajiraje was speechless. He could see that the Sultan meant every word of what he was saying. It took Ali Adilshah some effort to bring his vexation under control and continue in a softer tone, 'You will have to forgive me, Raja sahib, but time is slipping out of my hands. It's only on account of our old association with you, and considering that he is your son, that we want to give him another chance.'

'I'm listening, huzoor.'

'I do not demand that he should return to me all the forts and towns and coastal belts that he has snatched away from us. He can keep them for himself. On top of that, we shall bestow generous gifts upon him.'

'Huzoor?'

'If he dreams of becoming the king of the margatthas, we shall not stand in his way at all. In fact, we shall happily felicitate him for it.'

The sudden spin that the Sultan put on the conversation confused Shahajiraje for a little while. However, his long years of experience as a statesman and military commander made him suspect that a catch was coming soon. But before he could gauge the direction of the conversation, the Sultan resumed, 'Please listen to this carefully. The reign shall be Siva's. He will live in palaces, and rule over his men and his territories, but the flag that flies on the palaces and the forts shall be the green banner of the Adilshahi Sultanate.'

The Sultan's words embarrassed Shahajiraje, but before he could say anything, Ali Adilshah went on, 'I know full well that it will be a difficult task to bring your arrogant son around to agree to this suggestion. That is why, if you think it will help, you may travel to your land of Maharashtra. If you can persuade him to see where his welfare lies, it will be good for all parties concerned. But if you can't, I can only see death dancing over his head.'

Sultan Ali Adilshah spoke in the voice of one who was pronouncing a grim verdict. The atmosphere was so tense that even breathing had become difficult. To release the tension a little, Shahajiraje said, 'May I clear a doubt, huzoor?

'Go ahead.'

'It's been twenty years since I visited my native land. If I go now, and if my mind betrays me and I do not return, what then?'

Shahajiraje's query provoked a hearty laugh. 'My dear Raja sahib,' the Sultan said, 'the loving father that resides in your heart, the father who is ready to sacrifice his all for the welfare of his progeny, he will ensure that you return.'

'I haven't understood your drift, huzoor.'

'Well, it's quite obvious, isn't it? Although your son Sivaji is in the twelve Maavals, there is your younger son Vyankojiraja, with all his pomp and paraphernalia spread out here in Karnataka. With Vyankoji lording it over hundreds of thousands of hons here, how can you compromise his life by staying behind in Pune? Rajaji, I have no doubt that you will not want to tarry there. My advice, therefore, is that if you want the days left to you in this world to be spent in peace, you will have to take the proper steps now. Go to Maharashtra immediately and bring the flambeau back.'

'What flambeau?'

'Some seventeen or eighteen years ago, on the banks of the Tungabhadra, as you were bidding Siva goodbye, you handed over to him a torch which was a symbol of the flaming dreams of independence—in your lexicon, a battle against foreign dominance.'

'Huzoor, you have been entertaining a lot of misconceptions about me. The fact is, our Shivaji has been of a rebellious temperament since birth. I can take no credit for making him so.'

'Of course, I agree that he is a born rebel. But the flambeau that he holds … who set it alight? Plundering our treasury, raiding our forts almost every other week to plant the flag of insurrection, all this uproar and clamour in the name of independence—do you think I do not understand their undercurrents?'

The maturity and powers of perception that the Sultan displayed in their meeting shook Shahajiraje. This heir of Mohammad sahib was not the mere profligate that Badi Begum had imagined him to be. He definitely knew how to hold the steed of power between his thighs and take it forward with wisdom.

31

THE FATHER'S RETURN

SUMMER OF 1662

For the past four days, Shahajiraje had been plagued by uncontrollable hiccoughs. He couldn't get the thought of Shivaji and the Maaval region out of his head. That morning, after finishing his morning prayers, he brought up the subject with his wife Tukabai. 'Can you guess, Rani sahib, how many years have rolled by since I last visited the land of my birth?'

'How many?'

'Twenty-two full years, would you believe it?'

'Bai ga, could this really be true?'

'It's such a long time since I have had a glimpse of Shivba and Jijau.'

'You should certainly have made more of an effort.'

'True, but was it even possible, Rani sahib?'

'Why not?'

'The constant snake-and-mongoose confrontation between Shivba and the Adilshahi sardars, the almost daily needling by both sides, my incarceration, Fateh Khan's Purandar campaign, the schism brought about by the Afzal Khan episode … there was never any end to my worries.'

'Yes, that's quite true.'

'I've also had long-term and bitter enemies like Mustafa Khan and Afzal Khan to rob me of any complacency. Then there are those Muslim sardars of the south who are forever watching my every move in the durbar.'

'But you could still have squeezed some time out, perhaps?'

'Unlikely. I also had to steer clear of those snakes in the grass, Baji Ghorpade and Khandoji Khopade, waiting for an opportunity to put me in the dock. Even if I had set out on a pilgrimage, those backstabbers would have brewed a poisonous story around any meeting with Shivba and poured it into the Sultan's ears.'

Shahajibaba's eyes turned moist at the memory of the twelve Maavals. Running his hand over his grey moustaches, he groaned, 'Oh lord, breaking away from the land of your birth, getting uprooted altogether from the soil … the pain of it can be sensed only by one who has suffered it. How do I tell you, Tukausahib, of the memories of Maaval that haunt my nights, filling them with sorrow? In dreams, my unbridled mind would go galloping towards the Chandrabhaga and roll in its water, place its head at the holy steps of Mahavitthal there, play cymbals and drums at the doorstep of Tulza Bhawani, dance all night at the festival of the holy Mother … It would soak in the flow of the rivers Mula-Mutha, Bhima and Gode; it would go crazy, utterly crazy as it blew with the wind in the hills and dales of the Sahyadris …'

Perceiving the state of her husband's mind, Tukausahib suggested, 'Raje, why don't you seek permission for a trip home? The Sultan would not be awfully upset, I'm sure.'

Shahajiraje chuckled as he responded, 'This is exactly what the Sultan wants me to do—make a visit to the twelve Maavals.'

'Isn't it wonderful, then?'

'Yes, it is. Besides, our Vyankojibaba has no previous acquaintance with his motherland. This would be a good occasion for all of us to make a visit. I hope we can catch young Shivba at Rajgadh, though.'

'Why should he not be there? Shaista Khan is coiled like a snake at our Lal Mahal in Pune, so where else will Shivba be if not in Rajgadh?'

'But can we be sure of that?'

'Why not?'

'Aho, that is Shivba. Not even the god of nature can know which way the golden eagle goes flying. There's no knowing where it may be perching now.'

An extremely confidential meeting was in progress in Shaista Khan's private hall at Lal Mahal. Among those present were several senior Mughal chieftains, including Shaista's son Fateh. A number of spies were also in attendance, carrying intelligence from different parts of the twelve Maavals. Shaista told his muneem joyfully, 'Don't be tight-fisted. Open up your purse and let the money flow. Let there be extravagance of all kinds. Organise spectacles with dancers, prostitutes and courtesans in every street and lane of Pune.'

'Huzoor?' the muneem queried, swallowing hard.

'Yes. Let the outside world believe that I and my chieftains and my soldiers indulge in perpetual merrymaking. It is important to bring that shrewd margatthya Siva's guard down. We keep up this pretence of frolic and revelry, lure him out in one of the valleys and finish him off!'

'But Abbu,' Prince Fateh said, 'earlier you had planned to launch a full-blown invasion in the broad light of the day upon his Rajgadh fort!'

'Son, for the margatthas, Rajgadh is their Kailash, the mountain on which Lord Shiva resides, and it is an extremely difficult fort to attack. But the important question is, is this Siva present at all in his capital?'

Noticing the astonishment on the faces of his councillors, Shaista went on, 'That cunning fox is only pretending that he is ensconced in the comfort of Rajgadh. In actual fact, most of the time he is gallivanting across wide swathes of this land. What do you say, my secret agents?'

'Huzoor, you are absolutely on the mark,' said Ahmad Miyaan, chief of the Khan's espionage wing. 'Till very recently, he had secreted himself for a good three months in an ordinary, extremely small fort called Vardhangadh near Satara.'

'Vardhangadh?' Shaista looked questioningly at a senior sardar named Babul Khan.

'Khan Sahib, this Vardhangadh can hardly be called a fort. It is just a stubby little hill, a day's ride from Satara in the direction of Mahuli ghat. Cross the Krishna on the road to Mandesh, and you will see this hillock on the left. We had received news of this earlier too, and it astounded me. Why would a sensible king like Siva play this childish game and while away three months on a tiny mound like Vardhangadh, shunning much bigger forts like Rajgadh, Torana and Purandar?'

'If I know Siva at all, I can tell you that this is not a childish whim. There is a deep game here, a very deep one. We must find out what his purpose was, what his purpose is.'

It was after twenty-two years that father and son would meet. The very thought had banished sleep from the eyes of both. Shivraya was overcome by emotion every time he pictured meeting the man who had moulded him.

Despite the pressure of so many enterprises, despite the anxiety caused by Shaista Khan dispossessing him of his palace in Pune, the king was determined to suspend all his worries to celebrate the arrival of his father. 'I don't care what Shaista is doing,' he declared. 'The be-all-and-end-all of my life, my revered father, is going to be here with me and I have decided to set aside all other engagements, big and small.'

Soyrabai and Jijau were delighted to hear this.

'While pursuing one campaign after another, I hadn't allowed words like rest or enjoyment anywhere in my lexicon; now, however, I have resolved to put all work away and follow my father like a shadow for the three or four months he is here.'

There was a constant movement of heralds to and from Karnataka in preparation for the senior king's arrival. Jijausahib bustled around procuring ingredients for the dishes that her husband loved. There was a religious belief that when people of a family meet after a long time, this reunion should happen at a place of pilgrimage. Accordingly, Shivraya decided to meet Shahajiraje in the durbar of Mhalsakant in Jejuri.

Shahaji arrived at Tulzapur in the company of his wife Tukabai as well as his sons Vyankoji and Koyajiraje. Shahaji's wife Tukabai and Vyankoji's wife Deepabai had also come along. An impressive contingent of a thousand horsemen on Turkish steeds rode before and behind them. Their luggage was carried by a sizeable caravan of mules, ponies and bullock carts. Accompanying them was the senior king's famed official Raghunathpant Hanumante along with his brother Janardanpant. A large administrative team travelled with them.

They paid their obeisance to Ma Bhawani at Tulzapur, fed a thousand brahmins and distributed alms. Then the royal family set off for Pandharpur, this time in the company of Balaji Aaoji, the commander-in-chief of the Swarajya army. To ensure that his father's journey was safe and comfortable, Shivaji had dispatched a regiment that consisted of a cavalry unit, an elephant squad and a large battalion of clerks and attendants. He now waited excitedly at Jejuri for the moment when he would finally set eyes on him.

After what seemed an interminable wait, the auspicious day dawned. As previously arranged, Shahajiraje was escorted to a seat placed for him on a platform under a huge umbar tree in the premises of the Khandoba temple at Jejuri. Two other palanquins followed immediately, bringing Tukabai and Vyankojiraje. The climactic moment arrived when Shivraya climbed the nine hundred thousand, steps immortalised in countless songs, to reach the Khandoba temple.

His eyes swept over the scene that had been laid out under the ancient umbar tree and came to rest upon on a tall, strongly built, broad-chested gentleman dressed in a silk robe, and wearing a mandeel, the royal headgear. He had large, soulful eyes, a wide brow, an aquiline nose and a magnificent salt-and-pepper beard. At sixty-two, Shahajiraje's personality exuded a charm and mystique that one usually associates with world explorers. As for Shahajiraje, his eyes first narrowed and then widened to take in the fair, lustrous youth with a tapering beard who was walking towards him with leonine grace.

Shivraya paused for a moment, looked his father full in the eyes and saw them fill up. His own turned watery too, blurring everything that lay before him. Shahajiraje stood up like a man in a dream. Every pore of his body was tingling. Was this the eleven-year-old boy who had clung to him during that distant farewell on the banks of the Tungabhadra? The person standing before him now was a thirty-two year old man who had, with the heroism of his deeds, the generosity of his heart, hard labour and acuity of vision, scaled such heights that the Sahyadri range itself was honoured to call him a beloved son.

This son of his was now the source of courage among his soldiers, the ruler of the hearts of the poor multitudes, the companion of the peasants, the future of the Sahyadris, and the doom of the Mughals and the

Adilshahis. When Shivraya came rushing up to him, Shahajiraje spread out his arms and exclaimed, 'You have become as big as the sky, my boy!' Father and son leapt into a tight embrace, making utterly futile attempts at holding back the tears that had come gushing out. Their sobs broke out carrying a tinge of sorrow, but mainly joy.

Shivraya then suddenly shook himself out of his father's grasp and went down on his knees to place his forehead at Shahajiraje's feet. When the latter bent down and held his son by the forearms to lift him, Shivraya resisted the effort. Instead, he collected the dust from underneath his father's feet and applied it to his forehead. Overwrought, Shahaji forced him up, embraced him again and remonstrated, 'Why are you doing this, Shivba? You are not a child, but a king in your own right.'

'In the presence of your revered feet, I am just a child, Abasahib,' Shivraya said in an emotion-laden voice. 'Your example, your shade, your affection have shaped me in ways that I have no words to describe. The resonance of your deeds and the power of your blessings have kept me going all my life.'

In the meantime, Jijau and Tukabai had sought each other out and were immediately locked in each other's arms. It was a day of great good fortune for Jijausahib. She too was setting her eyes on her husband after more than two decades. But the focus of attention for all present was the father-son duo.

Rituals were performed to drive evil influences away. Balls of curd-rice and knots of turmeric were tossed at them; an ascetic brought out a broom of peacock feathers and swept it over them. The royal family then walked towards the sanctum sanctorum of Lord Mhalsakant. Shivraya slowed his steps to let his half-brother Vyankoji catch up and put an arm around his shoulder. Although he was only a year older, he took his responsibility as the elder brother quite seriously.

The residents of Jejuri had assembled a band which played several auspicious musical instruments with gusto. They had decorated the temple premises with flowers and leaves and coloured powder. A wide and shallow bronze vessel was placed before the statue of the deity and filled with clarified butter. The royal guests, as well as Jijausahib and Shivraya, were made to look into it and see themselves reflected as a family.

When father and son sat before the idol of Malharirαya, among the brahmins conducting the prayers was an energetic young man with an expressive face. He said that he was from the village of Mahur in the Sashti region near the island of Mumbai. He rested his gaze on Shahajiraje and said in a whisper loud enough to reach his ears, 'Maharaj, the knot of your dhotar has loosened. It needs fixing.'

'Oh, really?' Shahajiraje said and got up hurriedly but carefully, holding on tight to the garment. He went to a dark corner of the temple where the brahmin followed him and began helping him tighten the knot. The king then mumbled into the man's ears, 'What game are you playing, Dighe? Since when did you start this pantomime of officiating as a brahmin priest?'

'Maharaj, this is all part of my service to Shivajiraje.'

'And why corner me like this?'

'Maharaj, when you move out of the temple, please look to the west when you are on the first step downwards. You will see three Musalman men begging for alms under the lemon tree.'

'So, what about them?'

'They are three of Shaista's cleverer spies, here to get a whiff of what gets cooked between you and your son. Also, please don't labour under the delusion that Shaista is relaxing in Pune, indulging in pleasures of the flesh.'

'The scoundrel has been frothing and fuming night and day, toiling to cause grievous harm to Shivajiraje.'

The meaning was quite clear. The enemy's men were moving incognito among the king's relatives and well-wishers swarming around the temple premises. Each step had to be carefully placed and each word carefully uttered.

The great prayer meeting got over and rough-skinned palanquin-bearers began carrying the members of the royal family down the steps in soft, rhythmic movements. Although Shahajiraje was a big man, they were transporting him with delicate elegance on their broad shoulders, the muscles of their arms and calves flexing with every step they took. The men running alongside the palanquin with parasols of honour were in fact members of Shivaji's espionage squad. Underneath their flaring tunics they carried sharp weapons. Their job was to ensure the security of the royal family.

Shivraya himself had refused a palanquin despite his father's attempt to persuade him, and chose instead to walk with the palanquin-bearers. He held his father's velvet shoes to his chest. Walking alongside was his way of expressing not only his respect, but also his joy at this long-awaited reunion. All eyes were turned towards his unshod feet. Each time he stubbed his toes or stepped upon sharp pebbles, the expression on his face suggested that he would willingly endure more of it. The poignant scene reminded many observers of the devotion of Lord Rama towards King Dasharatha. Nobody had seen or even heard of such filial devotion in recent times.

It was a grand procession that journeyed through Purandar-Narsapur on way to Rajgadh. All along the route, people had erected huge arches, welcoming their senior king home. They had not forgotten the favours that he had bestowed on the sons of the soil and this was an opportunity to display their gratitude. It was through the good offices of this benevolent king that young men of thousands of Maavali households had found respectable employment in armies ranging from the Nizamshahi troops of Daulatabad to the Adilshahi forces in Bijapur and Bengaluru. The women of the region were so charged with emotion that they poured their all into the rangoli patterns they had created along the king's path.

When Rajgadh was only seven miles away, Shivraya got off his steed. Shahajiraje was shifted to a beautifully decorated howdah mounted on a majestic elephant. With him sat Jijau, Tukabai, Deepabai and Vyankojiraje. Once again, Shivraya walked barefoot alongside the elephant most of the way. Koyajiraje often gave him company in this exercise.

When Jijausahib stepped out of the big shrine in the palace the next day, she carried on her face a glow of satisfaction that nobody had seen earlier. Shivraya touched her feet and walked with her towards the front hall. 'Matoshri,' he said in a confessional tone, 'what I am about to say should not be considered as mere praise, but a statement of fact. '

'What is it, Shivba?'

'When I think of the relationship between you and Abasahib, my heart melts. Lord Rama and Sitamai suffered exile for fourteen years, and here you meet Abasahib after a gap of twenty-two years. Lord Rama had Sitamai for company throughout his exile, but you two were denied each other's company and yet you suffered it all with fortitude. When I think of this sacrifice, I wonder if any god or goddess could have withstood competition with you. How can anyone regard the two of you as mortal human beings at all?'

'Well, then?'

'There is divinity that resides in you; how else can one explain such courage and resilience?'

'Did we have any other way out, Balraje? The cradle of Swarajya had to be kept rocking; a radiant, extraordinarily gifted son like you had to be brought up so that this dream could be turned into reality. That was why, perhaps, god did not leave us with any alternatives to choose from.'

'You must have spent the entire night talking.'

'No, Balraje, every single day and every single night of the past twenty-two years have been spent under the scorching summer sun; we spent the night dousing each other with tears.'

A grand durbar had been organised that day. The impoverished multitudes of the state had begun flooding in a couple of days in advance from every corner of the Maavals—Nashik-Sangamner to Pen-Nizampur to Phaltan-Indapur—to catch a glimpse of their senior king. It was an age since the old among them had last set eyes on their champion; for the young, it was giving physical form to a legend. Jijausahib personally supervised the serving of meals to these thousands of her husband's devotees. Before entering the durbar hall, Shahajiraje gave alms to the poor and indigent who lined his path. The brahmins had been served their meals earlier.

The durbar began with Netaji Palkar gifting lavish silks to Shahajiraje as well as a gold-hilted sword on behalf of Shivraya. Shahaji himself had brought a huge variety of rare and priceless objects from Karnataka for his wife, son and daughters-in-law. He honoured them all by presenting them with gifts. He used the occasion to felicitate the great scholars and other accomplished persons assembled in the court. Shivraya too presented gold ornaments and other precious gifts to his father and his two mothers. Vyankojiraje and Koyajiraje were also felicitated with expensive clothing and adornments. The king accorded special honour to his father's administrator and scholar Raghunath Hanumante. Sweets were distributed to all and sundry.

The evening winds had begun to blow when the royal family finally found some time to breathe. The senior king and Shivraya sat relaxing in the front verandah. Shivraya used this opportunity to unburden his heart of the weight it had been carrying for years. 'Abasahib,' he said, 'I want you to forgive me with a large heart.'

'Why do you speak of forgiveness, Shivba?'

'I have committed serious offences against you, Abasahib.'

'How can you say that? I can't think of another father with a son who has brought such honour to his lineage. I consider myself blessed.'

'Abasahib, so often have I been guilty of disobedience. So often have I raised arms against the Bijapur Sultanate. You protected me by painting my activities as the delinquencies of a foolish prince and ignored them yourself. At your age, you were humiliated to the point of being thrown into prison, all because of my insurgencies.'

'There is no reason for you to feel guilty. I am well aware of the distress and danger you invited upon yourself for defending your faith and laying the foundation of Swarajya. That a valiant, world-renowned warrior like you should have been born in the Bhosale lineage can only be the result of some past merits.'

'Abasahib, you are my inspiration and my conscience. All that I have accomplished, I have done by keeping your image in my mind's eye.'

'Shivba, son, I pray that your victorious banner is unfurled across the length and breadth of this land. May your dominion expand, expand, expand so much that the waters of the Tapti in the north should flow by your desire and the sea at Rameshwar in the south should thrill at your sight.'

As the father and son talked, the two mothers walked up to them, treading softly.

That night, dinner was a grand and lively affair. The event of the entire royal family sitting down together for a meal had created an ambience of rejoicing and exuberance. They sat on planks of sandalwood, before each of which were drawn colourful and intricate rangoli patterns. The air was thick with the perfume of incense sticks.

As they sat consuming delectable dishes, they exchanged jokes and stories and lines of poetry to the accompaniment of much laughter. The conversation eventually turned in the direction of political intrigues and power equations. Vyankoji's wife belonged to the Ingale family. She was beautiful to look at, with delicate features and an arresting personality. Her eyes glittered with native intelligence. As they sat eating, she looked at Shivraya with awe and respect, voicing an opinion that she had held for a long time, 'Bhavoji, whenever the stories of your wonderful exploits fall on my ears, I feel both blessed and thrilled.'

'Why would that be, Vahini?'

'The astuteness with which you measured up your enemy Afzal Khan, the delicacy with which you handled the circumstances and saved both your life and the Swarajya, and finally the efficiency with which you finished off that wicked man, it was a riveting performance, grand enough to become the subject of an epic. I was completely swept off my feet.'

'Waah, daughter-in-law, well put,' Shahajiraje endorsed her remark, echoed by his two queens.

'Ranisahib, please finish your meals first,' Vyankojiraje admonished. 'Elders say that women should not blabber while they are eating.'

It was as if someone had tossed a handful of salt into a sweet dish. The royal family was flustered. Shahajiraje took his son to task immediately. 'What kind of talk is this, prince? Insulting your wife in this manner! What was it about her statement that you found objectionable? Afzal Khan's slaughter or Shivba's valour?'

'It's not that, Abasahib. But Ranisahib here is in the habit of showing off and talking quite unnecessarily.'

Vyankoji's utterly gratuitous and churlish remark marred the bonhomie that had reigned till then. The meal was finished in an embarrassed silence, after which the senior king left for the rear hall, accompanied by Jijausahib and Tukabaisahib following. The rest of the assembly retired to a hall by the side for a round of paan and after-dinner conversation.

As the conversation progressed, the assembly unwittingly divided into two camps. In a voice loud enough to reach Shivraya and his friends, Vyankoji said, 'Some people might consider it an act of heroism, but tell me if there is great gallantry here: you grant a person safety of life, invite him unarmed into your pavilion, pounce upon him when he is distracted and tear his entrails out. If some want to consider this an act of valour, they may go ahead and do so, but in my eyes it is nothing but treachery.'

Startled by the logic of this allegation, the audience turned their eyes involuntarily in the direction of Shivraya. The king then said in a soft voice, 'Vyankoba, let me tell you just this much about your great hero. When Afzal Khan entered the hills of Pratapgadh-Jaavali, do you think he came with the intention of reciting the verses of the Holy Qur'an to the mountains and gorges of the Sahyadris? My dear brother, there is something that you should know—'

'Aha, and what's that?'

'Even before I buried my wagh-nakh, my secret steel nails, in Afzal Khan's belly, he had gathered me in a bearhug. With all the strength of his enormous arms, he was squeezing the life out of me. It was only by the grace of Maa Jagdambe that I managed to free myself of his murderous embrace.'

'Waah, Shivajidada,' Koyajiraje burst out in appreciation. 'You absolutely had to do what you did in self-defence. The gods themselves have done so on innumerable occasions!'

As Shahajiraje and Shivraya sat discussing the western sea-coast and the increasing belligerence of foreign powers there, Shahajiraje said, 'If you want to smash the growing power of the Portuguese in Chaul and Vasai, there's one thing you may do.'

'What's that, Abasahib?'

'Mhatari's beyt, the hag's island, as it is called—along with Mazgaon, Parel and all its neighbouring marshlands—should all be brought under control.'

'You are speaking of the archipelago of Mumbai with its six islands?'

'That's right.'

'Quite recently, the Portuguese drained and filled some of the marshland, constructing a strong station there. They have erected huge defensive walls around it. Besides, they have built a fort near the little tongue of land called Kulaba. And now, look at the cheek of these firangis!'

'Why? What have they done?'

'What can you say about these impertinent foreigners? This land belongs to us, its natives. The Portuguese crossed the seas, constructed Mumbai on our land, fortified it, and then gave it away.'

'What do you mean?'

'On the other side of the seven seas, the Portuguese king gifted this Mumbai to Charles II of England as part of the dowry of his daughter Catherine. This is what is called being generous at somebody else's expense!'

Sonopant Dabeer was always submerged in work in the king's private office. Among many other duties, it was his task to track and record the deep movements of the English and the Portuguese, their open and secret political activities and their plans for the future. He would assiduously gather from his well-placed spies any tidbits of information that they could glean on this subject and put them into special folders. At the king's instruction, he brought a folder over and pulled out a hand-drawn map for Shivraya and Shahajiraje to examine. After poring over it for some time, Shahajiraje shot a question at his son, 'Have they, or have they not, actually tossed Mumbai into the English bag as yet?'

'No, Maharaj, not yet. The Portuguese viceroy of Goa is adamant that an important station like Mumbai should not be made over to the English.'

'Ah, that's interesting.'

'But the king of Portugal believes that he cannot take back what he has declared as given as part of his daughter's dowry. Retracting from this sacred word will bring shame on his name. Therefore, it will certainly go to the English, tomorrow if not today.'

'Which means that it still hasn't been officially transferred, doesn't it?'

Shahajiraje seemed to be harping on this question. This bemused Shivraya for a moment, but in the next instant, his eyes suddenly began to sparkle. With a smile playing at the corner of his mouth, he looked at Jijau and Tukabai and declared, 'When the Portuguese formally hand over ownership of the islands of Mumbai to the English, it is going to be a dazzling ceremony. I propose to be present there as a guest, whether I am invited or not.'

It was now a month and a half since Shahajiraje had come, and the prospect of his return was looming on the horizon. Despite his grief at this imminent separation, it was evident that once he took leave of his father Shivraya would turn around and plunge into action. The roots of his next adventurous campaign were already spreading deep and wide in his fertile brain. Countless plans and stratagems took birth in that creative flux, and more sleepless nights followed.

Poverty had to be banished from his Swarajya. The army had to be strengthened on a sound foundation and, particularly, sturdy forts had to be built along the coast. But where would the funds come from? Years of poverty under the merciless sun and rains had sapped the spine of the Maaval peasants. The only way that expenses could be met for such grand dreams was by looting some city of gold.

The king would often voice these thoughts among intimate associates like Netaji Palkar and Moropant Peshve. Even when he was dining or resting, he would make cryptic references to 'a visit to a city of gold', leaving his audience flummoxed. Jijabai and the younger queens had also overheard mention of this golden city, but nobody had any inkling about what its name was or where it was located.

The frequency of conversations on this subject between Shivraya and Netaji increased. If a third person happened to be present, the two would communicate through enigmatic codes. Increasingly, Bahirji Naik and Vishwasrao Dighe, the chiefs of the Swarajya's espionage wing, would make secret trips to Rajgadh in the dead of the night and disappear before dawn, without anybody being the wiser.

The bold enterprise involving the golden city would require a minimum of seven to eight thousand horses. Lately, the king had begun talking about a battalion of some five thousand foot soldiers too.

32

UNDER THE SHADE OF THE BANYAN TREE

In the woods at the foot of Rajgadh was a temple called Gaibi Maruti, sacred to the occult Hanuman, in which deity people had a lot of faith. Tukabai decided to visit this vibrant shrine. Velvet-roofed palanquins carried her, her daughter-in-law Deepabai, Shivraya's queen Jaishribai and Vyankojiraje down the fort, where the ladies spent a long, devout interlude in the sanctum of Lord Hanuman.

Lunch was arranged in the Shivapattan palace close by. It hadn't taken long for Shivraya to notice the chill in the wind blowing through the royal family. Vyankojiraje had made it a point to take offence over every little thing; accordingly, the king had advised Jaishribai to give personal attention to every aspect of hospitality.

It had been decided that they would leave for the upper fort after lunch, but suddenly, Vyankoji found the natural beauty at the foot of the fort far more attractive and announced that he would stay behind. As Jaishribai had plenty of work pending at the fort and couldn't tarry, she assigned the task of hospitality to the retinue of servants at the lower palace and left. In the early forenoon of the next day, Koyajiraje came down the fort in a flutter.

He addressed Vyankoji straight away, 'Why did you stay behind, dada? Our Abasahib and the others have been waiting for you since morning. So many prayers and rituals at the fort which require your presence have been suspended!'

'You are welcome to all the fanfare and camaraderie at the fort, Koyaji. Please tell everyone there that I do not propose to stir out of the Shivapattan palace here. I don't want to listen to all that fake, syrupy talk anymore.'

'Why are you doing this, Vyankojidada? It's after so many years of separation that the royal family has come together. At dinner last evening, Jijausahib felt the absence of both Tukabai ranisahib and Deepa vahinisahib so deeply that she could hardly eat.'

'Yes, well, maybe that's true.'

'How can you say this? We have travelled such a long distance because of the love that we bear for one another. Your coldness felt offensive to me too.'

Just then, as arranged, Tukabai and Deepabai came to the hall, dressed in their finest clothes. Vyankoji cast a sour glance at their gold-embroidered sarees and heavy jewellery. Tukabai had dressed according to her husband's preference, which included a gold band over her forearm that was crafted in the Indori style. Along with her many ornaments, Deepabai had woven a string of fragrant golden magnolia flowers in her hair. When they saw Vyankoji's irritated face, they both felt their spirits plummet. Next came the growl that they were fearing, 'Where are my dear mother and my queen off to, dressed so nattily? The festivals of Dussehra-Diwali are so far away!'

'Raje, there is a major puja at Rajgadh today, and a number of prayers and rituals are lined up,' said Deepabai.

'You should come too, prince. Our family is waiting for you to appear at the upper fort.'

'Don't you people ever tire of the conversation up there? There's just one single topic that keeps getting repeated.'

'What's that?'

'It's just going to be eulogies sung for my dear brother Shivaji: his valour, his administrative acumen, his great conquests, and so on. And the rest of the time it will be about what a wonderfully far-sighted, wise man our Abasahib is. Has he brought me all this distance only to hear about Shivba, Shivba and more Shivba? It's oozing out of my ears now, all that glorification!'

Both Tukabai and Deepabai were stunned at the bile that was spilling out of Vyankoji. All the enthusiasm of the morning dissipated immediately.

Trying to salvage the situation, Tukabai said, 'The strain of so much travel seems to have tired the prince. You stay here and rest, while the two of us go to the upper fort.'

'Yes,' Deepabai chimed in, 'there are all those prayers and ceremonies. We can come back—'

'Matoshri, why should you waste your time here at the foot of the fort? Better that you gather all your things and carry them up at one go!'

'And you?'

'Once you get up there in time for all those programmes laid out there, my horses will also set off from here.'

'Where?'

'To meet some of our relatives in Shirval and then head for Bijapur. A two-day journey, perhaps.'

'These people on the fort, they are not our relatives, are they?'

In response, Vyankoji raised his eyes to the sky in irritation and disdain, turned around and walked away.

Tukabai's feet had grown heavy; her eyes brimmed over. She turned towards the inner courtyard, with Deepabai following. In a hoarse voice, she said, 'Soonbai, it's best that we remain here. If this discord worsens, the senior king will be terribly upset.'

'God showers all kinds of blessings upon some people; but among them, there are those who suffer from this disease of ingratitude. They keep wailing about what they do not have.'

'Who are you talking about, Abasahib?'

'This perpetual grouse that Vyankoji has: look at all that Shivaji has got! And the complaint that he doesn't have any successes to his credit! His mind is in a permanent state of protest and grievances.'

'What's the remedy, then, Abasahib?'

'Look, Shivba, wallowing in the luxury of the bedchamber on soft mattresses and eiderdown cushions does not bring accomplishments. In order to make success your handmaiden, you have to sail into the elements and battle it out with sun, wind and rain. You have to walk through thorns and display your mettle before the maiden consents to walk with you.'

'What you say is true, Abasahib.'

'Vyankoji, really, has no excuse for whining. All that I had given you to start with was a few villages in Pune and Supe, and a province that had been robbed of its spirit. Technically, Sinhgadh was yours, but even that was really under the ownership of Adilshah. But in these fifteen-seventeen years, you have created a magnificent kingdom here in the Sahyadri range with a hundred forts and more coming up. You have thrown your net in the waters of the sea and terrorised the firangis on the coast. You have established your own navy—'

'All this is simply the outcome of your blessings and good wishes, Abasahib, nothing else.'

'In contrast, there, in Karnataka, Vyankojirao has been spreading his legs in the safety and comfort of the shade I provide. All the wealth that I have accumulated by the strength of my arms—Bengaluru, Balapur, Nandi, Kolar Basavapattan, Arni, Jinji, Tegnapattam, Hoskote and Porto Novo near Tanjavur—all the grandeur and privileges that this wealth brings, they have all come to Vyankoji on a platter. When he has all this paternal inheritance coming his way, why would he want to struggle and strive?'

'Well, all right then, Abasahib, I will agree that our family too has not remained untainted by schisms, bickering, discontent and envy.'

'What can one do, Balraje? These days, domestic intrigues too have become political machinations.'

'Why does our brother Vyankoji behave so whimsically, Koyajibaba?' Shivraya asked.

'Why do you say this, Shivajidada?'

'Don't tell me you haven't noticed it, dada. His capriciousness causes Abasahib a lot of discomfort, one can see. Although he may not admit it openly, deep inside he is upset, I am sure.'

'If he carries a grudge, it is not difficult to see why.'

'Why?'

'Ambition is one of the prime jewels that royal princes wear around their neck, but not all of them possess the ability to satisfy it, and thus, wear it with confidence and grace. When this happens, the jewel, instead of being an object of beauty, hangs heavy around the neck as disquietude and defeatism. It can drive the person who wears it quite mad, that's for sure.'

'If all this unrest and discontentment exists even while our Abasahib Shahajiraje is alive, what shape will it take when he is no longer with us?'

'There's nothing you can do, Shivajidada. Our Vyankojirao also wants the fame and adulation that has come your way, but he does not want to break sweat earning it. It's like a rabbit of the woods wanting the power and dominance that the eagle of the sky enjoys.'

Members of the royal family would often assemble in one of the inner halls or at the main shrine, discussing their joys and sorrows. Jijau, Tukai and their daughters-in-law would always be present at such gatherings. There was no saying when such an opportunity would arrive next.

One day, Jijau said to Shivraya, 'Shivba, these days of joy are numbered; before you even know it, you will find that you have run out of them. Therefore, do not delay matters.'

'What matters, Ausahib?'

'It's been an age since your father's feet have trodden this land. Utilise this opportunity to take him on a tour of all the important stations that you have established in this region.'

This very thought had been on Shivraya's mind, but it made his heart swell with pride that his mother thought it important too.

As he travelled around the kingdom with his father and showed him the new world he had brought to life, Shivraya was transported to seventh heaven. Shahajiraje inspected the infantry battalions and cavalry units of his son's army, as well as the new shipbuilding yards that had come up in Panvel and Chaul. He saw the work on the harbours that were being constructed at a number of places along the coast. He met scores of excited and enthusiastic labourers, ironsmiths and carpenters who worked on these sites to materialise the dream of Swarajya and exchanged pleasantries with them.

As they were returning from Chaul, Shahaji's eyes were inexorably drawn to the well-protected walls of the Portuguese fort. He remembered that stormy night of twenty-seven years ago. In his mind's eye, he saw the sky coming down in torrents as a young father stood at the entrance of the fort, holding a febrile five-year-old against his chest. He was in a panic for fear of the little boy coming to grievous harm if he were exposed to the elements any longer. The memory of that episode brought tears into the senior king's eyes.

In the company of his son, Shahajiraje also visited Purandar, Panhala, Vishalgadh, Rangana and Torana. Inspecting the stables at these forts, he was impressed by the health of the animals he saw there. 'Shivba,' he said, 'we are legless when we enter the battlefield. The legs of the horses we are riding become our legs too. It thus becomes the prime duty of a king and a general to ensure that the horses who carry the warriors—as well as the elephants and bullocks that transport the bulk of the armaments—are in perfect health. I am very pleased to note that you do justice to this aspect of kingship and generalship in your Hindvi swarajya.'

When he set out to visit the Rayari fort, Shahajiraje's two daughters-in-law Soyrabai and Jaishribai gave him company too. From the Songadh fort near Mahad, they travelled through the inner furrows of the mountains. They went past a crag and reached the village of Paachaad, from where Shahaji had his first glimpse of the fortress that Shivraya had lately christened as 'Raigadh'. The sight of its massive, incomparable ramparts left the senior king amazed. For the rest of the day he ambled across the battlements of Raigadh, and drank in greedily the magnificent view of the gorges, the impregnable walls and the forbidding bastions.

The royal family went over to the Konkan side of the fort and prayed at the temple of Shirkai Devi. Turning towards Shivraya and Jaishribai, the senior king said, 'Soonbai, for many years, this fort was under the control of your family, the Moreys. This is the first time that I've come here, Shivba, and I've observed it closely.'

'So, Abasahib, what do you think of it?'

'Well, the air here is full of the fragrance of flowers like jai, jiu and jasmine, mixed with the aroma of dry grass. The presence of this beautiful fort amid this wilderness of mountains puts me in mind of a lotus in the middle of a vast expanse of water.'

'Waah, Abasahib, well put. This fort has always been the pride of its rulers starting from Raja Bhoj right up to the Moreys. It seems to have hypnotised you too.'

'Yes, lad, that's true. It can hypnotise a poet, but at the same time, it has the capacity to awaken the fount of valour in a warrior too. Look at how the mountains are mounting guard in all directions! And all of it is the unsullied gift of nature.'

As he was examining the precincts of the Raigadh fort, Raigadh was often in the back of Shahajiraje's mind. He said to Shivraya, 'You have set up your capital in Rajgadh as of now, but you may want to consider shifting it here to Raigadh.'

'Why do you say that, Abasahib?'

'Look, our Rajgadh is surrounded by a large number of villages and hamlets. What's going to happen to them in the event of an enemy invasion? Essential supplies will be blocked from all sides. At the same time, these poor peasants living on the hills and in the canyons and valleys will be tormented to apply pressure upon you to bring you to your knees. What does rajdharma—the duty of a conscientious ruler—tell us to do?'

'I wait upon your words, Abasahib.'

'Rajdharma says that the heat of the battle should in no way singe the common folk. It's the king and his coterie that should absorb the main shock of the conflict. From this perspective, Raigadh seems to be the ideal place for your future capital. A bit of refurbishing, some shaving of crags, a few new ramparts and bulwarks … and this fort will become invincible.'

The senior king was also deeply impressed by the transformation that had been wrought on the Pratapgadh fort atop the Bhorpa mountain. He congratulated its architect and engineer Arjoji Yadav for the miracle he had performed at such short notice. He also bowed before the statue of Ma Bhawani that had been brought over from Nepal and poured milk over it as a ritual ablution.

Climbing down from Pratapgadh, the two kings visited the site of Afzal Khan' s assassination. As Shahaji cast his experienced warrior's eye on the landscape, he visualised the manner in which Shivraya had taken advantage of the lay of the land and the surrounding vegetation. A nostalgic smile played upon his face as he thought of his Bhatwadi campaign.

As he walked around the spot where Afzal Khan's shamiana had been pitched, he breathed a sigh of wonderment and said, 'The doughtiness you displayed in killing Afzal Khan was of no mean calibre, Shivba.'

'Why do you say that?'

'I've spent most of my professional life in Bijapur, son, so I know what a frightful phenomenon Afzal Khan was. Night after night during your battle at Pratapgadh I stayed sleepless, sending prayers to as many gods as I could remember.'

'What was so frightful about Afzal Khan, Abasahib, that it could banish sleep from the eyes of an audacious warrior like you?' Shivraya asked with genuine curiosity.

'Son, the people of Bijapur had taken for granted that Afzal Khan would return from the campaign flaunting the banner of victory, dragging Shivaji behind him, dead or alive. Afzal Khan had never heard the words "withdrawal" or "defeat" in his entire military career. What you did was the inconceivable: at the very last moment, you uprooted the man's arrogance and ground him into the mud. Despite all your courage and planning, without a generous helping of luck, this stunning achievement would not have been possible.'

'You think so?'

'Absolutely. Afzal Khan was no ordinary warrior by any measure. Even today, people in Bijapur whisper that if he had been alive, he would one day have ascended the throne of Bijapur.'

Before they could register it, four months had rolled by since Shahaji had set foot on Maaval land. Vyankojiraje, of course, had been an unwilling guest from the very first day, and had therefore departed with his wife for Bijapur a fortnight earlier. Shahaji's sentiments about leaving, however, were diametrically opposite. It was only the piling up of important work back in Bengaluru-Bijapur that compelled him to set a date for his return. Otherwise, the bonding between Shivaji and Shahaji had been so organic and so multi-corded that the thought of departure was gut-wrenching for both father and son.

Time was of the essence now, and neither missed an opportunity to seek out the other's company and engage in urgent consultations. 'Abasahib,' Shivraya could not prevent himself from musing aloud one day, 'we should really have moulded history along the lines that you had indicated immediately after Afzal Khan's annihilation.'

'What are you referring to?'

'Abasahib, if those plans had been implemented, the explosion would have sent half the world into convulsions. Even that officer of the East India Company, that Oxenden fellow, had sent this letter to his home country on December 10, 1659, by the English calendar. In effect, the letter said that a huge cavalry commanded by King Shahaji from Karnataka in the south, and tens of thousands of horsemen and foot soldiers led by the adventurous Shivaji from the Maaval region were expected to come together. They would descend upon the Adilshahi Sultanate and revolutionise the political map of the country.'

Shahajiraje's eyes turned moist at the memory of that occasion. 'If the world had been as shiny as the wings of a dream, it would have been a prettier place.'

'Abasahib, this firangi's apprehensions were not baseless. We had agreed to a plan, and were quite prepared to carry it out.'

'True, Shivba. Even now, the master plan we had chalked out floats like a grand dream before my mind's eye. I, with my men from Karnataka, and you with your army from Maaval: if our two forces had come together with all the fervour that was racing in our blood then, we might even have got the Mughals to wind up their durbar in Agra and Delhi, and sent them scurrying to Kabul and Kandahar!'

'But it didn't happen that way.'

'Destiny has a role to play in everybody's life. That golden beam of light reaches only a select few at the right moment.'

'What was it, then, that jammed the wheels of our ambitious chariot?'

'At first I didn't know how, from where or whom Badi Begum got wind of the flame of revolt that we were kindling. I didn't know whether it was the alertness of the enemy that paid off or one of our own had stabbed us in the back. But once Begum Sahiba sensed that their Sultanate was in danger, she moved swiftly in the jagirs close to Bankapur and Bengaluru. Before our excited horses could even storm out of their stables, their muzzles were throttled and the Maavali men who were to rise up in revolt with us were rounded up. The grief of that once-in-a-lifetime opportunity slipping out of our hands is heavy indeed, but I carry a heavier grief.'

'What grief is that?'

'Our achievements we can flaunt to the world, but some humiliations have to be swallowed in solitude. The person who stymied our effort at writing a fresh chapter in history and transforming the future of our land was not an alien, but someone very close to us. He alerted the enemy at the last moment and blew up all our dreams.'

'When do we meet next?' Jijau asked.

'When?' As he repeated her words, lightning seemed to run through his body. The question was simple, but the edge that it carried was sharp enough to pierce his entrails. He did not have an answer. He was already past sixty, and now he was going back to the kingdom of his son's sworn enemy. The mission for which the Sultan had allowed him the Maaval sojourn had been impossible to fulfil; even an effort at articulating it had been impossible from the very first day. He could never have delivered to the Sultan the result that he desired. Shivaji was not born to live out his days as anybody's slave, nor to acknowledge the ascendancy of any power but that which his people had vested in him. Now that he was returning empty-handed, it was impossible for Shahajiraje to anticipate what political manoeuvres would be played out against him.

'When do we meet next?' Much as he tried to keep the pain out, the poignancy of his predicament spilled out into his voice. 'Jiurani, I do not have an answer to this gigantic question of yours. I don't even know whether we will meet again in this life—'

'Please don't utter such words!' The distress that marked his response brought a flood of tears to Jijausahib's eyes.

'I am only being honest, Jiu. It is unlikely that, despite desiring it from the bottom of my heart, I shall have the good fortune to witness our Shivba's climb to the pinnacle of success. But whether I am around or not, I want you to protect this jewel of ours with all your might. Let him flourish in the shade of the sandalwood tree that you are for him.'

'What are you saying, Maharaj? If age is the monster that will ultimately consume you, do you think I am immune to its ravages?'

'I know you are not, but this sandalwood tree called Jijabai has no right to wilt until such time as our dear son achieves the greatness he is born for, until he ascends the throne of a Chhatrapati. You may take this as my command: you must be present when this boy of ours occupies that seat of honour.'

It was after a stay of three months that the senior king's caravan descended the steps of Rajgadh. While Jijausahib and Tukausahib were carried down in palanquins, he himself was so full of energy that he began to walk down briskly. The parting was more excruciatingly painful than any member of the royal family had imagined it would be. Little Sambhajiraje had decided to give his grandfather company during his descent. He would sometimes traipse on his own tiny legs and at other times travel in the old man's arms, exchanging countless hugs and kisses with him.

It was still quite early in the morning when the retinue reached Shivapattan and made their obeisance to the gods in Jijau's palace shrine. Three decorated and caparisoned elephants stood by the stream that was still gurgling with water. As he was placing his foot on the first rung of the ladder to climb up to the howdah, Shahajiraje stopped and turned around. When his eyes fell on Shivraya, the dam that the two had been holding back with herculean strength burst.

Shivraya rushed towards his father and they gathered each other in a tight embrace. There was no holding back the flow now, nor the sobs that accompanied the tears. When Shahaji noticed his grandson clinging to his feet, he released Shivba and took little Sambhaji again in his arms. 'My flourishing household … my wife, my daughters-in-law and my grandchildren,' he groaned, 'the grief of having to leave them all behind and travel back to an alien country! Lord, don't pronounce this punishment for the worst of my enemies. How helpless one is before Fate!'

'Maharaj,' Jijausahib said in a voice to which the steel had returned, 'please set off with a smile. They say that one shouldn't travel with a heavy heart.'

'What can I do, Ranisahib? It is agonising, this moment of parting. Who do I try to console? This little grandchild of mine? Or our Shivba here? Or, really, my own self? There's one satisfaction I carry with me, though … I could not have left my son and grandson in more competent hands than yours, Jijausahib.'

The caparisoned elephants and the camel squad led the way, followed by the cavalry. The royal family stood rooted to the spot for a long, long time, looking with streaming eyes at the wake that had formed in the distance. The cloud of dust dispersed in due course, but the yearning would remain, perhaps forever.

33

SETTLING ACCOUNTS WITH SHAISTA

APRIL 1663

Two English agents and six clerks of the Bijapur Sultanate had arrived at Raigadh on an errand. The king took a personal interest in ensuring that no outsider ever got wind of what was happening in his capital. He had, therefore, decreed that while the firangis could move freely in and out of the royal office, they would not be allowed to stay in the fort overnight. For facilitating this mandate, a waada had been built in Shivapattan which functioned as an excellent guest house for foreign agents and emissaries.

Firangi traders and officers had lately begun to hold Shivraya in awe and fear. There was a time when the Englishman Henry Revington of Rajapur had enjoyed immense clout among the European merchants and officials of the region. He had, after all, dared to point a cannon at the Maratha chest. But the manner in which Shivaji had punished him for his foolish swagger had set a cat among the firangi pigeons.

Revington had been publicly humiliated and thrown into a prison near Mahad. Within six months of his confinement, he fell ill and was reduced to a pitiable state. He wrote distressed letters to all, including the chief of the Surat warehouse, begging them to intervene on his behalf. However, considering that he had been running an illegitimate racket which supplied guns and ammunition to Indian clients on the sly, the Surat authorities didn't offer much help.

Finally, tiring of his incarceration, and rendered desperate by ill-health, he began sending pathetic letters of regret to Shivraya, begging forgiveness for all his misdeeds. Shivraya's heart ultimately melted and he granted the man pardon, releasing him from captivity on a set of strict conditions. Revington left for Surat, where his health showed no signs of improvement. One day, news arrived on the Konkan coast of his passing away. Since then, the Europeans operating on the western coast had resolved not to interfere in native matters—particularly never, ever, to fall foul of Shivajiraja.

Servants had been assigned the job of heating water for morning ablutions in the emissaries' waada at the crack of dawn. But on that particular morning, the English representatives from the Rajapur warehouse and a few Bijapuri officials were absolutely adamant about not wanting to take their bath indoors. The monsoons had just withdrawn and nature was at its most alluring all around the base of the fort. The greenery everywhere and the sound of the brook close by was too enticing for them to resist and they went for a swim. Since they were assumed to be representatives of some royal house, the attendants did not dare hold them back.

When some of these emissaries had swum a short distance downstream, something caught their attention that left them gaping open-mouthed. Further down the bank, they saw some three or four hundred boys engrossed in making leather knapsacks. Behind them was a kind of factory where these freshly made bags were stacked in large heaps. The astounded observers could see that the leather-workers had already made some seven or eight thousand knapsacks as well as other bags that could be strapped under the armpit. It was obvious to them that the work was going at a frenetic pace.

Soon they understood that bags were being produced in such large numbers for some military operation that was to take place soon. Was the king planning a march on some faraway land on a major campaign of conquest or plunder? When they returned to the guest house, the officer-in-charge Gauroba Dangata noticed the glitter in the eyes of his guests and instinctively knew its cause. In an effort to assuage their curiosity, he let it slip in casual conversation that the king was planning a major increase in his cavalry force, and that would need enormous quantities of leather items like saddles, bridles, reins and fodder-bags.

The guests did not respond, but the smile seemed to ask, 'Do your horses eat grams and oats by the sack?'

News of the whispers that were exchanged in the guest house reached the king's ears, as they were bound to. Leave alone the cavalrymen, even the king's senior ministers had no idea what project Shivraya was preparing for in the workshop erected next to the stream. What was their king up to? There was Shaista, ensconced in Pune, making life miserable for everybody; instead of grappling with that urgent problem, why would Shivraya engage in this seemingly purposeless activity of secretly manufacturing thousands of backpacks and shoulder-bags?

When Jijausahib saw the anxious face of Gopalrao who had just come from the office, she asked, 'Gopalrao, we hear that some twelve thousand of Shaista Khan's soldiers have arrived in the upper reaches of the Konkan coast around Kolaba!'

'Matoshri, that's last week's news.'

'So, what new information have you brought about Rahimatpur in the ghats, Pant?'

'Ausahib, around seven thousand horsemen have infiltrated Rahimatpur too. They have even erected tents there. I wonder what that Khan's plans are!'

'He's planning a major assault on the Swarajya, it appears,' Soyrabai piped up from behind.

The two turned their heads to see where the voice came from. Jijau was visibly delighted to hear her daughter-in-law making political comments. 'It is good, Soyra,' she said, 'to see you analyse the situation with such sharpness.'

'Actually, my brother Hambirdada came to visit the king a couple of days ago. In his opinion, Aurangzeb is applying pressure upon Shaista Khan to launch a massive invasion of the Swarajya,' Soyra elaborated. 'There is a strong possibility, therefore, of Shaista opening up two fronts at the same time.'

'Ah! So, one attack coming down from the ghats, and the other coming up from the Konkan coast … they want to catch us in a pincer move!'

As if these pieces of information were not sensational enough, there was another bombshell that exploded in the evening from the direction of Sinhgadh. The matter needed such urgent consideration that every moment lost measured an eternity. Jijausahib threw her silk stole over her shoulder and prepared to set off with her two daughters-in-law for a meeting with the king. Surprise of surprises, they had hardly stepped out of the palace when they espied the king riding in astride his handsome white horse, accompanied by a bunch of sardars.

An unspoken message was exchanged between mother and son, and the king headed straight for the private hall of the palace. The moment she caught Shivraya alone, Jijau rushed towards him, placed a loving hand on his shoulder and said, 'Balraje, the news is not good at all.'

'Could you be talking about the three traitors at Sinhgadh, Ausahib?'

'Precisely, son. Sinhgadh fort is the very breath of our Swarajya. When I heard that they wanted to present this jewel as a gift on a platter to that wicked Shaista Khan, I was terribly agitated.'

Deeply moved by his mother's anxiety, the king put her at ease by saying, 'Matoshri, praise be to Ma Jagdamba and the bravery and alacrity of our espionage wing. When I got to hear of this despicable betrayal a day and a half ago, I immediately took preemptive steps. Our stout-hearted men threw a ring around the perfidious three and their associates, and put them in solitary confinement. Our Tanaji has posted a round-the-clock guard on them and completely quashed their malevolent moves.'

'Brilliant, Balraje, absolutely brilliant.'

'Your blessings, Maasahib.'

'But why did you take so long to reach here in spite of so many messages?'

'Our Netaji Palkar—'

'What about him, Balraje?' Jijau's heart had jumped to her mouth.

'No, no, no cause to worry now, Matoshri, things are under control, but Netaji has had a close shave with death. It is our good fortune that providence has spared him; he is safe now.'

'Arey deva! What are you saying?' Despite the assurance, Jijau's heart had begun to thump wildly. 'I want to hear the details.'

'Well, as you know, Netaji has been mounting incessant raids upon the Mughal establishment and tearing chunks of flesh off them. His intrepid squads have thwarted Mughal operations everywhere in the region, turning Shaista Khan wild with rage and frustration. Therefore, unbeknownst to anyone, he handpicked a force of eight thousand horsemen and placed them under the command of fifty sardars. Their single mission was to annihilate their most ferocious enemy—Netaji Palkar.'

'Aai ga! Such venom!'

'Can't blame the Khan, Maasahib. Netajikaka has caused immense torment and heavy losses to the Mughal forces. There have been occasions when their entire army has gone thirsty and hungry for days at a stretch because of Netajikaka's sabotage. You will remember that when Shaista Khan was coming from Aurangabad, Netaji had plundered his camp on the Bhima bed and left them no choice but to sleep on the freezing sand for the entire night. They say that on that night, Shaista's wife had declared her desire to feed on Netaji's fried innards.'

'Yes, but what about the latest episode?'

'Netaji has been pillaging Mughal posts with such vigour and relentlessness that the Mughals began sending squad after squad to hunt him down somehow. In this latest development, Netaji gave them the dodge, and taking the Paranda-Ausa route past Solapur, galloped in the direction of Bijapur. Even as they closed in on him, the Mughals alerted the Bijapur forces on the other side.'

'Aga bai! It was a murderous entrapment!'

'Yes, that it was. Netaji racing away, and an entire cavalry of vengeance-driven Mughal soldiers hot on his heels! They were quite close to Bijapur when disaster struck. A Mughal spear found its mark on the rump of Netaji's horse and brought it down. Although he recovered quickly and sprang to his feet, he found himself surrounded by nearly two thousand enemy soldiers. The battle was so fierce that his protective ring of three hundred Maratha horses was slaughtered in no time.'

'Three hundred horses and men slaughtered?'

'That's right, Matoshri. And had it not been for divine interference, we would have lost a priceless jewel to the jaws of Death. He was saved only because of the intervention of a close friend.'

'And who was that emissary of god?'

'A person whose entire family has sworn their sympathy for the Swarajya in spite of earning their bread at the Adilshahi till.'

'Are you speaking of Rustam-e-Zamaan?'

'None other, Maasahib. He took Netaji into his protection. He deluded the Mughal sardars with some ingenious double-talk. He also threw in the scare that twenty-five thousand Maratha men were stationed down the road, and could cause them a lot of discomfort. He assured them that he would put Netaji in chains and advised them to turn back.'

Jijausahib could not hold back tears of gratitude as she cried, 'Waah, waah! What a blessing this prince of brother Randullah has been!'

'No doubt at all, Matoshri. Rustam-e-Zamaan used his ready intelligence and courage to deflect a terrible tragedy in the making. Otherwise there would have been no saving one of our greatest heroes of Swarajya!'

'Balraje, there are mountains of adversity that stand before us. That ruthless uncle of Aurangzeb refuses to get off the chest of Pune, where he has been sitting for so long. He has been busy deluding people into believing that he is sunk deep in sloth and merrymaking, but the facts on the ground are frightening.'

'You have something to suggest, Matoshri?'

'Yes. Look at the multipronged crises that this man has been creating for us. He very nearly cost Netaji his life. He has planted thousands of his soldiers in the Rahimatpur ghats on the one side and in the Konkan region, via Chaul, on the other. He tried to infiltrate the Sinhgadh fort by trying to buy over our men. If we do not tighten our strategies and take some countermeasures, we may have to pay a heavy price for it.'

'What you say is true, Matoshri. If we don't go on the offensive at this stage, we run the risk getting stamped out where we stand.'

'That's my point, Balraje. The situation demands that we gather our courage and hit back in some way.'

This strong signal coming from Matoshri impacted Shivraya deeply. Despite the lateness of the hour, the gravity of the current circumstances was being discussed threadbare among the gathered chieftains. In the midst of heavy demands upon his time, Shivraya squeezed out a few moments to write a letter of gratitude to Rustam-e-Zamaan. He thanked him profusely for all the favours that he had done for the Swarajya and beseeched him to take personal care of the wounded Netaji.

The urgent confabulations went on for the second day running, the issue under discussion being how to respond to the gathering crises. That was when a message arrived from the office superintendent. The brother-in-law of Mukunda, the gardener at Lal Mahal, had arrived and was requesting an audience with the king. When Shaista Khan had snatched away Lal Mahal, he had dismissed every single member of the palace retinue who had worked under Jijausahib and Shivraya.

The only exception he had made was with Mukunda, who had won him over completely with his exceptional gardening skills. Shaista had been so deeply impressed with Mukunda's maintenance of the rose garden near the palace that he had patted him on the back and declared that such gardeners could never be found in Delhi or Agra.

On hearing Mukunda's name, Jijausahib said, 'That's a good man. But what is his brother-in-law doing here?'

'Well,' said the king, 'Mukunda is our well-loved retainer. Perhaps, his relative has simply come to pay his respects to us.'

The king immediately ensured that arrangements were made for the man's stay. After a while, Balaji Aaoji came running from the office and said, 'The guest seems to have an urgent message to convey. Mukunda had wished to make this visit himself, but refrained because he did not want to excite Shaista's suspicion. Hence he sent his brother-in-law.'

'A message from Lal Mahal?' Everyone was immediately alert.

The man was admitted into the king's presence at once. Without wasting much time on overture, the man began, 'Everywhere on the banks of the Mula-Mutha, you find hordes of tanners washing bullock-skin and buffalo-skin in the pools, drying and tanning it to prepare leather. Hundreds of leather-workers have been put to task. A number of water-carriers have also been appointed to help the work move faster. They've been sewing large twin-bags that can be placed on the backs of buffaloes, one bag hanging on each side, for carrying water. Public announcements are being made everywhere in and around Pune that hundreds of male buffaloes will be required on an urgent basis. Mukunda dispatched me for delivering this information to the king.'

Even as everyone sat wondering what Shaista was up to, Shivraya stood up, swept his eyes over the assembly and said, 'When an army sets out on a major campaign, and the route runs through water-scarce lands, such bags are absolutely essential for carrying water in sufficient quantities.'

The eyes of the listening sardars lit up.

'But where does Shaista propose to go after making such massive preparations?' Moropant wondered.

'Well,' said the king, 'if Shaista is making such extensive arrangements for transporting enormous quantities of water on buffalo-back to accompany his army, he could well be planning an assault on Rajgadh.'

'If this is true, Raje,' Jijau voiced her opinion, 'why should you wait for the fox to stir out of its burrow? Would it not be better to trap it right there and finish it off?'

'What you say makes sense, Matoshri. It appears that we are left with no choice but to get into the camel's stable and thread a rope through its nose!'

Once this bold decision was taken, the king and his sardars began to act with firm resolve.

Shivraya journeyed by night to Sinhgadh with his intrepid army. He decided to make a brief halt at Khedebehara near Shivapur for feeding his horses. Whenever he was travelling to and from Rajapur, his favourite watering hole was the waada of Bapuji Mudgal Deshpande. This time around, he also wanted to pick up Bapuji's two sons Babaji and Chimnaji for the campaign that was brewing in his head. Despite the lateness of the hour, he was given a warm welcome. Refusing to partake of a late dinner, he settled for a glass of jaggery water.

As they were preparing to depart, there was a commotion outside. The Raja soon learned that it was caused by the arrival of an old friend. As the footsteps of a large number of people rushing towards the upper mansion echoed through the night air, he looked out of a window to see a few palanquin-carriers. They were mopping themselves as they stood next to a palanquin that they had just lowered. Curious to know who the guest could be, he threw a look at the door of the front hall.

That was when the king heard the booming voice of Netaji Palkar, followed by the man himself. But this doughty warrior entered leaning on the shoulders of Chimnaji and Babaji. An attendant walked alongside, carrying a crutch. Every one of Palkar's limbs was swathed in bandages. A keen observer would have noticed him wince often, much as he tried to conceal his pain. Clearly, his wounds were still raw.

The king leapt out of his seat, dashed towards Netaji and held him in his arms. Netaji's recent brush with death had whipped Shivaji's emotions up, involuntarily tightening his embrace of his commander-in-chief. 'How are you, Raje?' Netaji asked, a little out of breath. 'And how's Ausahib's health?'

'Netajikaka, how many days have passed since the assault on you?'

'About ten or twelve days, I think.'

'And where did you set out from?'

'I was near Bijapur a couple of days ago.'

'You really are the limit, Kaka. With your wounds still raw, why did you have to undertake this painful palanquin journey across such a long distance?'

'Raje, that poor man Rustam used the same argument too and went on his knees, almost, to keep me there till my wounds healed somewhat. But my simple question is: how can a fish live out of water? Living so long in a faraway land, so far away from you, was impossible for a person of my temperament. I then pestered your friend till he gave in and arranged a comfortable but swift palanquin journey that would get me here in these two or three days.'

Shivraya was in a hurry to depart. After some more casual conversation, he said to Netaji, 'Look, commander-in-chief, the first thing you must attend to now is your health. This waada is as sacred to the cause of Swarajya as any temple can be. I advise that you take complete rest here and stir out only when you are fully recovered.'

He then held Netaji's hand and rose from his seat, saying, 'I should be off, then.'

'Off, yes, but where?'

'I've told you I'm in a hurry, haven't I?'

'Raje, don't duck my question, understand?' Netaji said in mock irritation.

'I'm not doing anything of the kind.'

'Of course you are!' Netaji said with a laugh. 'Seeing the glitter in your eyes, my heart has begun beating faster too. Therefore, out with it! What is this big hunt that you're setting out on?'

'Netajikaka, you will have to forgive me, but however much you insist, it will be impossible to take you along in your current state of health.'

'What rubbish! I've just made this long trip in a palanquin, haven't I? And I can tell you, I could have been a flower on a prayer-platter so comfortably did I travel. Therefore, Raje, you may call it my obstinacy, if you wish ... but you are not setting out on any hunt leaving me behind here.'

'Netajikaka, please don't make unreasonable demands. Stay, and recover your health. Your wounds are far too raw to be exposed to the rough and tumble of our adventure. I value our commander-in-chief far too much to expose him to pointless risks.'

'Raje,' Netaji said with a twinkle in his eye, 'I am not a child. I know what hunt you are setting out on and in which jungle.'

'Really? Tell me, then.'

'You are going to pounce on that wild animal called Shaista, and you want me to stay warming my rump in this waada. Well, you are the king and I am your humble servant. Go ahead, if you want to, leaving this old man behind. But let me tell you this: the thought of missing out on such a critical battle happening in my immediate vicinity is going to do my health no good. You may be sure that, when you return, you will find me worse off than I am now. A better cure for me is to be in the thick of the battle, sword in hand, performing whatever small service I can. It is your decision.'

Shivraya's feet turned to lead. 'Netokaka, why are you being so stubborn?' he groaned.

'Why not? You tell me, honestly, with a battle raging within striking distance, which self-respecting warrior would want to stay wrapped up in blankets? Would you?'

Shivraya was left speechless by this argument. Mopping the moisture off his brow, he said in a soft voice, 'I am heading towards Sinhgadh right now to make preparations. For this night, at least, you should stay behind and shake off the tiredness of your journey. Arrangements will be made to take you to a certain spot by tomorrow afternoon.'

'Thank you, Raje,' Netaji responded in a relieved voice.

'Since you are so adamant, you are being given this opportunity to participate in the campaign, but on one condition.'

'What is that?'

'Considering the injured state you are in, you will not be placed anywhere in the lead; that will not help either of us. You will have to stay behind at the appointed spot, sword in hand.'

'That's perfectly fine, Raje. Your wish is my command.' A fleeting thought then brought a wry smile to his lips as he said, 'But this is a strange, scenario, isn't it? Shivaji at the head of the campaign and Netaji bringing up the rear ... inconceivable, isn't it?'

The image brought a loud laugh out of Shivraya. Feeling immensely proud of Netaji's indomitable spirit, he said, 'Don't worry, Kaka. The spot where you will be placed needs the services of matchless warriors like you. Your presence will work to the benefit of all.'

'How's that?'

'When your brave soldiers clash swords with the enemy, their morale will hit the skies when they know that their audacious leader is with them in this enterprise.'

On reaching Sinhgadh, Shivraya paid a visit to the dungeon where the traitors had been incarcerated. In the light of the torch, he saw the three turncoats sitting desolately with their heads bowed. If they had gotten away with their nefarious plans, calamity would have descended on the Maratha cause. The offenders could not find the courage to lift their heads; the king too had no desire to talk to them or linger there for long. However, as he walked out, he could not hold back the disgust that had welled up in him.

'See, Moropant?' he said to his companion. 'How readily some people can sell their souls to feather their own nests!'

'Don't think about it, Raje. However expensive the cloak that you throw on a mouse's back, it cannot give up its essential nature and refrain from nibbling at it.'

The war council, sitting around a rough map of Pune spread upon a table, lasted all night. The actual population of Pune was not more than fifteen thousand under normal circumstances, but it had been flooded for a few years now with an avalanche of more than a hundred thousand Mughal soldiers, plunging the life of its inhabitants in complete disarray.

Carefully tying up all the loose threads of his imminent adventure, the king said, 'Keep this in mind: Shaista and his men are in the middle of their Ramzan fasts. Which means that after sunset, when the fast gets broken, the soldiers go on a rampage of feasting. Therefore we may conclude that, during the holy month, Muslim soldiers are not placed on guard duty. I propose that we take full advantage of the presence of the Maratha soldiers who will be doing the evening shift from sunset onwards.'

Chimnaji Bapu said, 'Raje, we have spent our entire childhood romping around every nook and corner of Lal Mahal in your company. This knowledge will be invaluable to us two brothers on this operation.'

'Yes, of course. Remember this too. Jaswant Singh's ten thousand men are guarding the entire area extending from the Sinhgadh slope right up to the village Donaje in the distance. We must ensure that these demons get no wind of our movements. If these forces on the periphery of the town get wind of our presence, our entire operation will get blown away.'

The day finally dawned. The king took his bath and paid obeisance to Goddess Bhawani. Shaista Khan was no ordinary foe. He was no less than Aurangzeb's alter ego, as valiant as he was sharp and alert. He had proved his mettle in the battlefield of Chittagong in faraway Bengal.

Tall, lithe and strong as a whipcord, he had the swordsmanship to best four or five opponents at one go. Mounting a raid on an enemy like him would require as much skill and resilience as raw courage. If it succeeded, it would be an achievement of the highest order. However, if it failed, it could only mean painful death for the raiders. Shivaji was fully aware of this.

34

NOSE-RING FOR THE CAMEL

APRIL 5, 1663

One thousand five hundred Maavalis came out of Sinhgadh in the evening. As they stepped out of the fort gate, they kept off the open road and took to unbeaten tracks. There were those ten thousand Mughal soldiers of Jaswant Singh that had to be dodged. Like cattle returning home from a day of grazing in the jungle, the Maavalis were moving with rapid steps. They had deliberately chosen a roundabout route on the right that went past a few gorges.

Sticking to the edge of hilly ridges, they travelled through the jungles of Kondhanpur, Shindewadi and Yevlewadi. While they were still on elevated ground, they hit the Katraj pass. They came down it to the western side of Kondhva and moved along the banks of the Ambil stream. Every moment and every inch beyond this point was chiselled in stone in Shivraya's mind. It was the eighth night of the waxing moon in the month of Chaitra. As the Maavalis were descending the Katraj pass, they had the moon for company.

The atmosphere in Pune was that of celebration. Since it was the holy month of Ramzan, there were large and small gatherings of devotional qawwalis at numerous places. Added to that, it was the evening period of Goraj, which the natives considered auspicious for marriage. As a consequence, there were plenty of wedding processions moving with their bands of musicians from one hamlet to another. It was also time for change of guard, when those on evening duty took charge from their daytime colleagues. The city was throbbing with activity.

Netaji sat concealed in his assigned spot in the middle of a grove. When Shivraya's horse came and stood before him, he struck a light to see the king's face. Even though he snuffed it out immediately, he could not hold back a smile and an amused comment: 'Waah, Raje, with your fair complexion, your sharp nose and that fancy Rajasthani turban and tunic, who will doubt your claim to be Jaswant Singh's brother?'

'You are indeed a mind-reader, Netokaka. It is as Jaswant Singh's brother Madan Singh that I will be visiting Lal Mahal on some official work, you may say.'

Netaji had with him a thousand soldiers. While the king was on his assigned task, if there was any kind of betrayal or slippage, it would be the job of Netaji's company to rush forward and bail him out of any difficulty he was caught in. Considering that Jaswant Singh's men had surrounded the Sinhgadh fort, it had been decided that the return journey to the fort after the raid would not be along the Donje bullock cart track. If a skirmish broke out around the palace and it became necessary to enter Maaval territory from the other side of the river Mula, Moropant Pingale's thousand horsemen would be there, scattered thinly over the area, to help them escape. If the raid was successful, the king would take the route that ran through the Katraj pass. It would then be Netaji's responsibility to offer protection to the returning raiders.

'So, Netokaka, are all the fruit-trays and sweet dishes ready for Khan sahib's felicitation in the marriage procession?'

'They are, Raje, stop worrying. If the Khan tries to escape from this side, he will find a fully equipped reception party waiting for him.'

'How's that?'

'We've picked up three hundred bullocks from a village in a corner of the Katraj forest and shifted them up to a nook atop the mountain. We've got the herder boys ready; they will drive the bullocks in whichever direction we want them driven.'

'Excellent, excellent.'

'My subedar has reported that the cans of oil needed for the manoeuvre have been transported up there too.'

'And the torches?'

'Rags wound around bamboo twigs, like you make dolls. Everything is in perfect readiness,' Netaji assured the king. 'Most of the animals we have gathered are well past their prime, so they are not of much use. Their horns, however, are long and sharp. The fire will not cause them any discomfort at all, don't worry.'

The Mughal army had established a number of checkposts all around Pune to exercise rigorous control over traffic passing in and out of the town. Anybody wanting to enter would be subjected to intense questioning. For the past two years, it had been difficult for well-built Maratha men to gain entry. The guards were instructed to confirm the person's identity and the exact nature of his work beyond doubt before they let him in.

A crowd of two hundred men converged on one such post, creating a flutter among the soldiers manning it. The men were dressed in colourful tunics and barabandi jackets, with fancy turbans placed cockily on their heads. The jollity with which they carried themselves confirmed that they were members of a marriage procession. The guard on duty asked their leader, 'Where are you off to, friend?'

'Khan sahib, you must join us in our celebration. Here, please have some jalebis and give your blessings to the newly-weds.' A few packets of crisply fried jalebis were passed over to the guards on duty.

'Thank you, and congratulations,' said the head guard, accepting the sweets with alacrity. 'But where has the groom disappeared?'

'The wedding party entered the town quite early in the afternoon, Khan sahib.'

'Oh, I see. Where are your passes?'

'Here, sir, here they are, all signed and stamped by the kotwal.'

'Well, all right, you may go in.'

The permission letters had in fact been procured a couple of days in advance, with a little bit of under-the-table greasing of palms. Thus, the 'marriage procession' from Maaval entered the city. Some of the king's horsemen had also bought some old saddles and riding equipment from the army market and then, posing as Mughal horse-grooms, managed to slip past the guards without arousing any suspicion.

Meanwhile forty-odd soldiers, dressed in Mughal uniforms and armed with spears and swords, descended on another guard-post.

'Where are you coming from?'

'We were doing duty all day at the Katak post.'

'Well? And now?'

'What now? The guard has changed, so we are going back to our barracks. You fellows have been indulging yourselves on Ramzan sweets, while those of us who are not Muslim do double-duty on account of your festival.'

The group simply walked past the post, as if it was the only thing expected of them.

Aurangzeb's coronation, incidentally, had taken place in the month of Ramzan. The anniversary was being celebrated across the empire for four days with great fanfare. Lal Mahal, therefore, had become the centre of unbridled merrymaking for all of Pune. Starting from six in the morning, there would be bands playing and people setting off fireworks every three hours. There were festive camel circuses, edge-of-the-seat horse races and lively swordsmanship contests all across the city, which had the imperial soldiery literally dancing down the streets. Once the fast was broken at sunset, gourmet feasts of spicy Mughal cuisine replete with kebabs and biryani would be served everywhere, leaving the revelling soldiers heavy-lidded with indulgence.

Most of Shivraya's co-conspirators had arrived in the vicinity of Lal Mahal by dusk and sat outside exchanging pleasantries. The raid was to be conducted late in the night. The residents of Lal Mahal appeared to be in a happy, semi-drowsy state after the day's fasting and feasting. Sounds of laughter and congenial chatter, particularly of the womenfolk, came floating out of the arched windows.

The prominent participants in the evening's adventure lay concealed in the darkness behind the palace. The brothers Babaji and Chimnaji were imparting to their accomplices little nuggets of information on the layout of Lal Mahal. They had spent many years of their childhood running around the halls and through the passages of the palace; there was not a patch of it that they didn't know intimately. Besides, just a month ago, Bapuji had refreshed his memory by working as an apprentice to Mukunda, the gardener.

'Like his brother-in-law Shahjahan, this Shaista also relishes the company of nubile women. He is often found in their company.'

'Bapu, who's interested in his sexual escapades?' Yesaji Kank intercepted. 'Tell us of his whereabouts.'

'That's exactly what I'm doing. He is always surrounded by two or three dozen Uzbek women. They are handsome, tall and well built. They are also expert riders and swordswomen.'

'Ah, really?'

'Shaista's bedroom has two zenana sections on either side—the far side is occupied by his daughters and daughters-in-law, and the nearer side houses his begums and a couple of dozen concubines.'

'But how can such a large assemblage of women manage to fit in there?' Chandji Jedhe asked.

'The Khan has restructured many of the palace rooms. He's created new rooms just by dropping thick curtains or blinds to serve as walls. The patios, front and back, are guarded all through the night by these Uzbek women and some eunuchs armed with long swords, so better be careful.'

This brought a snigger from the men in the bushes, although a suppressed one. They couldn't afford to reveal their presence to the enemy.

Shaista had a harem of nine official wives and a dozen concubines. As with the wives, the concubines had also been carefully selected from around the world for their beauty and suppleness of body. Their job was to give the Khan a massage of perfumed oils and indulge his every desire.

Next to the Khan's bedchamber were the bedrooms of his princes and his daughters. This complex of numerous comfortable boudoirs had been created by demolishing and then restructuring the original halls by creating partitions using thick silk curtains and reed-blinds.

It was past midnight now. The music had hit a crescendo and then fallen silent. The festivities of that particular evening had been of the excessive variety; the Uzbek women guards too had ingulged in all the dancing and drinking and feasting. As a result, when they resumed their duty as night-guards, they were more than a little fuzzy-headed and wobbly-legged. There was also the bother of rushing for the pre-dawn breakfast before fasting began. The eunuchs had snuffed out the lamps, enveloping the palace in near-total darkness.

So much for the Khan's personal bodyguard. As for the palace guards, a number of small tents had been erected for them on the palace grounds. After the endless festivities of the day, including the liberal consumption of meat and drinks, several of them were sprawled in these tents snoring. Those who had turned up for duty were sleep-walking too.

Post midnight, the shadows around Lal Mahal suddenly started to sprout feet. The guards at the rear of the palace were fewer in number. They saw an extremely impressive-looking Rajasthani sardar dismount from his frightfully expensive black horse. The soldiers accompanying him moved with great discipline and alacrity and helped their master dismount, after which they withdrew a step and stood with their heads bowed in deep respect. The guards watching this display were overawed.

'Could this be Raja Jaswant who has come over?'

'Looks like it. For some secret consultation, perhaps.'

After a quick exchange of murmurs, the guards bowed low to welcome the sardar and his servitors who were dressed in long, embroidered tunics and colourful turbans. There was grace and authority in the manner in which Shivraya walked into Lal Mahal.

Shivraya had stood waiting for what seemed a long time in the darkness, sword in hand, eager for the action to begin. As he had done in the Afzal Khan encounter, he wore chain-mail under his loose Rajasthani tunic. A similar lattice of interlocking steel-rings functioned as a skull-cap, hidden under his exuberant turban. A company of two hundred men were now ready to enter the inner quad of Lal Mahal. Chimnaji, Babaji, Chandji Jedhe and their group waited in a state of extreme alertness, staring unblinkingly at the rear wall of the palace that lay in semi-darkness.

In a corner of the palace backyard stood Mukunda's squat little cottage, with its roofing of curved earthen tiles. His merchandise of saplings, fresh flowers and fragrant gajras allowed him a free run of the entire palace. When he heard the sound of a throat being cleared in the darkness outside, he sneaked out and signalled to the three shadows standing at a distance to follow him. He took them to a spot from where he unearthed some digging tools that he had concealed earlier in the day and handed them to Babaji, Chimnaji and Chandji Jedhe. He then took them to the wall that lay in the darkness ahead.

'Where do we begin the digging?' the three asked. 'How do we get into the waada?'

'Here's the wall, don't you see? There was a small trapdoor here earlier that Begum Sahiba had walled up a few months ago out of fear.'

'So, shall we get busy with our picks and shovels here?'

'Yes, but do it in small bits. We don't want the guards to hear any movement.'

The sound of the midnight drum reverberated through the air, but once it stopped, work began in a hurry. The idea was to dig a hole in the newly made wall that was big enough to allow men to pass through. However, it needed to be done with extreme caution, so as not to alert the guards. The three men began using Mukunda's tools to scrape the cement out of the joints and dislodge the bricks one by one. But for all their care, they couldn't make it an entirely soundless exercise.

The women guards inside the palace had fallen silent, but a groom and a eunuch lay twisting and turning in their beds because of the excessive consumption of biryani. When one of them stood up to let out a burp, he heard the sound of soft hammering outside. 'There's something suspicious happening there, for sure,' they decided. Not wanting to take any chances, they rushed to the door of Shaista's bedchamber, but the thought of waking him up at this late hour gave them cold feet. They did the next best thing by rousing Shaukat Shah, Shaista's young son who was sleeping outside the zenana. Shaukat was too young to have any second thoughts about dashing into his father's chamber.

Shaista was stretched out on his sandalwood cot in his usual state of debauchery. Merely two in a bed was never enough for him. To his left lay two of his wives, and two more women to his right, all in a state of disarray. They had brought into bed the stale fragrance of the flowers woven into their hair, which, along with the wearers, was a necessary soporific agent for Shaista. At his feet lay a beautiful concubine who had dozed off while pressing his legs.

Waking Shaista from his beauty sleep was considered a major offence, but the young prince was too naïve to bother and he banged on his father's door urgently. An extremely heavy-lidded and dangerously provoked Shaista rolled out of his bed and bumbled towards the door.

'What?' he barked at his son, while the groom and the eunuch stood trembling behind him.

'Abba huzoor, these two men heard something suspicious,' he said, pointing at the cowering pair.

'What?' The bark was now several decibels higher.

'Huzoor, just listen!' they begged.

As their luck would have it, the sound had simply disappeared. After straining his ears for ten or fifteen seconds, Shaista pushed his son aside and delivered a slap each to the two minions, raging with all the displeasure of a roused bison. 'You shit-scared rascals, you! Who appointed cowards like you as guards?'

'We swear, huzoor, there were suspicious sounds coming from the rear wall.'

Wild with rage, he held the two by their collars and shook them like a cat would shake a rat. 'Who the devil would want to enter the palace through the rear wall, you imbeciles? Siva? His grandfather? And how would they get past the ring of guards?'

Four more grooms and some women-guards came over to swell the crowd, which riled Shaista still further. 'The mere name of that rat is enough to make you shit water! If you dare to bother me again with your sissy prattle, I'll have you all flayed!' With that, he went back into his chamber, banged the door shut and strode back to his bed. The women around him, though, were trained pacifiers. A bit of mollycoddling, and he was soon snoring loudly.

The two minions who had raised the alarm had barely settled back into their beds when the sounds resumed. By then, however, the Maavali infiltrators had managed to knock a large enough hole in the wall. It was then that the drum marking the passage of three hours after midnight was heard. Taking advantage of the sound, Shivraya's associates quickly entered the palace premises through the hole.

Around that time, a few of the cooks had begun to stir and move towards the kitchen with lamps in their hands. They had to prepare the pre-fast breakfast for the royal household. Just then, heavy rags suddenly fell upon their lamps, snuffing them all out. The men were completely blinded for a moment. They heard the heavy tread of hundreds of running feet and saw, in the dim light filtering through the blinds, that they were surrounded by a huge crowd of armed men with their faces covered. Only one of them managed to shriek 'Allah!' before the swords descended and made short work of them all.

Time began to fly in the darkness. The swords of Babaji, Chimnaji, Chandji and their men swung furiously, clearing the way for the king and his Maavalis to go leaping up the staircase. They had Mukunda the gardener to show the way. The king himself, of course, knew the layout of the palace like the back of his hand. He had been familiar with the walls, the doors and the carved casements since childhood.

Mukunda led Shivraya straight to the zenana, where they expected to find their main prey. The footwear that the Maavalis were wearing had metal studs nailed to their soles, which made a distinctive clatter as they ran. The Uzbek female guards, now sure that a bunch of foreign feet were inside the palace walls, pulled out their swords and rushed towards the sound. A good three dozen of them emerged from the darkness and broke upon the advancing Marathas. They were strongly built, well-trained women and pushing them away was impossible. Swords clashed and a violent skirmish ensued. Within minutes, the floor was littered with at least a score of bleeding bodies, three of which belonged to Maratha men.

Chimnaji was using his sword to rip apart the silk curtains and clear the way. A number of the women sleeping in the hall were trampled under the pounding feet of the raiders, and they cried out in pain and terror. The king then noticed the entrance to another hall and assumed it was the Khan's boudoir. As he rushed forward with his men, a young prince got up with a start and pulled out his sword. But before he could lift it, a Maavali foot brought it crashing down.

The young man was Prince Fateh Khan. When he saw the place swarming with armed and agitated men, his courage deserted him and he froze. At that very moment, his wife Nusrat Begum who was dressed in flimsy night clothes shrieked and leapt at her husband to protect him. Chandji instantly placed the tip of his sword against her nape and growled, 'If you shout, you are dead. Release that bastard Shaista from under you.'

'Ya Allah!' the girl cried, 'please have mercy. This is not Shaista sahib. This is his son Fateh Khan. He has done no wrong. Please, brother, we have just got married!'

Shivraya held the young man by the throat and said, 'All right, then, tell us where your father is.' The girl registered the ferocity with which the words had been spat out. Instinctively choosing her husband's safety over her father-in-law's, Nusrat said, 'Come, huzoor, I'll take you to him, but please don't harm my husband!'

When she pointed to the grand bedchamber, Shivraya and his men dashed into the darkness inside. When Shaista Khan's wife Dulari Begum heard the commotion outside, she began shrieking in terror. Taking her husband in a tight embrace, she screamed, 'Treachery! Treachery! Help!' Her scream woke the Khan and the other women on the bed too. When the startled Shaista opened his eyes, he saw steel flashing at close quarters. A lump formed in his stomach and he bellowed, 'Ya Allah!'

Shivraya sprang forward and pulled away the bedclothes that had covered the sleeping party. Shaista frantically reached for the muzzle-loading pistol that he kept under his pillow, but it slipped out of his trembling hands and clattered to the ground. Dulari Begum hustled the other women into forming a human shield around her husband's body.

A few of the intrepid Uzbek girls rushed in with their swords and pandemonium broke loose in the bedchamber. Fateh Khan, seeing the women leap into the fray, was charged with a new fervour and dashed towards his father's chamber with a few soldiers. Destiny, however, was not on his side. Chandji Jedhe's sword came flashing down and separated his head from his shoulders in one swipe. Taking advantage of the melee, Shaista scurried out of the rear door and ran down the verandah, screaming, 'Help! Help!'

Shivraya and his men instantly went after him. The worry that his prey could slip away had brought fresh vigour into the king's limbs. The women had shrewdly snuffed out all the lamps, but the king swung his sword left and right andbrought down all obstacles that stood between him and his running quarry.

Much had happened on the palace premises since the scrimmage in the inner chambers. The guards had all been jolted out of their sleep, and were running this way and that or gathering in the palace quad, shouting, 'Enemy! The enemy has raided!'

There was an arched window in a passage that looked out on the courtyard. A few persons who were fleeing the Maavali raiders grasped the upper end of the door-frame next to it and jumped out of the window. Shaista's jump coincided exactly with the swing of Shivraya's sword. The sword missed the Khan and hit the door-frame while Shaista's hand was still gripping it, severing three of his fingers at one blow.

However, he did manage to leap out and land with a heavy thump on the ground below. Despite the immense pain of the fall and the severed fingers, Shaista thought it wiser to lie there unmoving, as if dead, till such time as the raiders withdrew. If he made the slightest sound, a hundred swords would fall upon him and chop him to pieces. 'Let's move out, my brave men,' Shivraya shouted. 'Shaista has been wiped out.' Shaista Khan's astuteness had saved his life.

Mayhem ruled the the palace premises. Cries of 'Enemy! Enemy!' were rising from every corner. To escape detection, Shivraya and his men picked up the same cry and raced out of the palace precincts. Before the combat had begun, he had assigned an important job to one of his lieutenants—the security of Mukunda. The gardener was to be moved out of the palace grounds along with his entire family. The king had told his men, 'Our supporters should not be made to suffer for the help they have given us.'

The sun's rays began to dissipate the darkness of the sky and the night of torment. The bedlam that had begun in Lal Mahal in the small hours and unspooled in increasing madness and havoc seemed finally to have ended. The Khan's family and their guards were scared out of their wits. At first light, a bedraggled man was seen hobbling up the courtyard to the door, his clothes blood-spattered and one of his arms swathed in rags from the elbow to the tip of his fingers. Onlookers would have found it hard to believe that this broken, beggarly looking man was none other than their glass-chewing, fire-breathing master. The hair-raising raid and his inability to stand up to it had crushed his self-esteem.

The dismal state of their chief broke the spirit of the sardars and the soldiers too. As for the various wives, concubines and other women, the shock of the blitzkrieg had rendered them speechless. Nusrat Begum had fainted at the sight of the decapitated body of her husband. Dulari Begum had suffered the double blow of losing a son and also a son-in-law. She stared uncomprehendingly at the devastation around her. The scene of the battle was not a sight for the weak-hearted.

Nobody had had the time or the strength to clear the staircase, the passages or the bedrooms above of the mutilated corpses of the couple of dozen Uzbek women and the score of slain guards. Pools of blood everywhere, headless and limbless bodies, entrails spilled out of torn abdomens—the goriness of the slaughter in this place designed for the ultimate comforts of life was a contrast the women of the Khan's household couldn't stomach. Eventually, the horror-stricken women recovered enough to start lamenting, 'All this destruction has been wrought by that hound from hell, Sivaji.' Nusrat, however, was beyond consoling.

Physicians were called over immediately to effect whatever repair could be managed on Shaista's injuries, particularly his maimed hand. The loss of blood had been substantial. Someone asked, 'But where has our friend Jaswant Rathod disappeared?'

'That rascal may well be hand-in-glove with his brother in faith, Siva. Together, they could have hatched this plot to hurt Khan sahib.'

The morning had not advanced much when a large contingent of horsemen arrived from the direction of Sinhgadh. Jaswant Singh dismounted from his steed and went in to meet his chief. Shaista Khan somehow reined in his rage and said in a cutting voice, 'Hello Ranaji, how did you drift this way?'

'Khan sahib, how is your health?'

'Forget about my health. I had heard that you thwarted Siva's march on Pune and got martyred in the effort! So, how did you return?'

Jaswant Singh's face turned dark with humiliation. The women too had begun to openly hurl abuses in his direction.

Just then a havaldar came rushing in, bringing more news that served as a slap on the face. After Shivaji had bolted from the palace, a company of Mughal soldiers had set off in pursuit. It was clear that the Marathas were headed for the Katraj pass and the jungles beyond; despite the difficulty of the trail, the Mughal men decided to go after them and finish them. Seeing the Maavali flambeaux receding into the darkness of the forest, they rushed forward to overtake them and slaughter them. What they found at the end of the chase was not the fleeing enemy, but a herd of cattle with oil-soaked rags flaming on their horns. All they had got in return for their valour and enterprise was broken jaws.

During these few years of stay in the city, Dulari Begum had begun to regard Pune as a veritable heaven and dreamed of settling down there for life. She had even undertaken modification and repair of the palace to fit it out to her taste. But here she was now, staring at the corpses of her young son and son-in-law laid out before her. With extreme bitterness and sorrow, she said to her husband, 'My lord, if one day I am able to chew a kebab made of Netaji Palkar's liver, I shall be satisfied.'

It was with the greatest difficulty that Shaista Khan managed to see another night through in that haunted palace. On the third day after the night raid at Lal Mahal, he crossed the Mula with a heavy heart and made his way towards Aurangabad with as much haste as he could muster.

When Aurangzeb heard of the most daring and damaging raid that anyone had ever mounted upon a Mughal post, he was in Lahore. He had just returned from a pleasurable holiday in Kashmir and was en route to his capital, Agra. So mortified was he by this incident which had irrevocably sullied the prestige of his empire that he ate nothing but fruits for the next couple of days. Finally, he took a hard decision and ordered the transfer of his uncle to the provinces of Bengal and Assam.

When Shaista Khan received his transfer order, he was overcome with a sense of disgrace. He did all that was in his power to have the order rescinded, but the Emperor was so upset by the dishonour that Shaista had dragged down upon the Mughal name that he snapped his lifelong ties of affection with his uncle. He sent a firman to Aurangabad, demanding Shaista's presence at his new post as early as the fastest horse could take him.

Shivraya had plans for getting his Konkan campaign started within a week's time. Rajgadh was in a mood of unrestrained rejoicing. Alongside the celebrations, the king held a durbar in which vital decisions related to the Swarajya were taken. Also, on this occasion, Mukunda was felicitated by Jijausahib, who conferred gifts of expensive clothing on the gardener, his wife and his children. Looking at the completely overawed man, Shivraya said, 'If you have any desires at all, Mukunda, please feel free to express them without any hesitation.'

'I have no wishes at all, Raje,' Mukunda replied, placing his head at the king's feet.

'How can you not place your demands, Mukunda? The debt of gratitude that the Swarajya owes to you is the size of a mountain.'

As he stood, the cynosure of all eyes at the durbar, he had a quick, whispered discussion with his wife. Once again he bowed before the king and said, 'Raje, this poor servant of yours has just one request. Before this moment, garlands of flowers grown by me were placed at god's feet in the palace at Pune. Please allow me to continue enjoying this privilege in your shrine here at Rajgadh. I want nothing else.'

The king whole-heartedly accepted Mukunda's request on the spot. He also gifted to the gardener three villages in perpetuity.

35

TOWARDS THE CITY OF GOLD

'Matoshri, a kingdom cannot be run without funds. If Aurangzeb were to come galloping into our land tomorrow, if he were to encircle us, we will need plenty of resources to withstand the pressure of thousands of his horses.'

'Truly said, Balraje.'

'Which is why, it's good to hit really hard when you hit, instead of exchanging innocent punches. The Mughals certainly need to be taught a bitter lesson.'

After a brief silence, Jijau breathed a deep sigh and said, 'Once you are back from your campaign, please have me escorted to Bijapur. I can't take your father off my mind these days. A strange discomposure seems to have overtaken me. Why does he visit me so often in my dreams lately? And look at the form he takes! He comes sitting haughtily on a horse, and doesn't miss an opportunity of teasing me, even in my dreams. Makes a big show of bowing before me just to make fun of me!'

In a more serious vein, she continued, 'When I think of his recent arrest at Bankapur, my heart fills with dread. Why would the Shah commit this fiendish act?'

'Matoshri, please stop agitating yourself with these unpleasant thoughts. It isn't really an arrest; just a pretence of keeping him confined to his quarters for a couple of days.'

'How humiliating this experience must be for a self-respecting person like him! To be punished with confinement after ruling over Bengaluru for so many years! And that too, for utterly trivial reasons!'

'Ausahib, Adilshah had sent Abasahib to Maharashtra with the express purpose of getting us to accept the suzerainty of the Bijapur Sultanate. He was bound to be affronted when both father and son dismissed the proposal.'

For the past month or two, Rajgadh had been sizzling with secret confabulations and all-night vigils. The Raja was clearly planning a major campaign, but whether in the north or in the south, nobody had any inkling. The visits of sardars like Parsoji Naik, Santaji Bobade and Naro Bapuji had become more frequent. True to his reputation as a born nighthawk, Bahirji Naik would suddenly appear at the fort after the sun had set, and disappear into the sky like a bird at the break of dawn.

At the base of the Rajgadh fort, Parsoji and Santaji were busy training the fifteen hundred youngsters who had been recruited into the army. The boys were mostly natives of the villages nestled in the gorges and ravines of the Sahyadris. They had grown up swinging from the branches of tall trees and scaling vertical cliffs from peak to abyss. They were next taken to the vast fields at the foot of the Torana fort where they camped for six months under the open sky. They were drilled there in horse riding, spear wielding and sword fighting.

Knowing that the departure of their lord from the fort was imminent, the queens bustled about looking after his every need, big and small. Putlabai sat for hours in the shrine, praying and fasting for her husband's well-being. Meanwhile, Soyrabai and Jaishribai constantly hovered around the king, ready to satisfy his every whim, spoken or unspoken.

Finally, the afternoon arrived when a contingent of ten thousand of the Swarajya's best horsemen rode out of the gates of Rajgadh. 'This time, there will be no kettledrums, no horns and trumpets, absolutely no fanfare as we leave,' Shivraya declared. 'This campaign of ours is utterly different from the ones we have mounted before. I have spent countless sleepless nights in the last two or three years contemplating the rich and thriving land we are headed for. Keep in mind that it is the enemy's City of Gold.'

The ten-thousand-strong cavalry galloped through gulches and gorges, and over densely forested mountainsides. Before they halted for their supper, many hills and valleys had been left behind. As they rode carefully in the darkness down a rather slippery trail into the valley below, Netaji Palkar's attention was drawn to the lights of what seemed to be torches twinkling here and there on the slopes of the massive mountain range on the right. A nameless anxiety crept into his mind.

Soon, they were riding across meadows on level ground, Netaji's horse cantering alongside the king's. The wind had begun to bite, but clearly, that was not what was bothering the commander-in-chief. 'Something on your mind, Netokaka?' the king asked with a smile.

'Cast your eyes to the right, Raje, and look at those twinkling lamps and torches. That insane Jaswant Singh is still parked around Sinhgadh with his massive army of forty thousand horses.'

'Forget about all that, Netokaka,' Shivraya said, unconcerned. 'For how long has he been sitting on the siege there, would you say? Three or four months?'

'A little more than a year, Raje.'

'And even so, the fort remains where it is and Jaswant Singh remains parked on the lower slope. Keep sitting there for as long as you want, I would tell him,' the king said with a laugh.

On December 6, 1663, the king was in the Lohgadh-Visapur region, where he ordered the fort-keeper to scour the stables across the ghats and around their bases. He was instructed to buy four thousand of the best horses he could find—young, spirited, strong and with the stamina to do long-distance runs. The rumour mills had begun to turn. The king wanted to go riding down the Umberkhind pass, perhaps? He had also wanted to bring the Portuguese down a few notches by plundering their harbours, hadn't he?

The king's ten thousand horsemen halted at a fold in the valley. After darkness descended, the army came to life. A fresh lot of four thousand horses was inducted into the cavalry; they were handed over as additional beasts to four thousand riders. When they were on the move, these spare horses would run alongside their own animal. Now there were fourteen thousand horses cutting through the jungles in the darkness of the night. They knew as well as their riders did that there were many such nights of incessant, surreptitious running ahead.

The king had deliberately chosen the period immediately following the winter season; that would ensure the water-bodies in these jungles were alive and flowing. Maps had been prepared that marked a river or a pool or a jungle spring beside which they would rest during the day. As soon as evening came, man and animal would shake off their laziness, flex their muscles and race for four continuous hours before a halt was called. The horsemen would then dismount next to a convenient water source, pull their skillets out of the saddlebags and set alight makeshift hearths for cooking frugal but nutritious meals of millet bhaakari and pithle made from gram flour. Sometimes it would be just bhaakari and onions. After the animals had been fed, horse and rider would lean against each other and stretch out to rest their tired muscles.

While the others snored, sleep was often reluctant to visit Shivraya and his commander-in-chief. After making the rounds of their open-air camp, they would sit together—discussing, planning and dreaming. There was forward movement every day, but their destination remained a deep, deep secret. Even when the two talked about it, they would do so in codes.

'Four weeks you had said, Raje, hadn't you?' Netaji queried.

'Yes. The first three weeks are going to be in and around our region. Then, we bow before Lord Mahadev and drink in the sight of the Jyotirlinga to our heart's content. Our fourth week begins right from those steps. That leg of the journey is by far the most menacing, because that is where the land goes sloping sharply down from the mountains. The rest of the distance our panting and frothing men and animals will have to cover in just a single week.'

'And the distance will be as much as what we have put behind us.'

'Exactly. We will have to stake our lives on reaching our destination in seven days, come what may. If the enemy blocks our way, he must be slaughtered and the journey resumed. Agility is of the essence; otherwise, even our horses will not have a chance of returning to Rajgadh.'

It was as if a gong had been sounded for the two o'clock hour. The men quickly sprang to their feet and the ride resumed. The sound of hooves reverberated through the jungles like the buzzing of a million bees. When the dawn wind began blowing, it infused fresh energy into the riders and their animals. They would see the sun rising as they rode and feel the temperature rising in the jungles. This morning's ride would carry on for a good seven hours or so.

Some among the four thousand riderless horses turned unruly from time to time and tried to plow their own furrow, inconveniencing the horseman in charge. At such times, the horseman transferred his saddle to the wayward horse's back and rode the animal some distance with liberal use of spurs. That usually drove all thoughts of defiance out of the animal's system.

There were occasions when the companies halted for an hour or so in the shelter of some wood, but only if there was a village or a fort or some human habitation in sight. Otherwise, they would ride on for another three hours. This land close to Khedebehara was Shivaji's territory, administered by the Deshpande brothers.

Naro Bapuji and Chimnaji Bapuji Mudgal Deshpande had the charge of two thousand five hundred horsemen each. However, the two were befuddled. They had left behind the town of Tikona and its market. Even when they had arrived close to Lanavali, they couldn't fathom what their destination was.

'Dada, where is the king leading us?'

'It's a wealthy city along some bay, they say.'

The four deputy commanders had come together during a break. The excuse was to share some tobacco, but the actual motivation was to try and solve a riddle. Where, exactly, were they heading with such a huge army? Wild surmises were being made among the rank and file of the company, and the conjecture that found the largest number of takers was that their king was likely to move towards Khambhat-Gujarat. When they saw Netaji Palkar approaching, the four young men surrounded him immediately and began to pester him. 'Netokaka, let us into the secret too. In which direction is this adventure taking us?'

'What can I say, friends? I am as much in the dark as you are,' Netaji responded with a perplexed smile. 'Never in my life have I seen the king mount such a major campaign with such secrecy.' Not merely the sardars, but even the army animals knew that Netokaka was virtually the king's shadow, the very beat of his heart. How was it possible, then, that he should not know?

The clerk accompanying Netaji fished out a sheet of blank English paper from his bag along with a quill and handed them over to Netaji. Netaji drew on it a thick, wriggly line like the trail left by a worm. It stood for the Sahyadri mountains. All that lay below the line was the Konkan region, with Borghat in the middle. Moving upwards along the line, one encountered the Rajmachi fort. Resting his finger on the spot, Netaji said to his sardars, 'We ride for two or three days in utter secrecy, crossing all these ghats on the way, to reach this point.'

Riding along the ridges of the ghats was an arduous task and a dangerous one. A few nights of travel would take them to Bhimashankar and Naneghat. There, on the other side, was the town of Junnar that lay in a big Mughal province. It was quite obvious even to the casual observer that Shivraya had planned this swift, silent movement through the jungles with meticulous care. Knowledgeable guides had been recruited who were thoroughly conversant with every forest path and mountain pass.

However, climbing down the ghats and moving along the coast, both were equally fraught. Crossing the valleys that lay beyond Junnar, one ran into the formidable Mughal post of Sangamner. Both these stations had a huge reserve force of Mughal soldiers. If they got wind of the Maratha horses moving cunningly through the jungles like wild cats, the entire campaign would fall apart. On the other hand, the areas of Vasai, Virar and Nalsopara were crawling with Portuguese guards; there were few who hated the king more than the Portuguese.

From Karjat onwards, the army moved along the Sahyadri foothills and crossed Murbad. On the Dolkhamb route, they came upon a small village called Asangaon. In comparison to the hilly region they had just traversed, the terrain after Murbad was flat and low. This made travelling during the day risky; there were no hiding places suitable for a large army, and chances of being spotted were strong. Consequently, day-long halts were made in the jungles next to a stream or a river, although these failed to provide adequate rest. When the army entered Asangaon after three consecutive nights of sleeplessness, they found shelter next to a sufficiently big stream. The men and animals stretched themselves out and soon began to snore.

Their passion for expanding the Swarajya had, as it were, pronounced a curse upon Shivraya and Netaji Palkar: rest and relaxation would not come anywhere near them. They were aflame night and day like burning torches. Consequently, while their fourteen thousand men and horses surrendered themselves to sleep at Asangaon, Shivraya and Netaji stood on guard under the dense shade of a mango tree.

'We do have a big cavalry, kaka,' the king said, 'and we are carrying quite a bit of luggage too. All this jungle crossing is getting really tricky.'

'What can one do, Raje? You had insisted on carrying about fifteen thousand empty bags. That is bound to slow down the movement of our horses.'

The king then revealed the reasons for the additional load. 'The wealth that lies scattered across the city of gold keeps the heart of the Mughal dominion beating,' he said. 'After we clean it all up, it will be dangerous to tarry there even for a moment. Every minute that we can save from our raid and plunder will be indispensable to our escape.'

The exchange of opinions between the two continued late into the night. 'Kaka,' the king said gravely, 'the journey ahead is going to be particularly tense. Although our spies are on the alert in every little hamlet hereabouts, the fear remains.'

'What fear?'

'Well, what if we accidently run into a Mughal squad of five thousand or so?'

'We'll simply chop them down, what else?'

'Kaka, kaka,' said the king with an indulgent smile, 'you seem to forget that we are not out to do battle, but to raid this city of gold, gather all the wealth that lies there and carry it back to our own capital city with all possible speed.'

The discussion went on.

'The blessings of the Lord of Kailash have always been with our Bhosale lineage. One of the twelve Jyotirlingas is bound to fall on our way. It doesn't seem proper that we should pass it by without offering our obeisance to Lord Shiva.'

'What you say is quite true, Raje, but climbing the Kasara ghats with all the additional load on their backs is not going to be easy for our horses.'

'Kaka, we need to split our force into two units. If one happens to fall into enemy hands, the other should be able to mount an assault upon them.'

The wise king and his valiant general had finally arrived at a mode of operation. Accordingly, Netokaka left the camp with five thousand horsemen laden with heavy baggage. Their fast horses took the jungle track on the other side of Kadsaar and moved towards Kolvana. They crossed Javhar-Mokhada and began galloping in the direction of Ramnagar.

On the third day after the bifurcation of his army, the king took a holy dip in the Narmada at a spot on the bank beyond Nashik and paid his obeisance to Tryambakeshwar very early in the morning. The keeper of the Tryambak fort had done the job assigned to him. He had scoured the markets and gathered for the king four hundred strong and well-built bullocks of the finest breed.

'Maharaj,' he informed the king with justifiable pride, 'these animals are extremely tenacious and sturdy. Whatever load you place upon their backs, they will go prancing through the hills and valleys like a herd of deer.'

The high mountains and gorges around the Tryambak fort were soon behind them. The king's army was traversing the Utaar pass at a fast clip. The wind blowing in from the west was keeping both men and animals sharp and alert. It was in this nippy air that the trail finally revealed its secret destination to the Maavali raiders.

'Briskly, briskly, my fellow soldiers. The city that has been touted as the golden city of the Mughal Emperor is none other than Surat. It is this city that we are out to plunder, so that we may bring relief and prosperity to our own Swarajya.'

'Well said, friend. Move with sprightly steps. Future generations will beat their pots and pans as they sing of our Enterprise. They will proudly proclaim to all that their ancestors had participated in this legendary campaign.'

Gusts of enthusiasm were blowing through the men. Joy and excitement were at their peak.

Parsoji Mahadik asked Moropant, 'What would you say is the population of our Pune?'

'Twelve to fifteen thousand, perhaps.'

'And how many are estimated to live in this seductive city called Surat?' Santaji Bobade asked.

'Well upwards of two hundred thousand!'

The mighty river Tapti gathers its water from the mountains of the Vindhya and the Satpura ranges and then abruptly descends to lose itself in the Gulf of Khambhat, also called Cambay, in the Arabian sea. Along its banks and very close to the sea was a beautiful trading township called Suryapur, which later grew into a city that came to be called Surat.

Among the harbour cities on both coasts of India, Surat was regarded as the most vibrant and prosperous. In fact, it was counted among the richest ports of the entire world. The operations of a few of Surat's merchant princes like Veerji Vohra, Haji Zahid Beg and Haji Kaasam were so extensive that even the Portuguese and the English bowed before their might. They readily confessed that no trader of their land could match them in the sheer scale of their enterprise or the volume of their turnover.

Surat brought more tax revenue to the Mughal empire than other major cities like Lahore, Calcutta or Delhi. That was why it was regarded as the most affluent of all Mughal holdings. Ever since Emperor Akbar had first annexed the town and the harbour, Surat had maintained its reputation as a place of luxury and opulence.

Twenty-eight miles from Surat was a settlement called Gandiv. Three horsemen from this post galloped into the Surat fort and broke into a gathering where Inayat Khan was making merry with his friends over bottles of wine. 'Huzoor,' they screamed, 'the huge army of some Mughal sardar has arrived in our town. They are carrying a lot of paraphernalia with them.'

'So, what's biting you?'

'Huzoor?'

'Royal guests of this kind keep materialising every now and then. And what do these Delhi people want? Song, dance, revelry, a little bit of gold and some jewels. They must surely be the greediest people in the world!'

The three horsemen seemed quite unimpressed by Inayat Khan's placatory words. When they remained rooted to their spot, exuding anxiety, Inayat Khan lost his cool and snapped, 'What's wrong with you, idiots? Why are you so agitated?'

'Forgive our impertinence, huzoor, but these sardars have with them an army that is at least ten thousand strong. And while they swear loyalty to the Emperor, they do not at all look like natives of the banks of the Ganga and the Yamuna.'

'Well, then?'

'We were wondering whether it could be that Maratha king Sivaji who has come to plunder our city.'

'To plunder? Even assuming for a moment that it is the margattha king, how did the thought of plunder enter into your heads?'

'He has ten thousand horses—'

'All right, and what else?'

'He seems to have brought with him a few thousand spare horses and hundreds of bullocks. Why else would he bring along so many unloaded animals to such a distant land?'

This last piece of information roused the first misgiving in Inayat Khan. It did seem like some mischief was brewing, after all. Being a vibrant and bustling city, Surat never ran short of gossip or sensation. Countless ships came and went every day, pirates occasionally paid visits, and squabbles sprang up over the distribution of property and profit, keeping its inhabitants on their toes. But the arrival of a huge army with thousands of horses and hundreds of bullocks to spare was an event with no precedent.

Inayat Khan hastily climbed up to the terrace of his mansion and scanned the direction in which the main harbour called Suwali lay, about fifteen miles to the west of the city centre. During high tide, a number of boats, big and small, would sail up the Tapti. Regular water-transport facilities existed too. As Inayat Khan peered into the distance, he noticed a big crowd of people rushing in from the docks towards the city. He also noticed the white traders clambering onto their horses in front of the warehouses and milling around in confusion. Even as he watched, he heard agitated cries from the marketplace, of 'Run! Run!! Shivaji has arrived!!!' and 'Allah! Save us!!!' The shopkeepers had hurriedly begun to close their shutters.

Inayat Khan stood frozen on the terrace for a little while. He could see the panic in the city quickly building up to a crescendo. His men began coming in with the information that people, after loading their belongings on horse-carriages and bullock carts, were scampering out of the city.

The very first breeze that blew in from Surat delighted Shivraya. Work immediately began on the erection of tents in an open space on its outskirts. Hearths began lighting up for the preparation of the evening meal. Meanwhile, reports arrived on the mayhem that was building up in the city at the news of their arrival.

Large rugs were spread out before the king's tent where a quick war-council was held. Commander-in-chief Netaji Palkar and the deputy commanders of the cavalry, Naro Bapuji, Chimnaji Bapuji, Santaji Bobade and Parsoji Mahadik, sat around the king while the others sat facing them. Briefing them on the defensive fortifications of the city they were about to enter, the king said, 'The Surat fort is invincible. The protective wall that runs around it is formidable, extremely formidable—sixty feet high and forty-five feet wide.'

'What's there to it, Raje? If the need arises, we can throw ladders and climb over the wall into the fort,' was Netaji's characteristic response.

Bahirji Naik, dressed as a mendicant, sat in front of the king with a bunch of hand-drawn maps. He had made the square in front of the big mosque in Surat his home for the past few months and had spent time roaming the lanes and by-lanes of the city, ostensibly begging for alms. He now possessed information that hardly anybody could match and was dispensing it to the king and his colleagues as they sat in conference: how the influential Dutch, Portuguese, Chinese, African, French and English traders had erected their massive shops and warehouses; how business worth hundreds of thousands of rupees was being transacted every day;

who the really powerful business families were; and who enjoyed what kind of reputation not only within the city, but across the world.

The king himself had done a great deal of painstaking research before he had set out on this campaign. He joined Bahirji in tutoring his colleagues on how the city was built and how it came to function as a vibrant hub of regional as well as world trade. After several historical upheavals, in the fullness of time, this small trading settlement that sat on the right bank of the Tapti had established its dominance as a major port of cosmopolitan reach and significance.

He told them about the commercial links between Gujarat and the Malabar port deep in the south. Boatloads upon boatloads of merchandise were unloaded on the Surat docks and transported to inland provinces and stations like Patna, Lahore, Delhi, Agra, Kashmir, Bhaganagar, Golconda and Bijapur. Both native traders and their foreign counterparts had constructed huge structures in the city to support their enterprises. They had made liberal use of dressed stone and baked red bricks to raise these mansions and warehouses. Bahirji presented his maps before the gathering, indicating the precise locations of these grand buildings.

Shivraya, Netaji and Bahirji bent over the maps, absorbing it all with hungry eyes. The Red Gate, the Delhi Gate, the Sahara Gate, Udhna, as also the market around the Burhanpur Gate: all these landmarks were carefully pointed out to the concerned sardars. They were also briefed on the lanes, the squares and the important buildings that they would encounter. The motive behind this exercise was to ensure that there was no room for confusion or error, and if mistakes were made, that they knew how to help each other.

The king and his commander-in-chief were ambling around the camp. Half of the cavalry that had travelled with Netaji had arrived at more or less the same time as Shivraya and his company. The deputy commanders were also on their rounds in different parts of the camp.

The British and Dutch warehouses had established themselves quite expansively in this city. The British warehouse was now in its fifty-first year of existence. This strong, double-storeyed building was the headquarters of their commercial activities. The chief administrator at that time was a person named George Oxenden, who also had charge of all the British trading stations in the region, including the formidably fortified harbour in Bombay. Thinking of their strong defences, the king remarked, 'It will not be difficult to mount a raid on the rest of Surat.'

'That's quite true, Raje. The Mughal subedar Inayat Khan is a corrupt, unreliable and self-centred person, they say. A very acquisitive—'

'Your information is correct. Which is why, I am not worried about Inayat Khan. But the British official Oxenden and the officials of the Dutch warehouse here are going to be tough people to crack.'

'Raje, a word from you, and we will crack all of them.'

'Although we want all the plunder we can gather here, we are still governed by the ethics of kingship. We do not seek the notoriety of cruel and wicked bandits. Even if our Hindvi swarajya is small in size, our vision and our policies are going to gain renown across the world. And we must plant our feet carefully in the business enterprise of the world.'

'Can you elaborate, Raje?'

'Netokaka, the problems of administering a state cannot all be resolved by the stroke of a sword. On the contrary, there are occasions when many matters have to be handled with a cool and wise head.'

It had started turning dark. Puling the reins of his horse, he said to Netaji, 'All right, Netokaka, let's now wind all this up.'

'We will, of course, manage the best speed we can, but ransacking this huge and affluent city will take a minimum of six or seven days—'

'Our job is not merely to sack Surat, but to carry the booty tidily away on horseback. Till such time as all this wealth is deposited at the foot of Rajgadh, we shall know no rest or relaxation.'

'Huh? But how can we pull it off at this pace?'

'Eating and drinking on one's feet, and stacking up the loot in an orderly fashion. The blowing wind and burning flame do not pause or rest; we, too, have to forget that the human body needs sleep. Without dallying or slackening, we have to finish gathering all our booty in three days' time, and vanish across the horizon of this land by the evening of the fourth day at the latest.'

The king had taken on a near-impossible enterprise. Everyone heard with rapt attention how he proposed to wrap up this unprecedented operation.

'Look, the very moment the Surat administration got wind of our presence here, that very moment, lightning-fast horses would have been dispatched to Ahmedabad. By the morning of the third day since our sack of Surat begins, these horses would have touched the precincts of Ahmedabad.'

'Arey deva! So fast?'

'Absolutely! These horses are not going to stop even for a wink of sleep till they present themselves to the Mughal subedar at Ahmedabad. After that, it will be just one single cry all over the strong garrison city: Shivaji's raid on Surat. The garrison head will not take more than five or six hours to get his troops in order. They will then mount the wind and come blowing in like a storm to settle scores with us.'

In a short while, Shivraya held a second meeting of his sardars. In the flickering flame of the lamps, the king's face looked as if it was carved in steel. His eyes shone with an unshakeable resolve. 'The enemy forces are bound to reach here on the fifth day; otherwise that Aurangya will chew his generals up like carrots and radishes. The Mughal forces, therefore, are not going to bother about the blood they draw out of their horses' nostrils as they fly in this direction.'

'That sounds completely reasonable, Raje.'

'Of course! Destiny has provided us with just four days to finish our campaign and depart. Wasting a single moment on idle chatter is a crime. Let's catch the wind by the scruff. Let's empty out this opulent enemy city and vanish!'

36

THE SACK OF SURAT

JANUARY, 1664

Shivaji and his men had pitched camp at Gandiv on the outskirts of Surat. On the evening of the king's arrival, the Reverend Father Ambrose, priest of a famous church in Surat, paid him a visit. As was the norm, the priest did not have to wait long to get an audience with the king. Father Ambrose possessed an attractive personality. His strong physique, thick neck, and thinning hair on a wide, pumpkin-like forehead, along with the soft expression on his pious face, left a positive impression on the observer.

Father Ambrose wore the dark-brown cassock favoured by the Jesuit priests of those times. After shaking hands with the king, he pulled out of his pocket a small, palm-sized velvet bag with a golden string. He undid the string and fished out a longish emerald carved in the shape of a peepul leaf, designed to be worn as a plume. With the greatest courtesy, he offered the ornament as a gift to the king.

'Please forgive me, father,' the king said, in a polite effort at refusal.

'No, no, please don't say no. I am offering this gift as a father would bestow it on a worthy son. The intention is as innocent as that.'

In the face of such persistence, the king was left with no choice except to give in. 'Thank you, father,' he said as he accepted the precious jewel, 'I welcome your gift with all my heart. I also assure you that this brilliant gem shall adorn the crown.'

'Thank you.'

'Now you can tell me frankly, father, about the reason behind this priceless gift.'

'Great king, our poor Christian brothers who reside in this coastal region have built a beautiful church in Surat. Prayers are offered there to Jesus Christ every single day. Our request is that the sanctity of this place of worship be maintained.'

'Had you made sufficient enquiries about me, Father, you would not have felt the need for this gift. You may return without any worry or fear. Forget destroying a place of worship, whether this army of Shivaji passes through the territories of friend or foe, it never so much as damages a single tile of any holy place.'

'Thank you, great king.' The priest was overwrought by the ease with which the king reassured him of his respect for all places of worship.

Wherever Shivraya travelled, it was his habit to gather all the information there was to obtain about that place. Not only did he have the details of the wealthiest households and warehouses in the town, he also knew the addresses of its good, compassionate, altruistic and public-spirited citizens. On the very first night of his stay in Surat, the king was informed by Bahirji, 'Raje, a very generous-hearted broker used to live here. People regarded him as god's own man.'

'What are you saying, Bahirji? A broker known for his generosity? Who was this paragon?'

'Mohandas Parekh was his name. A very wealthy man. Whenever a young woman's marriage was held up by dowry issues, he would immediately step in and play the role of a father or a brother.'

'That's good to hear, Bahirji. I shall be delighted to make the acquaintance of such a person.'

'Unfortunately, he passed away a couple of years ago. Half the population of the city cried inconsolably at his untimely death. Even the Dutch and the Portuguese were reduced to tears.'

'Waah, Bahirji, such large-hearted philanthropists are always an asset to the place they live in.'

The king turned to Netaji and said, 'Kaka, please go and visit the family of this wonderful man tomorrow. It is our duty to protect the home and belongings of such a person. Place a few of our guards in front of his door. In all the hustle-bustle of our campaign, his property should not suffer the tiniest harm.'

The king then sent a strong letter to Inayat Khan, the Mughal subedar of Surat, that read:

> We have arrived here to raid the city. Do not, for a moment, think that our intention is to burn and raze. On the contrary, your Emperor Aurangzeb has for several years been perpetrating brutal persecution and injustice upon our poor subjects; we are here to mark a protest against this savagery that is being unleashed on our people. However, it is our desire that the common people of this town should not suffer on account of our campaign. My advice to you is that you should gather the world-famous and wealthy traders of Surat like Veerji Vohra, Haji Zahid Baig and Haji Kaasam, and bring them over for an audience. We can discuss the ransom money to be paid by the city. This amount may then be gathered and handed over to us without delay. This will spare both parties a lot of pain and discomfort.

'What if this Inayat Khan does not pay heed to your advice, Maharaj?' Netaji asked.

'How can he not? The persecution visited upon our subjects in Pune, Supe and Konkan by the Mughal overlords will have to be compensated. Inayat Khan has to be told that if he does not pay the ransom, all of Surat will go up in flames and fountains of blood will spring up everywhere. As the representative of the empire at Delhi, he must decide whether he wants to save his skin from the flogging that the Swarajya army can deliver or submit to being flayed.'

An emissary from Inayat Khan arrived late in the evening with the intemperate message, 'Why are you so hungry for ransom?' The king was so incensed that he arrested the messenger and put him in chains.

The tension of the past month and the taxing journey to Surat had drained the king of his last ounce of energy. As soon as he lay down on his bed that night, he sank into deep slumber, the kind of sleep that he hadn't enjoyed for months together. In any case, as there hadn't been any gesture of compromise from the city, all that his men could do now was to gather the wealth and depart.

Darkness began to melt very slowly on Wednesday morning, as a strange wind blew in from the nearby coast. The city of gold was still submerged in sleep, even as the moist, nippy air of the departing night triggered off a cacophony of crows and sparrows. The king and his lieutenants finished their morning ablutions in the darkness behind the tent partitions. Even in this foreign land, the Maavali water-carrier squad had made available a regular and abundant supply of water.

The tent-master had been very keen to erect a handsome, regal-looking tent for his king, but Shivraya took him to task. 'Haibatrao,' he said, 'do you consider your king as some kind of Sultan? I am the king of the poor who throw rough blankets and rags around themselves. So, why would I want a tent decked up with the moon and the stars?'

'Forgive the impertinence, Raje. It shall be as you desire.'

Looking into the predawn darkness, the king said, 'Go along, and hurry. Even a moment's delay may cost us our lives. Go to Surat and erect a shelter in front of the Burhanpuri gate; not a fancy one, but enough to provide some shade.'

'Just as you wish, Maharaj.'

While the king was distributing the work at hand, Netaji had split the army into four companies of two thousand five hundred horses each and placed them under the command of his lieutenants. A miracle had occurred during the night. Thousands of men who had been doing the rounds of the weekly animal markets of Baglan, Ramnagar and Kolvan, posing as cattle traders, had suddenly oozed out of the dark jungles and reported at the Maratha camp. These four thousand men were given the four thousand riderless horses that had been brought along; they leapt onto these beasts with alacrity.

The spirited warhorses too had felt incomplete without a rider astride them. Once they felt the load on their back and the pull of the reins, they came to life and snorted in delight. Suddenly, all around them rose the cries of 'Har har Mahadev' and 'Shivaji Maharaj ki jai'. Netaji gave the king an extra-stiff bow and Shivraya leapt onto his horse. He immediately took a round of the assembled force and looked closely at his battle-ready soldiers. Satisfied, he rode to a piece of elevated ground nearby where Netaji was waiting for him.

Only a few torches had been lit. The dull-orange light from the flames made the king's face look like molten gold. 'Friends,' Shivraya began his address from the mound. 'It isn't greed that has brought us to raid this land, but the pressing need for resources that can help us fly our banner of Swarajya a few notches higher. So many of our forts remain half-constructed; our army needs better weapons and equipment; we are yet to match the strength of the firangis on the waves, and our shipbuilding activities have been stalled—all because of a lack of funds. For the past four years or so, Aurangzeb and his wicked sardars like Shaista Khan have rendered us helpless in our own land. Shaista has caused immeasurable harm to us.'

'But Maharaj, you did teach that demon a lesson by storming Lal Mahal! Who will forget that audacious act?'

'The intention was to slaughter him, but all we could manage was to chop off a few of his fingers. Besides, that other demon of Aurangya, Jaswant Singh, still encircles our Sinhgadh like a snake. It therefore becomes our bounden duty to retaliate, to destroy an enemy who has not only attacked our lands but continues to keep our people under his yoke wherever possible. There is no doubt that the men who have travelled to this Mughal city of gold for the meritorious act of emptying it of its treasure are fortunate.'

'Shivaji Maharaj ki jai!' rose the roar from the front ranks, and it went rolling backwards as the others began echoing it with vigour.

'My brave Maavali soldiers,' the king continued, 'you have to keep one thing in mind. The city of Surat must be sacked; there are no two opinions on that. But care has to be taken that no poor and innocent people of the city are harmed by excesses of any kind from our men, even in the heat of the expedition. Obviously, if someone obstructs us or raises his arms against us, he has to be brought down, but I repeat emphatically that no non-combatant or indigent person should suffer so much as a touch of your fingers.'

'Har har Mahadev!' Fourteen thousand horsemen leapt forward on their dancing horses. They had shaken away the last traces of sleep from their joints; some were excited to the point of standing up in their stirrups as their animals raced ahead. The darkness that had covered Surat was now getting shredded like a worn-out piece of cloth. The Maratha cavalry swept over the outskirts of the city even before it was fully light. The exit gates and checkposts in all the eight directions were immediately taken under control. The guards who had raised their arms in resistance were immediately put to the sword.

Cries of 'Ya Allah! Ya Khuda!' could be heard everywhere. The traders' neighbourhoods outside the walls of the city were surrounded on all sides. Shrieks of fear were heard from every house. The terrified merchants stuck to the doorsteps of their mansions like lizards. A number of them, in their state of panic, tied their gold coins up in a bundle and tried to whisk it away, but were stopped by the Maavalis and relieved of their burden.

Shivaji had instructed his tent-men to erect a wall of canvas-sheet along the trees by the side of the Burhanpur gate. He then seated himself in its shade, waiting for a reply to the notice he had served to Inayat Khan, and through him, to the traders. The Maavalis were waiting in a state of complete readiness with riderless horses and bullocks giving them company.

The king sat waiting at the Burhanpur gate, but he received no reply from Inayat Khan. The three biggest traders had not reached out for any negotiation either. All the prominent merchants of Surat, however, were at their wits' end. What could unarmed civilians do in the event of an assault such as this except to rush to their rulers or their representatives for a solution? Hence Veerji Vohra, Sayyad Baig and Haji Kaasam set out in search of Inayat Khan, only to find that instead of standing with his sword unsheathed in defence of his city, the subedar had disappeared into some rat-hole in the depths of the Surat fort.

Jaws clenched, Shivraya gave the order, 'Netokaka, Chimnaji, enough is enough. The time has arrived to tell these sons of the Goddess of Wealth that we carry sharp swords in our strong fists. Bellow out our war cry of 'Har har Mahadev' and begin the assault on this golden city of Aurangya.'

The wait was over. Sakya the bugler raised his horn and blew mightily into it, at which signal the Maratha cavalry raced into the streets and lanes of Surat and began their loot. Netaji Palkar was in the lead, followed by Chimnaji Bapuji, Naro Bapuji, Santaji Bobade and Parsoji Mahadik, along with their horsemen.

Soon, dense clouds of smoke began bursting out of the city's thoroughfares and alleyways, announcing that the arson had begun. By afternoon, a chilling silence reigned over the city. The smaller traders had abandoned their shops and houses and scurried away. By evening, havoc had been wrought. The Maratha foot soldiers filled their sacks and bags with jewellery and gold and emptied them out at the feet of their king. The heaps soon began to grow larger and larger.

Now that the raid was well under way, swords were bound to come crashing down upon the rich men's havelis and warehouses. It was terrifying to realise that cartloads of money would not provide them with safety of life. And if safety of life was not assured, what would they do with all their millions? Frightened out of their wits, these men tied up as much of their wealth as they could carry in two hands, and towing their families along, made a beeline for the security of the fort.

When Inayat Khan was finally convinced that a force of about fourteen thousand men had raided Surat, and that this force belonged to Shivaji, his hands and feet had turned cold. He immediately took his harem consisting of a cantankerous chief wife, six junior wives and fifteen other women, and sought refuge inside the fort. For his personal security, he posted a thousand-odd men of the army under his command around the fort. He then went up to a casement window on the upper floor of the palace and began observing the rampage that was playing out on the streets and lanes of Surat.

When his wife Gulbano saw the tumultuous scenes that were being enacted in the city and the cowardly manner in which her husband had secreted himself in the fort, she said severely, 'I had always thought of you as the subedar of this city—'

'That I very much am, foolish woman! Do I look a havaldar to you?'

'Shivaji has arrived with a big army for pillaging the city. So, why are you hiding here like a terrorised rabbit instead of pulling out your sword and resisting him?'

'What can you understand of my worries?'

'Does Shivaji frighten you so much?'

'It's not Shivaji. It's the thought of Alamgir Alampanaah Aurangzeb that petrifies me. I fear that he may have me trampled under the feet of an elephant.'

'For what offence?'

'Shivaji will devastate Surat and disappear, and only I will be left to answer the Emperor's questions. There will be an investigation and the cat will soon be out of the bag.'

'What cat?'

'I have been telling the Delhi administration that I have an army of five thousand men for the defence of Surat, whereas, in fact, I have just eleven hundred.'

'And the rest?'

'Only on paper. I have been pocketing the salary of four thousand soldiers and getting away with it so far. But after Shivaji's raid, there will be a proper inquiry, and my goose will indubitably be cooked.'

When the traders reached the fort, Inayat's guards blocked their passage. 'Tell Khan sahib that we need security,' they pleaded. 'Our lives are in danger.'

When the soldiers sent this message to their master, the chief administrator came down with a reply. 'There will be a security cess,' he declared. 'Khan sahib says that he will consider offering security to those who are willing to pay the price for it.'

'Arey!' screamed the incensed traders. 'What is this man? The subedar of this city or some demon? He wants to lick the butter off a dead man's brow?'

The guards, however, refused to act on their own and let them in. As the clamour of the city began reaching their ears, the panic of the traders mounted. The weak and dependent members of their household began to plead, 'Motabhai, Devarji, Dadaji, please think of our lives first. Money can always be earned later.' There really was no other remedy left. The traders paid heavy compensation to Inayat Khan for the securing the safety of their loved ones, after which the corrupt subedar let them enter the fort.

Around that time, George Oxenden, the chief administrator of the British warehouse, arrived at the gates of the fort with a dozen or so horsemen and bowed respectfully before Inayat Khan. His otherwise pink face had turned red as a beetroot. His thick, blonde moustache, beard and side-whiskers were wet with perspiration and laden with dust. 'Khan sahib,' he shrieked, 'Give us protection, or we will die.'

'Are you so frightened, my friend?'

'Huzoor, you are the subedar of this city, its protector. It's your duty to give us security.'

'That, of course, you shall get, but it will require protection money, as you people call it. How much have you brought?'

Finally, after a lot of haggling, the rapacious subedar offered to provide Oxenden with six soldiers in exchange for hundreds of thousands of rupees. The Englishman's disillusionment was complete. He turned around in fury and walked out of Inayat Khan's presence. As he stepped out of the fort gate, he growled, 'That stupid rascal! When he can't save his own skin, what security can he give us?'

Oxenden then began making vigorous preparations to confront the developing crisis. A boat called *Lirdam* had recently brought merchandise that had been unloaded at the company's docks in Suwali and now lay anchored in the river Tapti. The Englishmen quickly loaded the goods at the Suwali harbour onto another boat called *Harlem*.

Oxenden ran from pillar to post to ensure the security of the company's property and strengthen the defences of his warehouse. Come what may, he resolved, they would stand up to this Maratha assault. 'Resistance,' he told his colleagues, 'and counter-assault! We shall protect our possessions to the last breath. Go instantly to the harbour and bring over our six cannons. Mount them around our warehouse.'

Oxenden gathered around him his own eighty guards, fifty armed men of the boat *Lirdam* and a bunch of Indian soldiers. He was determined to protect the warehouse from the plundering Maratha horde at all costs. To underline his willingness to fight if the occasion arose, he took two hundred armed men with him and marched down the streets of Surat with his bugles blowing.

Meanwhile, the king had dispatched his men to the English and the Dutch with the warning, 'You either pay tribute to us or we know what to do with you.' The Maratha agent who was sent a second time to the English warehouse now stood trembling before Shivraya. Perceiving his frightened state, the king asked, 'Ganpatrao, why do you look so shrunken?'

'Maharaj, those red-faced Englishmen are extremely rude.'

'Why? What did they say?'

'They … they said that if I return to them with the same message, they would … shoot me dead.'

Everyone present was stunned at hearing that insolent message. Netaji Palkar, who had just arrived, was especially livid. Boiling with rage, he turned to the king and said, 'Maharaj, just give the order. If I do not stuff the body of that rascal Oxenden with sawdust and throw it at your feet, I am not my father's son.'

Shivaji swallowed the bitter medicine with some difficulty, released a sigh and said, 'Netokaka, in such matters, it is extremely important to stay calm and wait.'

'But Maharaj, why should a person like me even stay alive to hear such impudent language?'

'Staying alive is important kaka, if only to wait for the auspicious moment,' Shivaji said, trying to hide his inner turbulence behind a smile. 'These days shall pass too. When the ships of our Hindvi swarajya begin dancing on the waves, when the coasts of our motherland fall under our control, we shall set sail on the waters and blow the ships of these Englishmen to smithereens with our cannon. We shall riddle the bodies of brazen Englishmen like this Oxenden with our bullets. But you will have to wait for this scene to unfold.'

As often happens in a conflagration, the moist also gets burnt with the dry. In the pyromania that gripped Surat, the establishments of ordinary traders too suffered incalculable harm. Quite a number of Surat's poor also saw their belongings going up in flames. The evening wind that blew through the city was cold. The persona that now took charge of the king's psyche was that of a yogi, a sage, a mystic.

'There is this feeling of repugnance that rises inside me for all the chaos and destruction we have let loose in the city. I can't bear the lamentation of these innocent souls. Aho, we are no dacoits that have come from across the seven seas! I am a king. Netokaka, Tanaji, this burning, this assault and battery must stop immediately!'

'How can we retreat after having taken things so far, Raje? It may be seriously damaging to our enterprise.'

'Netokaka, this subedar of Aurangya called Inayat Khan is an utter imbecile. He has no concern for the welfare of his people or the tears of the poor. It doesn't seem proper to me that we should punish the citizens of Surat for the wickedness of this monster.'

'Then, Maharaj, what exactly are your orders?' asked a confused Tanaji.

'Withdraw your swords and rein in your horses from tomorrow.'

'But why?'

'Because when I see the people here who have been drained out by poverty and crushed by tyranny, my heart bleeds. You tell me, what has been their crime? Our targets are the moneybags, the usurers, the rich and the opulent. But our exercise of dealing out to them a brutal, if well-deserved, punishment is also inflicting untold hardship upon the common people here. Their wails of grief weigh heavy on my heart.'

Shivraya was undoubtedly a courageous warrior and an aggressive fighter, but there was a deep corner of his heart that was occupied by humane sentiments, a vigilant conscience and sage-like compassion. When the spirit overtook him, he would forget altogether about personal gain and loss, friend and foe. He would turn tender and moist with the milk of human kindness.

His sardars, however, were in a fix. They didn't know how to handle this yogic mood of their king. Withdraw all of a sudden? Stop the campaign halfway? Dust their hands off and move away?

That night, the king's mind was ripped apart by contradictory impulses. Many enterprises of the Hindvi swarajya lay suspended only on account of financial constraints. Shaista's occupation had laid waste to the land and the harvest; forts had to be built, and a bigger army raised; the possibility of a prolonged assault from a powerful enemy like Aurangzeb was strong; under these circumstances, raiding an opulent city governed by the Mughals was ethically altogether justified. But then again, what of the innocent, the poor and the destitute who were getting caught in the crossfire?

The night had advanced, but sleep refused to visit the king. He lay tossing and turning on his bed under the temporary shelter, hounded by distressing thoughts. For no ostensible reason, his thoughts drifted to the

Pemgadh of his childhood. Suddenly he heard the sound of hoof-beats and saw Shahajiraje riding towards him. Shahaji stopped his horse next to little Shivba, dismounted and took his son in his arms. Gravely addressing the little boy, he said, 'Shivba, you have to search and search for the auspicious moment, for the arrival of good things. Bad things, however, come in unannounced and stick to you like leeches. Alert! Be alert!!'

The king got up with a start, eyes wide open. It was pitch dark outside. In the distance, the fires that had been lit earlier in the evening were still burning. Netaji's horse was doing the rounds of the lanes and thoroughfares of the city. Shivraya asked for Tanaji Malusare who, as it turned out, was sitting nearby. He immediately presented himself and bowed respectfully, saying, 'What are your orders, Maharaj?'

'Today, from this moment onwards, please stay close to me.'

On Thursday morning, out of the smoke and dust of the city, a horse-carriage emerged from the side of the fort and made its way rapidly towards the Maratha camp. Atop it fluttered the green flag of the Mughal Sultanate. The carriage stopped a short distance from the camp. When Netaji stepped out of his tent and noticed the Mughal pennant, his face lit up. He immediately became hopeful of a speedy resolution to the face-off. 'Good,' he muttered to himself, 'finally some sense seems to have dawned and the subedar of Surat has sent an emissary to settle matters.'

The carriage was given permission to proceed to the king's tent. A tall young Jew climbed out of it. Slim and fair, he looked attractive in a red tunic worn over tight-fitting pajamas. He came and bowed respectfully before the king. He and his two associates were made to stand a few feet away from the king. Looking towards Balaji Aaoji, Shivraya said, 'Notice the sauciness of our Inayat Khan? Half the town is burning, the traders are in a state of agony, we are troubled too, and this presumptuous fool sends an agent, that too so late, to discuss the way out.'

The Raja signalled to the Jewish youth to step forward. As was his wont, he was sitting on a wooden bench under a tree. He had only a sheet of canvas stretching over his head, with all the four sides open to the wind. The young man came closer and bowed again.

The Raja made a sign to the messenger to speak. The young man seemed to shift uneasily, not knowing how he should begin. He held a bouquet of roses in front of his loose-fitting jacket. Clutching the bouquet tighter, he bowed and said reverentially, ‘My name is Yatin and I am Inayat Khan sahib’s agent—’

‘Waah! Half the city has been reduced to ashes, the poor are distraught, and Allah grants your subedar the good sense to send a person like you for talks with me?’

Bowing again with extreme courtesy, the young man said, ‘Our Inayat miyaan says that King Shivaji is among the greatest persons in the world. Whatever mistakes have been made, the people of Surat have committed them—’

‘So?’

‘So, Inayat sahib has instructed me to first beg the forgiveness of an angelic person like you—’

‘What exactly do you want?’

‘Your good wishes, your mercy and your blessings.’

Hunching his shoulders and bending low, Yatin stepped forward, and in the blink of an eye, he thrust the bouquet forward, inside which was hidden a sharp dagger, its tip peeping out viciously, lunging towards the king like a hungry hyena. But Tanaji, standing next to the king with an unsheathed blade, had been alert. He lifted his sword and brought it down upon the arm that held the bouquet with such force that it got severed from the body, falling to the ground. The momentum of the lunge, however, had sent the man crashing into the king, throwing him off balance. The blood spurting out of the stump dyed the king’s tunic red.

Pandemonium broke loose. The news that a dastardly attempt had been made on their king’s life set the Maavalis on fire. Some spiked the news with the rumour that the king had fallen. Swords descended on the people who had been rounded up the previous day. Four of them lost their heads and twenty-four their arms. Mercy and humaneness were immediately discarded as cowardly sentiments and the Maratha swords swung wildly, sparing none that fell within their reach.

The ungovernable wrath of the Shivraya's soldiers was fuel enough to set alight all the palaces and mansions that had escaped the previous day's depredations and soon the entire city started going up in smoke. The nights of Thursday and Friday were for the Suratis the stuff that nightmares are made of. Flames rose from every quarter; grand buildings belched out smoke. While the blaze of the fires turned the nights bright as day, the smoke in the daytime was so thick that it gave the sun little chance to make its presence felt.

Veerji Vohra's haveli was next to the Dutch warehouse. His property was estimated to be worth upwards of eight million rupees. The precious stones and jewellery that he had hidden in the walls of his mansion and in his basement were no less than the treasures of Allaudin's cave. The Maavalis raked in jewels that weighed nearly eighty kilos.

'But, Raje, it looks like an extremely big quarry is slipping out of our grasp.'

'Who is that?'

'The other major trader of Surat named Sayyad Baig. His haveli adjoins the British warehouse. The walls of his house, his attic and his basement are all stacked to the brim with diamonds and gold.'

'But Netokaka, why do you need my permission for looting Sayyad's house? Take your weapons, arm yourself with pickaxes and crowbars, and dig out all the wealth that lies concealed inside.'

'What can I say, Raje? That Baig happens to be the next-door neighbour of the white Englishmen.'

'So what? Go catch him by the scruff of his neck and drag him into our presence.'

'Can't do that. For the past three days, he has shifted with his family to the English warehouse and sits under their fans cooling himself.'

Thus the king and Netaji decided to mount an attack on Sayyad Baig's haveli and a unit of thirty-five horsemen was immediately dispatched for the job. They started using crowbars and pickaxes to bring down the outer walls, but Baig seemed to have anticipated such an eventuality when he built those walls. He had, therefore, reinforced them with steel bars and steel doors which were then secured from the inside with several steel latches. The few blacksmiths who had accompanied the raiding squad did all that they could to penetrate Baig's defences, but they found that one armour-plate led to another and then another behind it. Reaching the wealth that lay locked inside seemed almost impossible.

The blacksmiths began retiring with swollen, painful arms. The Maavalis with their pickaxes dug on till their backs turned stiff. Finally, tiring of these efforts, they decided to use fire as their weapon. They doused the neighbouring house with oil and were about to set it aflame when around thirty British horsemen emerged from the warehouse. The two forces clashed, sparks flew and many blows were exchanged, but neither group could overpower the other. Finally, as evening fell, they withdrew to lick their wounds, their pride more or less intact.

The next day, the front of Baig's haveli presented an unusual sight. It was being guarded by forty or so English horsemen. Their stance clearly proclaimed that they would not let the Marathas get into Baig's house, whatever the consequence. When Shivraya got to know that the Englishmen were were standing in the way of his soldiers, he was furious. He sent a strongly worded message to George Oxenden that read, 'We intend to plunder Baig's house. If you obstruct us in this exercise, send us three hundred thousand rupees as compensation for our loss.'

The messenger who was to carry this missive asked, 'What do we do if the English turn down our demand?'

'Tell them that if courteous words don't persuade them to get out of our way, we shall then arrive on horseback and slaughter every Englishman at their warehouse.'

Since tempers were running high, Netaji himself stepped forward to carry the message. When he met Oxenden, the Englishman complained in an aggrieved tone, 'Look, your Marathas were trying to get into the neighbouring haveli and were on the point of setting it on fire. If they had done that, our warehouse would also have been reduced to ashes. It was important for us to safeguard our possessions.'

'Sahib, why are you making this foolish effort to plant your feet in two boats? You can either cough up the three hundred thousand to compensate for our loss or get out of the way and let us do what we came to do.'

'Look, I am helpless in this matter.'

'If that is how you see it, we shall burn your warehouse down too.'

'Then you may tell your Raja sahib that he is welcome to launch his attack on our warehouse. But he must know that our British men will fight to their last breath, every one of us, to protect our property.'

It was evident that the English as well as the Dutch were willing to give their lives in defence of their properties.

That night, Netaji and Tanaji entered the king's tent with unsheathed blades, placed them at his feet and said, 'Maharaj, we find the insults heaped upon us by these English monkeys intolerable. Just give us permission.'

'For what?'

'To bury all these Englishmen in the sand of Surat and dispatch them to their maker. Let's finish the matter once and for all.'

The king's luminous eyes were, however, looking beyond them into the future. He said, 'My valiant friends, by all means keep the blood racing through your veins. But wait for a while. It will come—the moment will surely come when we shall slaughter these firangis not only on land but also on the waves that they are riding today. Please be patient.'

At around dawn on Saturday, a few horsemen arrived at the camp from the Gujarati town of Bharuch, sweating and panting in spite of the chill morning wind. These Maavali spies had travelled with such haste over such a long distance that their horses too were frothing at the mouth and perspiring profusely. Underlining the urgency of their message, they said, 'Please take a quick decision, Raje. A Mughal army of twenty thousand has set out from Bharuch yesterday to settle scores with you.'

'Under whose flag?'

'The old man Mahabat Khan himself is leading this enterprise. The danger is grave.'

Even before the sun was up, instructions went out to the men to begin packing. The loot that had been gathered over four continuous days of plunder had been heaped up close to the king's tent. The very size of the mounds of gold, jewellery and other expensive articles was astounding. It appeared impossible that the spare horses and the bullocks they had brought along would be able to carry such a load on their backs. Another five thousand animals could easily have been put to use. Seeking a resolution of this new worry, the king asked Balaji Aaoji, 'What do you think we should do, Pant?'

'Raje, let's carry only the best of the stuff. We will have to leave the rest behind.'

'All right, Pant. Let's pass it all through a sieve.'

People were immediately put to work for separating the really valuable items from the less expensive ones. Darkness had begun to dissipate and the first rays of the sun were creeping in. That was when the king was struck by a new thought. Looking around with a pleasant smile at the sardars gathered around him, he said, 'Wait, gentlemen, we cannot step out of Surat without fulfilling an extremely important duty.'

'Raje, let's hurry. Why are we dragging our feet during these final moments?' Netaji asked.

'Do you remember, Netokaka? During the siege of Panhalgadh, the Bijapuri army decided to continue their encirclement of our fort with redoubled vigour in spite of the monsoons? And they had done it all with such secrecy that our spies never got wind of it. That caused us a lot of harm, even if it was temporary.'

'That's true,' Balaji agreed. 'You had turned utterly furious.'

'I had dragged Bahirji Naik over the coals for that blunder. I had castigated him with the harshest of words. Today, however, if you ask me to identify the person most responsible for the success of our Surat venture, it has to be Bahirji.'

Everyone broke out in loud applause, and Bahirji's friends gleefully slapped him on the back with a loud 'Waah, Bahirji!' Bahirji himself bowed low before the king in gratitude and said, 'Nothing extraordinary about it, Maharaj. I was simply performing my duty.'

'No, no, Bahirji, for the last eighteen months or so, you completely submerged yourself in work related to our Surat expedition. You came and lived here for so many months at a stretch, gathered information on who had hoarded how much wealth and exactly where—every palace, every cellar, every trench, every wall, every fold and corner of the battlements. It was because of the detailed intelligence you supplied that we could see such a major enterprise through within the short period of four days. The credit for the efficiency of our operation goes entirely to you, Bahirji.'

The king spoke with great feeling. Removing an expensive necklace, he put it around Bahirji's. He also presented to him other ornaments and honoured him in the presence of all his men. After this short felicitation, they got back to their work of packing and winding up the camp.

Meanwhile, some four or five thousand of Surat's poor had gathered around the camp. They had spent their entire life in huts made of bamboo and mud, never even realising that the merchant-princes of their city had amassed such unimaginable quantities of wealth in their palaces and mansions. The king had made his decision. He got his men to load as much as they could of the more valuable loot on their horses and bullocks. The rest of the stuff was to be left behind for the poor to distribute amongst themselves. Never in their wildest moments had these destitutes thought that they would benefit from such a windfall.

The fully loaded animals were now waiting for the signal to begin their journey back home. The bulk of the plunder was placed on the backs of the bullocks that had been bought at Kolvan near Ramnagar, with fully loaded bags hanging on either side. The faces of the Maavali soldiers were glowing with satisfaction and pride at the sheer quantity of the wealth that they had been able to gather. Only Netaji looked a tad crestfallen. It had been his keen desire to attack the English warehouse, and Shivraya's refusal to allow him that pleasure still rankled. The king gave his disappointed general a smile and a pat on the back, saying, 'Don't be so disheartened, Netokaka. The annihilation of the firangis has only been postponed from today to tomorrow. As soon as the opportunity presents itself, we shall slaughter them on land, or give them a wet burial in the sea with the gods of the fishermen as witnesses.'

The faces of both Netaji and Tanaji broke into bright smiles. 'While sacking the city of gold was important,' the king said, 'getting all this wealth to Maaval quickly and safely is more important. As we set out, let's together shout out our gratitude to Ma Bhawani!'

37

A MOUNTAIN UPROOTED

FEBRUARY 5, 1664

The town of Shivapattan, at the foot of Rajgadh, lay submerged in darkness. Just a little past midnight, a small bunch of horsemen came down the fort and arrived at the bank of the stream. The presence of an audacious woman was a particularly noticeable feature of the squad.

That intrepid, straight-backed lady sat astride her horse, peering repeatedly into the dark vegetation around her. There were three or four tracks that came from different directions and met beside the stream, all leading up to Rajgadh. It was difficult to estimate which path Shivraya would take, which was why the horsewoman was looking in all directions. 'As Ranisahib is aware, whichever way the king comes,' said the soldier, 'he is sure to stop here awhile on his way to the fort to pay his respects at the temple of Gaibi Maruti.'

The king and his men had reached Khedebehara around supper time the previous evening. The horses were tired after having done a very long stretch; the king had therefore decided to halt for an hour or two to give the animals some fodder and also some rest. The evening meal was taken in the waada of Mudgal Deshpande. The soldiers and animals stretched their limbs for a bit, and then the army again set off for Rajgadh a little past midnight. A new energy could be noticed in the movement of the entire company, man and beast alike.

Even during the return journey, the king had many things to worry about. Bringing the loot back securely and depositing it in safe places was critically important. Accordingly, he had already stashed good portions of it in Lohgadh, Visapur, Rajmachi and other such forts en route, making foolproof arrangements for the safety of each hoard. So thrilled was he at the success of this major expedition that the king had begun to see treasures even in the mountains that he met on his way. However, without a doubt, his ultimate bliss would arrive when he reached his destination and received the blessings of the queen mother Jijausahib.

It was dark when he folded his hands before the statue of Gaibi Maruti. That was when his attention was drawn towards the figure of the lady astride the horse close to the door of the temple. As he glimpsed her face in the orange glow of the torch, he called out in a surprised voice, 'Who's there? Is that Jaishri Ranisahib?'

'Yes, Maharaj,' came the reply as the lady stepped forward respectfully and bowed at the king's feet.

Shivraya's astonishment hadn't lessened. Why would Ranisahib wait for him in this dense jungle at this time of night?

'Did you spend your night in the palace at Shivapattan, then?'

'No, Raje, I came down from the fort at midnight in the light of the flambeaux.'

'Very strange!' the king exclaimed, and asked in jest, 'The blood of the Moreys of the Jawali jungles doesn't let you stay still, does it?'

'There was really no other alternative, Maharaj,' Jaishribai replied, her voice turning hoarse. The king peered into the queen's face in the light of the torch. Her eyes were red and her face tense with an unstated grief. Something unimaginable had happened. The king's breathing stopped. 'Tell me, Ranisahib,' he said. 'What is it?'

'What do I say, Raje? And how do I say it?' The queen made a strenuous effort at holding her breath under control and then sobbed, 'It is our duty as members of the royal family to select words with the greatest care and arrange for you to be escorted to the palace.'

'What … does … that … mean?'

'Maharaj, the protective shade of our father has disappeared from over our heads, ho! Raje Shahaji Maharaj has left us all and departed for his heavenly abode!'

Shivraya was reduced to the state of a massive pillar shaken loose by an earthquake and collapsing along with the roof that it held aloft. The extremity of the grief had discomposed even a stout-hearted person like him. He was on the point of losing his balance altogether when Jaishribai stepped forward and held him in her embrace.

Shivraya broke into a sweat at the heart-rending news. His eyes began streaming and a wail of anguish escaped his lips, 'Aaba! Abasahib!! Why did you do this? Why have you deserted us?' He was overtaken by uncontrollable sobs. 'Abasahib!' he groaned, 'the tree of our labour has not even blossomed; the dreams of our mission are yet to take shape! Why should you have left for the celestial world before even the spires of our destination could be spotted on the horizon? Why did you do this?'

'Maharaj, you must dam your sorrow. Please, compose yourself.'

'This thunderbolt has broken my spine, Ranisahib. How can I go up to the fort in this crippled state?'

'Please, please, Raje! Fortitude!'

'Fortitude? What fortitude? Who, after all, was Shahaji Maharaj? Who? If they want, the gods and goddesses should dare to ask this question of Shivaji. Go! Go and seek endorsement from the prosperous city of Bijapur, whose seven or eight thousand soldiers he slaughtered in the battlefield of Bhatwadi. And yet, the same city grovelled on the earth before his blood-soaked sword and invited her vanquisher to become her protector, her commander-in-chief! Took him to her battlements and anointed him the Supreme Commander of her forces! That was Shahaji! The man who had compelled Emperor Shahjahan to abandon the grandeur of Hindustan and wander among the rocks and ravines of the Deccan for two full years … that was my father Shahaji Maharaj! The hero who taught our Maratha braves the art and science of guerilla warfare … that was Shahajiraja. He was the magical substance that brought lustre to the kunku that an epochal woman like Jijausahib wore on her brow; he was the great preceptor who gave shape to the life of this Shivraya. The passing away of such a champion is like the sky disintegrating over one's head. Have mercy on me, Ranisahib, I am so shattered with grief that I don't have the strength to move an inch from this spot.'

'Maharaj, it's not as if we cannot conceive of the dam of grief that has burst open in your heart, but you will simply have to wipe your tears and rise. You must come up to the fort.'

'How can I come up to Rajgadh, Ranisahib? How can I lift my eyes to look at Matoshri's bright, blank brow? You tell me how this son can find the strength to do so. You please return to the fort; as for me, it's asking for the impossible.'

Jaishribai, however, could no longer withstand the flood that had risen inside her. Crying incontinently, she said, 'Raje, you have just said that the passing away of your revered father has brought the sky crashing down upon your head … but if this calamity were to make mother earth also disappear from under your feet, if a situation arose where our queen mother, our Jijausahib, were also to be whisked away from you?'

'What are you saying, Ranisahib?' Shivraya sprang up as if lightning had struck him.

'Yes, Maharaj. Your mother has gathered the senior king's mandeel and robes to her bosom and set out to become a sati. The sandalwood pyre would now be ready for her to climb upon.'

Every single palace, mansion, temple and shrine atop the fort had sunk into the black gorge of grief. When the news of Shahajiraja's passing away had reached the upper palace at around midnight, the wails of sorrow that erupted from its chambers had sent violent tremors through all of Rajgadh. Later, around dawn, when news spread about Jijausahib gathering the late Maharaj's royal clothes and preparing to climb the pyre to become a sati, it was as if the double blow had shredded the heart of Rajgadh to ribbons.

In the month gone by, Shahaji was returning from Bankapur and had stopped by Hodigire, a small village in his principality. It was a particularly beautiful place that lay in the Davangiri area near Shimoga, and the king loved relaxing there. The intention was to go hunting in the jungles there in the company of his usual set of friends, beaters and horn-blowers.

When the king noticed a deer in the vegetation quite a distance away, he spurred his horse in its direction. The horse shot off instantly, but as luck would have it, one of its legs got caught in a vine that ran across the jungle track and another in a hole, the kind that jungle rats make by hollowing the ground. The horse lost balance and stumbled forward wildly, dislodging the rider, saddle and all. The animal managed to find its feet and leapt forward, unaware that the rider's foot had got caught in the stirrup and he was being dragged along through the rocks, tree-roots and bushes. By the time his friends were able to reach him, the king had suffered serious injuries all over his body, particularly his head, and was bleeding profusely. He was rushed back to the waada and a team of physicians was called. They tried to stanch the flow of blood and dress his wounds with herbal paste, doing all that they could to revive him. But the wounds were so severe that he did not survive the night.

It took a few days for the news to reach Rajgadh. Along with the jolt of the tragedy, the residents were also discomposed by the absence of their king. They had no idea where the latest campaign had taken him and when he would return. Matters became particularly alarming when Jijau decided to become a sati. Their only hope was that she would wait for the king to return before she took this extreme step, but she announced that she was not waiting for her son and ordered the sandalwood pile to be stacked up. The decision petrified her household and caused widespread panic among the citizens of Rajgadh. The news spread like wildfire, bringing thousands of the nearby villagers keening, lamenting, into the fort premises. The grief of the royal family at the palace was, for the folk gathering around, their personal grief too.

Jijau's grief, of course, knew no bounds. When tragedy had struck her mother's house, it was Shahaji who had held his pregnant wife to his chest and given her strength. He had wiped the warm tears off her cheeks and said, 'Jiurani, I am fully aware of the mountain of grief that sits in your heart. It is very difficult to absorb a catastrophe of this order, but you have to find the courage to outlive it.'

'To what end?' the enervated queen had asked.

'So that the seed growing in your womb grows, takes birth and becomes tall enough to touch the sky. You will have to dissolve the painful knot in your heart and live on to welcome the little prince and rear him for greatness in times to come.' The manner in which the king had seen his queen through the most gut-wrenching episode of her life had no parallel anywhere.

Jijau stepped out of the palace, holding her husband's clothes close to her chest. There was an impenetrable firmness in her eyes and steps.

When they saw the sati-to-be walk towards the stage that would transport her to heaven, her daughters-in-law came running to her side—along with other women, young and old, who resided in the palace—with loud moans and ululations. To those who had still not given up their effort to dissuade her from this precipitate step, she said, 'Don't insult a sati by blocking my path.'

'Don't say this, Matoshri!' they wailed.

'Just let me go. Why are you trying to stand in my way? My lord has already set out on his journey towards heaven.'

The king climbed up to the fort very early in the morning. The sky was laden with thick clouds that made a clear view of the ramparts impossible. All of Rajgadh was submerged in a pall of grief. The poor farmers and herders of the nearby valleys who had crossed ravines, traversed dense jungle and clambered up to the fort at night to be by the side of their devoted king during his time of despair now numbered in the thousands.

In the open space outside the palace, Matoshri's forehead was being daubed with vermilion, while the gathered women were keening inconsolably. When Jijausahib saw Shivraya approaching, the tears dammed in her eyes burst out. The king leapt forward and held her by her wrist, asking, 'Ausahib, what is this you are doing?'

'It is the religious duty of the wife to join her late husband as sati, Shivba.'

'But in such a tearing hurry?'

'I had asked for the death of a suhaagan from Goddess Jagdamba, for the privilege of dying while my husband was alive. Such a woman has the good fortune of forearms jingling with bangles and of kunku smeared on the brow and in the parting of the hair. She walks a path painted with turmeric and vermilion, her toe rings chiming pleasantly. But such an auspicious death is granted only to a fortunate few. I was not destined for this privilege, but I can choose to follow the king in his footsteps.'

'Ausahib, how can you be so hard-hearted as to begin walking to your pyre before I had even arrived? What was the hurry?'

'Balraje, I wanted to avoid you.'

'Why?'

'While you are otherwise hard as steel, your heart melts for the parents who brought you to life. You are exceptionally emotional.'

'That does not explain your haste!'

'I was absolutely sure that my desire to give my lord company on his final journey would be altogether unacceptable to you. You would create a furore and obstruct me, and I hadn't wanted that to happen.'

'What are you saying, Ausahib?'

'That's it, Shivba. I don't want the flaming pyre to be doused by the flood of your tears.'

Shivraya closed in on his mother and went down on his knees, enfolding her legs in his embrace. 'Please listen, Ausahib!' he screeched piteously. The cry reached the ears of the gathering and their stomachs turned in agony. Here was their king who always roared like a lion before making the toughest enemies bite the dust, a king whose deeds and capabilities were known and discussed even in the faraway European countries. Here was the epitome of an inconceivably brave warrior combined with the essence of a compassionate and imperturbable sage. Yet, his utter devotion to his mother had turned his strong heart to water and it now streamed out of his eyes in an unbroken torrent. The sight could not but melt the hearts and wet the cheeks of all who stood around.

The mother, however, was unmoved. 'Raje, get out of my way,' she said in a steady voice. 'Let me go. In any case, life and death are inexorable events.' Refusing to look anyone in the eye, Jijau tried to move forward. In the face of this pitiless resolve, the king was crushed. He tightened his hold on her and wailed, 'Matoshri, you have shown me today that this prosperous king of Rajgadh is worse off than a beggar on the street.'

'You are just back after a tiring ride from Surat, son—' Jijau tried changing the subject.

'Don't talk to me of Surat and all its wealth!' he cried. 'Placed against the blessing of a mother's shade, all the wealth of the world is no more than coal to me.'

'But why this insane obstinacy, Shivba? What do you hope to gain by blocking my passage to the pyre? Why should I continue to live?'

'Matoshri, I was a lad of barely seven or eight years when Shahjahan of Delhi exiled my father from this land. I was deprived of the great man's shade from that day onwards. Despite being in a faraway land, he dedicated his life to the dream of our own Maharashtra and launched the struggle to realise it. I have not recovered from the shock of my father's shade being withdrawn from my life, and here you talk about setting out to give him company. As I try to absorb these two massive shocks, I wish the earth under my feet would crack and happily swallow up this Shivaji. How do I tell you, Matoshri, that even the great treasure of the love of these millions of people has now turned worthless?'

'Son, we are all travellers on the road to the other world. It is so much better to undertake this journey in the company of one's husband. Death is not something that can be dodged. If not today, it'll happen tomorrow.'

'Please don't say this, Matoshri! Do you think that it is poor Shivaji alone who understands the value of having a great mother like Jijausahib? When I walked into the embrace of Afzulya at Pratapgadh, or when I disfigured the Mughal city of Surat three hundred miles away and brought the plunder home, or when I barged into Shaista's bedroom after leapfrogging over his security ring of a hundred thousand soldiers, I was never afraid of death, nor of the Sultan's dungeon. I didn't care for their snarling canines or for their fire-belching cannons. Who do you think stuffed this five-arms-tall bag of flesh and bones with this miraculous chemical? If it wasn't you, who was it?'

'Shivba, I too feel it was merit earned across ten lives that gave me a valiant son like you, but that doesn't give you the right to stop your mother from earning the merit of becoming a sati.'

'Listen, Ausahib. The mission for which you taught me to live and to struggle, I am nowhere near reaching its banks. The enemies outside our walls have not yet been eliminated; there is no saying when Aurangzeb's massive army will come thundering down to wreck this edifice of Swarajya. As for the enemies within our walls, some of our own so-called friends and relatives, these charlatans still sit tight wearing the armour of envy under their tunics! If you leave us, the shrine that lies inside me will be burnt to ashes. If that happens, what will be the point of this Shivaji living on?'

'Shrine?'

'Yes, what else? Shahaji Maharaj, the king who turned his life into a wasteland to realise his dream of Swarajya was my god Pandurang, and he is gone. If his wife, the goddess Rukhmai, should also disappear in his wake, what will I do with their devastated city of Pandharpur? What will I do with all this royal splendour? Living the life of a penniless hermit in the jungles would be so much better!'

Just then, four-year-old Sambhajiraje came running in with cries of 'Aabaa! Aabaa!!!'. He hadn't seen his father for months together. Shivraya lifted him up and held him close to his chest. As he ran a loving hand over the child's head, Sambhaji turned towards Jijau with a look of surprise. He had never seen his grandmother in this attire: a brand-new sari, her forearms loaded with bangles, her brow smeared with vermilion. 'Aaba,' he asked, 'when did Aajisahib get up without waking me? And where is she off to dressed like this?'

The king put him down in front of Jijausahib. 'Shambhu baal,' he said in a poignant voice, 'before you came to be four years of age, you would ask me where your mother had gone, and I had to lie to you about her. Sometimes I would point towards the sky and tell you that she was there in the kingdom of the gods, sometimes behind the clouds, sometimes in the land of the moon and stars. I would tell you that once her work there was over, she would come back.' Tears were streaming down Shivraya's face. 'Go, now, go forward and ask your Aajisahib where she is off to.'

Little Sambhajiraje ran with tiny steps towards Jijausahib and let out a childish squeak, 'Aajisahib!' The sheer innocence in that call caused Jijausahib to break into a shudder. She immediately lifted the child into her arms and held on to him for life, showering countless kisses and tears on his soft cheeks.

All of Rajgadh was drowning. The tears that thousands were shedding was flood enough to douse the sandalwood pyre that had been set alight.

38

WAR CLOUDS GATHER IN SOUTH KONKAN

OCTOBER 1664: THE FIRST FORTNIGHT

A dense crowd of noblemen, grandees and sardars had gathered in the durbar, leaving not an inch of standing space. They stood with anxiety writ large on their faces. This was the kind of scene which made Sultan Ali Adilshah sick with exasperation. He was also tired of the increasingly frequent episodes of openly defiant raids on the Bijapur Sultanate by Shivaji and his daredevil Maavalis: sometimes the ravaging of the Paranda-Solapur area, at other times risk-free hit-and-run raids and the unrestrained despoiling of Adilshahi posts in south Konkan and Goa.

This incessant stream of bad news, the litany of devastation and defeats, seemed to have reduced even the hefty pillars, the sinuous arches and the beautifully carved roof of the durbar to a mirage. Someone or the other storming in and picking up the challenge with a show of outrage and bluster had become a regular feature of the court these days. Of late, Ali Adilshah had begun to feel a sense of deep loathing as he sat on his throne, and his consternation had reached intolerable levels.

Five years had now passed since Afzal Khan had accepted the challenge of destroying Shivaji and lost his life in the bargain. He was followed by Siddhi Johar who first made a show of valour and ultimately made a fool of himself. And now, here was Khawaas Khan with the same bluster and inflamed rhetoric. 'Just wait one more month, my lord!' he growled.

'If only there were some deed that could match the bombast of words!' the Sultan groaned.

'Why not, huzoor? I am not fool enough to get my fingers chopped off by that hellhound Siva. On the contrary, I shall chop his head off and make his family mourn him for the next seven generations.'

He ran his rancorous eyes over the court and let out a scornful laugh as he said, 'I do not need the help of the Delhi Emperor's armies or of any other sultan. Even if the sun of the sky were to enter the battlefield on Siva's side, the sunset of Siva's life cannot be dodged.' Khawaas Khan's proclamations certainly looked far more potent than his big, bullock-like, flabby body.

The Sultan noted the fidgetiness of Bajiraje Ghorpade who was standing in the front row of courtiers and gave him a nod. Bajiraje said in a voice that dripped vanity, 'The good news today is that, even if delayed, Shivaji's downfall has begun. His half-brother Vyankoji is going to fight alongside us.'

'Waah! That really is great news.'

'Also, the days of Shahajiraje's haughtiness and deceit are now over. Vyankojibaba is now a free bird. Who can dare to obstruct his flight?'

The chief Qazi then got up and ran his fingers through his white beard as he said, 'Huzoor, I am a man of religion and can speak only of the welfare of Islam. So many orators have lit the durbar with their fluorescent talk, but what did the Sultanate gain out of it all? If the greatest heroes of this court march into the Twelve Maavals to annihilate that savage Siva Bhosale, they not only depart heavenwards but also wreck our entire armies. Huzoor, I now have a request for you. For the next few days, refrain from moving around Bijapur seated on a caparisoned elephant, looking at the sky. It will be more meaningful if, like a common man, you roam the lanes and alleys of this city barefooted.'

'Stop your babble, Qazi!' many shouted. 'Have you lost your mind?'

'It's not I who have lost my mind, but all of you. Fools, when our Sultan walks down our roads, he will see the miserable state of the thousands of orphans of the martyrs of this land. He will understand more keenly the pain of their helpless widows. When he sees their suffering, he will realise the urgency of burying that demon Siva alive.'

Among the audience, listening carefully to the Qazi's open challenge to the Sultan was an agent of Aurangzeb. His assignment was to pay particular attention to all that was being discussed on the explosive subject of Shivaji.

Earlier, he had related to the Adilshahi durbar an event that had occurred in the Agra court. Aurangzeb had shown less than lukewarm interest in celebrating his forty-seventh birthday; on the contrary, he had spent time drawing up plans to teach Shivajiraja some decisive lessons. He had also declared his intention of appointing a powerful and dauntless sardar to rein in the Maratha storm that was raging in the Deccan. It was his desire to whip up in the region a turbulence that would utterly overpower it. Accordingly, he had sent to both Kutubshah and Adilshah a harsh letter that read:

> It was because of your secret support for that village lout named Siva that he dared to mount a raid on our Surat. Your impotence is the real reason our wealth in the Deccan is getting decimated by the million. You will have to pay heavy compensation to the imperial treasury for your misbehaviour; otherwise both of you will be erased from existence in the near future.

Aurangzeb's agent had himself broken into a sweat as he read out the missive. He continued:

> Siva has today become a bone stuck in the gullet of the Mughal, Adilshahi and Kutubshahi governments. We can neither eat properly nor even breathe. This margatthya has raised storms of skullduggery and revolt in all of Hindustan. He is the punishment meted out to us for our indiscipline. Understand that destroying and burying Siva is not merely my command, but the command of Allah.

Ali Adilshah had raged inside, but he had been equally frightened too. Shivaji's menace was increasing by leaps and bounds, hollowing the Sultan from inside. To add to his woes, the grand robes of his sardars were all soiled to the extreme by ineptitude and failure. Scanning the durbar with a stern look, he said, 'Keep this important thing in mind: till recently, Siva's acts of plunder were committed only on land, but of late he has entered the waters too, like the Fish Gods of the Puranas. What do you say, Wazeer-e-Aazam?'

'Huzoor?'

'Even at the height of his troubles with Shaista Khan, not to mention the siege of Panhala, that man was not relaxing in the ghats. Quite on the contrary, for the past three years, he has been steadily chewing and digesting the coastal areas of Hindustan.'

'Yes, huzoor.'

When the Sultan placed his finger on the increasing strength of Shivraya on the sea, Khawaas Khan was left with no choice but to concede the point. 'Yes, huzoor,' he said. 'The Bijapur Sultanate once had total control over the coastal towns of Basnoor, Karvar, Goa and Kudaal, right up to Rajapur. If one ignored the tiny encroachment of those red-faced Portuguese on the Goa stretch, nobody had the courage to stop the gallop of the Adilshahi horse all across the western coast.'

'Wazeer-e-Aazam, for how long will you keep swinging on that bough of the past?' Adilshah's light-brown pupils flickered. Looking into the eyes of his senior sardars, he asked, 'Does anybody in this durbar even know what games this Siva is playing and with what daring? Yes?'

The stunned grandees remained silent. Ali Adilshah flared up at this frigid response from his sardars and their shameful ignorance of the state of affairs. He could no longer hold down the bile that had been rising inside him for some time. Setting his jaw and looking daggers at his men, he roared, 'Who do you think is nursing demoniacal dreams of pouring molten lead on the waves off the Maalvan coast for making formidable forts? It is this mutinous brat of Shahaji. This margattha bandit who goes around looting our coastal warehouses and markets, he has also been establishing a firm control of Maratha officials on our sea posts like Rajapur, Vengurla and Kharepattan. And now, wazeer sahib, what have all these manly sardars of our durbar been doing?'

Feeling the brunt of the sarcastic words that their sovereign was spitting at them, the noblemen of the Adilshahi court hung their heads in abashment. Their dispirited eyes and shrunken bodies riled the Sultan further. 'What Karbala are you now waiting for, Wazeer miyaan? Forget your brazen talk and hollow intentions. If we want to slaughter that rascal at the earliest, I can think of no battlefield except one.'

Believing that their Sultan alone had the magic formula for destroying their enemy, the assembled courtiers all looked at him with great expectation. 'If you really want to eliminate him fast, you cannot ask for a better battlefield than Kudaal-Vengurla. We have our Khem Savant there, and the Portuguese and the Dutch at their Vengurla stations. We have the Englishmen too, and many other sworn enemies of Siva scattered around in the region. Siva is a thorn embedded in the feet of natives and firangis alike; everyone is sick and tired of him. That is why, Wazeer-e-Aazam, I advise that it is on the soil of Konkan that Siva should either be buried or burnt alive.'

On the one hand, Shivaji's many exploits had reduced Bijapur to the state of a boat caught in a storm; on the other, far to the north, Aurangzeb sat in his Deewaan-e-Khaas of the Agra fort, frothing and fuming in anger. During the past year, Shivajiraja had created mayhem everywhere. He had bored through the security ring of a hundred thousand soldiers in Pune and penetrated the bedroom of Uncle Shaista, chopped the worthy's fingers and vanished into thin air. The consequence was that Shaista had to slip out of the city in utter humiliation.

Then there was that strong but foolish Jaswant. What was the sense in setting up a siege around Sinhgadh and then sitting tight, doing nothing for months and months together? The most shocking of his failures was the quiet passage of thousands of Shivaji's men through the dense jungles that lay within shouting distance of Jaswant's army camp. Subsequently, that devil had travelled three hundred miles and ransacked the richest of the Mughal cities in the subcontinent, dragging the Emperor's prestige through the slime, with the entire world watching.

Again, while that idiot Jaswant sat encircling Sinhgadh, what did this Siva do? He raided the other important city of Ahmednagar, denuded it of immense wealth, including a herd of expensive Arab and Turkish horses, and once again delivered a stinging slap on the face of the grand Mughals. The news of defeat and humiliation arrived every single day, exasperating Emperor Alamgir beyond endurance.

Meanwhile, in Bijapur, the Sultan's invectives in the durbar that day were enough to give the attendant grandees gooseflesh. As was true of his predecessors, extreme alertness and deviousness ran through Ali's blood. Like his ancestors before him, he had become remarkably cunning and calculating. During the Panhala campaign, the corrupt Siddhi Johar had gathered considerable wealth from Shivaji in the form of bribes. In the correspondence that had happened between the Sultan and Siddhi, the former had ordered the man to deposit all that wealth in the Bijapur treasury. Predictably baulking at the idea, Siddhi Johar had gone to the extent of abandoning his loyalty to Bijapur. He had openly declared that he was a servant of the Mughal empire and not the Sultanate.

Ali had been so incensed by Siddhi's treachery that he had secretly sent his henchmen to Kurnool and arranged for that grandee to be poisoned to death at a banquet that he was attending. The Sultan was also cunning enough to let the story circulate among his sardars, creating a culture of fear in the court. Consequently, there was no one left in the durbar who would dare to get into an open conflict with his highness.

Lately, the Sultan had observed a strange restlessness in Baji Ghorpade and Lakham Savant. The distrustful looks that Ghorpade and Khawaas Khan had been exchanging hadn't escaped the Sultan's notice either. If an army had to be dispatched for hunting Shivaji down, this lack of faith among his senior generals wouldn't help one bit. He, therefore, invited the two to his palace later in the night. Waving his hand in the direction of Ghorpade, he asked, 'Yes, Bajiraje, why were you looking a little distraught in the durbar today?'

It was like sprinkling oil over an open flame. Bajiraje threw a look of contempt at Khawaas Khan, his thick whiskers bristling as he spat out, 'Huzoor, I think this Islamic game of sending only Muslim generals to annihilate Shivaji should stop.'

'What do you want to say?'

'History is witness, huzoor, to the fact that a powerful Maratha can be eliminated only by another Maratha. Not even a big emperor can bring into play that degree of meanness.'

'Huh?'

'Zill-e-Subhaani, whether it is the Bijapuri Sultanate or the Mughal Empire, so far only Muslim generals have been dispatched to subdue Shivaji. Look at Afzal Khan, Kartalab Khan, Shaista Maamoo, Faazal

Khan … the list goes on. Which of these generals has been of any use, tell me?'

'Baji miyaan, I think—'

'Please hear me out, huzoor. If you wish, I can swear on your Allah along with our three hundred and thirty million gods. Only another Maratha can effectively perform the holy feat of snuffing this Maratha out. Keep all your sardars in the durbar. Just give me some ammunition, and your treasury. If you think that I am greedy for treasure, don't give me that either. I swear by my gods that I shall happily stake my Mudhol estate on the success of this sacred task.'

The bitterness in Baji's voice astounded the Sultan. In a bemused voice, he asked, 'Tell me, Bajiraje, why does your land have such a rich harvest of hatred against one's own brothers?'

'Mutual hatred is a virtue that the Maratha blood possesses. If the great Lord Rama had taken birth in the land of the Maavals instead of in Ayodhya, Ravana would most certainly have assigned the task of destroying him to Lakshmana. And Lakshmana would have removed that thorn in Ravana's heel with the greatest ease.'

Ali, with his native intelligence, could clearly read the situation. Both these generals were putting themselves forward for the task of eliminating Shivaji—one on account of baseless conceit and the other because of the disease of jealousy. Reprimanding the pair, he said, 'Both of you are caught in the tussle of proving that one is smarter than the other. But keeping in mind the experience of all of us sultans, I am absolutely certain that Shivaji is smarter than the two of you put together.'

'Huzoor?'

'Zill-e-Ilaahi?'

'Which is why I advise that you should dissolve your differences and come together. If that doesn't happen, this dreadful pattern of Shivaji's victory and the slaughter of our generals will continue.'

'Please stop worrying, huzoor. An outsider can never know how eager the city of Mudhol is to uproot and destroy Shivaji, and what kinds of preparation are already afoot. In the name of the Nelagudi Mahadev, I give you my word that Shivaji's end will be dealt by the blade of Mudhol. You may write it down, if you please.'

Ali Adilshah was happy to note the hatred for Shivaji that permeated Baji's words. 'So, Ghorpade,' he said, 'how much time do you want?'

'Sultan sahib, you want to pair me with Khawaas Khan for this enterprise, but I ask for an uncluttered field, for once. You won't even know the depth of the pit that we shall dig in the jungles of Mudhol for interring Shivaji's entire family.'

'Waah, Bajiraje, waah!'

'Shivaji, now, has just a few days to live. You may write this prophecy down,' growled Baji with immense confidence.

Khawaas Khan was extremely eager to get a taste of the Hindvi swarajya. He had already set out from Bijapur with a force of nearly fifteen thousand horses, drawn from the royal as well as army stables. Very soon he would be joined by companies led by other sardars. The news was being continuously relayed to Shivraya through his network of spies.

Around this time, the king was busy reviving the projects that had been suspended in the Konkan areas ranging from Mahaad and Chiplun to Rajapur. He received the worrisome report that Khawaas Khan was getting into a big deal with the Portuguese of Vengurla. Evidently they were planning something really vicious together, a blow that would seriously harm the prospects of the Hindvi swarajya.

All in all, the situation in Konkan was turning more and more dangerous by the day. Five or six years earlier, Khem Savant had faked friendship with Shivraya and taken full advantage of his trust. He had, among other betrayals, continued imposing his tyranny upon the people of the land. With the slightest change of wind, this Savant had now begun to turn his back upon Shivraya and developed an intimacy with the Dutch. These days, he was often seen moving around in the company of Khawaas Khan, as well as the Dutch.

These contrary winds gave the king no peace of mind. In an effort to scotch unpleasant developments, he and Netaji brought out their ten thousand horses and raced night and day through central Konkan to arrive at Vengurla. All hell had broken loose at the very pronouncement of Shivaji's name in Vengurla. Even before the Maratha horses had galloped in, a pall of fear had settled upon the small bunch of villages. Over six months ago, that man had stormed Lal Mahal in Pune and driven Shaista out with a few fingers missing; he had plundered the great harbour at Surat and brought home unimaginable wealth. Stories of these exploits and many others had burnt Shivaji's image into the minds of commoners across Hindustan and his name had begun to invoke terror among all who anticipated an assault on their lives or property.

At the news of Shivaji's arrival, the Dutch warehouse at Vengurla soon descended into panic. It took only minutes for the warehouse to empty itself of both native and foreign traders. 'Shivaji has come! The Maratha conqueror has come!!!' was the cry that resonated in the air. There was nobody there who had not heard of the punishment that Shivraya had meted out to the officials of the English warehouse in Rajapur. Recalling this, the firangis in the Dutch warehouse were the first to flee; among them was Verspreet, the officer-in-charge of the warehouse.

Within no time, the number of boats and rafts bobbing on the creek and at the mouth of the river shot up. Fearing for their lives, firangi horsemen and foot soldiers began to jump into the water to get to a boat. Many others, after hurriedly grabbing whatever clothes and valuables came to hand, began disappearing into the coconut and arecanut groves.

Wearing a loose robe, with a peacock feather stuck in his expensive European hat, the Dutch officer Verspreet stood on the deck of a dhow and tried to steady his hands as he looked through his monocular tube at the Vengurla coast. His wife and children were trying their best to stay down and out of sight of anyone observing from the shore. The name of Shivaji had terrified them out of their wits.

As Shivraya sat in his office tent that night going through some papers, an urgent missive reached him from Panjim. The Portuguese men handed it over to the king and disappeared immediately. Quickly reading through the dispatch, he tossed it across with a laugh to Netaji who was sitting next to him and said, 'Do you remember, Netokaka, how much wealth we had gathered from our Surat raid?'

'It was around thirty to thirty-five hons.'

'And look at this now. Without any labour, without any fisticuffs, these large-hearted firangis are offering us a lure of … make a guess, how much?'

'How much?'

'Fifteen hundred hons!'

'Who's doing this?'

'The Portuguese governor.'

'Such a huge amount! And what's the favour they seek?'

'For breaking the spine of the Dutch in Vengurla. For wiping them out.'

Both heaved simultaneous sighs. Such an offer was unheard of. As they looked at each other, eyes twinkling with humour, Netaji couldn't help asking, 'These Portuguese are mad enough to come to you with such a huge bag of money. So, Raje, tell me. What do you propose to do?'

Suddenly, the laughter in Shivaji's eyes was replaced by anger and contempt. He said in a serious voice, 'These firangis, particularly these Portuguese, should have at least a semblance of sense in their dense heads. They should know that Shivaji is a king; he is no warehouse trader to take such assignments from others.'

Soon, the king realised that there was more scope for humour in the offer than insult. He shrugged away his anger and began laughing again quite heartily, Netaji joining him in the fun.

Turning serious again, the king said, 'Netokaka, I have begun to see quite clearly the direction in which the future lies. Our empire shall spread not so much on land as on these turbulent waves of the sea. The big ships and boats anchored in the sea are going to determine the fate of people on the land. Hence, it becomes our pleasant duty to take care of our rivers and our boundless ocean. We must take urgent steps in this direction. The day on which I can snatch back our coasts from the jaws of these firangis … that will be the most auspicious day of all for me.'

Perceiving the firm resolve of his king, Netaji threw his own die on the table. 'Fine, Shivba, so why should we wait?' he asked excitedly. 'Let's step out now and swallow up both the Dutch and the Portuguese at one go.'

'Such haste won't do, Netokaka. Ships open or close their sails after testing the direction of the winds. This hurry is not going to help us achieve our objectives. Instead of helping us, it may well snatch away what we have in hand.'

'But what's the harm in being a little adventurous?

'We have to move forward in a disciplined manner, after carefully examining the circumstances. If, in undue haste, we agitate the Portuguese, the Bijapuris, the Goans, the English and the Dutch at one go, there is a possibility of all our enemies in the Deccan gathering together under the protective umbrella of Aurangzeb. Therefore, it makes more sense to smash the anchors of these people one by one as and when circumstances permit, thus moving our own boat forward with discipline and control.'

39

SHIV LANKA

OCTOBER 1661

That dark night, the two armies stood face to face on opposite banks of a river at Kudaal in south Konkan. Both had planted themselves on the heath next to the water with their respective pennants fluttering in the wind. Evidently, Shivraya and Khawaas Khan were biding their time to lock horns.

On one side of the river spread Khawaas Khan's camp; the flaring torches and the lamps inside the tents had given their canvas walls and roofs a deep orange tinge. Right next to Khawaas Khan's pavilion were the tents of eminent sardars like Shaikh Miraan, Siddhi Sarvar and Shah Hazrat. Four days had gone by since they had pitched their camp; Khawaas, therefore, had had plenty of time to ready his men for combat.

But what were these powerful Adilshahi warriors waiting for? What could be the mystery behind the delay in their mounting an assault? Trying to form an estimate on the basis of the activities he could see on the other side of the river, Shivraya said to Sonopant Dabeer, 'I can imagine only two possible reasons for the enemy continuing to play the waiting game.'

'What are they, Raje?'

'They don't seem to be mentally prepared to launch their assault for the next five or six days.'

'And the other possibility?'

'Going by Khawaas Khan's past record, he seems to be a close calculating person. He is not the kind of general who will line up his army and then do nothing for no ostensible reason. He is certainly waiting for someone.'

The two forces thus continued to stand on either side of the river, measuring each other up and growling.

Govindrao Vishwanath Prabhu was the king's lieutenant who was in charge of all matters related to Vengurla. The king had called him over to Kudaal for discussions. As the two sat together in a tent, the king said, 'Pant, for the past few months I have assigned one single task to you.'

'Yes, Maharaj.'

'The mission of building a fort as strong as that of the Siddhis at Janjira has robbed me of my night's rest.'

'Keeping that in mind, I have been rigorously examining the coastlines here.'

'Keep doing that. Visit the Koli villages, the fishermen's settlements of the Tandel community. Their boys, who spend their entire lives swimming in the sea, will be of immense use to us. They are bound to be familiar with every rock and gulch that lies under the water.'

'Of course, Raje. From our Kandalgaon right up to Shirola near Vengurla, we have already set our boys to work.'

'Govindpant,' the king said in a disappointed voice, 'when I see the firangi sailors at work, when I observe the dominance that they exercise over the waves, I am filled with deep regret over the naval impotence of our Hindu kings.'

'Raje?'

'There was a time when our Indian kings had performed wonderful feats on the seas. There was this dynasty of the Cholas that ruled over Tamil Nadu about five hundred years ago. Their ships would sail vigorously up and down the ocean right up to Sumatra and Jakarta and run trade enterprises of the highest order.'

'Yes, Raje.'

'May the pandits with their moth-eaten heads rot in hell for declaring sea voyage a sin. That single pronouncement inflicted immeasurable damage on the naval prowess of our people. They sliced off the wings of our seafarers, body and mind. Our ships that had soaked the waters and moved with the winds of many seas now lay decaying in junkyards. They simply rusted on the shores and turned to dust. All the skill and valour of the seamen of those times simply died an unmourned death.'

The king placed a map in front of Govind Vishwanath, which he instantly began examining with great interest. With a smile of satisfaction, he asked excitedly, 'Who prepared this map for you, Raje?' He went on looking into it greedily, with a small smile playing on his face. Seeing the way his face had bloomed, the king said, 'Pant, do you recognise some of the marks on this map? Tell me honestly whether the riddle is solved.'

'Yes.'

'Get up, then, Pant. Let's go there immediately.'

'These signs point to very nearby places, but—'

'What "but", now?'

'Our eyes are those of ordinary people, yours are the eyes of a visionary. Their flight is that of an eagle. However, as you suggest, I believe we should go there. My father had taught me that the distance between the eyes and the ears is just four fingers; therefore Maharaj should see these places in person and confirm these guesses for himself.'

'Sure, let's do it; but which part of the coast is this, anyway?'

'Raje, on this side here I see the hamlet of the Kolis and the Kunbis, the fishermen and the peasants. On the other side is Deulwada. The space in the middle is marshland, very sandy too.'

'Ah, I see. And these streams on either side, any idea about them?'

'This body of water to the north should be the Kurali creek, and to the south may be the rather wide creeks of Kolamb and Kalaval. In fact, no "may be" … they most certainly are, my heart says.'

'Aha!'

'Maharaj, this coast is called the Maha-lavan, or just Maalvan.'

'Maha-lavan?'

'Yes, "lavan" means salt, and "mahalavan" would mean a big deposit of salt.'

'Oh, I—!' Small furrows had sprung up on the king's brow.

'Have I made some error, Maharaj? You wanted to say something and you stopped.'

Maharaj smiled wanly and said, 'You said that the coast is both marshy and sandy; so how can a fort be built there? Pant, I want a rocky place, nicely spread out.'

'If that is true, Raje, I can tell you with certainty that this will turn out to be your dream coast. All the same, the best thing would be for Maharaj to see with his own eyes.'

There was an unusually bright sparkle in the king's eyes. A smile flashed between his moustache and beard. Bubbling with enthusiasm, he said, 'There's no tarrying now, no wasting of time. Let's rush to that place now.'

The king instantly sprang to his feet.

'You mean right now?'

'Yes. How far is it from Kudaal to Maalvan?'

'It will take us three hours at the most, but—'

'Why "but", now?'

'Riding out just on a whim … shouldn't the king worry about his safety?'

'Why should you ask that?'

'You have already spread out your foot soldiers, horsemen and battery of cannon all over the battlefield of Kudaal here; the enemy has laid out its own army on the other side. Don't you think that sneaking out quietly like this may turn out to be inauspicious?'

'Do not fear, Pant,' the king replied. 'Our Swarajya army is soaked as much in courage as it is in discipline. That bodes well for our chances in this battle, if nothing else does.'

The king made ready to leave along with Pant and sent a message informing his chief sardars of the expedition. It was pitch dark, but the glow of the torches and the oil drums with wicks flaming inside them carried by the guards of both armies was visible everywhere. From a distance they looked like the glittering eyes of jungle cats.

Two hundred horses were carefully eased out from among the seven or eight thousand spread over the camp. The horsemen slipped out in twos or threes, running their hands lovingly over the animals' muzzles, letting them know that they should soft-foot it out without neighing or sounding their hooves. The company gathered at a watering hole a mile away. The king had taken care to ensure that the enemy ranged on the other side of the river didn't get wind of their movement. He didn't let the rest of his own men become aware of it either.

Once they were on the slope outside Kudaal, the horses bolted. Within minutes their bodies had turned warm with all the exertion. As the night faded, they pulled up at a mound bulging out of a potters' village on a headland, a tongue of land stretching out into the sea. The sea was just a mile away. Govind Vishwanath had deliberately made the king halt at the edge of the mound.

By morning, news that spread that Shivraya had incarnated himself right behind their village. These Koli and Kunbi boys had been hoping for years for a glimpse of the great king; they had also been participating in the enterprises of the Swarajya. When they heard of his arrival, they went running up to the mound in the company of many others, young and old. The young Koli lads had grown up running up and down the beaches. They were on intimate terms with the fish, the tortoises and the rocks in the belly of the waves that rolled up on the coast.

Many of these youngsters of the Konkan coast had worked as labourers in the ships of the Malabaris, the Arabs and the firangis. Some had become tandels, captains of boats, and travelled to foreign shores. They were completely exhilarated by the thought of having their own sea fort and operating their own merchant ships, not to mention warships that would all belong to the Swarajya of their great king's conception. They needed no persuasion for joining Shivraya in his struggle for realising this dream. Present in this wildly excited crowd were brave and experienced tandels like Shiva Koli, Gunjaji, Saoji, Ghangaji and Taasaji and officials like Prabhu Desai and Sardar Tamroji Munje.

Dawn had brightened to early morning; the darkness had dissipated. The coast that lay a mile ahead was now clearly visible to the naked eye. How magnificent, how peaceful, how blue the water looked from this distance! As he scanned the sea, the king's eyes were arrested at a point. There he could see what could well have been a huge, black elephant that had dipped its head in the water. The king's fertile imagination saw the elephant lift its trunk and sprinkle water all over its massive back. He didn't have to be told that what he was really seeing was a huge, black rock that extended in width to about a mile. The waves were tossing water at its base as if they were washing the feet of a mighty god.

Shivraya's broad chest swelled up with a giant inhalation of wonder. He could feel his heart turning somersaults inside him. Finally releasing his breath, he whispered in a hoarse voice, 'Aho, Govind Vishwanath, a jet-black mountain spread out in the sea!'

'Maharaj, it is called Kurtya's island.'

'Waah, this place is beautiful! I don't know why, but this entire landscape seems to me auspicious and sacred. Even the wind that blows here has an aroma of its own. Come, Govindrao, come Munje, come Shiva and Gunjaji ... boys, let's get started! Why should we stop here?'

In no time, the horses had galloped through the green coconut groves right up to the tip of the tongue of land that ran into the water. Meanwhile, tandels like Shiva, Gunjaji and Taasaji had arranged for a number of dhows, boats, rafts and dinghies to be brought to the shore. The king was the first to get into a dhow. He looked carefully at the water around him and then climbed down. He asked Gunjaji and Shiva, 'Boys, how did you procure this dhow for me? Also, did you look carefully at what lies between the shore and the rock?'

The Koli boys felt quite embarrassed. They had understood the reason for the king's unhappiness. Even though the water on the surface looked unruffled and blue, right below the surface lay rocks, big and small, which made the passage of even a big boat to Kurtya's island impossible. The only way that one could go past the row of rocks was by using light boats, canoes, rafts and floats. It would be best to move forward with utmost caution.

The surface was calm. Only the tips of the rocks were visible above the water. On the seabed below was coral and mossy sand. The king began his journey aboard a raft among a flotilla of small boats. A little ahead, they discovered that the passage between the rocks was too narrow and even a raft would not be able to make the crossing. The king was stuck. Taasaji then arranged for a boat that could accommodate only two or three passengers.

The king got off the raft into water that was chest deep. He heaved himself onto the small boat, uncaring of the expensive clothes he had on which were now dripping with seawater. On the shore, he had removed all the ornaments on his body and handed them over to one of his attendants.

He had also taken off his chainmail armour, royal headgear, waistband, and all the other items of clothing that he could do without.

Shivraya finally reached his destination. The water, sand and slime sticking to his clothes made him look like an experienced seafarer. The very first step that he took on the rock transported him into another world. He instantly began racing like a young boy towards the elevated part in the centre. His thoughts went back to the time when he would run up the Rohideshwar mountain sixteen or seventeen years ago. The Koli and Kunbi boys too raced up with the king. Once he was standing on the highest point, the king looked around in all directions.

His eyes were closely examining the surface of the rock that spread across about fifty acres. Roughly half of it was above the water and the remaining twenty-five acres were covered by the crystal-blue water of the sea. The king walked into the water till it was knee-high and walked around over the rough, undulating surface of the rock, twisting and turning as it demanded. If there was some source of fresh water on the island, it would be just perfect.

In the afternoon, the Koli-Kunbi boys and men undid their little bundles of food to reveal bhaakaris made of rice, fresh and dried fish, and some vegetables. Some sat by the waves on the edges of the rock while others stood around as they polished off the food in the company of their king. Even as he ate, the king continued to observe every little rise and fall and fold of the rock face and the water that surrounded it. The clouds were busy playing their catch-me-if-you-can games in the sky, making the rock sometimes look like a giant black whale.

The king's eyes travelled a short distance into the sea, where he watched the waves rolling towards the shore. As he watched, he was struck by a thought. He called over the boy who had travelled with him on the small boat and explained something to him. He told him to instruct the others that they should all take their boats and rafts a specified distance into the sea, then turn around and travel back towards the island.

As they had been directed, the boys took their canoes, rafts and boats up to the specified point and turned around to cut through the water and reach the island. But suddenly, the speed of that returning fleet slackened. Even the sturdier boats were getting obstructed when they were at a distance of about six miles from the rock. They found themselves involuntarily being turned around instead of moving straight ahead. The king was thoroughly flabbergasted by what he saw. The huge waves rising there were simply not allowing the boats to move in the direction of the island but turning them back like frightened little whale calves.

The wind had now begun blowing in from the west. The team that had entered the water returned in their wet clothes. The faces of Shiva, Gunjaji, Taasaji and the others looked crestfallen as they exchanged whispers with each other. Noticing their downcast faces, the king asked, 'What, boys! Why this disappointment on your faces?

'Raje, we concealed nothing. We had given a clear enough picture of the underwater rocks that surrounded the island to Govind Vishwanath buva and warned him that the king would not like this place.'

'Forgive us, Raje,' groaned a few voices from behind, 'we searched everywhere for fifteen days, from Vengurla and Nivati right up to the Kurli creek, but we could not locate a suitable rock inside the water.'

The king's face was, however, blooming with joy. He smiled as he looked at the natives, beckoned to Tamroji and Govind Vishwanath and broke out in an exuberant voice, 'Come along, Pant. Call the people over to the shore. Call over the horns and trumpets and drums. Boys, play your tambourines and buy all the sweets that you can find in the markets nearby. Dance, eat, celebrate!'

'Wh-what exactly has ha-happened, Raje?' asked the men, deeply perplexed.

'The place that I have been seeking for the past few years, I have finally found it!'

Everyone assembled there was utterly flummoxed at the sight of the king in such a state of euphoria. Addressing the seafaring boys, the king said, 'Arey, you should understand that the submerged rocks around it are actually the perfect defence for the fort that will stand atop the island. Tomorrow, when foreign ships sail in to attack the fort, they will simply not be able to come anywhere close to it. They will have to anchor their ships and gunboats far into the sea. If they try to close in, the sharp rocks under the water will rip their hulls apart. As for the bigger boats that try to approach, they will be blasted away by the guns on the fort.'

'Waah, Raje, waah! What a delightful find!' Everyone, including Govind Vishwanath, now looked mirthful and festive.

'If you comb a hundred other shores, you will not find a place to match this. That sea fort of Janjira always rewarded me with failure, and I had wanted to build one that would be several notches stronger than that. Finally, I have located the perfect site for erecting my dream fort. We shall immediately begin the construction of our very own Janjira. There is no stopping us now.'

For the next two or three evenings, the king's trips from Kudaal to Maalvan continued. Once the sun had set, once the daytime face-off between the armies had cooled off, once it was ascertained that everything was under control, and it had turned sufficiently dark for him to slip out of the camp without being noticed, he would ride to the village on the headland.

As he stood on the magnificent rock of Kurtya in the afternoon hours, the king's mind was flooded with ideas and calculations related to the kind of structure he wanted to raise there. He had a few friends among the Portuguese in Goa; very soon he would have the best architects, the best masons and the best equipment to get the work going.

Shivraya dispatched three or four experienced stonemasons from Vengurla to gather information from experts on fort-building from all over Goa. He made furious calculations around the expenses that construction of the fort would incur. The constant whirring of his versatile brain allowed him no time for rest. His curious eyes roved everywhere, all the time.

Before he had set out for south Konkan, the king had dispatched a cavalry of five thousand from Rajgadh to Janjira under the captainship of a newly appointed official named Dattajipant Wakenvis. After the bitter experience of the betrayal of Shyamjipant Peshwa, Janjira had become a running sore for Shivraya. Actually, even before that, there was this settlement of some fifty-odd villages on the Janjira coast that was known as Habshan. Five years earlier, he had driven out of Habshan the Janjira Siddhi who had run to take refuge in the fort. But once inside, the Siddhi was beyond reach and had happily cocked a snook at all who tried to grab him.

Shivraya sat lost in deep thought. Emerging from his meditation, he said in a ringing voice, 'I shall build such a strong sea fort here that its stone walls will be as tough and impenetrable as an elephant's back. The jointing will be so faultless that it won't leave a single gap even to accommodate a blade of grass. If required, I shall pour huge quantities of molten lead and steel into the walls, but my new Janjira will be so grand and so strong that … how do I put it, friends? If a hundred thousand horses were to gallop in from Delhi and Agra and descend upon it, or if the armies of the English or the Dutch or anyone else were to cross the seven seas and suddenly launch an attack, I would not worry. The sea fort of my dreams is going to drain the biggest braggarts of their ambition and hauteur.'

Everybody bustled around in their desire to convert the king's dreams into reality. Strong and weak, young and old, rich and poor, all of them put their shoulder to the wheel. One thing, however, was clear. The building of the fort would require money to flow like water. The king was not alone in worrying about this.

One day, a chieftain from Bednoor came to meet the king on the Maalvan coast. The substance of his secret conversation with the king soon came to light. A large herd of elephants was to be dispatched from the jungles of Bednoor and Bankapur. What the pachyderms would do on these coasts, however, still remained a mystery.

One morning, a small procession of decorated bullock carts, horses and palanquins arrived at the door of the king's tent. They were a party representing the affluent saahukars, the moneylenders of the Konkan region whom Govind Vishwanath had invited for an audience with the king. The three prominent members of this group were Kuse Saahukar of Kaandalgaon, Malpe who lived next door, and Saapale Saapalkar of Rajapur.

During the Middle Ages, religious traditions had thrown manacles around the limbs of the daring navigators, tandels and entrepreneurs of the sea coasts. Any human interaction with the sea was declared as sinful. Sailors and even labourers who worked on seafaring vessels were declared as so polluted by the high priests that they were prohibited from so much as sharing a meal with others. Whether he was a kshatriya or even a brahmin, no matter his status in society, if he ventured into the sea or ran any kind of maritime enterprise, he was branded as an arch-sinner.

Such was the pernicious notion that the bone-headed touts of the gods had inserted into religious practice.

But there were some daring entrepreneurs in Konkan who had rejected this religious decree that was so palpably obstructive of human progress. They had made their obeisance to the Sea God and set up successful businesses that drew their sustenance from the sea. People like Kuse, Malpe and Saapale were lords of the sea who owned at least a dozen ships each; these vessels sailed frequently to Sri Lanka and even the Arab coasts.

The king began the meeting by saying, 'You rejected the obnoxious tradition of branding sea travel as sinful; you entered manfully into the sea and into overseas trade, thus bringing prosperity not only to your families, but also to the entire community, nay, the entire country.'

'Waah, Raje! The god of the sea himself speaks through your mouth.' These impassioned words of Shivraya were like honey dripping into their ears. Saapale Saahukar removed his cardboard cap from his head, wiped the sweat off his brow and said, 'You speak about all that we have suffered to this day. Our sin of trade across the sea has been visited upon our children. Our entire family is ostracised. Your wise pronouncements have brought hope back into our hearts.'

'Gentlemen, if you want high-quality enterprise, you need the finest warehouses and shops. For that, you need harbours that function under your control. For the safety of these harbours, you need secure sea coasts, and for the security of these sea coasts, you need to build strong, steely sea forts.'

The three financiers sat listening, mesmerised.

'It is our intention to build a sea fort right in front of Maalvanwadi on the rock island of Kurtya. It will need to rain money if we wish to see this enterprise through. We shall, of course, keep sending resources from Rajgadh as and when needed. We shall also collect taxes from the country around us. But this project is so massive that we will need all the support we can get.'

'Helping you in this endeavour is for us a means to repay our debt to the ocean that has brought us all this wealth,' the three declared in unison.

'How many years will this take?' Saapale asked. 'A dozen or more?'

'How can you speak of a dozen, Saahukar?' the king shot back. 'Once the work begins, we have to finish it in two years' time. Three at the most.'

'How is that even humanly possible, Maharaj?' Malpe burst out. 'Even the construction of a decent waada eats away half a dozen!'

'Rubbish! Not more than three years. We just don't have that kind of time in hand.' The king let out a hearty laugh. The three moneybags were now absolutely overwrought.

'Our only issue is the expenditure,' Shivraya reiterated the central point. 'Its mouth is as big as that of a python. We shall need funds all the time in limitless quantities.'

'We are there, Raje, we will always be there,' Saapale said on behalf of the trio. 'Frankly speaking, for the first time ever, we now have a king who is willing to leap a thousand steps ahead of the regressive faith that has muzzled all maritime enterprise and seeks to rewrite the norms of business and progress! Why are you talking about money, Raje? Just as people toss coconuts into the sea during Narali Poornima, the festival of the full moon, we shall toss our lives into this initiative.'

Shivajiraja was ecstatic. He was moving rapidly towards the realisation of his Swarajya by climbing up these rungs of success one after another. There were always multiple horizons dancing before his ambitious, pioneering eyes. His heart and mind soared over several peaks of enterprise, progress and knowledge simultaneously in the manner of a restless eagle.

Soon he had thousands of people working in and around Kurtya, expediting the construction of his dream fort. He had arranged for the transportation of a herd of thirty to forty elephants from Karnataka to the shores of Maalvan. The battlefield of Kudaal was simmering too, with valiant men like Netaji and Tanaji manning the front. This battle had to be won at all costs.

As he got astride his horse after the meeting with the saahukars, he noticed four spies riding in his direction. They had brought an urgent letter from Moropant at Kudaal. As he quickly read through it, despite all his efforts at keeping his face impassive, he couldn't conceal his agony.

It was as if his mind and heart were being pulverised. What to say? Who to say it to? He had heard gossip floating around on the subject of Moropant's letter, but he had dismissed it as bazaar talk. In any case, how many months had passed by since Shahajiraje's demise? Barely seven or eight! And now, for Shahaji's blood to come riding to Kudaal at the head of a four-thousand-strong army? To openly cross swords with his half-brother? Oh, Ma Bhawani, who should he be fighting against? Who should he clash against? The enemy, or his own brother?

Shivraya was unable at this moment to work out which way his destiny lay. In one direction stood the pinnacle of success, which he just needed to leap forward and embrace, and in the other direction was this biting wind that had come blowing across many a gorge and hill to test his mettle.

40

THE BATTLE OF KUDAAL

OCTOBER 1664: THE END

The king leapt off his horse and the groom took the reins from his master's hand. As the pageboys came forward with their salutations, Siddhi Hilaal too came along, bowed respectfully and said, 'Rajaji, some lady belonging to a regal household has come to the old Kali Maata temple behind the hill.'

'Hilaal sahib, that is not merely a temple; it is a sacred spot that devotees from all across the world visit. Hundreds keep coming and going, so what is special about this lady?'

'She was requesting for an audience with you.'

'Ah! We'll see about that.'

The king stretched himself out on his bed. There was a light wind blowing outside and the king's eyelids were heavy with exhaustion. Ordinarily, he would have passed into slumber, but this evening, the news that came from Kudaal had unsettled him. And now, this mystery woman! She could be a lady from some powerful family of Varhad, someone had said. But whenever a woman was involved, the king would be alert.

There were always some louts in politics who had no faith in the strength of their arms, so they often used a woman as bait to lead their enemy into a trap. Even the Puranas spoke of the vish-kanyas, the venomous maidens, in the land of the gods. A few years ago, an ill-wisher had brought over the beautiful wife of a sardar from Wai for a meeting with the king, so that he could later defame the king for unseemly conduct. The king, of course, had seen through his game and exposed him, getting the man thrashed in the bargain.

Hilaal rushed forward and placed something in the king's hand. 'Forgive me, huzoor,' he said, 'that lady has sent for you this Vyjayanti garland, as you call it.'

The king froze where he stood. He held it in a palm that had turned callous from holding horses' reins and swords. He then raised it towards his eyes for closer inspection and noticed the gold threads running through the silk rope. His eyes filled with tears. This Vyjayanti garland came from the main shrine in his own palace at Rajgadh. Which lady of the house had arrived so suddenly after travelling so far across the mountains?

The Raja said, 'Hilaal sahib, please keep the horses ready just before dawn tomorrow. We should reach the goddess's hill before the first rays of the sun.'

'As you command, huzoor.'

'We will find out who this lady is, of course, and also catch a glimpse of the goddess. One hardly gets the opportunity these days.'

The king's retinue galloped out while it was still quite dark. Who could this lady be? Soyra? Jaishri? Putla? Someone else? It was most likely to be one of his queens. In the matter of travelling long distances, and that too on horseback, his queens were exceedingly adept. Their mother-in-law Jijausahib had trained every one of them in horse riding and sword fighting. As Lakhojibaba used to teach his tiny daughter how to use a sword in the open spaces of the waada at Sindkhed, Jijausahib had thought it important to pass these skills on to her own daughters-in-law in the mango orchard of the Shivapattan waada, without making any noise about it.

'Girls,' she would tell them, 'the daughters and daughters-in-law of a peasant household have a lifelong association with sickles and scythes and shovels, because they have to sow their crops and bring in their harvests. You have got married not to Shivba, but to a double-edged sword. Our enemies are dangerous people. If they ever attack, you must always be ready to hit back at them with vigour and skill.'

Even before the first rays of the sun had broken out, the king stood at the doorstep of the old temple. The squad of horsemen that had accompanied the royal lady stood outside the temple. He acknowledged their smiling salutation and entered the temple where a radiant-looking lady was placing flowers at the feet of the irate-looking goddess. The king called out, 'Soyra Ranisahib! How come you are here?'

'Why? Didn't you get the message?' Soyrabai came soft-footedly up to the king and went on her knees to place her forehead at his feet. Rising up with a smile, she said, 'I've come with my retinue to go towards Karvar, for the holy sighting of the Gokarn Mahadev.'

The king was thrilled at meeting a loved one after so many days. The priests of the temple and Soyrabai's maids rushed forward, and the king and his wife bowed before the goddess with fanfare. The day had begun to heat up and both were in a hurry to go their own separate ways. But the pair stepped outside the temple and sat for a while on a seat in an arbour that the servants had arranged for them.

From the time of the Pratapgadh battle, there had been months upon months of skirmishes, assaults, campaigns, and incessant galloping from one jungle or town to another—it was as if there was nothing else in life! Meeting his wife after so many rough months on the road, Shivraya was blooming with joy. With great curiosity he asked, 'How is Ranisahib? And how is our Shambhuraje?'

'He's become quite obstinate these days. Throws tantrums and listens to no one, not even his grandmother.'

'Practising sword fighting?'

'Doesn't want to, he says. Often plays truant from his lessons too. Says he doesn't get the same fun out of it as he does when learning from his father.'

The king laughed. As talk about the royal family went on, Soyrabai said in a heavy voice, 'It's now about eight months since Mamajisahib departed.'

'Yes. Nobody is as fortunate as I have been to have had such a revered father. It was a good thing that Matoshri could regain her hold on herself. Otherwise, she was all ready to travel to heaven holding her husband's mandeel—'

'But, Raje, my mother-in-law has still not found her peace. She knows best the state of an Arya woman after the passing away of her husband. Often, she wakes in the middle of the night and cannot rest after.'

'What are you saying, Ranisahib? What fears haunt her? She just needs to send me her orders—'

'I think she has often made the effort to tell you what lies in her heart, but—'

'What do you mean, Ranisahib?'

'Do you not know? Matoshri has so often told Maharaj that the black snake of Destiny may go to sleep once in a while, but that wild snake named Bajiraje Ghorpade knows no sleep. That poisonous creature wriggles day and night, consumed by his desire for revenge!'

'Her wish is my command. But what is it that compels her now to repeat this caustic warning?'

'She knows of every storm that routinely assails our Swarajya. She knows of the challenge that Khawaas Khan has accepted in the Bijapur durbar. She knows that Bajiraje Ghorpade and Lakham Savant have set out for the same purpose. She knows that my brother-in-law Vyankojiraje too is adding oil to the fire that the enemy has lit.'

The letter that Jijausahib had sent with Soyrabai was an elaboration on the same topic. It took no time for Shivraya to guess that Soyrabai's pilgrimage to Gokarn was only an excuse; her real purpose was to hand over to him the queen mother's stringent message. This was what she had written:

> My body was so eager to turn to ash along with your father's, but it was you who stood in my way. Whenever I think of that event now, my heart turns sour. I often wonder whether I took the right decision, and this disturbs me greatly.
>
> Now that your father is not with us, that Ghorpada of Mudhol, who humiliated the lord of my kunku by making him march from Jinji to Bijapur, that sworn enemy of ours, has now risen up to eliminate you. I've received information that he has left Bijapur well prepared for this task. That wretched blackguard has committed the sin of pouring poison into the sacred lamp of our shrine. Vyankojibaba, after all, has your father's blood running through his arteries. But this man has poisoned that blood by infusing into it envy and jealousy for you. Khawaas Khan, Baji Ghorpada, Lakham Savant and Vyankojiraje have joined forces, and that foursome is now marching to destroy you.

Even so, I am not worried. The blessing of Ma Bhawani is always with us. However, I am digressing from the main point, and that is your lack of compliance so far with your father's wishes. Vengeance must be wreaked upon this deceitful enemy who has risen up against our very existence; he has to be encircled and asphyxiated. I desire to add my own voice to your father's and say: only when this arch-enemy is rubbed out, and his wife and children bathe in their tears, shall my soul find the contentment of salvation.

How can you think of food when you see this treacherous foe playing out his moves? How does sleep descend upon your eyelids? Anyway, the moment you receive this letter, you must let loose the reins of your horse, unsheathe your sword and slaughter him before he throws the shrine of your palace into the all-consuming fire of his unquenchable hostility. May god grant you the good sense to choke him to death, even if it is late.

May all your desires be fulfilled and the important task of expanding the Swarajya meet with success.

— Jijau

The king stayed silent for a few moments. Ausahib's words were harder than a sledgehammer. He asked his senior queen, 'What's your opinion of this letter?'

'The words are bitter, Raje, but the message is crystal clear. That bitter gourd named Bajiraje … even if its seeds were to be planted in heaven, its inherent bitterness would never disappear. Your revenge should materialise before he can cause any further damage to the Swarajya.'

This stern memorandum from Jijausahib made Shivraya's head spin. Every word of the letter scourged him worse than a whiplash. Combined with that, this meeting with Soyrabai, a person who was so much a part of his intimate world at Rajgadh, happening after such a long time, and that too in a remote patch of a jungle, right next to a battlefield! But the king had no time to tarry. He bid his queen goodbye and gave the cavalry unit accompanying her requisite instructions. Confirming that she was supplied with everything she needed for her onward journey, he walked away with a heavy heart.

Taking Netaji with him, the king walked to the raised platforms where the cannon had been planted. However, he could not shake off thoughts of his extraordinary parents. He said, 'Netokaka, even if this Shivaji is a king, after all, he is a human being. And the people who suffer the pains of shaping this human bag of flesh and blood, those divine persons are called parents.'

'Absolutely true, Raje.'

'I often remember the agonies that they endured while bringing me up. I was a five-year-old child when, as misfortune would have it, Abasahib's army of three thousand fell into an enemy trap in the darkness of the night. The army was gone and destiny seemed to have turned its back on us. I remember a Portuguese fort on the edge of Chaul that dark and stormy night. On the one hand, it was raining cats and dogs, and on the other, Abasahib was shedding copious tears on account of my insecure state.

'Yes, Maharaj.'

'It is extremely difficult for a devoted and loving wife to spend even a single night without the presence of her husband, and yet my mother and my father suffered more than twenty years of separation so that they could save their jaageers and jointly perform the task of raising our Swarajya. What would have been the state of their minds? It was just a year ago that I crushed under my heel the crown that Ali Adilshah had sent to me of the commander-in-chief of the Bijapur army. I distinctly remember the glow of proud satisfaction that spread over the face of Shahajiraja, my father. The Sultan was furious when he came to know that I didn't care a fig for his lures and had refused to walk into his trap. It was on account of this anger that he placed Abasahib under arrest in the fort at Bankapur.'

'That was just for a day.'

'But humiliation is humiliation, Netokaka, whether it is for a moment or for a day.'

Regrets and anxieties seemed to have become the king's lifelong friends. Netaji pricked up his ears when he noticed a slight tremor in his king's voice. His own personal fears found voice when he said, 'What if that Ghorpada of Mudhol slipped in during the witching hour of the night and joined Khawaas Khan's forces here in Kudaal?'

The thought did startle the king a bit. Proven warriors like Khawaas Khan, Rustam-e-Zamaan and Miraan had already lined themselves up across the river with their horsemen and foot soldiers; their cannon had been mounted on their platforms, ready to fire. At such a time, if the powerful

Bajiraje's men were also to get into the mix, their power would increase phenomenally, making the battle quite an ordeal for Shivraya's men.

Then there was that Aurangzeb sitting on the bank of Agra, and he wouldn't sit still either. The king immediately sent for Bahirji Naik and spread a map out on a bench. 'What do you think, Naik?' the king asked. 'When might this Baji set out from Mudhol and join the ranks of the enemy?'

'Raje, he hasn't set out from Mudhol yet.'

'Really? Can we trust this intelligence?'

'Absolutely.'

'So, where is this man now?'

'He will stay in Mudhol for the next two or three days. He is not merely gathering food, fodder and other supplies to see him through his conflict with us but also heaping up gold provided by private financiers.'

'Ah, so Bajiraja has kept his flame of enmity alive and sparkling.'

'Of course. When he had the senior king arrested, and when he played his duplicitous game on the Panhala-Vishalgadh trail, Bajiraja was only fanning his ardent desire to see you destroyed root and stalk.'

'Does that mean this Khan will now sit with his eyes planted in the direction from where Bajiraje's army is going to descend?'

The valley—and the stream flowing through it—lay peacefully in the embrace of darkness. To the east was Khawaas Khan's camp, and on the western bank were the tents of Shivaji's army. It was quite a few days now since they had begun testing each other's patience, but there had been no friction worth noting.

Some Adilshahi soldiers had stirred out to answer the call of nature. Through the heavy gloom, they noticed some stirrings in the Maratha camp. Some more peering into the distance, and their jaws dropped. How could that be? How could darkness have sprouted hundreds of feet? As they kept staring, they discerned that the feet belonged to both men and horses. The Maratha soldiers, instead of riding on their animals' backs, were quietly escorting them out of the camp. More seemed to be following them.

Now fully alert, the Bijapuri soldiers ran to convey the news to their supreme commander; they were joined by other riff-raff like the water-carriers, kitchen-boys and stable grooms. When they reached the big Khan's pavilion, one of the excited boys mustered all his courage and asked the guard to rouse Khawaas Khan. Woken up from deep sleep, a groggy Khan lifted his sword and stumbled out. The small gathering in front of his tent immediately broke into a babble: 'Huzoor, Siva's soldiers are sneaking out into the darkness. It looks like they are moving out of their camp.'

'And it looks like Siva also may slip away with them.'

This information made the Khan roll his big round eyes in their sockets. Peering angrily into the darkness, he began grilling the boys to gather more details. 'All right, now, the men you are talking about, which way did they go?'

'Backwards.'

'So, where? Towards Rajapur and Ratnagiri?'

'A little to the side, huzoor.'

'Towards Goa and Karvar? How is that even possible? With our army lying in their way like a python?'

'Huzoor, a bit further to the left …'

After some more cross-questioning, Khawaas Khan understood that the night riders of the Maratha army had gone into the mountains. The boys seemed to be quite sure of it. Still groggy and upset at being yanked out of his sleep, he snapped, 'Idiots! Why would Siva want to go into the mountains and forests? To die by suicide?'

He then called over some of his officials and instructed them to interrogate the informants a little more thoroughly. 'Give them a belting if they have dreamt it all up!' he barked angrily as he went back into his pavilion. The officials could smell the whiff of smuggled firangi liquor on the men's breath. Their decision was made. They lined up the culprits and delivered five juicy lashes each on their buttocks.

Khawaas Khan's sleep, nevertheless, had been broken. He sent for his sergeant and began voicing the doubts that were bothering him. 'That creature from hell cannot be trusted. The demon seems to have a pair of wings along with his limbs. He can fly, and travel underwater, is what the firangi traders of the coast say.'

'It must be true, huzoor. After all, he did raid Uncle Shaista's bedroom in the middle of the night and chop his fingers off!'

As soon as it was light, Khawaas Khan dispatched his spies for conducting an extensive investigation of the Maratha camp. They were specifically ordered to gather clues which yielded any information on Shivaji's movements.

The Kudaal heath lay under a blanket of thick fog. The sun had crossed the horizon, but its rays were weak. Close to the Khan's pavilion, where a few long-muzzled cannons were lined up, a cannoneer was scouring the Maratha camp with a firangi telescope. As Khawaas stood outside his shamiana, fretting over the previous night's ruckus, the man called out, 'Huzoor, if you can come here, please!'

The Adilshahi commander-in-chief quickly went over and peeped through the telescope. A relieved smile spread over his jowls when he saw the Maratha flag fluttering in the distance. He saw the huts, the tents and the cannon all lined up, and among these he saw Shivaji himself moving around with a happy look on his face. 'The drunken fools!' he cried, with a strange mix of irritation and joy in his voice. 'My quarry is right there! Siva, my son! This time, there is no escape for you. Your death is certain. The only question that remains is—at whose hands?'

As the unhappy Bijapur men had rightly observed, darkness had indeed sprouted limbs. The Maratha men had quietly moved out of the camp in groups of fifty, climbed up the hillock nearby, and assembled on the other side to form a hand-picked company of two thousand tough horsemen. They were now moving in an orderly fashion up an incline, determined not to seek rest or recreation till they had their prey in their grip.

Netaji suddenly laughed. Looking at a flank of the Sahyadris to his side, he said, 'Whatever one may say, you do seem to put a lot of faith in this mountain range, Raja, don't you?'

'Of course, Netokaka, and why not? The Sahyadri is the loving father-figure of countless ascetics, scholars and other virtuous men. Besides, the armour and weaponry that the Sahyadris provide are by far the most precious strengths of Shivaji's arsenal. As long as I have the Sahyadris covering my back, my arms possess the power to squeeze the breath out of the toughest adversary that destiny may confront me with.'

Ordinarily, even strong Arab and Turk horses would have taken a day and a half, at least, to traverse the near-perpendicular cliffs, but these charged men and animals had crossed them within the latter half of the night. By the time the sun peeped out, they stood at the source of the river Ghataprabha.

They had set off at short notice in the middle of the night, carrying no paraphernalia with them. After hours of lung-bursting struggle, with not a grain of food inside them, when they drank the tingling-cold water of the nascent river, an irresistible languor overtook the travellers. They lay down along the bank of the water, man and beast, used each other as bolsters, and went limp. An hour or two of relaxing the muscles was completely in order.

As soon as Shivraya got off his horse, Netaji and Madaari Mehetar scuttled about, looking for something that the king could rest on. Finally Netaji pulled a length of sackcloth out of his saddlebag and spread it on the fine sand, upon which the king happily stretched himself out and went to sleep. Everyone else was snoring too. Netaji alone moved around with a burning torch in hand. He never rested, even if the gods advised him to, if the king's security was at stake.

They rested for three hours or so and wound themselves up for the next lap. This journey would be longer. From here on, and for the remaining distance, they would move alongside the banks of the Ghataprabha. The thick vegetation on both sides of the river gave the company enough and more cover to move without fear of being spotted by enemy eyes and therefore move rapidly.

After travelling for a few hours, they began to hear the distant rumbling of water falling from a great height. Netaji pulled a map out of his pocket and placed his finger on a dot marked 'Gokaak'. This rather large township was renowned for its huge waterfall, and that was the sound which had begun reaching their ears.

It had now become a routine for Khawaas Khan to peer at the army lined up on the other side of the river. He would then turn around, scan the outlines of the Sahyadri mountains and heave a grunt of disgust. Finally, he sent for his senior chieftains including Shaikh Miraan and Siddhi Sarvar, and barked, 'We have done enough of waiting. There on the slope in front of our eyes wanders our prey Siva, and all that we do is stare at his face through this telescope. This has gone on for too long. Let's leap at him while he's within our sight.'

'Khan sahib, a little patience is always advisable. Please remember the words of our Sultan. He wanted it to be a joint venture with Bajiraje.'

'Or else?'

'Else, it may just turn out to be a little beyond your capacity. It is easier to handle a wounded tiger than a wounded Siva who has eluded our grasp. That would be far more dangerous. Let's wait for Bajiraje to come down those mountains in front. A little caution cannot do us any harm.'

'Stop your cowardly prattle!'

'Huzoor, Bajiraje is Siva's kinsman. He is so unhinged by hatred for the man that he is bringing along eight thousand gold mohurs and thousands of fresh horses from his stables to help us.'

Mudhol was noted for the finest breed of horses in the region. Khawaas Khan had heard of Bajiraje having combed countless stables and assembled a cavalry of thousands for the purpose of settling scores with his bete noire. Baji had vowed to next appear at the Bijapur durbar only after he had wiped out his most detested enemy. Khawaas Khan, also, was now desperate for Baji's reinforcements to arrive at the earliest. At the same time, he too was frothing at the mouth to close his fingers around Siva's throat and earn glory for himself.

41

THE BATTLE OF MUDHOL

When Bajiraje Ghorpade's company saw the walls of their city appear before them at a distance through the darkness of the night, they began moving with greater speed. As dawn broke, Bajiraje espied three dollies and a few palanquins belonging to his own royal waada approach with their waddling gait. As soon as they saw their master, the guards in front and the accompanying horsemen stooped, followed by the dollies and palanquins. Bajiraje's wife Latikaraje climbed out of one of the palanquins and stepped forward to place her forehead at her husband's feet. It was clear to Baji that his wife, in the company of their two sons Maloji and Shankaraji, had set out on a journey.

'Where are you off to in such a hurry and so early in the morning?' Baji asked his wife.

'Lakshmi Mata of my mother's house came to me in a dream four or five times. It has had me worried for the past few days. I thought it best to take her darshan and pacify her with suitable offerings.'

'When do you propose to return?'

'After the princes take their darshan of the goddess, they will, perhaps, wish to stay behind for a couple of days with my brothers. We shall return soon after.'

Bajiraje was returning home after a long time, therefore it was natural for him to feel a little upset at the thought of not having his family there. Disregarding the officials who stood around, Latikaraje held her husband by the arm and took him aside. 'Raje,' she said to him in an anxious voice, 'this conflict that you have been having with one of our kin is not wise. Whether it is the Bhosales or the Ghorpades, you do agree, don't you, that we belong to the Rajput clan? We share a close kinship!'

'Therefore I should go and fall at the feet of that conceited son of Shahaji? Is this what my darling wife thinks?'

'That's not what I'm saying, but fire feeds fire. So much better to hold the water of mutual respect in the cup of one's hand.'

'I have no thought in my mind other than uprooting and destroying Shahaji's entire family and serving the Adilshahi Sultanate loyally. All right, it's getting late—for both you and me.'

His wife's retinue moved on and Bajiraje's men reached the northern gate of Mudhol as the skies turned bright. As the company rode in, Gungajiraje saluted his dynamic and powerful brother with a flourish. Bajiraje's two-day stay in his ancestral waada was to be full of frenetic activity. He was due to fight the most momentous battle of his life. He was determined that he should fall short of nothing in this final showdown between him and his adversary.

To ensure a sufficient supply of food and fodder, dynamite and gunpowder, he had to raise funds from the market. He had taken upon his shoulders the responsibility of raising not a dozen or two, but eight hundred thousand gold mohurs. Accordingly, he had dispatched his men to Bagalkot, Kagwad, Belgaum, Jamkhandi and Gokaak, right up to Hubli and Dharwad, even before he had left Bijapur. After gathering all this wealth, he was due to leave instantly for Konkan.

He had not forgotten Ali Adilshah's pronouncement while bidding him goodbye, 'Shivaji's destruction is certain if Khawaas Khan and Bajiraje come together.'

Bajiraje had thrown all his resources of wealth, power and influence, even religion and black magic, into this campaign. Which was why, before he stepped into his waada, he had arranged for tantric prayers to be offered to the dark gods by a priest named Lingaji Bhat. He had met this celibate Deccani priest in the brahmin lane of Bijapur just a few months ago.

Impressed by the man's scholarship and skill in the art of pleasing the darker gods for boons and favours, he had tripled his wages and sent him over to his waada in Mudhol. Lingaji had immediately set about serving his master with instructions to use tantra, mantra and yantra for bringing about the total destruction of his arch-enemy Shivaji.

On the day of his arrival in Mudhol, Bajiraje rode out on his horse. Accompanying him was Lingaji, sitting on a Kathiawadi horse, wearing nothing but a knee-long dhotar. They went to a high point that lay on the far side of the bamboo grove near Mudhol. The scene that he witnessed in the valley below made Bajiraje's heart dance with joy.

He had poured huge wealth into the hands of Gungajiraja to procure for him seven thousand of the best horses that money could buy, and what lay before him was the outcome of Gungaji's efforts. Twirling his luxuriant moustache with pride and contentment, he said, 'Tell me, Swamiji, did even Chandragupta Maurya have such a magnificent cavalry as this back in his day?'

'Impossible, Raje! No one even in the Ramayana or the Mahabharata had a comparable fervour to annihilate his enemy.'

'What else can I do, Swamiji? That brat of Shahaji's is an obstinate and troublesome fellow. But this equine wealth of mine is very soon going to dance upon his head. Just watch how I grind his idiotic dreams of Swarajya to dust under the hooves of my thousand steeds.'

'I am dying of curiosity to know how such deadly hatred was born in the first place.'

'Forget it. There's nothing much to tell there. Besides, the story is very old. When I had arrested Shahaji in the jungles of Jinji and handed him over to Mustafa Khan, I screamed from the base of my lungs, told my idiotic Adilshahi friends, 'Listen, brothers, burn this poisonous creeper instantly.' But nobody listened to me. While that imposter was serving the Sultanate, his lout of a son was talking about creating an independent kingdom here in the twelve Maavals. Arey, when Afzal Khan was killed, thousands of Bijapuris had gathered on the streets, demanding punishment for the father, at least, if not for the son. They were bursting their blood vessels screaming, but what did Begum Sahiba and her foster-son do? Instead of offering him protection, they should have thrown him to the crowds! And we know what the crowd did to Murari Jagdev earlier.'

Listening to the incensed ranting of Bajiraje, Lingaji Bhat's body turned taut as that of a salamander. He shut his eyes and mumbled a mantra to bring down a curse upon the enemy. Addressing Bajiraje in a grave tone, he said, 'Never has there been such a congregation of malefic planets against Shivaji in the almanac before. Just a little effort from you, Bajiraje, and victory shall be yours.'

'That's true,' Bajiraje gloated, twirling his moustache again. 'The victorious end of all my efforts is not more than two days away.'

At this point, Gungajraja rode up to them and asked, 'So, dada, how big is the cavalry that is going to come down upon Shivaji's head?'

'Well, you see these seven thousand brand-new horses. Add to them my own three thousand and the ten thousand gathered in Konkan under Khawaas Khan and Bahlol Khan. You also have Shivaji's half-brother Vyankoji arriving with another four thousand—'

'Abababababa!' mumbled Lingaji Bhat in his Kannada tongue. 'With an avalanche of twenty-four thousand horses descending on him, that Shivaji of the margatthyas will get crushed like an ant, ho!' He then looked piously up at the sky, muttered, 'Purushyah Bhaagyam!' and counted the beads of his rudraksh rosary.

They had travelled the previous night across mountains that rose up straight as walls, and that too within a short time. No wonder the joints and bones of both men and animals had turned to jelly. That had been followed by a long gallop under the hot sun. In this state, Shivraya and his men came to the great Gokaak waterfall. It wasn't a stream, but an entire river rolling over the precipice. There was a spot below where the water had collected in a deep pool, made doubly inviting by the shadow of the neighbouring crag falling upon it. Horse and horseman instantly made a beeline for the pool and frolicked in it to their heart's content.

The sun hadn't altogether set on the other side of the mountains, but the shadows falling upon the river had turned quite dark. Refreshed and revitalised, the horsemen did three more hours of hard riding to reach their destination. The ancient town of Mudhol had been swallowed up by darkness by the time they arrived. The stone wall that ran around it stretched for about three miles. It was strong enough to do justice to a fort.

At the centre of Mudhol was Bajiraje's royal waada with three courtyards the size of a town square inside it. On all four corners were balustraded parapets which were patrolled by guards with burning torches. The city walls too were mounted by bastions, also manned by armed guards. Of the three entry gates, the east-facing one was the post of Baji's own brother Gungajiraje Ghorpade.

Bajiraje too had a small but efficient espionage department. That evening, they brought him a piece of unusual news. Baji knew that Shivaji had clashed with Khawaas Khan in the battlefield of Kudaal. But some travellers had told tales of an impersonator with an army of a thousand or so horses wandering in the neighbouring forests. Gungaji rushed with this intelligence to the waada, where his brother was engrossed in some important work. Raising his head a bit reproachfully, he said, 'I am very busy with some very important work. Why do you bring these stories of imposters and pretenders to me?'

'Just thought I should alert you.'

'Handle this kind of stuff at your level. But yes, it's good to be alert. Shivaji cannot be trusted.'

Bajiraje Ghorpade was an immensely strong person. Even at this age, he would run with the horses for miles together. He would dive into the waada well that was seventy hands deep and swim for hours. He had kept his body strong and supple with vigorous exercises. Since he had to leave for Konkan on a new campaign that day, he rose at midnight. As always, the first thing he did was to take a swim in the waada well.

When his well-built, seven-foot body hit the surface, it threw up a massive splash all over the well. Wrapping a thin, brand-new karvat-style dhotar around his dripping body, he went to the shrine in the waada to bow before Mahalingeshwar. He next took a darshan of the Nelgudi Mahadev that had been installed underground in a tunnel-like shrine. Lingappa was there holding a tray full of freshly collected flowers. After placing those golden magnolia and jasmine on the feet of the god, he stepped out. Very soon he would get astride his horse and set out on the campaign.

The entire establishment had woken up at dawn. The main entrance had been thrown wide open; the place was abuzz with the last-minute hustle before the departure. Suddenly, the sound of a thousand hooves rang out, pricking up everybody's ears. Next arrived a grand white horse, the size of a battlement that stood at the gate and let out an angry neigh. The waada's guards felt their spines go limp. If Shivaji had arrived at the heart of the town, it could only mean that he had slaughtered the guards who were minding the city walls. Also, it was done so swiftly that before wind of it could reach them, their nemesis had himself entered the waada gate.

As if performing a perfect dive into a pool, the king dismounted. His aquiline nose, piercing eyes, thick, tapering beard and silk attire were well known, but more than any of these, it was the radiance that sat on his face and was exuded by his personality that left no one in any doubt about his identity. The guards could do nothing except widen their eyes, drop their jaws and freeze like pillars. As he strode past the gate, Shivraya called out in a stentorian voice, 'Baji Ghorpade, come out. I have arrived.'

'Come, boy, come,' came the equally powerful response from the upper storey of the waada.

'Ghorpade, sarkaar! It is I, Shivajiraja, who stand at your door.'

'Come, boy, I've been waiting for you. You may call yourself a king if you wish to, but we are loyal servants of the Adilshahi Sultanate.'

'My father too has served the Sultanate alongside you.'

'Ah, talking about Shahaji, are you? Yes, of course, he had to be your father. It's the same inclination towards rebellion and treachery that runs through your blood.'

'Uncle, dear, all these Adilshahs and Mughals are, after all, intruders from foreign lands. We are the sons of this soil and its legitimate owners.'

'Look, boy, we can argue all day on this topic and never arrive at any conclusion. But you did take a long time coming here.'

With that remark, a sixty-five-year-old strode down the steps into the square: tall, generously built, muscular, supremely confident, and with the swagger of one who knew he possessed all these gifts. The squeak of his leather footwear provided the requisite menacing accompaniment to his materialisation. His intimidating eyes, his flaring nostrils, his darkly threatening eyebrows and his dense, bristling moustaches were enough to put the fear of god in even the stoutest antagonist.

Shivraya had crossed the threshold. He now walked warily into the tiled courtyard. When his foot touched a small stone statue of a tortoise on the floor, he bowed with reverence, then walked up to stand at a distance from the big man, straight as a ramrod. The two stood looking at each other in the manner of a snake and a mongoose measuring each other up. Meanwhile, the soldiers belonging to both sides were perplexed. What should they do?

Bajiraje growled, 'Shivaji, your father turned your head and set you on this path of vengeance. I always knew that you would come, just as Takshaka chased King Parikshit in the form of a venomous snake.'

The blade in Shivraya's hand glittered in the light of the torches. His lieutenants Netaji and Tanaji perceived the fire of vengeance that had lit up the body of their king. As Bajiraje stepped forward with his broad, jewel-hilted sword, Netaji and Tanaji ran their experienced eyes over his huge, crag-like body and their hearts missed a beat. It looked formidable enough to tackle four or five assailants together and grind them to dust. By comparison, Shivraya was lean and small-built, almost like a boy.

Bajiraje leapt off the low platform into the courtyard. When Shivraya stepped forward to clash swords with him, Netaji and Tanaji let out a loud cry of 'Har har Mahadev' and stepped in. His smile dripping with sarcasm, Bajiraje snarled, 'So, you brat of Shahaji, this is how, huh? All that talk of Swarajya for the world, and duplicity in private, that too suddenly sprung?'

'Ghorpade, your lordship, keep this in mind: the Bhosales never attack from behind,' Shivaji returned scorn for scorn. 'We demolish our enemy by aiming for his nose and guts. Disembowelling him from the front is our religion.'

'You have already demonstrated your perfidious nature, boy.'

'How?'

'By raiding the enemy's camp while he is still asleep; by trying to catch him unawares.'

'Asleep? Unawares? Could you be sleeping as you stand, uncle? And are you unaware of the nemesis that stands before you in your own yard, with your men standing around you? You make me laugh.' Shivraya then turned towards his men and said, 'Netokaka and Tanaji, sheathe your swords. If this Ghorpada is as strong as a bull, I have the agility of an eagle. The blood that runs through my veins is not that of a deserter in a field of battle. It is the blood of Shahajibaba who held five kings in disdain and held aloft the flag of rebellion till his last breath. And of my Matoshri Jijausahib who fed me live coals with each mouthful of bhaakari.'

'Enough of your bluster, boy. Lift your sword, then.'

'Indeed! The battle now is not between our armies, but between the two of us. On guard, then, wretch. May justice win!'

Swords clashed with a force that sent sparks flying. Old Baji Ghorpade's strokes were powerful and murderous, backed by the muscled weight of his body. Shivaji, on the other hand, was nimble and quick-footed. Netaji and Tanaji were all eyes and ears, eaten up by worry, now that their priceless jewel was at stake. The mortal combat raged on: Shivaji came up with lightning-quick feints but found his adversary ready to fend them off. A couple of times the old warrior came up with such vicious swings that, for all his sprightliness, Shivraya could count himself lucky to have escaped alive.

But then, he came up with a swift countermove that dodged Baji's thrust and delivered a blow that landed with full force on the old man's left shoulder. Wild-eyed, Baji looked down at his body, expecting to see a severed arm slipping out of his sleeve. The distinct stench of death assailed his nostrils. The very next moment, he had turned around and fled towards the wall at the back. On reaching there, he hit a spot that opened up a stone panel which allowed entry into a secret basement. As he went racing down the steps, the panel swung back into place. There he sat in the darkness, terrified at the prospect of what awaited him out in the open.

'Bajiraje!!!' Shivraya's roar came down to him from above, 'don't sit hiding there like a lily-livered skunk. Prove to me that you are a Maratha and step out!!!'

'Silly boy, there's pedigreed Maratha blood flowing in my veins. And there's no question of fear. Constructing defensive walls and secret tunnels, and taking their shelter in times of need, is very much a part of royal strategy. If you have the courage, open the panel and step down here!'

Within moments of saying it, he was completely petrified to see the heavy stone panel slide open. He then saw the basement light up with an orange glow and soon Shivaji was striding down the stone steps, while behind him Lingaji Bhat lifted a torch high. Baji was startled beyond measure at seeing the fiery face of his priest. Shivraya stepped forward and held the fallen man by his good right arm. He lifted him to his feet and dragged him up the stairs. Once out in the open, he tossed a sword in Baji's direction.

'Fight!' Shivaji commanded, throwing him an ice-cold look. With no options left, Bajiraje picked up the sword, gathered all the dignity he could muster and swung into action. The combat didn't last long. A fatal slanting swing of the king's blade found Baji's chest and ripped open the ribcage. Even as he knew that all was over, eyes flaming red, blood oozing from mouth and nose, the old man flung his sword with the last force of his dying breath. The blade found its mark and entered Lingappa's shoulder. The man was evidently made of sterner stuff than priests generally are. He went down on his knees and tried to stanch the blood that was now flowing out of his wound. The agony was unbearable.

The now-lifeless body of Baji Ghorpade lay on the ground. Shivraya ran towards the priest, loosening the broad silk sash that he wore around his waist as he ran. 'Are you seriously hurt, Vishwasrao?' he cried anxiously, as he began winding the sash around the fallen man's wound. Despite the excruciating pain that he was in, Vishwasrao Dighe managed to bring a joyous smile to his lips. This was a victory worth celebrating.

Gungaji Ghorpade, who had been fighting the king's men outside, heard that the winds of war and destiny had changed and all was lost. Within the waada too, it was all mayhem and massacre. Bajiraje's men began oozing out from every nook and corner and balustrade. Swords clanked and blood spurted. A few Ghorpades yelled from behind, 'Don't let Shivaji escape. Don't let him get away alive!'

Tanaji, Rayaji, Moropant and other warriors let out cries of 'Har har Mahadev' and leapt into the fray. However, this unexpected pouring out of enemy soldiers from the walls infuriated Tanaji. 'Rats hiding in crevices need to be brought out with fire, Raje,' he declared, and began setting alight the entire waada. Corpses were soon bobbing in the well next to the Mahalingeshwar shrine. A good four hundred or so lay scattered around Bajiraje's body. When some assailants ran out of the neighbouring alley, the Maavalis set the entire lane on fire, sending houses and shops up in flames.

Meanwhile, the thought struck Gungaji that the enemy should not benefit from the wealth that Bajiraje had painstakingly collected for the Kudaal campaign. Gathering a dozen of his men and all the gold that he could lay his hands on, he galloped across the river and reached a dense patch of vegetation on the far bank. Beyond it were the secret meadows where the seven thousand horses—the weapon with which the dream of annihilating the house of Shahaji was to be realised—were coralled.

The men who had been guarding the treasure rushed out at the sound of the clattering hooves. Gungaji shouted at the top of his voice, 'Arey, get up! Cut the halters and pull out the stakes! Release all the horses and scatter them wide in the jungles around here! Make the horses vanish before Shivaji arrives!' Gungaji himself began swiftly severing ropes and removing stakes. The other men got busy bringing down the fences around the stables and shooing the animals away, using whips to expedite their gait.

That was when Netaji got wind of what had transpired and made a dash for the meadows with his men. When Gungaji learned of Netaji's imminent arrival, he disappeared into the jungles. By the time Netaji reached the place, it was almost too late. Most of the stables were deserted. Nevertheless, he and his men started picking up as many of the scattered gold coins as they could and managed to round up over twelve hundred thoroughbred horses.

The mountain of gold mohurs that Baji had collected for obliterating Shivaji thus fell into Maavali hands. It had started turning hot, and precious time was slipping away. As the king made ready to leave the Ghorpade waada, a bunch of about fifty men, most of whom were Bajiraje's cousins, nephews and close friends who had been hiding in the basements all this time, rushed out for a final assault. But the men around the king were alert to all such possibilities. They quickly turned around and scotched this maniacal last-ditch attempt by slaughtering the assailants in whichever corner of the waada they found them.

As Shivraya's army was moving out of the precincts, the fallout of Bajiraje's seething, long-harboured hatred became evident. He had spread his personal abhorrence of Shivaji so wide and deep that, even as his army was withdrawing from Mudhol, bunches of agitated men would come screaming out of the city's lanes and take rash shots at the passing soldiery. The chieftains marching with the king's army were so incensed at this that they turned around and began razing the entire city to the ground. When they finally joined the rest of their colleagues, the once-prosperous city was going up in billows of smoke behind them.

Two horsemen were carrying an ingeniously crafted swing between them, in which they had placed the injured Vishwasrao Dighe. The wound on his shoulder had earlier been treated with herbs and potions before it was bandaged firmly. This was the best they could have done under the circumstances, but it was not enough to alleviate the valiant man's agony.

The king had finally fulfilled the commitment he had made to his parents. In the bargain, he was coming back with all the gold that Baji had stacked up, as well as those twelve hundred horses. But his mind was not on any of these gains at the moment. It would keep hovering around his loyal and much-loved official Vishwasrao who travelled alongside him, groaning and yelping at each clumsy step the horses took.

Ahead of them rose the range of the Amboli hills. Behind them lay a devastated Mudhol. In due course, they would cross the range and begin the descent into Konkan. The battlefield on the heath of Kudaal at the foot of the hills on the other side was waiting for them.

Khawaas Khan sat watching unblinkingly the Sahyadri hills that lay to his left. Since yesterday, he had been repeating Bajiraje's name almost as if he was counting the beads on a rosary. Adilshah had been wonderfully astute when he had brought the two together, removed their misunderstandings and underlined for them the importance of flexing their muscles together. Consequently, he was waiting most eagerly for the arrival of Bajiraje, for it would bolster his strength many times over.

This day, too, even before the sun had made itself visible, he had pulled out his telescope and peered at the cannon lined up in the enemy camp. In the soft light of the morning, he once again saw Shivaji making the rounds and yawning copiously. Once he had confirmed that Shivaji was where he should be, the rest of his day would flutter by like a lark.

The day after Khawaas Khan had located a convenient spot and laid out his cannon outside the Kudaal fort, he had been visited by Verspreet, the Dutch governor at Vengurla. The Dutchman had said to him wistfully, 'The day we hear of the elimination of that Siva and of the Portuguese at Goa, we Dutch here in Vengurla, and those Englishmen spread across the region from Kharepattan to Surat, are going to celebrate the event with far greater fanfare and fireworks and distribution of sweets than your Adilshahi army. But—'

'Why the "but", friend?'

'But your dreams of reducing him to dust are going to be very difficult to realise. That enemy of ours who rides roughshod over us is a clever, clever man. Don't forget that, Khan sahib.'

Khawaas Khan had thanked the governor for his visit that day.

It was evening when the boys of the artillery unit came running to him and said, 'Huzoor, look towards the mountain!'

Khan instantly waddled over to the cannons and pointed the telescope at the mountainside they had pointed at. It now lay in shadow, with the setting sun behind it. His heart leaped with delight when he saw not just a few, but an entire army of Bajiraje's men clambering down the slope like so many ants. He instantly went down on his knees and offered a prayer of thanks, mumbling, 'Ya Allah, a million thanks to You!'

Khawaas Khan suddenly bloomed. True, it would take five or six hours for an army loaded with war-paraphernalia to make the descent of those majestic mountains, but it was now only a matter of time. With the arrival of Bajiraje's forces, Siva's fate was sealed. He danced around in his tent, singing to himself, 'It's over, the wait is over. We shall come down upon Siva's army this very night. If we catch him alive, we shall put him in chains; if he dies, we shall put his body in a sack and lug it away.'

He was so fired up with the picture he had drawn in his head that he called his sardars over and instructed them to begin marching forward. Senior sardars like Shaikh Miraan, Siddhi Sarvar and Shah Hazrat remonstrated, 'Wazeer miyaan, how can you possibly uproot the entire army that has been laid out according to a well-considered battle plan? You can't treat our forces as a herd of goats or cattle!'

'You people have lost your senses. Look, look up at the mountainside and see who is coming! It's no less an angel from heaven than Bajiraje, and he's coming with ten thousand horses and a load of treasure. This is certainly going to be Siva's last night on this earth!'

Khawaas Khan was evidently in no state of mind to entertain any opposition to his plan, which was to move in the direction of the descending army of Bajiraje. They would then join forces and move stealthily along the foothills and through the jungle in the darkness of the night. That would take them behind the Maratha camp, where they would launch their surprise attack and decimate the enemy army. He had worked himself up into such a state of frenzied obstinacy that the sardars realised all arguments would be useless. They gave in to his insistence and went dragging their feet behind him.

Very soon darkness descended upon the hills. All that could be seen were the lights of the torches coming down the slope. The Khan sent some spies on ahead to inform Bajiraje's forces of their presence. The men returned after some time in a state of panic. 'Sarkaar,' they screeched, 'they look like margatthyas, all of them!'

'Fools!' bellowed Khawaas Khan, 'do you think Baji Ghorpade and his men have converted to Islam? Of course they are going to look like Marathas! But this time, they are our Marathas.'

It was at around ten at night that the Maratha horsemen descending the slope saw the climbing Adilshahi men and pounced upon them with loud cries of 'Har har Mahadev!' and 'Shivaji Maharaj ki jai!' The Bijapuri men were so totally flabbergasted at this unexpected turn of events that they completely lost their heads. Here were these Marathas leaping down upon them with murderous intent, and behind them was the jungle slope, down which it would be impossible to turn around and flee, particularly in this darkness. They saw some of their compatriots turn to the west at the foot of the mountain in an effort to escape the onslaught, and everybody followed suit. At around midnight, Shivraya received the information that a large number of enemy soldiers now lay trapped in the gorge that lay just beyond the valley.

The previous few days of constant riding had exhausted the king. A tent was quickly erected for him on an open patch of land. He now had a clear understanding of the desperate straits in which Khawaas Khan's men had been caught. He also heard that Miraan Khan's chest had been torn open by a Maavali spear. Knowing that his men would also be as tired as he was, he thought the matter carefully through and finally dispatched a herald to the gorge where Khawaas Khan was trapped. The man carried a letter to the Khan, which read:

> Khan Sahib,
> You have a big name and a big status to uphold. Allah-ta'ala has exalted you by bestowing on you the lofty seat of the Wazeer-e-Aazam of the Sultanate of Bijapur. That is the reason why I am inclined to grant you an opportunity to salvage your reputation. You have landed yourself in a deep, dark cave that is so narrow that it does not even give you the space to swing your sword. The place you have chosen as your refuge is the valley of death. Here is my large-hearted offer: disappear in the direction of the land you came from with all your remaining men before light returns. If you disregard my generous proposal and are seen anywhere in the vicinity, come dawn, you can't even imagine the state to which you and your men will be reduced.

Khawaas Khan's throat went dry. Circumstances were slipping swifly out of his hands. The news that his own spies had brought him hardly seemed credible. Wilting under the stress of it all, he asked again, 'Is it really true that Baji Ghorpade has been done to death? And that too by Siva?'

'Yes, Khan sahib. He has also burnt and razed Mudhol to the ground.'

'Ya Allah! How many Sivas has this godforsaken land got? Just this morning I saw one Siva with my own eyes, standing next to the cannons! And now you tell me that there is a second Siva who has come down the mountains after killing Bajiraje of Mudhol! And, by the way, who is this third Siva supervising the construction of a sea fort on the coast? How many more are hiding in this country of demons?'

This confusion as well as the darkness that enveloped him from all sides weakened his ability to form a clear estimate of the state of his army: how many of his men and officers had died, how many had fled. But going by the sheer number that he had at his disposal, he found it quite plausible to believe that he could fight back. Thus, in a moment of false bravado, he sent the messenger back with the immoderate message, 'Go, tell your Siva that we are not the kind to be scared by such empty threats. If he has the courage, he should show up tomorrow for battle.'

It was only as the night advanced that he began to get a clearer picture of his unhappy, vulnerable state. As Siva had said, there really didn't seem to be any space here even to swing one's sword. When his associates came to him in a panic-stricken state, he assured them, 'Don't be afraid. This is where Siva will come in the morning, and this is where he will die. This spot shall be sanctified by his death.'

When morning arrived, Khawaas did wait with a pumping heart for Siva to materialise in that frightful gorge, but no such thing happened. As the morning advanced and more information arrived, the picture began getting clearer. His impulsive decision of the previous night to rendezvous with Bajiraje had utterly destroyed him and his army. The moment the Maratha army at the Kudaal base had got the news that the Adilshahi base was in disarray, it had recognised an opportunity. A timely message from their leader in the mountains had only confirmed their suspicions. After that, in the darkness of the night, disaster descended upon the remaining Adilshahi men at the Khan's camp. Since they knew that offering even token resistance would be folly, they had abandoned the camp wholesale and run in whichever direction they sensed safety. The rout was complete.

When Khawaas Khan's men were being slaughtered in the mountains, Vyankoji was just a few miles away from Kudaal. However, when his advance guards came running back frantically to inform him that Khawaas Khan's army had fallen to pieces, he did the only thing that any person who was not a total idiot would do in such circumstances: he turned around and vamoosed.

After a very long time, Shivaji was not in any tearing hurry when he woke up. A large number of Adilshahi officials had been taken prisoner, some of whom were released on payment of ransom. Around noon, as Shivaji sat exchanging notes with his deputy Netaji, Rao Jedhe brought along with him a bunch of bedraggled Bijapuri prisoners. It was apparent that not all of them were insignificant footmen and water-carriers as they were claiming to be. The king, however, was in a generous mood. 'Release them,' he instructed. 'What's the point in flogging dead horses?'

But when the hugely relieved men began to disperse, happy that all the ash and slime they had smeared over themselves had worked, Netaji sprang forward, caught one of the retreating men by the scruff of his filthy collar and dragged him back before the king. The man cried piteously, 'Please Raja sahib, I am a poor man. I had just one animal with a pair of leather mashaks for supplying water to the army, and even that is gone!' Netaji, meanwhile, was sniggering in amusement. He signalled to the king to look at the man's hands.

Shivraya caught on and peered at them, only to realise that under all the grime and dung were expensive gems glittering on gold rings. The king laughed uproariously and said, 'My dear Khan sahib, it was only luck that made you the wazeer of the Bijapur Sultanate. And now you have been reduced to hiding behind the garb of a bhishti! Actually, that is the only job that you are capable of. However, your luck still holds. You have found me in a generous mood. Let the miserable man go, Netokaka!'

42

THE GLORIOUS DREAM OF SINDHUDURG

NOVEMBER 25 1664

'There, on the faraway coast of Konkan, Shivaji is raising his sea fort, and who is paying the price for it, pray? It's us! Can no one snuff out this rebellious rascal?'

It had now become a routine ritual of the durbar: the Sultan seething, and his chieftains counting their toes. 'Allah-ta'ala has blessed our Bijapuri Sultanate with many a thousand square miles of land, but there is one thing for which we have to look outside, and that is a sea coast. The coasts that we can lay claim on are the distant ones of Kudaal, Vengurla, Dicholi, Nevati, and that headland they call Dandi.'

'That's right, huzoor.'

'Do you have any conception of what will happen if Siva succeeds in making a sea fort on that patch of the coast? Of the disastrous consequence it will have for our Sultanate?'

The rumours of Shivaji building a sea fort had set the cat among the pigeons in the Bijapur durbar. Naamdaar Khan, Kabeer Khan and a few others suggested, 'Why don't we ask someone who has just come back from those parts? They will know what's going on there.'

'But whom do we ask? That wretched Khawaas Khan who fled the battlefield fifteen days ago after getting a drubbing?'

Sultan Ali Adilshah was in a state of deep depression as he spoke to the assembled chieftains and officials of the Adilshahi court. 'It seems impossible to fathom the nature of the road that goes in Shiva's direction. Whoever has set off that way with the resolve of bringing that rascal to heel has always managed to destroy himself instead. Just look at the list! Fateh Khan went to the Purandar battle and lost his life. A mountain the size of Afzal Khan was reduced to dust. That blackguard Siddhi Johar brought such shame upon himself that he never had the courage to show his face again. This last person who had left with a swagger, swearing vengeance, this Khawaas Khan ... he destroyed our army of thirty thousand, buried four of our stalwarts, and now hides Allah knows where!'

'Huzoor,' said the senior Qazi in a mournful voice, 'the road leading towards Siva has always been dangerous, but there are calamities looming ahead that we cannot disregard! If that Siva succeeds in building a fort on the coast, it may spell the end not only of the Bijapur Sultanate but of Islam in these parts.'

Ali Adilshah was faced by a crisis and seemed to have no answer to the questions that were raging in his mind. About a fortnight ago, news had arrived of the annihilation of his entire army on the battlefield of Kudaal. He had no idea how many were left of the thirty-five thousand that had marched out. On its tail came the terrifying news that Shivaji's enterprise of building a fort on the Maalvan coast had picked up speed. The task of immediately raising and sending another army to prevent Shivaji from going ahead with his plans looked completely beyond the Sultan's resources at the moment.

After a great deal of contemplation, Ali instructed his new wazeer, 'Whatever money is left in our treasury, send it to our Arab brothers in Vengurla, Kudaal and other areas of Konkan. Dispose of our gems and jewels if you have to. Tell them to distribute money freely. Give them gunpowder if they need it, but they must bring this project of that renegade Siva to an immediate stop.

The ordinary people of the Konkan region had, as it were, received a new lease on life from Shivraya's ventures on their coast. It had all begun with the king's visit to the Dandi-Maalvan coast and his immediate decision to construct another Janjira on the rock island of Kurtya, followed by the exciting news that construction would begin within a month. This news had spread like wildfire across a wide area that included Kandalgaon, Kuse, the banks of the Maldi, Kalawar, and then beyond to the Bharatgadh fort, the Nevati fort, Medha, Wayari, Kumbharmath, and a hundred other villages.

The people of those parts were ecstatic that this king of the common man would also become the 'Lord of Konkan'. Women and children, traders, shopkeepers, the labourers working in the depots, the Kolis who worked the coastline, the people of the nearby jungles—all of them were waiting for the day when the reign of Shivaji would begin on the red soil of Konkan.

The king had marked the second day of the month of Maarg-Sheersh for laying the foundation stone of the sea fort. The tempo of the preparations had peaked when there were barely four or five days left for the occasion. At the same time, the forts of the Arabs to the south of Maalvanwadi began bustling with activity. These stations were always manned by some three or four hundred Arab soldiers of the most despicable kind. Suddenly, the population of each fort swelled to nearly fifteen hundred. These hooligans then started patrolling the shores in their boats and dinghies with big whips in their hands and began throwing their weight around on the poor peasants, the fishermen and the young boys of Konkan.

The three-hundred-year history of these Arab ruffians had been one of tyranny and oppression. The coastal affairs of the Bijapur sultans were run by these petty Arab officials and soldiers, which had given them the license to indulge their propensity for violence and vandalism.

The month gone by had seen momentous developments that were certain to have a far-reaching impact on the region. Kudaal had fallen under Shivraya's control after Khawaas Khan had fled from the battlefield in ignominy. Khem Savant had tried to flex his muscles at Shivaji with his force of ten or twelve thousand infantrymen and had been roundly belaboured for his effort. Against the backdrop of these events, Shivraya's resolve to lay the foundation of a sea fort within a matter of two or three weeks seemed all the more courageous and admirable.

As the day for performing the foundation-laying puja came nearer, the shadow of fear looming over the proposed ceremony began to turn darker. Many doubted whether this event would be allowed to take place, because a strong wind of jealousy and rancour had been blowing through the palaces, the waadas, and the forts of the traditional power wielders of south Konkan. If Shivaji was allowed entry into these parts, they feared he would never withdraw. It was precisely this apprehension that had robbed sleep from the eyes of Antonio D'Mello, the Portuguese governor of Goa, as well as Verspreet, the Dutch commander of Vengurla.

Stories began circulating, gossip started spreading fast, and soon skepticism about the viability of the venture was rampant.

'It's simply out of the question. This land has been under the suzerainty of the Bijapur Sultanate for hundreds of years, and they've always been great friends with these Arabs.'

'You're right. It's for the Arabs, the Mughals and the firangis to control the forts. The job of the Marathas is to do their bidding and keep the forts secure. It's not our business to become kings and set out on campaigns. Service to these masters is where our right lies.'

'Let's see whether that Shivaji can place four slabs of stones one atop the other on the Kurtya rock. If he can manage that, I shall set afloat fifty-one fresh coconuts from my depot into the sea.'

People were not ready to stop being slaves. There could never be any shortage of congenital detractors or mean-minded naysayers. Shivraya, on the other hand, was quite determined to give shape to his long-cherished dreams.

As he lay stretched out on his bed, sleep continued to elude Shivraya. Excess of joy or sorrow is a known obstacle to slumber. On the morrow, he was due to officially inaugurate the effort that would lead to the fulfilment of a major ambition. In keeping with his philosophy and strategy of staying as close as possible to the people and the culture of the region where he was operating, he had instructed Govind Vishwanath, 'Look for a local priest to officiate at the stone-laying puja.' Then, noticing his downcast face, the king asked, 'What's the matter, Pant?'

'Maharaj, I feel ashamed to say this to you.'

'Huh?'

'I couldn't locate a single priest either in this town or in the neighbouring villages. They have locked their houses and vanished, every one of them.'

'Why?'

'Fear for their lives.'

'Who would harm them?'

'How do I say it, Raje? It was just a few weeks ago that you had thrashed the living daylights out of Khem Savant of Wadi in Kudaal. He had fallen at your feet and begged for his life. However, he was one of the powerful people here who strongly opposed the idea of your fort coming up here.'

'Arey Pant, why are you so hung up on Khem Savant? He has sunk out of sight, run to Goa. Going by the intelligence provided by our spies, the Portuguese too have refused to entertain him. If he is still searching for a roof to shelter under, what obstruction can he possibly cause?'

'Even if Khem Savant has himself disappeared, Maharaj, he has got his henchmen all over the place. Then you have the Portuguese, the Dutch and those Arabs; not one of them has warmed to the thought of a Maratha fort here. Adilshah's men are busy ensuring that some hindrance or the other can be created to thwart the fulfilment of your mission. These Arab soldiers have threatened the priests with dire consequences and driven them out of their villages.'

'Is that so?'

'Yes, Maharaj. They were told to their face that if they were found anywhere close to Shivaji's drama, their supply of victuals would stop. No more alms for them … they would beg for a fistful of rice and die begging!'

The argument of Shivraya's enemies was compelling: disappointing Shivaji would be bad, but disobeying the Adilshahi Arabs or the Portuguese and the Dutch would be far, far worse. The people there had grown up with the fear of the Adilshahi sword on their neck and the Arab spear in their chest. When the overlords began stringing insubordinate men up in the trees, they reasoned, Shivaji would be nowhere around to save them.

'Stop worrying, Pant. We will not allow these roughnecks to dictate terms here. We shall not let them rattle their swords and intimidate these simple, helpless folk. For all their machinations, we shall most certainly build our fort on Kurtya. The inauguration shall happen on the appointed day and within the appointed hour. Stop worrying.'

Around dawn the next day, the king reached the Rameshwar temple in the company of Govind Vishwanath, Moropant, a few Koli boys like Gunjaji, Yesaji and Taasaji, and the two priests Janam Bhat Abhyankar and his nephew Dadam Bhat. The plan was to proceed to the island immediately after finishing the prayers in the temple. The priest had just poured the libation over the pind and the king was engrossed in prayer when a commotion was heard outside. About half a dozen horsemen dismounted in front of the temple and entered in an agitated state. 'Raje,' they said in a panic-stricken voice, 'it appears that Adilshah has planned a big disruption to our ceremony.'

'What's happened?'

'There's a grand procession of some seventy or eighty elephants coming this way along the Bijapuri road through the jungles behind—'

'Elephants?'

'They are huge Malabari elephants, accompanied by a thousand-strong Kannada army carrying short swords.'

'Raje,' Govind Vishwanath broke in anxiously, 'please do something; else the inauguration will have to be abandoned.'

As he calmly tossed flowers over the pind, the king asked, 'What's the colour of the pennants they are carrying?'

'It's quite a strange thing. Red, with a stripe of green.'

This information appeared to delight the king. Turning to Moropant, he said joyously, 'Go, Pant, get going. Take the drummers and the horn players; escort the elephants to the site with pomp and show.'

'But what does all this mean?' asked a confused Moropant.

'Aho, these elephants have arrived to help us build our fort. They have travelled a long distance, from beyond the border of Badroor in Karnataka. Yellappa Nayak, the subedar of my friend Bhadrappa Nayak, has dispatched some of his own wonderful beasts at my request.'

The king had wanted this prayer before the foundation-laying ceremony to be a relatively private affair, but even so, a good hundred and fifty citizens had assembled at the temple. They clapped in delight when they heard that a huge team of elephants was rolling in for the construction of the fort. The king said, 'Friends, we are not erecting the wall of a mere house or a temple here, but a fort that will plant its feet in the waves of the sea. We shall need the help of the heads, the legs, the trunks and the backs of the strongest elephants to push and carry huge blocks of stones to the site. This is not a job for mules and donkeys.'

The dawn air had not lost its nip when the king's company left for the Maalvanwadi shore. They could hear the crash of the waves some distance away. Suddenly, all sounds were drowned by the thunder of a few explosions from the direction of the shore. The priests and officials riding with the king then noticed flashes of light shooting out from the Kurtya island against the ambient darkness of the sky and the sea. What was this new mischief? Could the Portuguese have marched in from Goa? Or the Englishmen, perhaps, had sent their gunnery from Rajapur? This did not bode well for the king's ceremony.

It was the king who reassured them. 'We shall need many tons of stone for constructing the fort. Instead of transporting it over long distances, we decided to gather it right here by blowing the rocks up with dynamite. Our stonemasons from Bankapur have started their work.'

Dadam Bhat, however, looked concerned. 'Forgive me, Raje,' he said, 'all of this hustle and hurry doesn't seem right to me.'

'Why? What's your worry?'

'Why should they have begun the inauspicious act of laying mines and blasting rock just before the ceremony, creating so much noise?'

'How can you say this, priest? After all, we do beat drums and blow horns before starting an enterprise, don't we? Besides, the work we have undertaken here is so sacred that nothing related to it can be considered inauspicious.'

The sky was bright when the king's company entered Maalvanwadi. Around the same time, another company entered from the other side, playing drums and tambourines and bugles. The denizens of the village were woken by this sudden noise and rushed out of their small houses. People in big and small groups came running towards the source of all this clamour. What could have happened suddenly, on this day of all days? Could it be the procession of a bridegroom come from another village?

But the procession they saw passing through the village made their jaws drop in amazement. There was a company of armed Maavalis strutting behind the drummers. Ringed by these men was a cluster of about two hundred Arabs who were being driven like cattle to the weekly market. They were bound together like cattle too, with a jute rope encircling their midriffs. Walking in front of this procession like the father of the bridegroom was Tanaji Malusare, sticking out his barrel chest and twirling his moustache as he marched. Some of the soldiers wielded canes which they would let fly at regular intervals on the dispirited Arabs.

Tanaji had raided the old Arab fort that lay on the shore of the Kolamb creek in the east. While a large number of its occupants had managed to escape into the neighbouring jungles, he had still managed to round up two hundred stragglers and trussed them up with sturdy ropes. These dark, hefty, crinkly haired thugs were used as cat's paws by the Adilshahi Sultanate as well as by the Savants of Wadi for persecuting the poor of the Konkan. Tanaji was relishing implementing his king's instructions to whip and parade them through the streets. The villagers who had lined up on the streets or were peering from behind their doors and windows were thoroughly enjoying the discomposure of their erstwhile tormentors.

When Shivraya reached the Dandi shore with his priests and associates as well as a huge crowd of the local populace, they heard five loud explosions emerging from the Kolamb creek. People turned their gazes to see the masonry of the old Arab fort flying into the sky. Even before the auspicious task of laying the foundation of Shivaji's sea fort had got under way, the last remnants of the Arab presence on the coast had been blown out of existence.

The sea water looked sparkling clear from the Dandi shore. The morning wind was invigorating and the red-gold rays of the early sun looked as beautiful on the waves as they did on the hills behind the festive procession. Bullock carts of different shapes and sizes had begun streaming in from the nearby villages much earlier in the morning, with passengers disembarking and joining the hordes that had arrived before them. It was a carnival of joy that the shore had not seen in its living memory.

A triangular block of rock was selected for the ceremony that would be performed on the shore. This was the moriyaachaa dagad, the stone that represented Lord Ganesh, the god of auspiciousness. Huge shamianas had been raised here and there on the sandy shore for providing shade to the assembled villagers and other guests. From there, about a couple of miles into the sea, the magnificent Kurtya rock could be seen, looking like a fabulous black elephant with its head immersed in the water.

Frenetic activity had begun from the previous night on the rock. Two hundred and fifty blacksmiths, five hundred masons and two thousand labourers had been transported to a neighbouring island. The king had made all possible arrangements for ensuring that the great task was well and truly launched on this day.

Suddenly the king's attention was caught by something that was happening on the waves. Three boats laden with Koli boys were making their way towards the shore and the lads on board were frantically trying to pass some kind of message to him. It was, however, impossible to hear them over the noise of the waves. Shivraya soon realised that they were making signals, pointing to something behind them. Peering into the distance and sharpening the focus of his eyes, he noticed a big ship anchored in the deeper waters near the horizon. The cynics in the crowd spotted the ship and instantly trotted out their doomsday prophesies.

'All right, now,' they gleefully told their companions, 'the time seems to have come for Shivaji to pay for his cockiness. That must be a foreign ship laden with soldiers which has sailed in to put this swaggering king in his place.'

The king, however, looked reassuringly at the gathering and said with a relaxed smile, 'No need to worry. That ship belongs to the Swarajya. Following my instructions, Dorojipant Phaakade and Mainak Bhandari had set sail last afternoon from the Rajapur harbour to arrive here.'

'Arey waah!' some of the assembled elders exclaimed, 'it seems to have a company of soldiers aboard it too!'

'That's not just a squad or two, but five thousand well-trained soldiers,' Shivraya said confidently, particularly addressing the doubters. 'These men are not out on a pleasure cruise, either. This army is not going to budge from its spot till the battlements of our sea fort are laid out and our ochre flag flutters atop it.'

In the assembly were a number of knowledgeable and experienced people, some of whom had seen the coasts and harbours of half the world, visited the capitals of many countries and interacted with many a sultan and emperor. They had been mesmerised both by the king's enthusiasm and his expert planning for the construction of this sea fort.

Govind Vishwanath had commissioned an elaborate map of the proposed fort, drawn by an artist, and put it on display in a corner of the main pavilion. It indicated that the fort in the sea was to be raised over an area of forty-eight acres. Its circumference would be about two miles and a half. The height of the outer walls would be twenty-five to forty arms and their thickness would be eight to twelve arms.

'Govindrao, if there are to be forty-two bastions on the walls, you will also need to man them with that many posts. So, the number of guards and soldiers you will require for the security of this fort is staggering!'

'What's the alternative, friends? Maharaj himself refers to this fort as Shiv Lanka. This means that it has to be strong enough to confront a couple of dozen foreigners and local rivals, doesn't it?'

For the puja, the king had wound a short dhotar with a serrated border around his waist. An elaborate ritual of this kind required the wife to be seated next to her husband; yet, the king didn't have even one of his seven queens with him. All that he had was a bit of arecanut fruit with some mantras pronounced on it and the thought of his wives in his head. Then, it was as if a thunderbolt had hit him: his entire being was pervaded by the thought of Matoshri. The one presence he deemed indispensable for such an unprecedented, incomparable event was that of his mother.

He found it difficult to control the anger he felt toward himself. He had thought of every block of stone, every peg, every hinge and every nail while planning the erection of his Shiv Lanka. How could it be, then, that he had not thought about the presence of his mother at this peerless event? If he had only sent her a message in advance, she would have happily ridden the wind to come and pat her son on the back!

The pensive king lifted his eyes towards the puja pavilion to see about a hundred horses pulling up. A hundred tall, well-built and red-faced Portuguese men dismounted, most of whom were expert architects and engineers. The king had hired them for five times the wages that the Portuguese governor gave them, with a lot of other facilities thrown in. They had, therefore, left their earlier employment and enlisted in the king's service for a few years. Arjoji had himself visited Goa, got the agreements signed and disbursed advance payments. A number of boats were ready to transport them to the site.

As they began leaving for the island, loud calls of the Kannada mahauts reached the ears. They were lowering their animals in the waves nearby. At the sight of water after such a long journey, the elephants had gone into a frenzy of delight. They scampered straight into the water, sat down in it with a great splash and immediately began giving themselves an elaborate shower with their trunks. These delightful scenes on the shore, as well as the panoramic vista of the sea spread out before him, again put the king in mind of his mother and his wives.

The punishing protocols of kingship take away from the king the comfort of carrying tears in his eyes. Even if they are the tears of joy, they can be misconstrued by the enemy to suit his own ends. In this moment, however, the absence of his mother was causing the king such agony that all protocols were broken. Quickly daubing the tears with the fringe of his stole, he looked up and straight ahead speechlessly.

What immediately struck his eyes was a magnificently built stallion of the Panchala breed, and Netaji Palkar sitting astride it with great pomp. Right behind him were another fifteen or twenty horses. The child sitting in front of Netaji quickly slipped down without the king noticing. Looking at Netaji's smiling face, the king got up and advanced towards him with a loud 'Come, Netokaka, come.' As he stepped forward to gather Netaji in his arms, he was arrested by the high-pitched voice of the child, crying, 'Aaba! Abasahib!!!' He looked down to see his son clinging tightly to his legs. Shivraya forgot Netaji and instantly lifted up his seven-year-old to hold him tightly to his chest. It was after an age that father and son were holding each other in their arms, rubbing cheeks against each other, laughing with unrestrained joy.

The horsemen standing behind Netaji parted to create a passage through which the king espied a palanquin decorated with gold leaf. It had an elegant, brocaded roof from which hung tassels of silk. A regal-looking old lady eased herself out and straightened up with the help of the palanquin bearers. When she threw a tender and adoring look at her son from that distance, the king felt a thousand streaks of lightning course through his body. This time, there was no effort at holding back the tears. 'Aausahib!' he cried as he lowered his son to the ground, 'Matoshri!' He sprang towards his mother who was waiting with arms extended to gather him in her embrace. She then cracked her knuckles against her temples and looked at him with unrestrained pride.

The long journey would definitely have stiffened Matoshri, but how different she looked since he had last set eyes on her! How swiftly age had now begun to show on her! The thought that his seemingly indestructible mother was quickly growing old hit the king like a sledgehammer. He held her by the arm and escorted her to the pavilion. Jijau's curious eyes, however, were bounding everywhere and taking everything in: the tide rolling onto the shore, the black rock that raised its head beyond the waves, the hundreds of labourers toiling away on their little assignments, the sheer variety of tools and equipment scattered around. The entire place looked alive and vibrant.

When she saw all that was happening around her, her heart swelled with immense pride. She looked at her son in the manner of a tigress returning to its cub after a long separation. She heard his voice telling her, 'Matoshri, only one in a hundred harbours would have this kind of site for constructing a sea fort!'

'There are three recent events, Shivba, regarding which any amount of praise will be inadequate.'

'What are they, Maasahib?'

'It was a good thing that you broke into the waada of our enemy across many lives, that wretch Baji Ghorpade, and slaughtered him. The second good thing was the way you meted out punishment to Khawaas Khan, handed him a shameful defeat and drove him out of Konkan in ignominy. Laying the foundation of this fort, of course, is the third one.'

'That's true, Matoshri. It was providential that I could chop off Khawaas Khan's tentacles and dislodge the Adilshahi forces from Kudaal in good time. Otherwise, work on this fort could never have started. And if it had not started now, we might never have had another opportunity, with all these native and foreign powers jumping in to help Adilshah.'

'What sweet words are being exchanged between mother and son?' Soyrabai Ranisahib's voice could be heard. 'Raje, there are others too who have come along with Matoshri!'

The king turned around to see that all of his seven queens had arrived. He could not conceal his delight when he realised that they had rolled their nine-yard saris tightly around themselves and made the entire journey on horseback, covering the five-day-long distance between Rajgadh and the Vengurla-Dandi coast within four days. Also, he could not but be astonished at the speed with which the palanquin bearers had moved, and the passion which had instigated them to sustain such a pace. They had sworn that they would deliver their royal load at the desired spot within the desired time. He happily slipped gold bands upon the wrists of all twelve of them.

Every one of his seven queens had been able to make it: Soyrabai, Putlabai, Sakvarabai, Kashibai, Gunvantabai, Sagunabai and Jaishribai. The one person who was not present on this extraordinary occasion was Saibai. When the thought of his late wife flashed through his head, he turned around to look at his son Sambhaji. It was through the child's eyes that his deceased mother was participating. Looking at them all with unbridled exhilaration, the king said, 'I have been thinking of all of you since the time I got out of bed.'

'Don't try to salvage the situation, Raje,' Jaishribai said with mock-anger. 'The fact is that you had forgotten about us.'

'What rubbish! People who occupy space in one's heart and in the air one breathes … how can they ever be forgotten?'

The king's exclamation delighted the queens. He went on, 'I have to admit, though, that because of the immense pressure of the thoughts and plans swirling in my head, I had forgotten to send someone over to fetch you.'

'Aho, Shivba, whose daughters-in-law are they, after all?' Jijau piped up with satisfaction. 'Why should they not have made their entry here like the whirlwind? Their mother-in-law has not taught them the skills of the kitchen alone. All that I learnt in the courtyard of Sindkhed, all the lessons in swordsmanship, the moves and the countermoves, the heavy horse riding: I taught them all that I knew and made sure they perfected these skills. For no one can know what can befall us at any time.' The young queens looked at her with gratitude.

'But do tell me, Matoshri,' the king asked, still bemused, 'how did news of all this reach you?'

'What do you think, Shivba? Your Bahirji Naik and the others, do they report only to you? As soon as I heard about this ceremony, I decide to set out immediately. Alone. I hadn't wanted to take the girls with me for such a long journey.'

'How, then, did you all come together?'

'I was just about to step out when I saw your Netaji's horse standing outside the door. He too had heard the news from someone and made a beeline for the palace. Once I knew I would have him for company, I decided that for a once-in-a-lifetime event like this one, the king should have his queens by his side. And they can claim this companionship by right. So, this was how things fell into place. And a good thing too! Because, without these girls, the grace and beauty of this event would have been lost.'

The king turned to Netaji and asked, 'But Netokaka, my information was that you were on your way to Bhimthadi, which lies even beyond Pune! How did you get to hear of it?'

Before Netaji could even get a word in, Jijausahib said, 'Balraje, if you can set aside your Matoshri for a moment, who do you think understands your joys, your sorrows, all the desires and ambitions that swirl inside your head better than this Netaji does?'

After a while, the royal family, the king's other loved ones and his close associates stepped out of the pavilion and into the water for the puja. Alongside the Dandi shore flowed a small stream; the company crossed this knee-deep water and reached the damp sand on the other side. That was where the moriya-stone had been placed, upon which some gifted sculptors had etched happy and auspicious motifs that included Shri Gajanan, the Remover of Obstacles, the moon and the sun, the linga, Lord Shiva's bull Nandi and some footprints.

Dadam Bhat was a little lame in one foot, but he had quite forgotten his infirmity in the excitement of the rituals he was so expertly conducting. The king had registered the impeccable quality of work that Dadam Bhat and his nephew Janam Bhat were delivering. He was aware that the priestly community of the Konkan shores had all but disappeared a couple of days ago fearing the Arab goons. Against this backdrop, the king was particularly impressed by the probity and courage of the uncle-nephew duo.

Tarpaulins were spread out on the sand and the puja began. The king undid the knot to bring out the arecanut he had tied to the end of his dhotar and placed it on a tray with a smile playing upon his face. The curiosity in many minds was as to which of his queens would sit by his side. Soyrabai, who was the nearest, simply walked towards him and sat down confidently, without looking this way or that. The puja began.

The tide had begun to come in and the sea was encroaching more and more into the land. The king's velvet-leather shoes were placed upon the sand. As the water came in, they began floating. As soon as Putlabai noticed it, she ran up to the shoes, picked them up and tied them up in the pallu of her embroidered saree. The shoes remained there till the puja got over.

A tent had been put up that the royal family could use during the time that they were there. Jijausahib and the seven queens went inside along with their maids to rest their limbs. The king's attention, however, was totally focused on the work in progress.

Officials of all ranks came to visit him in a regular stream. Doroji Phaakade and Mainak Bhandari got into a small boat from their anchored ship and came to meet the king. They bowed ceremoniously and responded to Shivraya's queries on the state of the weapons and gunpowder on the ship. The subedar of Murud had come over too; the king questioned him closely regarding the work on the Suvarna fort that was in progress there.

Whenever he could find the time, the king would chat with his son Sambhajiraje. Keen to know what the young boy's interests were, he asked, 'How is everything going for you, Yuvaraj? What weapons have you learnt to wield?'

'Abasahib, listen to this interesting story first. Before we came here, Netaji ajoba showed me a handkerchief which had on it a picture that our espionage wing had made.'

'Whose?'

'Why don't you guess?'

'Can't. I accept defeat, and you win. So, whose picture was it?'

'It was of that Emperor Aurangzeb in Delhi. Even in that picture, the wicked man's eyes looked so piercing and mean! And his long beard—'

'Yes, go on.'

'Aaba, that man must be wicked from birth. He refused to let go of me.'

'What does that mean?'

'He came to me in my dreams, the beast.'

'Oh, is that so?' the king asked, impressed. 'What were you doing in your dream, then?'

'How do I tell it, Abasahib? There was this huge palace and this big durbar inside. And in that durbar sat this arrogant Aurangya. I don't remember exactly, but there was an argument between him and you, because you had turned red-faced and stuck your chest out at him without caring for his words. I was there with you too.'

'Ah! So, what were you doing?'

'I too was holding the hilt of my sword, waiting for an opportunity to leap at him.'

'Indeed! What next?'

'Ask Aajisahib. Your Ausahib shook me awake, saying, 'Shambhubaal, why are you grimacing and biting your lips?' Otherwise, all may not have gone well with Aurangzeb.'

The royal family and the other guests listening to Shambhuraje laughed joyfully. Shivraya, however, was overcome by emotion and said, 'Waah, Yuvraj! Waah, little boy! While other boys of your age see peacocks dancing in their dreams, you dream of Aurangzeb's beard. At this auspicious moment, Baalraje, I read this dream of yours as a call to battle in times to come.'

It was after a long time that Matoshri Jijausahib had got an opportunity to observe Shivraya's working style from close quarters. The plans he was making for the new fort coming up here, the progress made on the construction of the Suvarna fort near Ratnagiri, his conversations with experienced sailors and traders, the extensive information that he possessed on matters related to the sea—Shivraya now seemed to be a repository of immense knowledge and wisdom. He knew about the direction of the winds, the art of navigation by the stars, the sailing and sinking of ships, the types, capacities, maintenance and speed of cargo boats, the renovation of harbour creeks, and the white and black business dealings of the firangis. He was a king who had the faculty of drawing the distant stars of his dreams down to the terrain of practicality. Conscientious and alert to his duties, he carried inside him the magic potion that could bring the greatest of deeds to fruition.

Deeply impressed by what she saw, Jijausahib said, 'Shivba, anyone who sees your passion and your efficiency will readily believe that you are an experienced navigator who has been sailing the seven seas of the world and exploring the mysteries of the ocean for twenty-five years, at least.'

'Have I another choice, Aausahib? In my opinion, a real king is essentially a good boatsman. He devotes his entire life to ensure that the little dinghies of the common people do not sink, and to help their small craft reach the shores of prosperity and contentment.'

The king's crowning achievement was that the people of Konkan had begun to love and respect him with all their heart. It was as if the stars of the sky had come down to their shore. That Friday, November 25, 1664, had turned out to be a truly blessed and fortunate day. Single-mindedly and tenaciously, Shivajiraja had laid the foundation of the Sindhudurg fort in south Konkan with the desire to replicate—indeed, improve upon—the Janjira fort of north Konkan. Only twenty days after destroying the thirty-thousand-strong army of Khawaas Khan, he had gathered his resources and brought the matter of the new fort so far forward; what else could it be called but a miracle?

An old woman in a peasant house by the creek asked her grandson, 'Bablya, what were the things that this king of yours turned upside down in a single day?'

'Aga aavashey!' remarked the grandson, 'when you decided to raise a barnyard wall for your buffalo, the entire lane had kicked up such a storm. And this here is a king, our Shivajiraja, no less. If he has set out to pour lead into the sea's belly and construct a massive fort, the world is bound to get reshuffled, isn't it? It's like tying buntings to the sky.'

The lovely evening wind captivated all hearts, although an occasional gust had a nip in it. It was after a long time that the entire royal family was spending time together. A mattress had been spread out on the floor and the king lay resting against a bolster next to Jijausahib. The waves crashing upon the rocks roared. No one in the world could be as happy and satisfied as Jijausahib was at this moment. Her son had done what he had said he would do. He had, as it were, thrown his saddle and stirrups upon the sea. Jijau said: 'If you promise to answer with complete honesty, I'll ask a question.'

'What a thing to say! Of course, ask, Matoshri.'

'It's been an extraordinary day, and you've added a golden feather to your cap. But I've been noticing since morning that a wisp of cloud keeps casting its shadow upon your otherwise sunlit face. So, what is bothering you?'

The king smiled knowingly. He had been sure Jijausahib's sharp, observant eyes would catch him out. He gave a soft sigh and said, 'I've just received intelligence from Aurangzeb's durbar at Agra. It's not public knowledge yet, but a wind from the north is going to blow viciously against the pennant of our Swarajya, and that's certain.'

'You have me worried, son.'

'The matter is about seven weeks old. When Aurangzeb's forty-seventh birthday was being celebrated, the Emperor took this momentous decision. He has appointed Mirza Raja Jaisingh to descend upon the Deccan with an army of a few hundred thousand, targeting our Hindvi swarajya in particular.'

'Mirza Jaisingh? I've heard his name.'

'Oh, he's a lion-hearted Rajput warrior. After seeing so many of his Khans and Shahs bite the dust, Aurangzeb has apparently lost faith in his Muslim brothers. It takes steel to cut through steel, he has learned. Therefore he has decided to enter Mirza Raja into the battlefield.'

'All right, so?'

'As an enemy, his prowess cannot be overlooked. It will be difficult to handle a general of his calibre in the theatre of war.'

'Shivba, where weapons are inadequate, intelligence can compensate.'

'Even that may not suffice in this case, Matoshri, because Mirza Jaisingh is a man of canine instincts.'

'Canine instincts?'

'A person who fights for his master with the devotion and obstinacy of a dog. Such people are dangerous, because they don't much care for fine calculations, but put their canines to full use. Once they get their teeth into something, like bulldogs, they never let go.'

It would certainly take a few months before an army of hundreds of thousands was ready to march down to the south. It would first have to be equipped with the armaments and the muscle that this enterprise would require, not to mention the arrogance and the regalia that was the hallmark of the Mughal army. This gave the king time to make quick, adroit moves and put a number of things in order. The Bhatkal-Kundapur shore to the south was beckoning him. At the same time, he was keeping a sharp eye on the activities of the Mumbai islands of the Portuguese. The stamping out of one Baji Ghorpade was not enough; there were other sparks that were still flying around. There were many missions to complete and many projects to be launched.

That night on the shore, however, was replete with happiness and gratification. There was just that tiny bite in the wind, as scenes of bygone days played themselves out before the inner eye of mother and son. The stars took some time appearing on the firmament. And then they began twinkling, weakly at first, but gathering strength as the sky turned darker. Jijausahib and Shivraya began recognising in them the heroes who had offered their lives as fuel to keep the torch of Swarajya burning bright.

There was the gallant Shareefji who was martyred while rounding up a herd of elephants in the raging battle of Bhatwadi; there was young Babaji Bhosale who, on the eve of his nuptials, preferred to embrace death in the Radtondi ghat during the Pratapgadh conflict; there was Siddhi Wah Wah, who offered himself at the foot of the Panhala fort; there were Shambhuji, Baji and Phulaji Prabhu who became human barriers in the Ghodkhind pass so that their king could reach safety; there were Godaji Jagtap, Baji Jedhe, and of course, thousands of other faceless young men who swelled the list of the martyrs who had sacrificed their all for giving shape and substance to the concept of Swarajya.

The night wind pushed a wispy cloud aside to reveal a particularly bright star, which performed the miracle of exuding a sense of calm even as it glittered. It attracted Jijausahib's notice by its sheer radiance; then her eyes filled up and overflowed. She immediately drew her son's attention towards it. Shivraya instantly felt his heart tighten and a lump form in his belly. He gathered all of his being into his eyes and stared at the star unblinkingly. He then held his mother's arm and said in a hoarse voice, 'Abasahib, the man who first dared to dream of our Hindvi swarajya!'

'Yes, Shivba. If only Fate had given the senior Maharaj a lease of just another eight or ten months for his sojourn on earth, the celebrations we had today would have acquired a rare significance and an added layer of fulfilment.'

The waves rolled in and out; their song rose and sank with the lifting and falling of the wind. For that magical night at least, the hearts of all present on the Konkan shore were overflowing with a sense of unmitigated triumph.

GLOSSARY OF INDIAN WORDS USED IN THE BOOK

Aai ga	Exclamation of surprise, embarrassment, usually used by women
Aaji	Grandmother
Aalam-Panaah	Address to the king/emperor. Literally, Shelter of the Universe
Aapa/Aapajaan	Address for elder sister
Aashaad	Fourth month of the Hindu calendar. Coincides with June–July
Aavashee/Aavashey	Grandmother
Abasahib	Address for father
Abba/Abbajaan/Abbu	Father
Aga bai/Ago bai	Exclamation of surprise, discomfort, used by women
Aho/Avo	Exclamation to attract attention. Equivalent of Hey, listen
Allah-o-Akbar	Literally, God is Great. Used as a battle cry
Ammi/Ammijaan	Mother
Arey	Exclamation
Arey deva	Exclamation of worry. Equivalent of Oh my god
Ashtagandha	A powder that is a combination of eight herbs. Applied on the as a teeka, a mark that the Hindus wear on the forehead
Aukshan	A ritual of waving a lamp around the face of someone as a mark of welcome
Ausaheb	Mother

Baal	Male child
Babhul	Vachellia nilotica, more commonly known as Acacia nilotica, and by the vernacular names of gum arabic tree and babul. Its thorns are hardy
Barabandi	A Peshwai tunic with 6 knots to be fastened at the chest. It also has a belt to be fastened at the waist
Bhaakari	Unleavened made of jowar millet. Staple food of the peasants
Bhavoji	Address for husband's brother
Bhishti	Water supplier who dispenses water out of a leather bag
Bhoi	Community of palanquin bearers
Chaataka	Jacobin cuckoo
Chacha/Chachajaan	Address for father's younger brother, also used for an avuncular person as a mark of respect
Chhatrapati	Royal title for a king. Literally, Lord of the Parasol
Dada	Elder brother; also used as an address for a senior person
Daroga-e-dak	The official in charge of posts
Darshan	Holy sighting of god or saint
Deen-deen	Literally, deen means religion. Here, deen-deen is a war cry of the Muslim army
Deewaan/Diwan	1. Accountant. 2. A low, long seat
Deewaan-e-Aam	A hall where the king gave public audience
Deewaan-e-Khaas	A hall where the king gave private audience
Deshmukh	The head of a few villages
Deshmukhi	The office of a Deshmukh
Dhow	Arabian merchant boat
Doley	Documents signed by the Sultan that allow the holder to act on his behalf
Durbaar	Also spelt as durbar, the king's court
Firangi	A term used by Indians for a white foreigner
Gadi/Gadya	Friend, partner
Gajra	A string of fragrant flowers worn on the wrist

Ghaagra	A loose petticoat worn by girls
Ghazi	A soldier fighting a religious war
Ghoongat	A sheet of cloth worn on the head by women, with one edge reaching up to the chin to conceal the face
Ghorpad/Godha	Iguana lizard
Gulaal	Red powder that is tossed in the air and applied to each other's faces during celebrations, particularly the festival of Holi
Habshi	Arabic term for a person from Abyssinia, today's Ethiopia
Hakeem	A physician practicing Unani medicine
Har har Mahadev	War cry of the Maratha army
Haveli	Mansion
Havildar/Havaldar	Sergeant
Howdah	Seat atop an elephant
Huzoor	Address of respect for a person of rank
Irali	A hood made from slit bamboo to use as a rain-cover
Jagir/Jaageer	A grant of the public revenues of a district to a person with power to collect and enjoy them and to administer the government in the district
Jaagirdaar	The holder of a jaageer
Jahaan-Panaah	Address to a king. Literally, Shelter of the World
Jai Bhavani	War cry of the Maratha army. Bhavani is another name for Goddess Durga
Jai Malhar	War cry of the Maratha army
Jai Shivraya/Jai Shivaji	War cry of the Maratha army. Literally, Hail Shivaji
Jambhul/Jaamun	Dark purple, edible berry
Janaab	Address of respect to a male. Equivalent of 'Sir'
Jhunka	Dish made of roasted gram-flour. Staple food of the peasant, particularly on a journey
Jowar	Millet cultivated in Maharashtra
Jyotirlinga	Devotional representation of Lord Shiva

Karbala	Battleground in Iraq where a fateful in which Hasan and Hussain, the grandsons of Prophet were defeated. Now symbolizes disastrous enterprise
Karvanda	A thorny shrub of the genus Carissa that bears sour, plumlike red to purple-black fruits
Khaavind	Lord and master. Also used for husband
Khuda-na-khaasta	Equivalent of god-forbid
Koli	Community of fishermen
Kotwal	The police chief of a town
Kunku	Vermillion powder worn on the forehead by women whose husbands are alive
Lezim	Folk dance of Maharashtra. The dancers carry a small musical instrument with jingling cymbals called the Lezim or lezium, after which the dance form is named
Linga	Penis. The symbol by which Lord Shiva is worshipped
Maamoo/Maamoojaan	Address for mother's brother
Maarg-Sheersh	Ninth month of the Hindu calendar, corresponding with November-December
Maashaa-Allah	Exclamation of admiration
Maavale	A term of endearment for mother
Maavali	A native of the Maaval region of Western Maharashtra
Maavashi	Mother's sister. Also used as a respectful address for a senior woman
Mahaut	Elephant driver
Mandeel	Headgear of a Maratha king. King Shivaji wore a Mandeel
Margattha/Margatthya	Derogatory reference to a Maratha
Matoshri	Mother
Miyaan	Address for a Muslim man, used either singly or before and after the person's name
Mohur	Gold coin. Also a seal of authority

Mrig	Technically deer. There is also a constellation by that name. It also refers to a period during the rainy months
Mujra	A low bow with the lifting and dropping of the right hand to show extreme respect, as before royalty
Muneem	Accountant
Paadava/Gudi Paadava	New Year's day in Maharashtra. On this day, gudi, or a cloth doll is hung to the door of Maharashtrian houses
Paan	Betel leaf, chewed with lime and other ingredients
Padishah	Variant of Badshah, or Emperor
Palaas	A tree that bears bright red flowers in March-April. Also called the flame of the forest
Pallu	The upper part of the saree, that is very often draped around the head
-pant	A suffix added to the name of a Brahmin male
Patil/Patlin	Head of a village. The wife of the Patil is also addressed as a Patilin
Paush	Tenth month of the Hindu calendar. Corresponds with December-January
Phugadi	A game, played usually by girls where two girls lock crossed arms with each other and spin together
Pithle	A liquidy dish made from gram flour
Pooran-poli	Maharashtrian sweet dish made from ground gram, sugar and ghee
Pora	Address for a boy
Pori	Address for a girl
Prahar	A three-hour division of the day. The day is divided into eight prahars, the first prahar being 6 a.m. to 9 a.m.
Qibla-e-aalam	Address to the king
Quawwali	A style of singing devotional songs, particularly popular among the Sufis
Raj-dharma	The duty of the king
Rangoli	Patterns drawn on the floor with colourful powder
Saahukaar	Moneylender

Sarkar/Sarkaar	Address to a superior authority. Also means administration
Sati	A woman who burns herself to death at her husband's funeral pyre. Such a woman acquires the status of a goddess
Seth	Rich trader or money-lender
Shaasan-kaathi	A long stick swung for sport and used as a weapon
Shab-e-baaraat	The night that falls between the fourteenth and fifteenth of the Islamic month of Shaabaan. Believed to be a night when Allah offers forgiveness to worshippers
Shamiana	A cloth and canvas pavilion
Shevai	A sweet dish made with vermicelli and milk
Shivaji Maharaj ki Jai	War cry of the Maratha army. Literally: Hail Shivaji Maharaj
Soon/Soonbai	Daughter-in-law
Subedar/Subhedar	The administrative chief of a suba or a province
Subhaan-Allah	Exclamation of appreciation
Suhaagan	A woman whose husband is alive. Among some Hindus, a widow is considered an inauspicious person
Swami	Lord. Title for a holy Hindu man
Swaraj/Swarajya	Self governance, independence
Tatya	An address to a senior
Tantra, mantra, yantra	By whatever means. Literally, either through black magic, the incantation of holy verse or through some mechanism
Teen Darwaza	Three Gates. Here, the name of a structure
Vaanar-wada	Vaanar means monkey. Here, the strategy used to drive away monkeys from the farms
Vahini	Elder brother's wife
Vish-kanya	Literally Poison-girl. In Indian stories, such girls were made to imbibe poison from early age, so that a time arrived when their slightest bite could kill. They were used as a lure against enemies

Waada	An extensively spread mansion
Wagh-nakh	Literally, tiger's claw. This was a weapon that was worn on the fingers and used by Shivaji to tear open Afzal Khan's entrails
Wazeer	Minister of a king
Ya Allah	Exclamation of anxiety. Literally: Oh my god
Ya Khuda	Same as Ya Allah
Ya Parvardigaar	Same as Ya Allah
Zenana	The women's quarters
Zill-e-Ilaahi	Address to a king. Literally, Shadow of god (on earth)
Zill-e-Subhaani	Same as Zill-e-Ilahi. Subhani is another word for Allah